Dear Reader,

WINGS IN THE NIGHT has become a tradition and, sort of, my signature series. I've certainly come full circle with this series. *Twilight Phantasies* will always be my first sale in my mind, even though I had to revise it before it was contracted, and in the meantime sold a different title. The two books sold only a month or so apart. And since *Twilight Phantasies* was the first one submitted, to me it was the first sale. (Hard to believe that was over thirty books ago!) I wrote a few more in the series, but then my heart was broken when Silhouette Shadows was closed, and for a few months I thought it was the end of the vampire series.

But then I was elated again when I was asked to write another, as a Silhouette Single Title. So elated that I hung up the phone and wrote a thirty-page outline by the end of the day, then overnighted it to my editor. The manuscript followed in eight weeks' time. That book was *Born in Twilight*. There is some special well of inspiration somewhere in the universe that feeds these vampire novels to me. It's not work to write them. I literally open a vein, if you'll pardon the pun, and they just pour themselves onto the page. I don't know why, and I don't know how. I just know that I have to keep writing them. I am so, so extremely honored that the next edition to this series, *Twilight Hunger*, will be released by MIRA. I still can't quite digest that I'm in the company of some of the biggest stars in the writing world. It boggles my mind.

What's really fun to note is that the big event that unfolds at the end of *Born in Twilight* is one of the trigger events that sets off the drama in *Twilight Hunger* (MIRA, March 2002.) So get ready to dig in.

And remember, don't read in the dark!

Maggie Shayne

DARK LOVER

I loved not the night
but he drew me,
With dark whispers beckoned me near
His shadows I thought
would subdue me,
Enslave me in chains made of fear

I wished not to look
but he wooed me,
His strong, gentle hand turned my face
I opened my eyes
and saw beauty,
Where I'd seen but a desolate place

I fled from the night
but he chased me,
He caught me in arms of dark steel
I sighed as I let him
embrace me
In his touch, at last, I could *feel*

I turned to the night
and he kissed me,
On his lips I tasted sweet wine
I opened to night's
sacred mystery
He took me, and whispered, "You're mine"

The night has become
my dark lover
By day but a dream, bittersweet
At sunset I run
to no other
My surrender to night is complete

AT TWILIGHT

MAGGIE SHAYNE

Published by Silhouette Books

America's Publisher of Contemporary Romance

SILHOUETTE BOOKS

AT TWILIGHT

Copyright © 2002 by Harlequin Books S.A.

ISBN 0-373-48458-5

The publisher acknowledges the copyright holder
of the individual works as follows:

BORN IN TWILIGHT
Copyright © 1997 by Margaret Benson

BEYOND TWILIGHT
Copyright © 1995 by Margaret Benson

Visit Silhouette at www.eHarlequin.com

Printed in U.S.A.

CONTENTS

WINGS IN THE NIGHT SERIES

Collected as WINGS IN THE NIGHT

Twilight Phantasies   Tamara Dey & Eric Marquand
Twilight Memories   Rhiannon & Roland de Courtemanche
Twilight Illusions   Damien Namtar (Gilgamesh)
                                & Shannon Mallory

Collected as AT TWILIGHT

"Beyond Twilight"   "Ramsey" Bachman & Cuyler Jade
Born in Twilight   Angelica & Jameson Bryant

"Twilight Vows"   Donovan O'Roarke & Rachel Sullivan

And available next month from MIRA Books

Twilight Hunger   Morgan De Silva & Dante

BORN IN TWILIGHT

This book is dedicated to you.

You who refuse to apologize for your choice of entertainment.

You who walk into a bookstore,
place your stack of romances on the counter and look
the clerk in the eye with your chin up and your spine straight.

You who—despite the opinions of pop psychologists—
know full well the difference between fantasy and reality.

You who have made romance
the world's top-selling form of fiction.

All of you who share the secret—romance novels are by
women, for women and about women. You and me.

No wonder some people are so afraid of them.

Chapter One

I am damned. I am damned. I am damned.

Those words were the only ones I could utter as I stumbled through the city streets that first night of my new life. My hair in tangles, my clothes torn and dirty. Passersby looked at me and then quickly looked away, their eyes flashing with alarm—or was it contempt?—as their steps altered to give me a wide berth. Almost as if they knew.

I'd been on the right path. Or I thought I had. Perhaps I'd been a bit too confident in my righteousness. Pride goeth before a fall, after all. But surely the sin of pride didn't warrant this severe a retribution. Surely it hadn't been the hand of God that brought me this low.

No. No, God had nothing to do with it. Nor Satan himself, but a monster. A creature far more hideous than even Lucifer in all his evil glory could ever be.

For thirteen years I'd been as pure and as holy as I envisioned the very angels to be. From the darkest night of my life—the night my mother had left me at the altar at St. Christopher's, promising she'd come back for me soon—I had done only good. Though I'd barely been old enough to know good from bad then, a nine-year-old child abandoned by her mother learns quickly enough. If I were only good enough, perhaps she would come back for me.

She hadn't. But it had only served to convince me that I *hadn't* been good enough. It only served to make me strive to be better.

The sisters had raised me well, taught me all they knew of the ways of truth and righteousness for His name's sake. And I hadn't left them when I'd come of age, but instead, had clung to the refuge I'd found among them.

My final vows would have been spoken a week from that horrible night. Just one more week. And I wondered, for just a moment, if I'd have been safe from the monster had I taken the veil sooner. Would my devotion have protected me then?

"I am damned," I muttered again, this time sinking to the steps of a beautiful cathedral. I didn't gaze up at the spires, or wonder at the beauty of the stained-glass windows. I couldn't. When I looked at the colors, my monstrous eyes refused to linger on the heavenly blues and greens and golds. They focused instead on the bits of scarlet-colored glass, and on those alone. And a hunger stirred from the very depths of my soul. A sinful hunger, one I could not—*would not*—assuage.

I'd gone out alone that wintry night, despite the sisters' dire warnings....

My soft-soled shoes made squeaking sounds as I raced down the steep wooden stairs from my cell. I was in a hurry to be off. It was snowing outside! The first snow of the winter, and how I loved it. I'd been pacing my chamber, unable to concentrate on my studies, or much of anything else for that matter. All I seemed able to do was glance at the small, white-faced clock on my wall, and scowl at its slow ticking, before turning back to my single window to gaze longingly out at the snow.

We were not a cloistered order, exactly. We did go out among the worldly, but only in service to the Lord, or when Mother Mary Ruth saw it as absolutely necessary. Tonight it was my turn to work at the shelter several blocks away. And while I knew I should be rejoicing in the opportunity to serve God by helping my fellow man in his time of need, I wasn't. I was rejoicing in the opportunity to go out in that brand-new snow.

I pulled a light shawl over my habit, which was a simplified version of the ones the true sisters wore. I'd have one like theirs soon. In just over a week when I took my solemn vows.

But my steps faltered as I reached the bottom of the staircase and saw Sister Rebecca, who was to accompany me to the shelter, leaning against the newel post and looking sickly.

"Sister, what's wrong?" I rushed forward, my heart sinking as much at the thought of having to stay in tonight as at the thought of Sister Rebecca being ill. We always worked in pairs at the shelter. Always traveled there and back together.

"Stomach virus, or so I suspect," she replied. She was young, like me. It had been only a year since she'd taken her final vows, and I sometimes thought it was a shame she'd never married or had children, as lovely as she was. And as I thought it, a small, niggling doubt tried to creep up my nape and into my brain, but I shook it off. This was the only life I'd ever known. I remembered almost nothing from before my mother left me here. I wouldn't know how to live among the worldly. Besides, I wanted to be *good*. And there wasn't a better way, was there?

"Don't worry," Sister Rebecca said, valiantly lifting her chin and trying to paste a smile over the grimace on her lips. "I'm not going to beg off. You've been looking forward to this all day."

Had I been so obvious? I averted my face. "No, Sister Rebecca. I won't have you going out when you feel so poorly. You should be in bed." I pressed a hand to her forehead, and felt heat there. Then I turned her around, and helped her toward the stairs. "Now, go on upstairs and rest. I can certainly tend to the needs of the homeless without a partner on the verge of collapse."

She stiffened, as I'd feared she would. "You will most certainly not go out alone! You know the mother superior's rules!"

"Surely she'd make an exception if she knew you were sick. She'd never insist you go with me."

"No. She'd insist you stay here."

"Lucky for me she's not here, then."

Sister Rebecca shook her head slowly. "Look at you! Your eyes are sparkling tonight. What has you so excited, Angelica?"

"The snow," I said, spinning around and stopping when I faced the window and could see the snowflakes pirouetting in the glow of the streetlights outside. "I want to be in it. Feel it on my face."

Her soft hand came down to my shoulder. "There will be other snow, Angelica."

"But this is the first," I said, and I faced her once more. "Please let me go. I'm a grown woman. Grown women traipse about this city by themselves every day."

"Not women of this order," she began.

"Well, technically, I'm not of this order...yet. So I can do what I want."

"Angelica..."

I stopped on my way to the door, and turned to face her.

She smiled, and I saw the fever in her pink cheeks and shining eyes. One strand of golden hair had escaped her wimple and curled against her cheek. "You're a very strong-willed young woman, Angelica," she said, but her smile remained. "And adventurous, and more than a little bit mischievous. I often wonder if you've given enough thought to the decision you've made."

But I only shrugged. "I'm going to the shelter. Mother superior can lecture me when she returns, but until then, I'm going out in the snow."

She nodded then, as if in defeat. "Hurry then. Don't miss your bus. If you do, you come straight back here—" But I was already out the door.

Oh, the snow! I'd always loved winter. I tipped my face up to let the icy, wet flakes fall against my cheeks and my nose. And even tasted them the way a small child might do. They coated everything I passed, like powdered sugar on parked cars and sidewalks and windowsills and front stoops. And I know I dawdled, because it enchanted me so. I remember thinking it was like magic, that first snow of the winter. Like a fairy tale come true. And I remember telling myself that I was far too old to be so giddy over a simple thing like snow. Dancing in it like a little girl. But I couldn't help myself. I *was* giddy.

And wrong, I was wrong to have come out alone, blatantly breaking the rules of the order. But I'd done so often enough in the past that the sisters must surely expect it by now. I disliked rules. I'd probably have to change my rebellious ways and conform a bit better once I took my vows, but I refused to do so until then. After that...

Again, that shiver of doubt. Again, I shook it away. I'd think about that later. Not now. All I wanted to do right now was walk alone at night, breaking the rules with every step, and enjoy the snow.

And that is precisely what I did. When I finally reached the bus stop on the corner though, it was only to see my transportation rolling away without me.

It threw me, but only for a moment. After all, I was almost a sister of the Order of the Sisters of Mercy. I was *good.* I lived my life serving God, and surely no one else did so with such enthusiasm as I. And certainly, wherever I went I was walking within the protection of His love. In fact, I'm sure I felt invulnerable, though where I got that idea, I do not know. It was not something the sisters would have taught me, not something I'd read in my studies. But I felt it, all the same. I felt surrounded by a protective shield that would let no harm come to me, and because of it, I foolishly decided to walk the six blocks to the shelter. And that, I later realized, was the foolish pride that led to my downfall.

He was waiting. Crouched in the shadows of a garbage-strewn alley. The monster called out to me as I passed, and my steps slowed to a reluctant stop. What a fool I was.

"Sister! Sister, please, help me."

My beloved snow fell in gentle puffs as I turned to look into the darkness, unable to see the owner of that plaintive voice. I stood a little straighter, feeling a hint of fear for the first time. "Who's there?" I called. "Come here, where I can see you."

"I can't. I'm hurt. Please, Sister. Don't let me die here in the cold. *Help me!*"

My fear did not evaporate. It was simply outspoken by my unwavering confidence. I was a servant of the Lord, and I would walk where even His most trusted angels feared to tread, if that were what was necessary. I'd help this poor soul in the alley. But

I'd be careful, cautious, wise. Tentatively, I stepped into the black-
ness, and an icy shiver raced up my nape, chilling me right to my
soul. And I should have known. I should have known right then
not to go a single step farther.

"Over here," he moaned, drawing me closer. Closer, until the
lighted, busy street was out of reach. And when I was close
enough, still blind in the darkness, he came at me. Bony arms
with the strength of Samson closed around me, nearly crushing
me, and a hand clapped over my mouth. I struggled. Mightily, I
struggled. For though devout, I had never been timid or weak, or
cowardly. I kicked at him with a force that surely should have
broken his shins. And I boxed his ears hard enough to knock him
unconscious. I twisted and pulled against his grip, and tried to bite
the hand over my mouth. But nothing I did to him seemed to have
any noticeable effect. He didn't flinch, or even draw a harsh
breath. My heart pounded so loudly it deafened me as he dragged
me deeper into that alley. And silently, I began praying. Praying
for salvation from this madman, praying for my life to be spared.
Lord, forgive me for that error. I should have been praying for
my immortal soul, not the preservation of this life, this body.

He threw me down among the rubbish so hard my breath was
taken away when I hit. And then he came down on top of me, as
I gasped for air among the fetid garbage. The stench was sickening. I caught my breath, parted my lips to scream, but he covered my mouth again. He sat there, straddling me, and with his
free hand he tore the wimple from my head, freeing my hair and
grasping handfuls of it.

"Black satin," he whispered as he fingered my hair. "And eyes
like onyx. You're perfect." I struggled beneath him. "Perfect. I
won't be alone anymore."

I still could not see him well. Only the shape of his face, and
the darker wells of his eyes were visible. But I could not escape
the feeling that he could see me perfectly.

"I've been watching you for so long, you know. I've chosen
you, of the many I've known. You should be grateful, Angelica,
for the gift you're about to receive."

I shook my head, but to no avail.

"Yes. Grateful," he went on. "No cloistered order for you, my perfect one. No vows. You're not meant for that. You're meant for me."

The monster bowed over me, lifting me slightly from my bed of refuse. He bent to my throat, and my stomach turned when I felt the touch of his cold mouth on my skin. With one hand, he forced my head back until I thought my neck would break. And then the moment I shall never forget for as long as I live. Indeed, the moment I'd never dreamed of. I thought he would rape me, murder me. I thought many things when that creature bent over me that night. But I never thought this.

There was pain—brief, shocking pain, when his incisors pierced the tender skin of my throat. And then that pain was gone, and I was left instead with the horror of what was happening to me. His mouth sucked at my neck as he drank the very lifeblood from my body. I could feel it, feel my essence leaving me through those two tiny holes in my throat. My mind swam, faded. Everything faded. The stench of the garbage and the chill of the cold winter night. The feel of those wet snowflakes on my face. The very ground on which I lay. Everything vanished, and I was left with nothing. Every aspect of me was focused on the part of me where this monster had fastened himself. My throat, and his mouth drawing the blood from it, were all that remained of the universe.

He lifted his head. I lay still, barely conscious, unable to move or utter a sound. He moved, and there was a glint of silver. I couldn't even feel alarm when it occurred to me that he held a blade. That he would finish me now. I could hear nothing. The sounds of the city could no longer reach my ears. Only his voice.

He lifted me, pressing my face into the crook of his neck, and he whispered, "Drink, Angelica. Drink....and live."

He forced me closer, his hand on the back of my head. And my lips touched warmth, wetness on his throat. I tried to draw away, but my weakness would not allow it. And the first taste of it touched my tongue, quickening my senses. A jolt, like a blast of icy wind, shot through me. I think my eyes shot wide. My lips parted on a gasp, and more of the thick, salty liquid surged into my mouth. Had I not swallowed, I'd have drowned. And if I'd been as devout as I'd prided myself on being, that's precisely what I would have done. Let myself drown in this cursed elixir. Gone willingly into the arms of the Lord rather than surrendering myself to the instinctive need to stay alive. But instead, I swallowed. And that was when I first felt the power of this devilish hunger. It shot through me, overwhelming all that I had ever been. It took control, a need I couldn't even identify. I closed my lips over the wound in his throat...and I drank. Hungrily, greedily, I drank, and as I did, my body came alive with sensations I'd never known. So gluttonous was I, that he had to push me away when the curse was complete. Push me, his unwilling victim, away from his neck.

And I lay there in the garbage. And my eyes cleared. I could see. I could see everything. Every aspect of his white face, and black eyes, and bloodstained lips. Every grain of sand in the bricks of the building beside me. Every star in the sky. My skin tingled with new life, new awareness. I *felt* in a way I'd never felt before. The shape of each snowflake as it hit my skin. Every molecule of chilly air that caressed my face. Every pebble and piece of trash that lay beneath me. I could identify each vile smell. And my hearing...I could hear the conversations of people passing on the street. The roll of tires on the wet pavement. The squeaking of snow-dampened brakes.

I heard the traffic light turn green.

"What is this?" I cried, and my own voice was so shockingly different, so vivid and rich and clear, that I pressed my hands to my ears and squeezed my eyes shut tight.

"You'll learn to control it," he told me. "You can close it out, hear only what you wish to hear. You'll learn. I'll teach you." He removed my hands from my ears, pressed them to the rubbish at my sides. "I'll teach you. You'll live forever, Angelica. You're not mortal anymore. You're like me now."

I opened my eyes. "Like you?" I was horrified.

"Yes."

And my heart seemed to stop beating as I realized what he had done, what I had allowed him to do. "I'm damned," I whispered.

"Come. Your first lesson awaits." He hauled me to my feet, dragged me toward the mouth of the alley, though I pulled against him. My habit was torn as he grabbed at me. "Strong," he whispered. "Already, you're very strong. You'll be even stronger, Angelica, after we feed." He stopped, holding me there at the mouth of the alley, and I watched his odd, black eyes scan the passersby.

"Feed?" I whispered, terrified.

"Yes," he said, and he smiled. I saw his teeth then, his fangs, razor sharp and glistening. "On them." He nodded toward the people who passed.

Horror enveloped my heart. He was a monster! A demon. A...*a vampire*. I shivered as the word whispered in my mind. He'd made of me another creature just like him. And I'd allowed it. I'd even taken part in it. I'd—

He caught me up in his arms, though I fought, and he carried me back into the alley. Slinging me over his shoulder, he clutched the side of the building and began to climb. Like a spider, he made his way to the very top, and I stopped my struggling for fear I would fall. Higher and higher he went, and the wind blew stronger here. My beloved snowflakes became weapons. Tiny arrows slung by the Angel of the Lord to punish me. Cutting my face with their biting touch. And yet I did not shiver or suffer from the cold. Only felt it more acutely than I ever had.

He climbed onto the roof, and then raced over rooftops, leaping from one to the next. I think I screamed as we seemed to sail through the night sky like true demons. I think I screamed. If so, the sound of it is only a vague memory now.

We made our way to the ground again, to the streets, and I knew where we were. Not far from the shelter where I'd been so arrogantly going this night. Oh, why had I been so rebellious? Why?

He pointed, and I looked. A handful of the city's homeless stood around a fire barrel, warming their hands near the dancing flames. Red-orange light painting their haggard faces and illuminating their tattered clothes.

"There," he said. "Our victims...ours for the taking, Angelica. Their lives will be no great loss."

The people I'd spent years trying to help. This man intended to feed on them, to use them in order to sustain his own cursed life. "No," I begged him. "No, please, we mustn't. It's a sin to kill!" For I knew that murder was exactly what he had on his mind.

He left me free to run if I chose. He must have known, animal that he was, that I could not. Like a great, stalking wolf, he crept up on them. But quickly. So quickly there was no time for me to shout a warning. And then, without hesitation, he grabbed one. There was a shout of alarm, and then the others scattered, vanishing in the night. And he held the man he'd chosen. A terror-stricken, aged face that I knew I had seen before. In the shelter. In the soup kitchens where I'd worked. I'd given him blankets, and that very sweater he wore. I'd prayed with him.

I raced forward, but too late. The beast had plunged his wretched teeth into the neck of the innocent old man. I battered his head, clawed at his face, but he only released his victim when he'd taken his fill. He lifted his head, and he smiled at me. And his lips gleamed scarlet in the firelight. I backed away, shaking my head, working my mouth but unable to speak.

The man whose name I could not recall slumped to the ground, eyes wide, but already glazing over. His face was the face of death, bathed in the dancing glow of the fire in the barrel beside him.

The monster licked his lips, and then with the speed of a striking cobra, snatched a handful of my hair and pulled, making me cry out in pain. "You shall never fight me again, Angelica. You're mine now. Mine, do you understand? All your life I've watched you, waited for you. You'll go where I go. Do as I say. Feed when I feed." He glanced past me, into the shadows, and that evil smile returned. "Even now your first victim waits. There, quivering in the night, thinking we cannot see him in the darkness." He stared down into my face. "I'll bring him to you, and you will take him,

Angelica. You will drain him dry, or suffer my wrath.'' And then he released me and started forward. I turned and saw the boy, a mere youth, dressed in tattered rags, crouching in the darkness, shivering and wide-eyed with fear. And I could not let that creature take his life. I could not.

My hand closed around a piece of wood that protruded from the fire barrel. The end I grasped was not burning, but as I pulled it out, I saw that the other end was aflame. With a low growl, one I could not believe came from me, I lunged forward, swinging my torchlike weapon with all of my newfound strength.

But it wasn't the force of my blow that did the deed. The flaming end of the club crashed against the vampire's head, knocking him to his knees. But I'm sure the damage I did was minimal. It was the flame. The blaze seemed to leap at him, fire licking at his hair, and then at his clothes. He surged to his feet, his lips parting in a snarl as he came at me. But the fire...I crossed myself as I watched it engulf him. It seemed as if he'd been doused in gasoline, the way the flames spread. I backed away when he reached for me. And that was all. He fell to the ground, and there was a surge of white-hot flames. And then nothing. The flames died away as if they'd never been. The tiny sparks and embers sailed into the night and blinked out, one by one. And not even ashes remained to soil the perfect white snow at my feet.

The boy in the shadows was gone, and I could hear his fleeing footsteps still reaching my ears as he ran. I staggered away, shocked, terrified, appalled. I had killed. I had been transformed. I was a creature like the one I had murdered. I was damned. Damned.

His hearing was excellent. Not preternaturally so, since he was still a mere mortal, but good enough to know what was going on. The bastards were going to kill him.

For three days, he'd been strapped to this table, inside this tiny cell. Poked and prodded by DPI scientists in white lab coats until there wasn't an inch of his skin they hadn't violated. Nothing. There wasn't a bodily fluid they hadn't taken samples of. Not one. But it wasn't humiliation he felt. It was rage. And this time, the bastards would pay. Jameson Bryant might not be a vampire, but he wasn't a child any longer, either. He was a grown man, and as of tonight, he was a man bent on revenge. He'd tear this building down brick by brick when he got free. He'd destroy the Division of Paranormal Investigations and everyone connected with it.

Jameson understood DPI's interest in him. He knew—had known since he was a boy—that he was different. His blood type was rare, shared with only a chosen few. The belladonna antigen made him a subject of study for these so-called scientists. The few, rare individuals with this blood type were the only mortals capable of being transformed. Being made over...becoming vampires. And every living vampire had claimed the belladonna antigen during their mortal lives.

DPI, in their quest to learn all there was to know about the undead—and thus enable themselves to rid the world of them— often used live research subjects. But they'd had their chance with Jameson long ago, when he'd been just a boy. And they'd nearly killed him then. Would have, if not for his undead friends. Roland in particular. Still, they'd had their time with Jameson Bryant. Surely there was no more they could learn from him now.

God, to think Tamara had once worked for these bastards! But she hadn't known. She hadn't known.

Jameson didn't know why every preternatural being on the planet didn't band together and destroy DPI the way DPI was intent on destroying them. They didn't deserve the constant harassment, the fear they were forced to live with due to this secretive government agency. Oh, certainly, there were evil ones among the undead. Just as there were among any race of beings. But for the most part, vampires were the best people Jameson had ever known. They'd taken him in when his mother had died. Practically raised him.

Well, if Roland and Eric and the others wouldn't raise a hand to bring this organization to ruin, Jameson would. It was time. Long past time.

They had their "specimens" he'd heard them say. The experiment had been completed in record time, and now they could go on with phase two, whatever the hell that was. Well. They weren't fools then. DPI knew from experience that Jameson Bryant's friends were not the kind of people they wanted to tangle with. And now they would "dispose of the subject" before any of his undead protectors were the wiser.

He pulled against the straps that held his arms and legs to the cold, metallic table. They had a surprise coming if they thought he'd go down without a fight. This might not be Jameson's first involvement with DPI, but it would damned well be his last.

One way or another.

"Jamey!"

At the harsh whisper, Jameson turned his head as far as the restraints would allow. And then he swore, because Roland stood at his cell, bending the bars apart as if they were made of rubber.

"What the hell are you doing here?"

"What the hell do you think?" Roland stepped into the cell and easily tore through the straps that held Jameson pinned down. "Are you all right, Jamey?"

"Fine. And it's Jameson now." He sat up, jumped down from the table and faced down the man he loved like a father. A man who was centuries old, but who appeared not much older than Jameson was now. Though a bit paler skinned, and with eyes that gleamed a little brighter than a mere mortal's would.

Roland smiled. "I keep forgetting. Look at you. You dwarf me now."

"What you keep forgetting, Roland, is that I don't want my friends risking their lives for me."

"It would have been riskier to leave you to them," Roland said, and he shrugged sheepishly. "Rhiannon would have fed me to her cat."

Jameson tried to hold on to his anger, but that was a useless effort. He could well imagine Roland's mate, Rhiannon, threatening just that, and since her "cat" was no less than a panther, it was a threat not to be taken lightly. Not that she'd ever carry it out. She adored her husband.

Jameson embraced Roland, who hugged him back just as

fiercely. It had been a long time since they'd seen each other. Jameson had been leading a fairly normal, mortal life in San Diego, under an assumed name, thinking DPI would never find him again. He owned a bar there, and profits were good.

And then one day as he'd locked up and headed for his car, he'd been grabbed by two thugs in dark suits, and the next thing he knew he was strapped to a table in White Plains. Talk about déjà vu.

"We can catch up later," Roland said, releasing him. "Eric is—"

"Eric is here?" Jameson asked, suddenly angry all over again. Damn, when would they learn not to risk their lives every time he got into trouble? "And Tamara?"

"She's waiting outside with Rhiannon."

Jameson backed away from Roland, stiff with renewed anger. "Dammit, Roland, how could you let Tamara come here? You know what could happen. What they'd do if they ever got their filthy hands on her again!"

"She wouldn't stay behind. You know her well enough to know—"

"Hurry it up, will you?" Eric appeared at the cell door, a small cut on his forehead trickling scarlet. "One of them got away, and—" He broke off, eyes widening slightly as they skimmed Jameson, head to toe. "Good God, has it been that long? Look at you!"

Jameson shook his head, wondering how the hell a thirty-year-old adult man could be made to feel fourteen again. He supposed it could only happen when the two who made him feel that way were several centuries older. It would probably never change, no matter how long he lived. Roland grasped his arm, and hurried from the cell, pulling Jameson along with him. They ran into the hall, following Eric, who led the way to the nearest window. He stopped there, pushing it open.

Jameson planted his feet, and looked from one man to the other. "You guys are kidding, right? We're on the tenth floor for—"

The two flanked him, gripped his arms and jumped.

Chapter Two

"Two guards dead," DPI supervisor Wes Fuller repeated, though everyone in this staff meeting already knew the body count. "Six others injured. And that bastard Jameson Bryant gone, free as a bird." He rapped the pipe, bowl down, against the glass ashtray, expelling the spent tobacco.

"Doesn't matter." Chief aide Stiles went over the checklist on his clipboard, nodding as he did. "We got everything we needed from him. Our theory was correct. Once they're transformed, the males are sterile. Beforehand, though, while they're still human—"

"Human my ass. They're only passing. Animals, all of them."

"Yes, well..." Stiles cleared his throat. "At any rate, before that kind is changed over, they're fertile. The belladonna antigen doesn't seem to affect the sperm count."

"That's what I was afraid of." Fuller pushed his chair away from the conference table, the casters squealing in protest of his bulk, and got to his feet. He turned his gaze to Dr. Rose Sversky, who was pushing seventy, and still the sharpest member of DPI's research team. She had snowy-white hair, cut short, to go with her pixielike frame. She ought to be wearing an apron and rocking grandbabies, not dissecting vampires.

"You have the data?" Fuller asked. "What's the breakdown?"

Rose adjusted her Coke-bottle-thick eyeglasses and cleared her throat. "Of the twelve thousand, five hundred female subjects we've tested and/or autopsied in the past two decades," she said, her voice clinical and cold, "just over three thousand still had viable egg cells in their ovaries. Ninety-eight percent of those had been transformed for less than a year. None of them for more than twenty-three months." She looked up from her notes, and moved her glasses down a notch to peer at him over the tops of them. "To break it down, Mr. Fuller, yes. It is entirely possible that a newly formed female vampire could mate with a mortal male, and produce a child."

Hilary Garner's pencil lead snapped off. The sound drew Fuller's cold eyes, and he scowled at her. "Try and keep up, Garner. We'll need these notes."

"Yes, sir." She blinked the horror from her eyes, and went to the desk for a fresh pencil. She'd only recently been promoted to this position, executive secretary to Weston Fuller. It came with a huge bonus in pay, terrific hours…and some frightening, sickening revelations as to what this organization was truly about.

She hadn't believed her friend and co-worker Tamara Dey, all those years ago, when she'd tried to warn her. She hadn't seen anything to indicate that what Tamara had said was true. The kidnappings, the torture, the murders.

Hilary paused there, staring down at her reflection in the solid silver pencil holder on Fuller's expensive desk. Caramel skin, and wide brown eyes with a few crow's-feet at the corners stared back at her, and her reflection whispered, "What the hell are you doing here?"

"Hurry it up, Garner. I haven't got all day."

Clearing her throat, Hilary snatched a pencil from the holder and hurried back to her seat beside Chief Fuller.

"Now then," he began, still addressing Rose Sversky, who looked far too sweet and far too old to be involved in a covert government agency. But she was involved. Up to her bushy white eyebrows. She was the world's top—and, Hilary thought, likely the world's *only*—forensic pathologist specializing in the examination of the remains of vampires. But Fuller was still speaking and Hilary was supposed to be paying attention.

"Suppose one of these females were to mate with a mortal who carried the antigen? What would the results be?"

Rose shrugged. "A baby, I imagine." She winked, and an uneasy chuckle went around the table.

"Yes, but what *kind* of baby?" Fuller looked around the room, eyeing each high-ranking agent at the conference table one by one. "Don't you *see* what I'm getting at here? Should these creatures find a way to reproduce, we'd be outnumbered within a few years."

"So what are you suggesting we do about it?" Every eye turned to Hilary when she blurted the question. Hell, she wasn't supposed to have any input at all here. Just sit quietly and take notes while the big boys made their plans. Rose was the only female at the table besides Hilary, and she was only there because they couldn't get by without her.

Wes Fuller leaned back in his chair, crossed his arms over his chest and looked at her as if he were awaiting an apology. Hilary sat up a little straighter, looking him dead in the eye, and not giving him one.

The tension stretched to the breaking point, and finally he came forward, slapping his palms on the tabletop and leaning toward her. "What we're going to do about it, Miss Garner, is find out."

"F-find out...?"

"Find out what the results of such a mating would be. Research, Garner. That's what we do here." He nodded to Stiles, returning to his former comfortable, almost lounging position in his chair as he made life-and-death decisions as though he were ordering lunch. "We have the frozen samples from Jameson Bryant, and you say they're fertile?"

"Yes, sir."

"Good." Then he turned his attention to Whaley, the eastern regional operative coordinator. "We'll need a female, newly changed over. Preferably close by so we don't run into trouble getting her here."

Whaley nodded once, sharply. "I'll put every operative in the area on alert. We'll have a subject within the week."

"Good." Fuller smiled grimly, then glanced into Hilary's eyes, making her feel dirty inside. "You have any sort of problem with this?"

She blinked, lowered her chin, said nothing.

"I hope not," Fuller told her. "Because we deal harshly with employees who can't stomach the work we do here, Miss Garner. Very harshly."

"I understand," she said, meeting his gaze once more. And she knew when she looked into those chilling eyes, that she did. She understood perfectly. If she tried to get out, tried to walk away…she would die. Or disappear, just like pretty young Tamara had done so long ago. And no one would ever be the wiser.

Fuller dismissed them, and one by one they filed out of his office. He stopped her at the door and nodded back at the notepad she'd left on the table. "Have those notes typed up and ready for me within the hour," he barked, and then he pushed past her into the corridor with the others.

Hilary only nodded and watched him go.

"Are you feeling all right, dear?"

She brought her head up fast, and searched Rose Sversky's aging face as she gathered file folders from the table. They were alone in Fuller's office, and against her better judgment, Hilary closed the door.

"Rose…how can you be a part of something like this?"

Rose frowned, scanning a sheet before closing a folder and adding it to her stack. "Something like what? It's research. It's necessary."

"It's more than that."

Rose looked at her then, *really* looked at her. She pulled her glasses lower on her nose, tilted her head back and seemed to search Hilary's face.

Hilary moved forward, as if by being closer she could reach the woman. "This place is a prison. Do you know they have prisoners in the sublevels? Locked up in cells like animals?"

"Of course I know, dear. I'm the head researcher."

She could have slapped Hilary and shocked her less. "You know?" Rose nodded. God, Hilary thought, she'd probably known all along. Hilary had found out only recently, and she'd stupidly assumed the kind-looking old woman would be as appalled and horrified by the news as she had been. "But, Rose..."

"But nothing. We're not talking genocide here. These are animals, not human beings. They *feed on* human beings. For heaven's sakes, it's them or us. Surely you can see that."

Hilary took a backward step, the wind knocked out of her. "But...but what they want to do! A baby, for the love of Christ! And what will happen to it if they succeed?"

"Not a baby. A pup. A young animal, no different from the rest." She slipped her glasses back to their former position, and sighed. "It would be the most incredible research opportunity we've ever had."

Hilary swallowed the bile that rose in her throat. This was the stuff of nightmares, and she was going to throw up. Was this sweet little old lady actually getting wistful about the chance to carve up a child? Her hands were damp with sweat and shaking, and she felt dizzy as a sense of unreality washed over her. Her knees tried to buckle. She braced a hand on the table to keep from falling down.

"Hilary," Rose began, taking a step forward, narrowing her eyes. "You do understand why this is necessary, don't you? Because, if you don't—" her face softened with a blatantly false smile and equally phony concern clouding her eyes "—I can arrange to have you taken off this case. Perhaps you weren't quite ready for this promotion. Not everyone can handle the research we do here, and DPI is quite aware of that."

Her voice had changed. Become sugary. And there was a dark suspicion behind that fake concern in her eyes.

Of course DPI is aware of it. And the ones who can't stomach the work here disappear without a trace.

Hilary swallowed hard, shook her head. "No, I think I understand it better now. You're right. It's necessary. I'm...glad we talked.''

"Of course," Rose replied, and her smile became a little more genuine. "Any time you have misgivings, you can come to me. All right?"

"Thank you. I'll do that." *And you'll run right back to Fuller to report everything I say. Hell, you'll probably add this little conversation to their file on me.*

Still smiling, Rose hugged her stack of manila folders to her chest and left the office. Hilary leaned back against the door, and tried to quell the nausea. She'd said too much, blurted her thoughts without thinking first. Let herself see Rose Sversky as a stereotype. A sweet old lady. Somebody's grandma. Mrs. Santa Claus. Dammit, she was nuts to have opened this can of worms with that woman. Rose had been aware of the atrocities DPI was sponsoring for years. Years! Hell, she was likely a part of them!

And what would she do now? Had Hilary saved herself in time, or had she given herself away completely? And what if she had?

She was scared. Jesus, she was scared.

Jameson and the others stayed a few days in Rhiannon's Manhattan penthouse. Heavy black draperies lined every window, with dark shades beneath them. And there wasn't a coffin in the place. Everyone slept in beds, by Rhiannon's order. She liked the good life, Rhiannon did. Satin sheets on every bunk in the suite.

Jameson had to smile at her antics. She certainly kept the conservative and staid Roland hopping.

Roland. How many times had he saved Jameson's life now? Three? Four? There was the time DPI agent Curt Rogers had kidnapped Jameson when he was—what, twelve? That prick had left him tied up in a condemned building in the heart of winter. All just a ploy to get to Tamara, of course. If Roland hadn't found him after he'd fallen down those stairs, though...

And then, later, after his mother died, that bastard Lucien had taken him, offered to trade his life for the dark gift. Once again, his friends had stepped in to save him. Rhiannon had nearly died that time in the effort.

And now, here they were again. Pulling him from the jaws of death in the nick of time. So certain that just because he was still mortal, he couldn't take care of himself.

Hell, he was half vampire already. He lived like one. Slept days, and worked nights. It had come naturally to him, after spending so much time in their company. Even when Roland had found Jameson's natural father for him, and sent him to live with the man in California, he'd stuck to his nocturnal ways.

Someday, he supposed, he'd ask one of them to change him over. Someday. Not yet, though. He still had a few mortal years left, and he'd like to see a lot more sunrises before he said good-bye to them forever. He liked a good steak, a glass of wine, and he wasn't ready to give it all up for a strictly liquid diet.

"You guys shouldn't hang out in the city for very long," he warned the others, as he paced the floor that night. Their third night here. "You know the place is practically lousy with those DPI bastards."

Rhiannon smiled. "I wish I would run into one of them." She licked her lips, earning her a scowl from Roland. It didn't faze her. She reached down and stroked a path over Pandora's head, and the cat batted playfully at her hand.

"You're right, Jamey," Tamara said softly, and she went to the nearest window to part the draperies and snap the shade so it rolled up on itself. Then she stared out at the glittering skyline. "But I don't want to leave until you do. I know you're still furious. And I know you want revenge."

He shrugged. "That's my problem. I'm not going to keep telling you, I don't want you involved in my troubles, Tam. You're going to get yourself killed one of these times, sticking your nose in where—"

"I had a dream."

Jameson stopped talking when she turned slowly, pinning him to the spot with her huge, black eyes. "Jamey, I had a dream... about you."

Eric lifted one brow at his wife's statement, setting aside the book he'd been reading. A new one on quantum physics. "This is the first I've heard of it."

"I didn't say anything the first time...but...I had it again, today." She swung her gaze to Jameson's, shaking her head sadly. "It wasn't visual. Just a feeling. A horrible feeling that something's going to happen to you, Jamey. Right here, in this city. So I'm not leaving. Not until you do."

Jameson lowered his head, seeing no sense in arguing with Tam. She'd been like a sister to him, even when she was mortal. Protective even then.

"Well now," Rhiannon purred, slinking across the room to stand beside Tamara with as much grace as that cat of hers. "I agree. We remain. If anyone touches Jameson, we..." She smiled that half smile that had been giving him wet dreams since the first day he'd laid eyes on her. "Take action," she finished.

Jameson grated his teeth. It didn't matter that he was taller than Roland, or that his muscles were more firmly developed from hours in the gym than Eric's had ever been. It didn't matter that he'd found a gray hair amid the jet-black ones last week, or that he'd celebrated his thirtieth birthday the month before that. They'd always see him as a child in need of their protection. Always.

He turned, stalked to the apartment door, picking up his coat on the way. "I'm going for a walk." Then he looked back at them, his hand still on the doorknob. "And if any of you follow me, I swear to Christ, I'll never come back."

"Jamey!" Tamara rushed forward, grabbed his arm as if to stop him.

"Jameson," he told her gently. "Look at me, Tamara. No, I mean *really* look at me. I'm not Jamey anymore." She did, her ebony eyes racing over his face, tearing up as she nodded. He ran his hand through her dark curls, and then lowered his head to kiss her cheek. "Please understand, Tam. I just need some space, okay?"

Her lower lip quivering, she nodded. "Be careful," she whispered.

"I'm always careful."

He turned and left the apartment.

He walked, alone and after dark, completely unafraid. Aside from his occasional run-ins with DPI, few people ever wanted to mess with Jameson once they'd looked him in the eye. He supposed the old anger showed there. And now, probably more than ever. Now that he'd been used, humiliated, as an adult this time, at their bloody hands. Oh, he knew about them. The way they'd had Tamara's parents killed just so they could get their hands on her. Used her, from the time she was a little girl, as bait, knowing she had the antigen, and knowing, too, that sooner or later one of the undead would show up to check in on her.

And when the one appointed to be her mortal guardian, kindly old Daniel St. Claire, had changed his mind, when he'd decided he couldn't go through with the plot to use the child he'd raised as his own, they'd had him killed as well.

They were ruthless, bloodthirsty animals. They hunted the undead like game, and when they found them, their experimentation techniques were utterly free of any hint of conscience.

The bastards.

Jameson wanted to know why they'd taken him this time. What kind of information they were seeking. Why they'd taken the particular specimens from his body that they had, and what they intended to do next.

He wanted to know. But how could he find out? That was what he needed to think about, and he needed to think about it alone. Outside, with the fresh, snapping winter air keeping him sharp, and without all those concerned, protective eyes watching over him.

He walked fast, enjoying the exertion and the chill. And he planned. Well, he supposed he might break into DPI headquarters and go through their files. Maybe tap into their computers and see if any information could be found there. Or perhaps he could just grab one of them. That Nazi-like doctor, Rose Sversky, for example, or perhaps Fuller's lapdog, Stiles. He could torture one of them into talking. Maybe even Fuller himself. Jameson smiled as he thought about the pain he'd like to inflict on that bastard, who'd done likewise to so many, for so long.

Whatever he decided, he couldn't do anything until he convinced Eric, Tamara, Roland and Rhiannon to get the hell out of here and leave him alone. If they stayed they'd get themselves tangled up in whatever mess he ended up creating, just as they always did, and he didn't want that. He didn't want his friends—family, really—put at risk because of his need to vent this old, ever-growing anger. His passion for meting out some long-overdue justice. He couldn't allow them near this. It was going to be messy.

So he supposed he'd have to wait, and…

Jameson came to a stop in the street, and stood silently, head cocked slightly to one side as the cold wind ruffled his hair and stung his cheeks. He'd heard something…something so faint no one else passing on the street seemed to notice. Or if they did, they didn't seem to care. He had to strain to catch it again, with the slow-moving traffic, and blasting horns, and hissing air brakes. Less noisy now than during the day, but not by a hell of a lot.

A second ticked by, then two. And then he caught it again. The sound was that of moaning. Agonized, pain-filled moaning.

And the voice was that of a vampire.

A little shiver crept up the back of Jameson's neck as he pinpointed the source of the sound. An abandoned building, several yards away from him. Crumbling brick and fingers of broken, dirty glass. Snow on the old stone dormers. Gargoyles lining the top, though little remained of those gruesome guardians now. You couldn't even make out their features aside from their snarling mouths, and angel's wings, dusted now in snow.

She was in there.

How he knew that—how he could even hear the sound of her voice—Jameson didn't know. It wasn't audible. Not to mortal ears, anyway. But that was just it. His *were* mortal ears. So why was he hearing her, sensing her there? Why could he *feel* her pain?

Jameson Bryant was not a fool. He'd encountered other preternatural beings before, those who were strangers to him. And he always avoided them. True enough, it went against their nature to harm one of their own—one of the Chosen. Those rare mortals with the belladonna antigen coursing through their veins. They always knew that antigen. Scented it or sensed it or something. And most of the undead tended to protect and watch over those mortals with the antigen. Dark guardians. Dark angels. His mouth twisted in a smile at the irony of that.

But there were exceptions to every rule. And there were monsters in every race and every species. He did not make a habit of walking up to strange vampires and extending a hand.

But this time was different. He was compelled, drawn by some force he neither recognized nor understood. She might be mad. She might be a killer. She might turn on him. But he had no choice but to climb over the graying boards nailed in the shape of a cross in the doorway of the ruined building, and make his way through the rubble, to where she was.

And when he finally saw her, his heart tripped over itself.

She sat, curled in the fetal position in a corner. Her black dress—or robe or whatever it was—was torn and tattered and filthy. As was her tangled ebony hair, long and dirty and covering her face. She was startlingly white. So very white she nearly glowed in the darkness like a wraith. And thin. Emaciated, even. Her hands...Jesus, he could see the bones in those chalk-white hands.

He took another step toward her, and her head came up fast, eyes wide and fear-filled. And as she stared at him, the clouds skittered away from the moon, allowing its light to spill through the broken glass, and bathe her face and her eyes in that ethereal glow. She was painfully thin, but even then, she was beautiful. The shape of her face, like a sculpture in the moonlight. High, sharp cheekbones, and a delicate jawline. Full lips, parted slightly, and a long slender neck that held him motionless as he studied it. Then she moved her head just slightly, and the light fell on her eyes, and he caught his breath. They were violet. Brilliant, vivid violet. So bright was their color that he'd have suspected it to be false if he didn't know better. Huge, luminous eyes that shone with color. Her thinness, he suspected, made those haunting eyes seem even larger than they were. And no doubt it was that same condition, and those slight hollows it caused in her cheeks, that made her bone structure seem like that of a goddess. Or an angel.

She wasn't an angel, though. She was a vampiress, quite possibly a dangerous one. He knew that.

And he knew a few other things, as well.

He knew this vampiress was on the brink of starvation. He knew she might very well be *beyond* the brink of madness. He knew he should leave.

And he knew, damned good and well, that he wasn't going to.

Chapter Three

I had wandered alone for three nights. Hiding out in the very filthiest, vilest parts of the city, for I felt this was all I deserved. I was a filthy, vile being now, wasn't I? Violated by a monster, and made into one just like him.

And I knew it was my fault. Because there had been a moment, one single moment in time when I could have said no. I could have chosen death and salvation over life—unending life and damnation. I didn't have to drink when he pressed my face to his throat. I didn't have to drink. But I had. I had. I'd been filled with an incredible, powerful urge not to die. I'd wanted to live! And so I had.

God had seen fit to test me before I pledged myself to Him. No doubt He had sensed my misgivings. My flawed faith. And I'd failed that test. Failed it miserably.

But there was one thing I would not, *could not* do. And that was to prolong this life by feeding on the living. The innocent. Lambs of God, flocks of them outside, even now. And I, the wolf, hungering for them. Starving for what was the very essence of them. God, how the hunger burned in me! I writhed with it. When one of them passed by the windows of my hovel, and the wind sharpened, I caught the scent of their blood, and my mouth watered. My eyes filled with tears. My flesh tingled and my nerves came alive, singing, and then screaming with need. With every part of me I wanted to take one of them, take them the way I'd seen that monster do it. Gorge myself at their soft throats and taste their salty skin against my lips. Sink these newly elongated, razor-sharp fangs deeply into them, and drink.

Something, some small part of the person I'd once been, remained alive in me, and it was that part I clung to, and drew on to sustain my resistance.

That part...and the crucifix I wore around my neck. The symbol of all I believed in. I ran my hands over the smooth grain of its wood, and studied the grimace on the face of the Christ, the one too tiny for me to have even noticed before. Those things kept me going. Though they did not keep me sane. Like a rabid dog at the sight of water, I do believe I was quite mad that night.

And then *he* came.

I smelled him, as I had the others. No. No, that's not quite true. It wasn't the same. His scent came to me more powerfully than theirs had. It tantalized my senses to an even greater extent, so that I curled into the corner, drawing my knees to my chest and hiding my face against my legs, and praying he would pass by. Quickly, before that succulent scent drove me completely out of my mind.

He didn't, of course. His scent came stronger and more delicious with every second. And then there was a sound. A small sound, his steps coming nearer across the littered floor. I looked up, and he was there, his breaths making little clouds of steam in the dark. Staring at me as if he'd never seen anything quite so pathetic as the picture I made there in the filth. And I wanted to scream at him. Get away! Can't you see what I am? Don't you feel the danger you're in?

"Don't be afraid," he said to me. I wanted to tip my head back and scream with laughter, but I hadn't the strength. This man, this poor, innocent mortal man, telling *me* not to be afraid of *him*. Such irony!

But I didn't laugh. I didn't make a sound, but simply sat there, staring at him. His beauty amazed me. I saw it—as I saw everything now—in greater detail than I'd ever done as a mortal. Even in the darkness of that wreck, I could see him. For I saw very well in the darkness now. His eyes—not coal-black. But dark, velvet brown. With blacker stripes, wavy stripes surrounding his pupils like rays around the sun.

He was like the sun...the sun I would never look upon again.

His hair was thick and he wore it long. I could see, even from this distance, its luster, its richness. It would feel like silk, that raven mass of unruly curls. His skin wasn't chalk-white and sickly like mine, but bronze, as if his body had been coated in honey just for me.

I licked my lips as my eyes feasted on the bit of flesh exposed at his muscled throat. And then I lowered my eyes, closed them. I wanted him. I wanted his blood, and I wanted his body. I, a virgin, whose intent had been to pledge myself to Christ, and to remain chaste until I died. I craved him with a hunger so carnal it shocked me. Was this yet another aspect of my new character? Was I to become a harlot as well as a demon and a murderess?

"Go away," I croaked. "You're not safe here."

But the man came closer, towering over me, and frightening me, until I recalled that I was stronger. Despite his size—and he was a big man, broad across the shoulders and very tall—I had nothing to fear.

He stood over me, staring down, those tiger-striped eyes of his soft with pity when they should have been wide with revulsion. "You're starving, aren't you?"

Yes, I was starving. And I could hear the strong, and steady thrum of his pulse now. The rushing river of the blood running through his veins. I could hear it!

"Please!" I cried, burying my face in my hands. "Get away! I can't stand it!"

And then his hand came to stroke the hair from my face. It slipped down to cup my chin, lifting my head until I stared up at him again. I could feel the warmth of that hand, suffusing my face. I could feel every line in his palm. "You're just a fledgling, aren't you?"

But my eyes had found the spot where his pulse beat in his throat, and for the life of me, I could not look away.

"I can help you," he told me. "It will be all right, you'll see."

"Go, please…" But my voice lacked conviction now as I thought of the taste of him. My mouth on his skin. The warm rush of his blood as I—

"I can't just go away and leave you here. You're suffering, I can see that."

I moaned low and deep in my throat, and the tears rolled from my eyes. Sobs tore at my breastbone, shaking my body, racking me. I wanted to take him more than I wanted to draw another breath. And yet I couldn't. How could I? He'd done nothing wrong. Tried to help me, even.

But my crying was the wrong course of action, because the big, beautiful fool put his strong arms around me, and I could feel every curve of the muscled firmness beneath his clothes. He drew me close, holding me gently, rocking me a little. Saying, "Shh, it's all right. I have friends who are like you. They can help you. I'll take you to them. It's going to be all right."

He went on like that, stroking my back and my hair. I had no idea why. But his movements made me insane with this unnatural need. Insane with lust for him, body and blood. And the two desires seemed to intermingle until I couldn't distinguish the carnal lust from the unnatural hunger. They became one. My face rested in the crook of his corded neck. My lips even touched his warm, salty skin, as he held me there. And it was the end. All I could stand. There was no shred of humanity left in me at that moment. I was simply a hungry animal, and he was my meat.

I slipped my arms around the beautiful man, opened my mouth and sank my sharp new fangs deeply into him. Skin, and muscle, and then the pop as I pierced the jugular. He gasped. But didn't fight me very hard at all. In fact he leaned closer, held me tighter, and I felt a shudder work through him. He groaned and threaded his fingers in my hair, and pressed his hips against me. I felt his arousal, the hard shape of him nudging me between my legs, and like a common whore, I arched against him.

I think, perhaps, he didn't realize that this would be the end of him. Not until I'd nearly drained him dry. That was when he began to twist in my arms, and pull. But as starved as I was, it was useless. He couldn't break my hold on him. Already, he was weakened from the loss of his luscious blood.

"No more," I heard him whisper, so close to my ear. "Please, no more."

But I held him tighter, and bit down harder, and sucked at the wounds in his throat all the more. His strength surged through me, filling me, warming me, bringing me to vivid, sparkling life again. And he said, "Damn you...you're...killing me," in a barely audible whisper.

That voice, that same silken voice that had been music to my ears, pleading now, for his very life, and reduced to this harsh whisper. I was horrified, and shoved him away from me. But he collapsed on the floor like a rag doll, and lay there, his eyes no more than glazed slits, staring up at me. And then they fell closed.

"Jesus, Joseph and Mary, what have I done?" I whispered, and I turned to run away.

"Hold it right there."

This voice had no music. No silk. It came harshly, cruelly, from just beyond the doorway. A voice that held authority, command and menace. I froze there, panic trying to chill my body, so recently warmed by my victim's blood. This newcomer couldn't see the man I'd just killed. Not from here. I hoped he wouldn't. I couldn't bear for anyone to know what I'd done, what I'd become.

He stepped into my range of vision, and he was pointing a weapon at me. A gun, of sorts.

"There's a tranquilizer in here," he said. "You come along peacefully, and I won't have to use it."

I eyed the gun, and then the man. "Come along...where?" I asked him. And then I licked my lips, and I could still taste that handsome one on my tongue. Shameful pleasure filled me at the taste of him.

"You're very young, aren't you? When did those bastards change you?" Suddenly the voice was filled with sympathy.

"Three nights ago," I told him quite honestly, seeing no reason to lie. The light the man held shone in my eyes, then, and glinted from my crucifix, and illuminated my tattered habit.

"For the love of Christ," he muttered. "You're the missing nun."

"Novice. Not nun. Not yet." I closed my eyes, averted my face from his light. "Not ever."

"I can help you," he said, and he clicked off the flashlight as if it were a sign of good faith. "I work for DPI—the Division of Paranormal Investigations. It's a government agency, Sister. We're doing research, and—"

"Don't call me 'Sister,'" I said. "Don't ever call me 'Sister.'"

"I'm sorry. Listen...come with me. We're working on a cure. There's a chance we can help you."

I narrowed my eyes and studied his face. "Where?"

"Our headquarters. In White Plains. It's not far, really. Come on, come with me. Let me help you. You want to be human again, don't you?"

I blinked, searching his face. Was it truly possible? Could I regain my mortal self, and with it, my immortal soul?

No! Don't trust him!

I went stiff as, very clearly, that satinlike voice rang in my mind. The voice of my victim. Not wandering through my head like a stray thought or a daydream. But speaking, weakly and breathlessly, in my mind. His voice. It was real.

I glanced behind me, and his eyes, though barely open, met mine, held them. *Don't go with him! Don't go....*

I snapped my head around, ignoring the dying man. Surely he was not the one I should be listening to right now. He'd admitted to me that he had friends who were...like me, as he'd put it. Other vampires. Was I to trust a friend of those creatures, those leeches in human form, those predators of the night? No. I hated them. All of them, and I hated myself for being like them. I wanted it to end! I could not exist as a monster. I could not.

"I'll go with you," I said. And the stranger took my hand.

Fool. I kept hearing his voice in my mind as I went with the stranger. Though it grew weaker and weaker. *Traitor. You're a traitor to your kind. And you deserve whatever they do to you there!*

I closed my eyes, tried to block out his voice.

I could have helped you. You'll wish you'd let me...I swear you'll wish...

And then nothing. Nothing at all. Had he finally died then? A heaviness like none I'd ever known filled my heart. I'd killed. Twice now, once for no more reason than to preserve my own life. I was damned, but perhaps the road to salvation was not entirely blocked to me. Perhaps this was simply a test, or a lesson I had to learn, before I could take my final vows. Perhaps there would be forgiveness for me still.

The stranger opened the door of his automobile, and I got in. And as we pulled away, I heard him again, that musical voice, perhaps its dying breath.

You were right, Tam. Dammit, I need help...I...I...

There was no more. Not another hint of life from that condemned building. A large tear rolled down my cheek as we rounded a corner and drove out of sight.

"Jameson? Can you hear me?"

"He's going to be all right, Tamara. We got to him in time."

"But Eric..."

"Shh. Let him rest. He's going to need all of his strength when he wakes. It won't be easy for him to deal with this. He wasn't ready, you know."

"I know." A hand stroked Jameson's face. "I'm so sorry," she whispered. "But we just couldn't let you go."

Jameson opened his eyes, and then blinked, because something was wrong with his vision. Everything was too bright. Too vivid. He quickly closed them again, startled. "What happened?" he whispered, searching his memory.

"You were attacked," Tamara said softly, and he was amazed that he could hear the very vibrations of her vocal cords as she spoke to him. The perfect hum of her voice. Like music. "You called out to me for help. We found you in—"

"Wait...I remember. That crumbling ruin." It all came back to him then, but as he held up a hand to stop Tamara from speaking, he turned it slowly, eyeing the white bandage on his wrist. When he looked at his other wrist, he saw another. "What's going on?" he said slowly, eyeing each of them, one by one.

Rhiannon sat in a chair on his left. She closed her elegant hand around one of his much larger ones. "Some renegade bastard drained you to the point of death, Jameson. We had no choice."

He shook his head, but even as he did, the truth was making itself a home in his mind. He couldn't deny it. Even without their worried, slightly guilty expressions he'd have known. He was feeling things. Every wrinkle in the sheet. His skin was alive, tingling, and he could hear the way the breeze outside fluttered over the single dead leaf that still clung to that flowering maple. How many stories below was that skinny tree, planted in a perfect circular opening in the concrete? Twenty-four?

Again, he looked at the bandages. "I don't understand," he said.

"You were unconscious," Tamara whispered. "Too weak to drink."

"So?"

"You were dying, Jamey—Jameson," she went on. "I thought..."

Eric turned toward the windows, gazing out at the night, not looking Jameson in the eye. "I had to rig up some tubing," he said. "For the transfusions."

"Trans...fusions?" He looked at Eric's back, staring until the man turned. "Eric?" Then he swung his gaze to Roland, who stood silently in a corner of the room, saying nothing, just watching, listening. "Roland? Jesus, are you saying that I'm..."

Roland nodded, just once. "Yes. Your mortal life ended last night, Jameson. There was nothing we could do to save it. The one thing—the only thing we could do for you, was give you another life to replace the one that bastard stole from you. A life of...unending night."

Jameson closed his eyes and swore. He heard Tamara's soft crying, felt Rhiannon's hand tighten on his.

"I can't believe it," he muttered. "God, I can't believe it." Then he searched their faces. "Which of you did this? Whose blood is running in my veins now? Yours, Roland?"

Tamara sniffed. "All of us," she told him, drawing his gaze to her tearstained face. "We all gave to you, Jameson."

He closed his eyes, shook his head, expelled his breath in a rush. "Dammit," he said. "I didn't want this. Not yet. Maybe not ever. Dammit—"

"Enough!"

His mouth snapped closed at Rhiannon's harsh command. She rose from her chair, leaning over him, eyes narrowed to slits, reminding him sharply of the way Pandora looked just before she pounced on an unsuspecting rabbit.

"We gave you life, Jameson. The alternative was death. You should be thanking us." She bent even closer, so her long, glistening black hair trailed over his face. "Unless, of course, you'd have preferred the second option. And if that's the case, it's not too late."

"Rhiannon!" Tamara shouted, jumping to her feet. "How dare you—"

Rhiannon straightened, tossing her hair behind her shoulders. "I dare, Tamara darling. I dare anything. You know that. And frankly, I'm a bit weary of this one's constant lack of gratitude." As she said it, she nodded toward Jameson.

He couldn't believe Rhiannon was this angry with him, but she was. Her eyes blazed with it, and when Roland came forward to slide his hands over her shoulders, she shrugged him off and walked away. She paced back and forth at the foot of his bed. "We took care of you when you were a child, Jameson," she said, her voice deep and smooth as black satin. "Saved your life for you on more than one occasion, risked our necks for you more often than not. Found your father for you. And yet all you've done is complain. We treat you like a child! We call you by the wrong name! You don't have enough *space!*"

Jameson sat up in the bed, pushing the covers aside, lowering his feet to the floor.

"And then," she went on, "you bumble your reckless way into still more trouble, and as you lay dying, with what could have been your very last breath, Jameson, you call out to us for help. What in the name of the pharaohs were you expecting us to do? We can't raise the dead! You asked for help, and we gave you the only help we could give. And still you complain."

"That's enough, Rhiannon," Roland said, and he said it sternly. She glared at him, but he didn't back down. "You know nothing about what Jameson is feeling right now."

"And you do?" she shot back.

Roland nodded, turning his gaze on Jameson. "I do. Rhiannon, and Tamara too, you both sought this life. I did not. It was forced on me, Rhiannon, when you found me near death on that battlefield in bloodstained armor."

"And on me," Eric said softly. "When Roland came to me in that filthy French cell, the night before I was to face the guillotine." He met Jameson's eyes. "I was terrified, then, of what I'd become. And though you know us, know us well, I imagine you're a bit frightened, too. You think that now you're a monster like we are."

A lump came into Jameson's throat, and his eyes stung. "I have never thought of any of you as monsters, Eric. You have to know that. It's just that...all of this..." He shook his head. "I thought I'd have time to get used to the idea. I thought I'd be the one to decide if and when I was ready for this." He lifted his head, met Rhiannon's haughty stare. "You're right, Princess. I'm being an ass, and I'm sorry. If it hadn't been for all of you, I'd be dead right now, and I was even less ready for that."

He could see her softening. Rhiannon liked it when he addressed her by her proper title. She was a pharaoh's daughter, after all. Not that she'd ever be likely to let any of them forget it. Jameson lowered his head, closed his eyes. "So I'm here. It's done. Can't be changed. I guess I might as well get used to the idea."

"You're going to be just fine, Jameson," Tamara told him. "I promise."

He lifted his head, met her eyes and thought this wasn't all bad. He'd be even more able to take on DPI with his new abilities. He flexed his hand, wondering just how strong he was now. Strong enough, perhaps, to go back to that towering facility in White Plains and tear it down, brick by brick? Strong enough to make the bastards tell him what this last round of tests performed on him had been all about? And then kill every last one of them?

"I imagine the first thing we'll need to teach you is how to guard your thoughts," Roland said, looking him squarely in the eye. "Although when they're as foolish as that one was, it might be better that we all know about them, hmm?"

"I don't blame you, Jameson," Rhiannon said, and her anger seemed to have been banked, for the moment, anyway. "I've been wanting to destroy everything even remotely associated with that organization of buffoons for years. But they all fight me." She jerked her head toward the others in the room.

"For good reason," Roland told her. "If we were to do that, we'd be making everything they believe about us, true. We'd become the heartless predators they claim we are. Deadly, destructive and dangerous. And they'd have all the more reason to mount a full-scale attack against us. Can you imagine, Rhiannon, what would happen if other branches of the government became involved? The military, for example?"

She tossed her head. "Bring them on."

Roland rolled his eyes heavenward, but Jameson laughed aloud. And then Eric was stepping closer, scanning his face. "Enough of all this," he said softly. "Jameson, tell us about the beast that attacked you. Who was he? Can you describe him?"

"Yes," Roland put in. "We can't let him go on—"

"Not him," Jameson said, getting to his feet and turning to face them. "Her." He saw the frowns on their faces as he went on. "And we don't have to hunt her down. She surrendered herself to a DPI operative right before my eyes. Turned herself over, without batting an eye. I think she bought what he was selling, about them being able to make her human again.''

"My God!'' Tamara got to her feet. "Who was she, Jameson? Did you know her? Had you ever seen her before?''

He shook his head slowly. "I think the agent might have known who she was, but I was barely conscious. I kind of came around when he told her to come with him, to let him help her.''

"It's better he found her than I,'' Rhiannon said.

"She was mad, I think,'' Jameson went on. "Filthy, her clothes tattered. She seemed very young…and I'm certain she was on the brink of starvation. I heard her crying, so I went to her. I thought I'd bring her to you, and you could help her.''

"And we would have, of course,'' Tamara told him.

"If I ever see her again, I'll wring her pretty neck.'' Jameson thought of how fragile she'd seemed…just before she sank her fangs into his throat. And then he thought a little further, and had to avert his face from the others.

She'd taken him someplace he'd never been. Shocked him at that first piercing of his flesh, but then…

Jesus, why hadn't any of them told him what it was like? Was it normal to react that way? He'd never been so turned on in his life as he'd been when she'd held him hard against her, and worked his throat with her mouth and her teeth. And he'd wanted it. Wanted her. And for a few minutes, he'd figured it would be all right. That she'd only take enough to keep her alive, and then she'd stop.

But she hadn't stopped. The bitch had tried to kill him. And he'd been hard for her right up until he'd collapsed at her feet.

Jesus.

"I'll kill her,'' he whispered.

"Vengeance is a wasted emotion, Jameson,'' Tamara told him.

"She tried to kill me.''

"Perhaps she didn't know better.''

"Or,'' Rhiannon put in, "perhaps she simply lost control of herself. It's been known to happen…in certain circumstances.''

Jameson looked up quickly, wondering if they'd all been privy to his every thought just now. But Rhiannon was looking at Roland as if he were a juicy steak, and he thought he detected a glint in Roland's eye, as well. Jameson decided not to say any more about his erotic attack. He tried not to *think* any more about it, either, but that was far harder than it should have been.

Time to change the subject. "Look, if DPI goons are out rounding up vampires for another group of experiments, maybe it's time you guys get the hell out of the city."

"Exactly," Roland said. "But don't forget, my friend, you're a vampire now, too."

Jameson frowned. Damn.

"Even should you decide to go ahead with your plans to learn what they wanted you for this last time they took you, Jameson, you have to agree, it would be better to wait. You need time to get used to your new nature. To learn to control it. To test the limits of your strength, your endurance."

He had a point there. Damn him.

Roland smiled, no doubt having heard *that* thought, too. "There is much you need to learn about being a vampire, Jameson."

"Hell, Roland, I know more about being a vampire than you think. I've been around you most of my life."

"Yes, that's true enough. But living the life of the undead is a far different matter than just witnessing it. You've discovered that already, haven't you?"

It was true. It *was* different, far different than he'd imagined it would be. His senses were altered, heightened somehow. And there were new ones to explore as well.

"All right," Jameson finally conceded. "All right, we'll all go. But I'm coming back. I'll find out what those bastards wanted with me, if it's the last thing I do."

Every one of them looked worried. Except Rhiannon. She wore her Mona Lisa smile. Very secretive. And Jameson wondered what the hell she was thinking.

Chapter Four

They took me to a large building, down in an elevator to a sterile white room, with a bed, and a chair, and little else. I was led inside, full of questions. How could they help me? What was this experimental cure that could return me to humanity?

I turned to ask my questions, only to see a solid steel door closing on me. No window in that door, and locks aplenty. I heard the locks turning, and a feeling of dread welled up inside me. I went to the door, tried to push against it, but it didn't give at all. And it should have. It should have. I was strong, stronger than any locks they could make. I knew that.

Ah, but that man, the one who'd brought me here. He'd injected me with something. A drug, he said, to prepare my body for the shock of becoming mortal again. And it had to be that that had taken away my strength.

And now I was here, locked in this room. A prisoner, for all practical purposes. And I recalled the voice of my beautiful victim telling me not to trust them. Not to go with that stranger.

God, had I made a terrible mistake?

I paced the room throughout that first night, and it seemed endless. And then finally the door opened, and a kindly, white-haired woman of tiny stature smiled at me.

"Hello," she said. "My name is Dr. Rose Sversky. I'll be taking care of you while you're here."

Taking care of me. This sweet, harmless-looking old woman. I nearly sagged in relief. I hadn't made a mistake after all. They would truly help me here.

"Why am I locked in like this?" I asked her. "It frightens me."

"Oh, dear, they really should have explained." Dr. Rose came in, closing the door behind her. "There are others here, others like you. People we're only trying to help." She shook her head, clicking her tongue. "But some of them...well, they can be quite monstrous, you know. They'd attack anyone, even one of their own kind."

I believed that readily. I'd fallen victim to one of them, and I had no doubt that they were all just as beastly. Just as horrible as I had started to become now that I was one of them.

"The locks are to keep them out, dear, not to keep you in. For your own protection, honestly. Someone should have told you."

I sighed hard, my relief palpable.

"Now, if you'll just hop up onto the table," she said, smiling her reassurance, "I can get started making you human again."

I obeyed hurriedly. The woman eyed my dirty habit, shook her head, and pulled a hypodermic from her pocket.

"How long will I have to be here?" I asked.

"Well, it might be weeks, to be honest. The process involves several steps, you know. But you needn't worry. We'll take better care of you than your own mother would. You'll see." The needle's tip sank into my arm, and in a few seconds, my world became dark and murky. I drifted into unconsciousness.

When I woke, I wore a white hospital gown. I had been bathed, and my hair had been washed and brushed. I felt oddly violated. I wondered what sort of procedure the kindly old doctor had performed on me, but there was no way of knowing.

Eventually, my door was opened once more, and a strong young man entered, handed me a glass of scarlet liquid and left without a word. Not a word. As if I were an inanimate object or a pet to be fed. I drank the cold stale sustenance he'd provided, but it lacked the invigorating warmth of blood drawn from the living. That warmth I still recalled suffusing my body as I fed at the throat of that beautiful man who'd offered to help me.

But I didn't want that warmth. I didn't want to prey on the innocent. I wanted to be mortal again, to have my old life back. And so I drank, and I prayed it would not be long I'd have to remain in this place.

Hilary Garner listened to Rose Sversky's report, and tried to keep a semblance of clinical detachment on her face. She wasn't certain she succeeded. But she tried.

"We've successfully harvested and fertilized a single egg from the subject. Only one. The implantation will have to go off without a hitch, and if it doesn't take, I'm not certain we'll get another shot. We may have to have another subject or two before we achieve success."

Fuller nodded, his narrow-eyed gaze slipping to Hilary's face every so often, as if he were watching for something. A slip. She kept her expressionless mask firmly in place. She'd show this man nothing. There was nothing she could do, anyway.

"Schedule the implantation for tonight," he said. "Let's get this experiment under way. How is the subject?"

Rose smiled her grandmotherly smile. "Irony always amazes me, Mr. Fuller, but this time it's overwhelmed me. The subject is a virgin."

Fuller's brows rose high. "You're kidding me."

"No. Other than that odd state of affairs, she remains completely cooperative. She still believes she's going to become mortal again. She won't give us any trouble."

"Don't get too complacent, Sversky," Fuller said. "She'll give us plenty of trouble once she realizes she's pregnant. And she'll have to realize it, sooner or later."

"Yes, well, she will if the implantation is successful."

Fuller nodded. "Best prepare one of the maximum-security cells for her. Once she figures it out, she'll fight us every step of the way." He shook his head. "A freaking virgin birth. Wasn't she some kind of nun before she was changed over?"

"Something like that," Sversky said with a chuckle.

"Will wonders never cease?" Fuller replied. He leaned back in his chair and began filling his pipe.

I was slowly going insane. Stir-crazy would be the closest term. I had no books. No television. No radio. I was allowed to bathe nightly. And my liquid meals were brought to me by soft-spoken, even respectful individuals dressed in white. From glasses, not warm bodies, I fed. And the sustenance was diluted. Thin and cold, and I began to suspect, laced with some sort of tranquilizer. Since coming here, I'd never once felt that odd surge of vampiric strength that I'd felt before.

I should have known, I suppose. I should have seen the signs. The heavily veiled disgust in the eyes of those caregivers. The glances they exchanged. When I objected to any of the conditions I lived under, I was told that they'd never be able to help me get back to being mortal again, unless I cooperated with them. So I did.

And oh, that was so foolish! So incredibly foolish.

I had no idea why they would want to do what they did to me. No clue. Not in my wildest imaginings could I concoct a reason. But it soon became apparent.

Months had passed before I understood what was happening. Truly understood it. My belly began to swell, and more than that, I could sense a life force within me. I could feel it there. A separate entity. Living, growing, inside me. I was, I realized, stunned, with child.

And as that knowledge came to me, I pounded on my cell door, screaming and kicking at it. But no one came to tell me why they'd done this to me. No one came near.

I sank to the floor only when I sensed daylight painting the earth, slowly stealing my consciousness. And this time, when I woke, I was in a far different place.

I was sealed in a dark, coffinlike box. Panic took a firm hold on me, and I beat against the lid with my fists, screaming until I was hoarse.

At last, the cover was lifted. I flew from my prison, only to be gripped by three strong men. I kicked and shouted. I asked them, pleaded with them to tell me why they'd done this, what their intentions were. But to no avail. I was injected with the familiar drug, returned to the pathetically weak state I spent all my waking hours in, and then they let me go. I slumped to the floor, sitting up, eyelids heavy, and warily examined the room around me.

The sterile white walls were gone now. I was in a dungeonlike cell, with barely any light. One of the men pulled me to my feet, and ushered me close to the rear wall, while another clamped shackles around my wrists, and then my ankles. I was chained, chained to the cold stone wall at my back.

A glass of the detestable liquid was pressed into my hand. The chain was long enough to enable me to drink. And yet I did not. I stared at the glass, and shook my head. "No," I told them, lifting my chin in defiance. "I won't drink. I'd rather die than go on living in this prison! Let me go. I demand you let me go!"

One of the men chuckled, and shook his head. "If you don't feed, you'll lose your baby. You don't want to starve your own baby, do you?"

I swallowed hard, tears flooding my eyes so that the men swam before me. I couldn't do that, couldn't starve my own child, and they knew it. They knew it.

Oh, God, what had I done? What had I done to deserve this particular hell? Only then did I fully understand what a grave mistake I had made. Willingly, even eagerly, I had made myself their prisoner. Their guinea pig. I could scarcely believe it was true. They saw me as a creature. A laboratory rat, and I was, from then on, treated as such.

I drank, because I had little choice, and so I lived. Lived on their drugged liquid, kept too weak to break my chains or fight my captors. Each night I remained chained to the cell walls. But the days were far worse. For each dawn, as soon as the day sleep overtook me, my vile captors took me down from my wall and sealed me inside that coffinlike box. More often than not, dusk would fall, and I would awaken still trapped in that tiny cement sarcophagus. I'd claw and kick and cry, and I'd hear them laughing as they passed me by, not letting me out until they were good and ready. It seemed they enjoyed my panic.

They no longer tried to conceal the disgust in their eyes. I was treated as an animal. For the sake of the child I carried, they continued to provide me with sustenance, and warmth, and sanitary conditions. For the sake of the child. I knew that. And I knew, too, with a growing sense of terror, that what became of my child once I'd given birth, was completely beyond my control.

And I knew something else in those long months of my captivity. Those long months of a loneliness more intense than anything I'd ever known. As the child grew in my womb, as I felt it there, living and even moving eventually, I spoke to it. Wrapped my arms around my swollen belly and cradled it. I even sang to it, in a voice that surprised me with its preternatural range and purity. I'd always loved to sing, but I'd never found such joy in doing so with my flawed, mortal voice. Now I thought I must sound like the very angels. And as the time passed, I came to realize that I loved the baby I carried. She—and for some reason, I was certain, even then, that she was female—she was the only living soul I spoke to in all that time. She was a part of me, my very heart. And I loved her with everything in me. Never in my life had I contemplated motherhood. I'd never imagined that I would have a child. But now, I could not imagine *not* having one. This one, whom they would try to take from me as surely as the sun would rise each morning. They would try to take her.

And I would die before I would allow that to happen.

Every once in a while, Hilary slipped down to the maximum-security sublevels, and checked in on that wide-eyed young woman they held there. And once, very late in the experiment, she heard something that made her heart trip to a stop in her chest. Singing. The purest, most angelic singing she'd ever heard in her life.

She crept closer to the cell, and peered through the mesh-lined safety glass. And she saw her. Pale and thin, except for her protruding belly. Her name was Angelica, though to DPI she was called by a number. Her hair shone like black satin, long and lustrous, and she had huge violet eyes. Their color no less than stunning, even through the tears that spilled slowly from their purplish depths.

She sat on the floor of her cell, chains dangling from her arms and pooled around her legs. She hugged her bulging belly, and rocked slowly back and forth, and she sang "Amazing Grace," so beautifully that it brought tears to Hilary's eyes.

And then she stopped singing all at once, and lifted her head. She stared right into Hilary's eyes from beyond that glass. And Hilary was unable to look away. She was so sad, so frightened and so utterly alone. It was horrible what this organization was doing to her. Horrible.

And if I try to help, she thought, *they'll kill me. They'll kill me. I'll disappear, just like Tamara.*

But the story went that Tamara hadn't disappeared. According to the DPI grapevine, all those years ago she'd become one of them. A vampire, like the ones she'd been trying to help. Could it be true? Could Tamara be out there somewhere?

She shook that thought away and looked back at the woman in the cell. But the plea was still there, in those violet eyes. And Hilary knew that she had to help. She had to try. She had to.

She closed her eyes, and turned away. And the singing began again, filling the entire sublevel with beauty. And as she passed other cells where other captives languished in despair, she saw them listening. Saw them closing their eyes and drinking in the beauty of that song.

Hilary ran from the cell block to the elevators, eager to shut out that sad, sad voice. But even after the doors slid closed, she kept hearing it. Ringing in her mind. And she saw those beautiful eyes, imploring her to act.

It was difficult walking into Fuller's office for the staff meeting that night. Harder than ever to keep her mask in place. But she had to. She made a valiant effort, too, she thought.

Until Rose Sversky's dire predictions filled the room, at least. "We can't take it C-section," she said. "They bleed like hemophiliacs. The mother would probably bleed out before we could get the child, and then we'd lose them both.''

"Then we go natural,'' Fuller said, tamping more smelly tobacco into that rank pipe of his as Hilary took rapid notes.

Stiles cleared his throat. ''Sir, you know that kind feels pain as if it were magnified a thousand times.''

"Like I give a damn,'' Fuller said.

Rose's eyes met Stiles's. Even the two of them, monsters though they were, were not quite as heartless as Fuller. They saw the undead as animals, yes. But even animals didn't deserve unnecessary agony.

"She'll need to be tranquilized,'' Rose said. ''With her preternatural strength, if she pushes, she could crush the child. We'll give her the drug, a far higher dosage than the daily one. Enough to render her semiconscious before we induce labor.''

"And what happens to the baby?'' Hilary whispered.

Again they all looked at her, but they were over being surprised at her ever-increasing interruptions.

"The baby will be our most prized research subject,'' Fuller explained. ''Ms. Garner, this is a first. A one of a kind. Will it be born a vampire, or a mortal, or some mutant cross between the two? We're going to learn more from this creature than...Ms. Garner?''

It showed in her face. That sick feeling that made her think she'd better get out of here fast before she lost control and broke into tears in front of all of them. She schooled her features, stood up slowly. ''I'm sorry, but you'll have to excuse me for a minute.'' She turned toward the door.

"Stomach bug, Ms. Garner?'' Fuller's voice was full of speculation, and the look in his eyes was deadly as she glanced back at him.

"Yes,'' she told him. ''The flu, I think.''

"It had better be.''

It was a haze of pain and horror and fear. The first drug they gave me left me nearly paralyzed. And the second one brought on the pain. I couldn't think. I couldn't see the walls I passed as they wheeled me along, strapped to a stretcher, into an elevator and up. They took me to a room with masked, white-coated people and machines and equipment of all kinds. And those masked demons surrounded me, staring down, snapping on surgical gloves.

They spoke, but I didn't know what they were saying, so dazed was I by the pain. I hurt, I only knew that. I thought my body would tear itself in half, and I screamed. I know I screamed.

And those white coats all around me, eyes eager with excitement. There was only one, the brown-skinned woman with the big doe's eyes, who might be different. I'd seen her before, the woman with the kind brown eyes. The kindest brown eyes I thought I had ever seen. She looked as horrified from behind her surgical mask as I felt.

Oh, and I was horrified, beyond all thought. Horrified, because I could barely move, could barely think. And all I could feel was pain. And I knew I was helpless to fight them. Helpless to protect my child. Utterly...helpless.

She stood beside my head, the one with the kindness in her eyes. She stroked my face, not speaking, but I could see the pity in her eyes when they met mine. And then there was relief, so swift and sudden I nearly floated off the table with it. Doe Eyes turned her head, looking down at the men and woman who stood at the foot of the table on which I lay. I followed that gaze, looking where she did. And I saw my child. The woman I'd thought of as a kindly old grandmother held her—a pink, wrinkled blur in her arms. A blur that squirmed and kicked and had jet-black hair stuck to her head.

And then that pretty one leaned close to me and whispered, "A girl. And she looks healthy."

I moved my lips, lifted my hands toward my child, my daughter. I tried to beg. "Please..."

And those doe eyes filled with tears. They met mine. Held mine. "Please," I whispered. "Help me...help...*her!*"

She looked at me, then at my baby as they carried her from the room, out of my sight. All of them, leaving me lying there. And I watched them go, as great heaving sobs that hurt as much as the birth had, tore through my body. I tried to sit up, tried with everything in me to tear free of the straps that held me down. But the drug made my efforts into a joke. A sideshow, as I cried in agony and they took my child out of my sight.

And then that beautiful, dark-skinned woman who seemed different from the others touched my face. I turned to look up at her, and her eyes, with tears swimming in and nearly spilling from them, met mine again.

"Help her," I whispered.

And slowly, almost imperceptibly, she nodded.

Then she left me to the orderlies, who arrived to clean me up and return me to my cell, I was left wondering whether I had imagined that nod, the assurance in those eyes. I prayed I hadn't.

The classified ad read:

Tamara, remember me? Eighteen years ago. You had the chicken, and I had the seafood. We both had the wine. A little too much. And the cheesecake was more than we could resist. All that cholesterol. It could cost me my life. Call me. 374-555-1092.

No one would have thought it anything unusual. But Tamara did. Eric paced, looking worried.

"Where did you get this?" Tamara asked, looking up at him from where she sat in the oversize house they owned just outside San Diego. Jamey had returned to get his affairs in order. Sold the bar he'd owned, traded in his car, bought another under an assumed name. He was making arrangements to hide his money as well. DPI must not be able to track him. He had to live the way the rest of them did now. In hiding.

"A vampire by the name of Cuyler saw it, recognized the name, tracked us down and sent it to us. She thought it might be meant for you. Do you think she was right?"

Tamara nodded slowly. "Of course she was right. This is from Hilary Garner. We worked together at DPI. I remember that night, we went out together. I went home alone, and had a flat. That was the night I was almost—"

"I'd rather not be reminded of what nearly happened to you that night," Eric said. He moved forward, stroking one hand through her hair. "This could be a trap, Tamara. Hilary still works for DPI."

She shook her head hard. "No. Hilary wouldn't do something like that. And look at this last line." Tamara held up the paper and pointed. "'It could cost me my life.' She makes it sound as if she's referring to the cheesecake, but she's not. It's there to let me know this is urgent." She looked into Eric's eyes. "I have to call her, darling. I have to."

He lowered his head, and she was glad that for once he didn't argue. "I was afraid you were going to say something like that." She held his gaze until she saw him conceding. He sighed hard, and nodded. "I'll rig something up, just in case. They won't be able to trace the call."

She smiled, and then kissed him.

Since his change, Jameson had been learning. Testing his strength and energy. Honing his mental skills. And he was decidedly happy with his progress. He could run nearly as fast as Eric. Climb and leap and jump as well as Roland. He could speak to any of them without uttering a sound. That was probably the most surprising aspect of his new nature. And the hardest to get used to. He could read their thoughts now just as easily as they'd always been able to read his. Unless they were guarding them. He'd become adept at erecting a mental shield around his mind, one that could bar entry to any vampire.

He'd expected to miss eating a good meal, but oddly enough, he didn't. His other senses were so finely honed, so much sharper and more acute than before, that he took sensual pleasure in everything. Sounds and sights, smells and feelings bombarded him constantly. The tastes he'd once enjoyed were easily replaced. Easily forgotten.

He did regret that he'd never have the chance to fulfill his dream of a "normal" mortal life. A life with a family, a wife, children perhaps. But then, that had never really been a possibility anyway. He'd always known that those rare individuals who carried the belladonna antigen had abbreviated life spans. Few ever lived beyond the age of thirty. Jameson was thirty now, and while he hadn't experienced the onset of any of the usual symptoms, it probably wouldn't have been much longer before he had. So his initial anger at his dearest friends was long since reduced to cold ashes.

The fury he felt for the woman who'd attacked him, though— that remained red-hot. Coals of that anger glowed in his soul, and it would take only a bit of stirring to bring them back to blazing rage again.

He'd been attacked, fed upon without his consent, made to feel helpless and nearly killed. Oh, how he'd like to run into that raggedy vampiress again. He was strong now, stronger than she would ever be, he was certain, since he'd been infused with the blood of the truly ancient. Rhiannon in particular. Yes, he'd like to see that tangled and tattered woman try to attack him again. He'd toss her away like a rag doll. Snap her like a matchstick. She would learn.

Of course, that fury would probably never be vented. She was likely long dead by now. Vampires, Jameson knew all too well, didn't tend to last long in captivity. Particularly when their captors saw them as useless once the experiments were done. Easier to simply let them die in an agony of slow starvation, or just tranquilize them with that drug they'd developed, and stake them out in the burning rays of the sun. Disposable experiments.

Somehow, it gave Jameson no pleasure at all to think of that bone-thin and chalk-white vampiress dying in such a way. No pleasure at all.

Above all the lessons he'd been taught by his friends was that he mustn't take blood from the living. The bloodlust could become overwhelming, and a vampire could easily lose himself in the act of assuaging his passionate thirst. Well, he'd witnessed that firsthand, hadn't he? And since he had no desire to kill anyone— anyone in San Diego, at least—he took his blood as the others did. From the stores they kept, robbed from blood banks and hospitals.

"Jamey, I need to talk to you."

He turned, saw Tamara entering his room in one of the many houses they all kept around the country, this one in San Diego. He really wasn't certain why they were still here. His affairs were in order. He had plenty of money and a good cover to keep him invisible from DPI's prying eyes. His lessons were pretty much complete as well. They could go wherever they wanted. He supposed they hadn't moved on yet because they simply hadn't felt the urge to do so.

Tamara still hadn't stopped calling him Jamey, and he'd all but given up hope that she ever would.

He frowned as he met her eyes, and a little trill of alarm rushed through him, because she looked...very upset. "What is it, Tam?" She approached him, gnawing her lower lip, but then stopped halfway, and gripped the back of an armchair as if for support. And this alarmed him even more. "My God, what's wrong?"

"Jamey—Lord, but I don't know how to tell you this...."

He went to her, gripping her shoulders and easing her trembling body into the chair she'd been clinging to. "Has something happened to Eric? Or Roland? Is Rhiannon all—"

"Everyone is fine, Jamey. But you...you won't be." She tipped her head up, her eyes probing his. "If you fly out of here in a blind rage, Jamey, you'll only end up getting yourself killed, and that won't help the situation. This is...it's horrible. If it's even true. If it is, we have to take action. But with thought, and planning, and extreme caution. I can't stress that enough."

He narrowed his eyes and stared at her. "I don't have a clue what you're talking about, Tam."

She licked her lips, closed her eyes for a long moment, then opened them again. "When DPI held you..."

As her words trailed off, Jameson snapped to attention. "When DPI held me?" he prompted. "Go on, Tam, get to the point."

Tamara cleared her throat, lifted her delicate chin, looked him in the eye. "You said they took...samples."

He averted his eyes. But Tamara's small hand came to his shoulder, and her steady gaze drew his back like a magnet. "I need to know...what kind."

"That's not something I'm going to discuss," he said. "Not even with you."

"Forgive me," she whispered. Then cleared her throat. "Did they take your semen, Jamey?"

"Tamara, for Christ's sake!" He turned away, pulling free of her gentle grip and pacing the floor.

"I must know."

He only stopped when he reached the window. He shoved the black chintz draperies apart, braced his hands on the wide sill, and stared out into the murky gray night. The clawlike fingers of storm clouds reached past the moon, breaking its light into thin, jagged portions. And the stars were invisible.

"Why?" Jameson whispered. "For the love of God, Tamara, why would you ask me something like that?"

"Because I've been told something too horrible to believe," she told him. She didn't cross the room, didn't come to put her hands on his shoulders as he'd half expected her to do. Instead she remained sitting in the chair nearest the fireplace. And when he turned to face her he saw her staring into the dancing flames. He saw the teardrops rolling slowly down her cheeks, reflecting the light of the fire.

"Tell me," he said.

She nodded once. "You remember Hilary? My friend from so long ago?"

Jameson tilted his head, searching his memory. "She worked for DPI," he said at last.

"So did I."

"That's different, Tam."

"Maybe not," she told him. "Maybe it's not so different at all." She drew her black eyes from the firelight, and turned her gaze to him again. "She told me they had taken your semen, Jameson. She told me they'd frozen it. She said their research had shown that some female vampires—very young ones—still had functioning ovaries.''

Jameson felt his eyes narrow as he stepped away from the window, closer to Tamara. ''What in hell are you saying?''

''The men—once they're brought over, they seem to be quite sterile. But you know DPI and their unending quest for knowledge about our kind. You know them, Jamey. They wanted to know what would happen if a female vampire were to have a child. And since they couldn't mate her with a male vampire, they decided that one of the Chosen would be the next best choice.''

Jameson stood in front of her now, between her and the hearth's protective screen. ''Are you telling me they intend to implant a woman with my seed?''

More tears. She bit her lower lip, then tipped her head back, staring up at the ceiling. ''No, my love. I'm telling you they've already done it.''

''Already...''

Tamara's head came level again, and she got to her feet. Her hands closed on Jameson's shoulders, and her grip was firm. ''Last week a vampiress being held in that place gave birth to a child, Jameson. Your child.''

''No!'' He pulled free of her, spun away. He slammed his fists down on the mantel, and the clock and other bric-a-brac lining it flew into the air and smashed to the floor. ''No, it's not possible.''

''I'm sorry,'' she whispered. ''It's killing me to tell you this, Jamey, but Hilary says it's true. They...they have your child.''

''I'll kill those bastards,'' Jameson shouted. ''I'll kill every last one of them, I swear!'' He stalked across the room, and yanked the door open, only to be met by a solid wall of resistance.

Roland, Eric and Rhiannon stood there, blocking his path. Jameson shoved his way past them all, but Roland gripped his arms and fought to keep him from leaving. ''Jameson, please! Just listen—''

''No. I'm through listening. I'm through letting you all treat me like a child. Jesus, Roland, don't you realize what's happening? A child—*my child,* Roland, if what Tamara says is true—is being used as a research subject by those monsters.'' He swung his gaze around to Rhiannon's. ''You were their prisoner once,'' he told her. ''You know…you know better than anyone, Rhiannon, what they're capable of. I have to get my child out of there. I can't wait.''

''Of course I know that,'' Rhiannon told him. ''And I agree fully that the animals must pay, Jameson, though these others will no doubt argue that point. We only want you to be aware, before you go, of some vital considerations.'' She stopped there, turning to Eric, nodding at him to go on.

Jameson stopped struggling and met Eric's eyes. ''First, just keep in mind that we only have Hilary Garner's word that this is your child,'' Eric said. ''And—''

''Do you really think that matters? *No child* deserves to be used the way they will use him…or her.…'' He turned to Tamara, whose tears flowed unchecked now. ''Him, Tamara? Or her?'' And his voice broke as he asked the question.

''Her,'' she whispered. ''A girl.''

''A daughter. Jesus Christ, I have a daughter.'' He felt dizzy, weak, ill.

''Maybe,'' Eric said. ''And we'd mount a rescue attempt no matter whose child it turned out to be. But Jameson, there's one more thing you need to be aware of before we move in.'' Eric licked his lips. Closed his eyes very briefly. ''You have to prepare yourself, my friend. We don't know what sort of child we'll find. Whether she'll be mortal or…or—''

''Or vampire?'' Jameson moved closer to Eric, searching his face. ''My God, Eric, you don't think…no. No, not a newborn vampire. That's too horrible for words. A child who lives on blood? A child who can never grow older?'' Jameson closed his eyes, then popped them open again and turned to Tamara. ''This Hilary, she saw the baby?''

''Only for a moment. She just glimpsed her, and says all she could tell for sure was that she was…she was beautiful. Dark curls. Like yours, Jamey.'' Her beautiful face fell then, into her delicate hands, and Tamara wept. Her shoulders shaking with it. Eric went to her, took her into his arms.

Jameson stepped away from them, looking back at them all. "You love me," he said, his voice coarse. "I know you all love me. But do you trust me?"

"Of course we trust you, Jameson," Roland said quickly. But Rhiannon was looking at him with wariness in her eyes. As if she knew full well what was coming next.

"I've never asked anything of you. I'm asking you now, and this means more to me than anything ever has. If you care for me as you say you do, then let me go after my daughter alone."

Tam's head came up sharply, eyes red and puffy and wet. "No!"

"This is my child," he went on. "My responsibility. For once, treat me as an equal. I am, you know. I'm your equal now. There's no more reason for all this protectiveness. None at all. And if you won't let me do this, if you won't trust me to save the life of my own child, then..." He lowered his head, shook it slowly.

"Then," Rhiannon said softly, "our relationship with this young man is going to be severely damaged."

Jameson met Rhiannon's eyes and nodded. "Yes. That's it exactly." Then he looked at the rest of them, each in turn. "Trust me enough to know I'll be wise, and cautious, and that I won't satisfy this rage that's burning inside me at the risk of my child's life." And then he went to Tamara, and he stroked her hair away from her face. "I want you to wait for me. If I need you, I'll call to you, I promise you that."

"Swear it, Jamey," Tamara whispered. "Swear to me you'll call us, if you're hurt or if you're taken. Or if things look too dangerous. Swear it to me, and I'll believe you."

"I swear, Tam." He stared down into her eyes. "You're more to me than a sister could be. Closer to me than my own soul, sometimes. You'd know if I were lying to you. I'll call if I need help. My pride won't get in the way of saving that child. I need to do this alone, Tamara. I need to focus everything on getting to her, not on worrying which of my friends will suffer or die in the attempt. Please..."

Tamara sniffled, brushed at her eyes but nodded. "All right then. Go. We'll be waiting."

"There are many of us, Jameson," Roland said. "There are others who will come to your aid. Damien, the oldest of all of us. The first, and the strongest. He'd come in a heartbeat. And his mate, Shannon. And so many others."

"It might very well take all of us to defeat DPI this time," Rhiannon said softly. "And if it does, we'll all be willing. Know that, Jameson. Say the word, and we'll be there."

Jameson nodded. But he had no intention of risking their lives unless he had to.

A daughter. A tiny, newborn child. His child was waiting, somewhere, for her father to come and rescue her. Her father. He closed his eyes as the enormity of it hit him. Her father.

As he turned to go, a single tear fell and rolled slowly down his cheek.

Chapter Five

I was hosed down like an animal, and then wheeled back to my prison cell. Men lifted me from the gurney, and carelessly dropped me into that box where I was condemned to spend my days. The coffinlike box with the lid that sealed from without. The place where I would lie, trapped and suffocating, until they saw fit to let me out.

And only vaguely did I realize as they shifted me into this tomb, that it was not dawn. Nor even near to dawn. It was still fully night, and the slumber wouldn't fall upon me for several hours yet. Surely the chains on the wall were preferable to being trapped in this box!

"Please," I said to the two who lowered me into my prison. "It's not daylight yet." My words were thick and slurring together. And I was still weak from the drugs they'd given me, still feeling the residual cramping from my enforced labor.

They did not answer me. Just lowered me into that box, and reached for the lid.

"No!" I tried to pull myself out again, tried with everything in me. Suddenly I was terrified of being sealed inside the tiny casket. I couldn't bear it. I wouldn't! It might have been some form of precognition that made me feel this panic, but whatever the source, I felt it, and I fought.

But it was little use. One orderly, a burly man in white, held me down as I kicked and clawed, while the second easily pushed the lid into place. I screamed. I howled and pushed at the heavy, perhaps lead-lined lid that held me prisoner, but my efforts were worthless and exhausting. I heard them working without. Heard the bolts they inserted to keep the lid down tight. And eventually, I stilled. I would have curled up into a tiny fetal ball if the space were wide enough to allow it. But as it was I could only lie flat in the darkness, with the ceiling only inches above my face, and my knuckles brushing the walls on either side of me. I pressed my hands to my flat belly, empty now of the child I'd cherished all these months, and I wept bitter tears, until it seemed no more remained.

There wasn't enough air. I couldn't move. I could only lie there in the pitch-black closeness, feeling the heat of that cramped space closing in on me. With my heart, my mind, I felt my child's presence. I knew she was near…but that faded a short while later. My sense of her grew slowly weaker, until it vanished entirely. Why I was so aware of her, I did not know. I'd felt her crying for me, and I'd known she was comforted in someone's arms. I'd sensed when she was wrapped in a warm blanket, and when she'd fallen into a contented sleep. And I knew now, as surely as I knew my own name, that she'd been taken from this place. Taken away, so far away that I could no longer reach her. And the tears I had thought were used up, renewed themselves, and spilled from my eyes.

I slowly realized the awful truth. These people had used me. And their use for me was finished. They had no reason to keep me alive any longer. And I knew with an instinct that struck me with mind-numbing fear, that the lid of this coffin was never going to open again.

How long, I wondered, would it take for me to die?

The white lab coat had belonged to the man who was now occupying space in the darkest corner of a supply room. As did the ID tag. Jameson knew this was not a foolproof plan, but not entirely a bad one either. He could read their thoughts. He'd know which of them were suspicious of him, and which believed his stories. He moved through the corridors of the fourth subterranean level of DPI headquarters in White Plains. The last place any of them would expect to find a vampire visiting of his own accord. He knew well enough that the captives were kept below ground level, and the more important the prisoner, the deeper he would be found. Like a living burial, life in this hole. He pushed a stainless-steel cart full of instruments, and he wore a pair of latex gloves, and he stopped on occasion to flip open the chart he'd stolen, and gaze thoughtfully at the gibberish scrawled there. All to add flavor to his charade. An extra white lab coat, and surgical mask and cap were tucked inside the coat he wore. And he knew from the blueprints he'd pilfered that there was a rear exit used only to remove the remains of those who died in captivity here. An elevator that went directly to that exit. And a large blast furnace in the room that elevator opened into. A crematorium, of sorts.

He passed a young woman…then stopped as he sensed her gaze on him, her approval of his appearance, the initial flare of attraction, and he turned to her, saw her glancing back at him, running one hand through her silken blond hair, and moistening her cover-model lips. "Excuse me, maybe you can help," he said. "I'm a little bit lost."

Her smile was quick and brilliant, and she was hoping he'd ask her to meet him after her shift. She was a lab technician, an up-and-comer, very talented. And utterly without morality. "Sure," she said, her gaze dipping only briefly to the ID tag on his chest. Seeing it dangling there was all the confirmation she required. She was a beautiful fool. "What are you looking for?"

"The uh—" He glanced around, made a pretense of being secretive, knowing full well that not everyone here would be privy to the most secret of information. Then he checked her ID tag, noted her security clearance was one of the highest and nodded. "The new mother?"

The woman frowned, and a bit of suspicion rose in her mind.

He heard her thoughts plainly. *Why would he be visiting that one? She's probably dead by now, anyway.*

"I'm supposed to take a few samples, and then move the remains down to forensics," he added quickly.

"Oh." The suspicion left her pretty face. "One level down, isolation cell 516-S."

"Thanks."

She was thinking maybe she ought to mention this man's mission to someone. Jameson turned once more, flashing his most brilliant smile, yet careful to conceal the telltale tips of his incisors. "Say, what time do you get off?"

"Midnight," she told him, a triumphant gleam in her green cat's eyes. "Why?"

Jameson stared into her eyes, and though he'd never used the mind control before, he knew he could do it, so long as the mortal in question didn't resist. And he sensed no resistance or fear in this one. He'd seen Eric do it. The trick took practice, and he hadn't had much. Still, influencing the actions of one mortal female shouldn't be too difficult. *Say nothing about me to anyone. Say nothing. Nothing.*

Aloud, he said, "Why don't you meet me in the parking lot at twelve-fifteen? We could go out for drinks...or something."

She nodded, her eyes eager. "That sounds nice," she said.

"Great." He turned and headed down the hall to the elevators. He passed several others, but none of them seemed at all wary of him. The woman he sought, whoever she was, was in all likelihood dead, according to the pretty technician. Why was she still here then? And would he find the child, as he'd expected he would? He'd thought they'd be together, sharing a cell at the very least. Now, he wasn't so sure.

Sublevel five was like a dungeon. And it was only seconds before Jameson knew this was where they brought the vampires when their use for them had ended. This was where the undead were left to die. The second death. The final one. This level was encased in concrete, and painted a dark green, like a basement morgue in a hospital. Each tiny cell had a door, and all the doors were sealed. And he could smell the stench of death heavy in the air.

He reached the door with the correct number. No guards on this level. Apparently, they assumed none was needed for dead or dying vampires. Jameson gripped the door handle, and it was with only a minimal exertion of his strength that he pulled it open, breaking the locks in the process.

He stepped inside, and caught his breath. In the far corner of the tomblike room was a box the size and appearance of a stone sarcophagus. Six inches thick. No baby in sight, and thankfully, no tinier, infant-sized deathtrap sat nearby. He'd thought to find the child with her mother. He'd obviously been mistaken. And if she were dead already, the woman would provide no clues as to where his daughter might be. Even if she were alive, he realized, heart sinking, she might know nothing. But he had to try.

Stepping closer, Jameson pushed the huge stone top aside, wincing at the grating whine of it. The sound was like a cry, and it echoed endlessly in this room. Within it was a smaller coffin, ordinary wood, though he sensed there was a layer of lead within it. This one was bolted shut, but he snapped the bolts like twigs, and wrenched the lid from the casket.

In the pitch-darkness, his eyes were as sharp as those of a cat. And she lay there, still and white, the sharp bones of her face protruding into her pale skin. Her hair spread around her in tangles. And he stared down at her in utter shock, and whispered, "You!"

Her eyes opened, their violet light so dulled he barely recognized it there. "Please..." she whispered, parched lips barely moving to form the words. "My...child..."

Why she made the effort to speak the words aloud when it was so difficult for her, he could not fathom. She could transmit her thoughts to him much more easily. Her. Why the hell did it have to be her? What twist of fate had brought this ridiculous irony about?

"Where is the child?" he demanded, gripping her shoulders, shaking her when she would have faded into slumber. "Where?"

She parted her lips, but only a low moan escaped them. Jameson shook her again, and she blinked up at him. "They...took my baby...they took her...."

"Took her where, dammit!"

Her eyes widened at the anger in his voice. And then she stared up at him as if seeing him for the first time. "You're alive," she said with a sigh, scanning his face.

"No thanks to you. Now, dammit, where is the child?"

Licking her lips, she shook her head. "I...they've taken her...away from here."

"She's not in this building?"

She shook her head.

"And you've no idea where she is?"

"No."

Jameson swore, spinning in a slow circle, then pacing away from the woman's intended tomb.

"Please," she groaned. "Don't...leave me here."

And then he laughed, a low, bitter sound that echoed from the concrete walls, and turned to face her again. "You want me to help you? Me, your victim, the mortal man you did your best to murder? Why the hell should I? You tried to kill me, lady. You drained me and left me for dead, and then you turned yourself over to these bastards. It's your fault they've got their hands on my daughter, and you deserve everything they—"

"*Your*...daughter?"

Jameson stopped speaking and stepped closer to stare down at the pathetic, yet somehow still beautiful woman, who was too weak even to sit up on her own. "Yes," he said softly. "My daughter. I was once a prisoner here, just as you are now. And it was my seed they used to impregnate you. She is my little girl. And I will find her."

She closed her eyes, drew a painful breath. "I...can help you."

"How?" He didn't think he believed her. Hell, he wasn't truly going to leave her here. Wouldn't leave his worst enemy to die this way. But she obviously thought he would, and she was trying

to convince him not to. Grasping at straws. Bluffing, in all likelihood.

"I..." She gripped the edges of the coffin, struggled to sit up.
And Jameson's hands moved automatically. It seemed they found
it a bit too easy to forget this woman had once tried to murder
him. He slipped his hands over her shoulders, grimacing at how
thin she was, and helped her to sit up. She had to cling to the
wooden sides to keep herself in that position, and her head fell
forward as if even holding it upright were more than she could
manage. "Please, if nothing else...take me out of this box."

He saw the fear in her eyes when she lifted her head briefly to
look around her, when she realized the box she'd been entombed
within had been sealed inside a larger one, made of stone.
"They're monsters," she whispered.

"Ah, so you've finally figured that out, have you?" Jameson
gathered her featherlight body into his arms and lifted her out of
the box. But when he lowered her feet to the floor, her legs buckled. She fell against him, and only his quick reaction kept her
from sinking into a heap at his feet.

He held her. And doing so stirred up unpleasant memories.
Memories of the last time he'd held her this way, with her face
pressed to the crook of his neck. Of the desire that had overwhelmed him when she'd put her mouth to his throat. Of how
much he'd wanted her at that moment. She'd been desperate then.
Starving. She was, if anything, more so now. He waited, tense
and expectant, his arms around her waist to keep her from falling.
Her body pressed tight to his. And he felt her lips touch the skin
of his neck, felt her soft gasp.

And then she turned her head away from his neck, and rested
her cheek on his shoulder.

Of course. She wouldn't attempt to overpower another vampire.
Particularly as weak as she was. It was that, nothing more, surely.

"Tell me," he said, "how you think you can help me to find
my child."

"My child," she whispered, not moving. "There's...there's a
link between my baby and me. I felt it...even before she was born.

I knew how...she'd look." She slipped lower in his arms, sinking toward the floor, and he was forced to hold her tighter, closer. "I knew she was female. I spoke to her...and she heard, I know she did." Her voice was so weak. But a whisper, and speaking was obviously a tremendous effort.

"Of course she did," Jameson said, not believing a word she said.

She lifted her head, met his eyes. "I could feel what she felt. I knew when she was here, and I was aware of it the instant they...took her away." Her head lowered to his shoulder again, and he knew she could hold it up no longer. She was very near death right now. "I'll know again, when we get close to her. I swear to Christ, I will."

Jameson tipped her chin up with one hand and searched her eyes, wondering if she might be telling the truth, nearly wincing at the agony he saw in their violet depths. And then he scanned her mind, not expecting to find much there, particularly if she were lying. She'd be smart enough to guard her thoughts if she hoped to fool him. But he was surprised, because her mind was utterly unguarded. Completely open to him.

He must take me out of this place! Yes, he's a monster...a horrible monster, just like the other...but even a monster is better than dying here. I'll run from him. I'll get away as soon as I leave these walls behind. And then I'll use this psychic bond to find my child by myself. I'll take her away from them...and away from him. His kind will never lay eyes on her. I'll protect her from all of them. And if I must feed on the innocent to do it, then so be it!

Jameson tilted his head, studying the brief, rebellious anger in her eyes. Shocked by the power of it. Hungry. She was so very hungry. And she thought him a vile monster. Odd, since if vampires were monsters, she must surely realize she was one as well.

She hated him. Hated what he was. Hated every one of her own race. She was a traitorous, murderous creature. And she wanted to take his child from him.

But the bond with the baby was apparently real. And he needed her if he hoped to rescue his daughter. The rest, he'd worry about later.

"Come on," he said, turning for the door. "Let's get the hell out of here."

She took a single step, and fell to the hard floor. Jameson looked at her, lying there, all but helpless, and slowly he closed his eyes, knowing full well what must be done. Hating it, but knowing it. He could not carry her from this place and risk being seen. She must wear the disguise he wore, and she must walk out on her own. And she couldn't do that in this weakened state.

He crouched and scooped her up into his arms, holding her like a child, and then he turned her face to his own throat, one hand at the back of her head, cupping her, supporting her. Sharing blood with another vampire...he'd been warned of the bond it could create. The attraction it could stir. The longing it would embed in the depths of his soul like an addiction. But it could not be helped. For his daughter, he must do this.

She turned her face away.

"You know what's necessary as well as I do," he told her. "Do it."

"I can't," she whispered, and he thought there might be tears on her cheeks.

"Do it, damn you!" And he turned her face to him again, pressed her tight to his neck.

She parted her mouth and sank her fangs deeply into his flesh, and Jameson drew a deep, shuddering breath. He felt her mouth working him there, hesitantly at first, but then harder and faster as the bloodlust overwhelmed her. He felt each movement of her lips, each lap of her hungry little tongue. And lust came rushing through him. Weakening him. He trembled with it, dropping to his knees and moaning, and still he held her there. His heart rate quickened, and his breaths came rapid and shallow. True, Roland had warned him how closely the bloodlust and sexual desire were linked in his kind. How the two intertwined to the point where they were nearly inseparable. But this was a thousand times more powerful than what he'd experienced with her before. And he hadn't expected it to be like this. Not like this. Not this urge to pull her closer. To do to her what she was doing to him. To take her, in every way he knew how, until, until...

She lifted her head, blinking and looking dazed. He hadn't had to tell her to stop. She'd done it on her own. And judging from the look in her eyes, he thought she'd experienced the same mind-numbing desire as he had.

As he...still did?

He swallowed hard, and got to his feet, lowered her to the floor, still shaking with unbelievable need. Her face was no longer chalk white, but was slowly becoming infused with healthy color. A glow. And her eyes were shining brighter with every second he spent looking into them. Her dulled hair took on a new gleam, and her hollowed cheeks began to plump right before his eyes.

God, she was beautiful.

He blinked the thought away. No time for this. Not now.

"I...feel stronger," she whispered, but the shock of the desire that had raged between them still showed in her violet eyes. "Thank you." She was bewildered. She had no clue what had transpired between them, was completely shocked over the feelings that had swamped her just now.

Looking back at her, he nodded and reached into his pocket for the second lab coat he'd brought along. He held it open for her, and she turned, swayed, nearly fell, but managed to catch her balance and thrust her arms into its sleeves. It wasn't starvation weakening her now. It was desire. And it disgusted her. Jameson watched her struggle with the buttons for just a moment, then ran out of patience and bent to do them up himself, effectively covering the thin white robe that was all she'd been wearing.

He then produced a surgical mask and a disposable paper head covering, a puffy thing with elastic. Quickly and efficiently, he wound her long, tangled hair into a bunch, snapped the cap over it and tucked the loose tendrils up underneath.

"That's going to have to do," he said, standing back and eyeing her, noting how those violet eyes stood out above the white mask she wore. "Come." He took her hand once more, pulled her out of the room, into the hall, and started down it. He looked down at her, saw her fear in her eyes. She was afraid of him. He'd sensed that from the start. And no wonder. She must expect some kind of retribution from the "monster" she'd once tried to murder. But right now, she was more afraid of the others who roamed this place. Her eyes were wide with it, and she was trembling.

He squeezed her hand for some reason he could not explain. Perhaps to calm her fears. It was cold, shaking. She didn't pull it away. "I don't know your name," he said softly. "Ironic, isn't it? We have a child together, and don't even know the simplest things about each other."

"I'm Angelica," she whispered.

Angelica. Angel, he thought. A dark, frightened, lonely angel. Stupid thought. She was no angel.

"I'm Jameson."

They reached the elevator that led to the furnace. No one should be there at this hour of the night. DPI didn't dare risk one of their victims waking—bolstered by the night—as they shoved him into the flames, and wreaking havoc on the attendants. They stepped inside, and the doors slid closed. "What happened to you?" he asked her as the car started upward. "How did you end up alone in that condemned building, half-starved?"

She lowered her head, shook it slowly. "I was mad. Out of my mind, that night."

The car jerked to a stop. Angelica was jostled against him, and he closed his arms around her without forethought.

"I'm sorry for what I did to you," she whispered. "It's my fault you're..."

"What, Angelica? A monster? That's what you think I am, isn't it?"

She looked up at him as the doors slid open, eyes widening. Yes, she must know he'd read her mind now.

"Just so you know, your plan to run from me as soon as we're out of here is never going to come about."

"What?"

Taking her arm, he led her from the elevator, and out through the exit. There were guards outside of course, but he kept close to the shadows, using trees and shrubs for cover. He stopped behind one, out of earshot of those sentries, and faced her once more. "Your maker should have taught you better, Angelica. Vampires can read one another's thoughts. Just as I read yours back there. Even a fledgling ought to know enough to guard them. You are not going to run from me once we're away from here. You're not going to find my child and take her away where I'll never lay eyes on her again. I won't allow that."

"You can't stop me," she whispered. "I can find her. I'm the one with the bond to my little one, not you!"

"Which is why," Jameson said as the guards in the distance turned away, and he started forward again, still holding her arm in a firm grip. "I've decided to keep you with me. Right by my side, Angelica, until we find our daughter. As my prisoner, if need be."

"No."

"Yes," he said, gripping her arm and leading her quickly across an open space before the guards could turn in their direction again. "But don't worry. I'm not nearly as monstrous as you seem, for some reason, to think I am."

I went with him. But only because I had no choice. I was still weak, and run-down, and he was obviously much stronger than I. I knew nothing, then, of my own abilities. Of the limits of my power, or the psychic part of my newfound senses. I only knew that I could die easily if exposed to fire, as my creator had. And that starvation could leave me weak and barely able to function. I suspected it, too, could kill me, but of course, I couldn't be sure.

So I went with this stranger. This vampire. This Jameson who claimed to have fathered my child. I went with him, thinking I'd certainly traded one hell for another, and vowing in silence that when I was strong, I would run. If he could read my thoughts, then let him. I would run from him, just as fast and as far as I could, at the very first opportunity.

I was afraid of him. When I'd put my mouth to his skin, a wildness had come to life inside me. A madness far more intense than what I'd felt the first time I'd taken from him. A passion that blazed like hell itself, and weakened me with its intensity. I was ashamed of the feelings that had overwhelmed me for this man. And what frightened me even more was that I'd sensed he'd felt them, too.

I must escape him.

But until then, I would bide my time. Use it to regain my strength and to discover the extent of my abilities. That way I'd be more able to rescue my child from the animals who held her.

Jameson was young, not more than thirty. He was human when I met him. I was certain of that. No vampire would have allowed me to do what I'd done to Jameson. He was strong, too. Broad across the back, and very tall. But I would escape him. When we were out of this place, I would get away. I had to, for my daughter's sake. And for my own.

He led me right up to the towering and obviously electrified mesh fence that surrounded this prison, and as I looked up at it, my hopes of escape faded rapidly. "What now?" I whispered, turning to look up at him.

He frowned down at me as if puzzled by the question. Then he reached up to pull the cap from my head, and remove the mask from my face, tossing them carelessly to the ground. "Now," he said, "we jump it."

I nearly choked as I stood there, searching this grim-faced man's countenance for some sign that he was joking. When there was none, I looked up at the fence, back at him, and slowly shook my head. "It's impossible."

"You have no idea how strong you are, do you?"

Well, of course, I did not. But I felt admitting as much to him would be a dire mistake.

"Just how long ago were you made, Angelica?"

I shrugged, turning my gaze to the fence once more, ignoring his question.

"Put your arm around my shoulders," he instructed, and though still doubtful, I did so. He slipped his strong arm around my waist, his fingers pressing into my belly as he pulled me firmly against his side. And that rush of desire for him returned. What was this madness?

Then he bent his knees, drawing me down with him. "Now...jump!"

He pushed off, and I did as well, nearly laughing at the idiocy of it all. I fully expected to hop perhaps a foot or two into the air, and then land right back where I stood. So I was ill prepared for the flight that followed. We sailed into the night sky like two rockets, propelled upward by no more than the force of our legs, pushing off. The mesh rushed before my eyes in a blur, and then we cleared it by several feet. And as the momentum eased and changed, and we began to plummet toward the earth on the other side, my heart nearly tripped to a stop in fear. My hair blew upward, and the night wind whistled past my ears. I peeked below us, saw the ground rushing at us at dizzying speeds, and I clung to Jameson and I buried my face against his shoulder, too afraid to look again. He closed his free arm around me, holding me against him as if I were a child. We hurtled downward, and I expected I would suffer incredibly upon impact.

But instead, I felt my feet hit the ground, and then my knees bent as the rest of my weight followed. My body absorbed the impact without pain. I stumbled and fell onto my backside, the motion pulling me out of Jameson's firm embrace, which was a relief and a disappointment, all at once. I felt clumsy, I recall, as I saw the grace with which he landed, squatting low and then springing upright again, all without wobbling in the least. And then he turned to me, reached for me and pulled me to my feet.

I could only stare up at the fence we'd just leaped, almost effortlessly. I couldn't believe....

"You didn't have a clue, did you, Angelica?"

Dumbly, I shook my head, then faced him and, realizing what I'd just admitted, bit my lower lip.

"Who made you?" he asked, searching my face. "What kind of vampire would bring you over and leave you alone?"

I met his dark eyes, lifting my chin. "You ask me things that don't concern you."

He blinked, but finally nodded and stopped waiting for my answer. Apparently he'd realized it was not forthcoming. Taking my arm, he led me through the parking lot to a small black sports car that seemed to be crouching there, waiting like a bandit in the night. It was completely concealed in the shadows.

He opened a door, and I slid into a seat so low that it seemed to rest atop the road. Then he slammed the door, moved away and got in on the other side, sliding behind the wheel. He started the engine and we rolled away, unnoticed. And when the place that had nearly been my deathtrap was finally out of sight behind us, I turned to him. "How will we find our child?" I whispered. "Where will we begin?"

He met my eyes, and his seemed to blaze in the orange-red glow of the dash lights. "We'll begin by finding out which of them knows," he said. I saw his hatred for my former captors— *his* former captors, if his story was true—flare in his eyes. Saw it for the first time. I knew that hatred well, for I felt it, too. "And then we take them. We question them, one by one, until we get the answers we need."

"They will never tell us," I said, shaking my head and losing hope rapidly.

"They will," he replied, and he fixed his eyes on the road ahead. "If they want to live."

Chapter Six

Jameson drove away from White Plains, and as he did, he tried to keep his eyes, and his mind, on the highway ahead of him. But that was useless, because his curiosity about the woman in the seat beside him seemed to gain strength with every mile that passed. He'd asked her about her origins. Twice now, and he'd been rudely slapped down on both occasions. He wouldn't give her the satisfaction of asking again.

But he couldn't help but wonder about her. What kind of woman had she been in life? When had she been changed, and by whom? And why did she seem to detest her own race so thoroughly?

She leaned back in the passenger seat, her head resting against the black leather, her eyes closed. She wasn't sleeping. No. Not at all. She was feeling. As Jameson let his thoughts slip unnoticed into her mind, he sensed her every aspect was focused on feeling that connection she'd described to him. The one that would tell her when her child—his child—was near. Her mind seemed almost to sniff the air through which they sped, to search every car they passed, and every building, and every field and every wood-lot. And the farther they went, the more desperate that search became, until he could almost hear her soul crying out to the child.

She'd taken only a very little sustenance from him. And he

realized now that it was not enough. She was draining her own energy, sapping her strength in this mental search, and as little as she understood about her own nature, Jameson was surprised at her ability to even try it. Instinctive, he supposed.

She was paling, now. Her eyelids twitched in protest, and a gentle shudder worked through her body. He wanted to despise her. And he should. He certainly should. She'd attempted to murder him. She'd handed herself over to his oldest enemies, allowed herself to be used by them, and because of her, they now had his child. The only child he'd ever have. In the hands of the people he despised with everything in him. All because of her.

And yet he didn't quite hate the woman. He shrugged and mentally shook himself. It was natural that he couldn't hate her just now. She was barely able to remain conscious, as weak as she was. Months of captivity, and God knew what kind of abuse. Pale and trembling and sickly. No, he couldn't hate any person in this kind of sorry state. Not even her. He'd worry about hating her later. No doubt it would come in time. He touched her shoulder.

"Angelica," he said, and then schooled his voice before going on. It should have the sharp ring of command, rather than that quiet hint of concern. "Stop, you're not strong enough."

Her eyes opened, but slowly, and she blinked at him as if rousing from a deep slumber. And then her gaze focused, her eyes narrowed. "What do you care how strong I am? You detest me, remember?"

"It's not something I'm likely to forget," he told her. "And my only concern about your strength, Angelica, is that you not waste all of it and kill yourself before I find my little girl."

Something flashed in her eyes. A fierceness that surprised him. Even when she'd attacked him all those months ago, he'd sensed no viciousness in her. Only desperation. This was quite different. Like a lioness eyeing a careless hunter and licking her chops. A half-dead lioness, still managing to stir up a healthy rage for what she perceived as a threat to her young.

"You need to understand something, *Vampire*," she spit at him, making even this harsh whisper sound violent. "No matter what

you do to me, no matter how you try, you will never have that innocent child. I am her mother, though not long ago I'd have believed it impossible. I am her mother. And I will raise her in a fine and moral manner. She will not be touched by the likes of you. I will not have her corrupted by your evil. If you want her..."
She closed her eyes, took a breath, as if the very act of speaking was draining her. "You'll have to kill me."

Jameson closed his eyes very briefly and shook his head as if to shake the confusion away. "The likes of me?" he repeated, searching her weary face in brief glances. "Angelica, you *are* the likes of me."

"No." She turned her face away from him, staring out the window into the night. "I'll never be like you."

"And how can you be so sure of that, when you have no idea what I'm like?" He turned the wheel, taking the exit that led to the isolated estate on Long Island, which through a series of tricky legal maneuvers and several transfers of deed still legally belonged to Eric. It had been so many years since he'd been sighted there that DPI had long ago stopped keeping the place under surveillance. Eric had been there, though. And he'd been busy.

"I know what you're like," she said, and her whisper was weaker now.

She was remembering. Remembering something that made her stomach heave and her heart race with fear. A dark alley, and an amazingly strong man, holding her down and—

"Stop it!" She snapped her head around to face him, eyes filled with fury. "Stop invading my mind, damn you!"

Anger rose up, but it was brief and gut level. She had every right to order him to keep out of her thoughts. He knew better than to read another's mind without permission. It was just that he was so damned curious about her, and...and those frightening memories he'd just glimpsed made him even more so. He sighed hard. "I don't like you, Angelica. That's no secret. But if you're to be of any help at all in finding our daughter, you're going to need to learn a bit more about your own nature. And I suppose there's no one else to teach you, so..."

She let her head fall back against the seat. "I don't want to know anything you might want to teach me."

He lifted his brows. "No? Not even how to guard your thoughts? Not even how to keep monsters like me from reading your mind whenever the mood strikes?"

She sent him a sidelong glance, filled with suspicion and mistrust.

"It's very easy, Angelica, and once the technique is learned, your thoughts will only be readable if and when you intend them to be."

Her head came around a little farther, eyes narrowed. "Black arts, no doubt. Sorcery. Satanism."

"I don't believe in Satan," he said. "So it can't be that."

"Heretic," she muttered.

Jameson shrugged. "Close your eyes and envision your mind as a house, your thoughts as its inhabitants. And you as the master of the household."

She frowned, not closing her eyes or doing anything he told her to. But she was filing it all away for later consideration, he thought.

"Others wish to invade your home, and it's your responsibility to protect those who live there. So you build a wall. Pick any material you like. Brick or steel or stone. But see yourself, very clearly, building that wall, making it solid and strong, raising it higher and higher, until your house is no longer just a house, but a castle. A fortress. Impenctrable."

A bit of the suspicion left those violet eyes. They widened, and for once, looked directly into his. And their impact, when she did, jolted him like an unexpected blow to the chest. When their gazes met, something happened. It was as if her eyes probing his were the trigger to release the memories he'd vowed to put from his mind. The feelings...the desire...the touch of her lips and...

He blinked, and jerked his own gaze back to the road ahead, breaking the powerful connection. He realized he'd missed his turnoff, and pulled a U-turn in the road and headed back the other way. Then, clearing his throat, he went on, trying very hard to pretend he'd noticed nothing unusual when their eyes had met. Her mind. He'd been telling her how to protect her mind. "See yourself as the keeper of the wall you build," he said. "You can send messages out to others at will, and—"

"I can?"

He glanced at her again. Wider now, those eyes, and filled with purple wonder. Moments ago they'd been passion-glazed as she felt the same things he had. But like him, she'd done her best to hide it. And focused instead on the words they'd been saying. Words, floating on the surface of a still lake, while the deeper waters churned into chaos just below.

She was looking so innocent right now. So surprised at what he'd told her. He caught himself halfway to smiling at her, and checked it with ease. "Yes, of course you can. And you can hear the thoughts of others as well."

"Yes," she said, very softly. "I do hear them. All of them, all the time. It's maddening. Like a constant roar in my head, with nothing clear. Everything jumbled and garbled. I—" She looked up quickly, as if everything she'd just said had tumbled from her lips without her consent. As if only just now realizing that she was speaking to him as if he were something other than a monster. And she clamped her jaw, gave her head a tired shake.

It angered him. But he spoke all the same. "Your wall will admit only the messages you wish to receive. All others will bounce off it like carelessly aimed arrows."

Her brows rose, and she looked at him, doubting, but hoping, he could see that much.

He shook his head, looking straight ahead and refusing to see that distrust in her eyes anymore. "Try it and see for yourself if you're so certain I'm a liar. Go on, do it. Concentrate. Build your wall."

Her lips thinned and she rolled her eyes, but seconds later, he saw her leaning back, relaxing, and focusing inwardly on the things he had told her. He gave her time, waited several moments, driving slowly and looking at the coastline as it came into view.

And then he sent his mind to hers, seeking and probing. And

he found her wall. Felt it there, a flimsy barrier. His stronger will could break through if necessary, but her defenses would get stronger with time.

"Very good," he said. "Not bad at all, in fact."

She looked at him through narrowed eyes. "You're trying to confuse me with all this nonsense."

"Am I?" he said. And then he focused his mind on hers, and without speaking aloud, said, *We're near the sea now, Angelica. See it, off in the distance?*

And he saw her stiffen, and turn toward him as if he'd spoken. Saw her flinch when she noticed that his lips were not moving. Saw her look off in the direction he'd mentally indicated, and notice the Atlantic shore.

"It's…it's uncanny. It's unnatural," she whispered.

"No, not to us it isn't. And it can be damned convenient. Especially when you find yourself in a scrape. You can send out your cry for help across the miles, and bring others to your aid."

She lowered her head, shook it. "I'd rather take my chances with my own trouble, thank you all the same."

"And why is that, Angelica?"

She lifted her brows and her shoulders at the same time. "Same reason it's unwise to deal with the devil, Vampire. He can't be trusted. Nothing made of true evil can be."

"So we're like Satan himself, now, are we? Made of evil? Not to be trusted? I didn't realize you were in such close contact with the Almighty, Angelica. Has He told you all this personally? Or are you judging me without divine assistance?"

"I don't need to judge you," she whispered. "You've already shown your true colors. You began as my rescuer and became my captor. I'll know better than to make the mistake of trusting your kind ever again."

"If I were untrustworthy, that wouldn't necessarily mean that all vampires were, oh Angel of wisdom. And while we're at it, let's set the record straight. I began as your rescuer, that's true. Then I became your victim when you tried to murder me. And then, dark Angel, I became your lover." He enjoyed the little gasp that statement instigated. He even smiled a little. "True, it was only in a test tube, but we mated, nonetheless. And now, Angelica, I am both rescuer and captor, but only to prevent you from playing the role of child abductor."

She lowered her head, closed her eyes.

"How can anyone so detest the very thing they are?" he asked, half to himself. "You *are* a vampire, Angelica. When you condemn us, you condemn yourself."

"I'm not the one who's condemned you," she whispered. "God has. And for some reason, He's turned His wrath on me as well."

He tilted his head to one side, saw the utter torment on her pretty face. "You believe this is some form of punishment from God?"

"It's hell," she whispered. "I died in that alley, and this is hell."

"What alley?" He knew...she'd been made in an alley, and against her will, quite obviously. But he wanted to know more. Wanted to know everything.

She averted her face, bit her lip, refused to answer him.

"You know, Angel, you're really without a clue. You have no inkling of what being a vampire is all about. You're jumping to conclusions without the slightest bit of evidence. Do you have any idea how self-righteous and arrogant that is?"

"I'm one of the damned," she whispered, her throat apparently very tight. "Do you really think I care if I seem arrogant to you?"

"Jesus Christ," he muttered.

She flinched and turned her head away. Jameson let the silence stretch between them. Then he saw their destination bathed in the headlights' white glow, and he nodded toward it, thinking he could change the dreary subject. "This is where we'll be staying, for now. A base of operations. At least until they catch on. It probably won't take them long."

She eyed the house, shaking her head. "I don't want to be here. I want to be out searching for my child."

He lifted his brows, amazed in spite of himself. "You can

barely function,'' he said. ''And you obviously aren't thinking clearly. You need to rest, and to feed. Give yourself time to regain your strength, and perhaps even learn a bit about your own nature. It's obvious you know nothing.''

''I don't want lessons, I want my baby!''

He swallowed hard as he faced the blazing purple flames in her eyes. ''So do I,'' he said. ''But it will be dawn soon. There's nothing we can do in the short time of darkness we have left. We'll start our search at sundown.''

She grated her teeth in frustration, but turned to wrench her door open all the same. Jameson gripped her wrist before she could jump out of the car, and she faced him once more. ''And I *do* mean *we,*'' he told her. ''Don't even think about waking before me and slipping away on your own, Angelica. The place may look decrepit, but that's an illusion. My friend Eric keeps it up, and his technological standards are the highest. It's a fortress, Angelica, and I hold the key.''

''I despise you!'' She wrenched her wrist free of his grasp, and turned to get out of the car.

Jameson held her there easily, preventing that. ''Close the door. We're not quite there yet.''

Scowling at him, she did.

The house was as frightening to me as anything could have been. I was terrified. Alone with a monster who seemed to know more of me than I knew of myself. A man who'd taken me from one prison only to bring me to another. This one looking as if it belonged to a band of witches in old Salem. But it didn't. It belonged instead to a band of vampires. And perhaps that was even worse.

We drove past a tall iron gate that hung open and seemed attached only by one hinge. Above us, an arch of black filigree spelled the name Marquand. The drive was littered with broken limbs, overgrown with weeds and lined with scrub trees and briars. And then the house itself loomed before us like a giant demon. It was a tower of gray stone blocks, and ivy had crept over most of it. Large timbers had been nailed over the massive front door. The wrought-iron railing was broken, and leaned over the chipped stone steps like a crippled old man leaning upon a cane. Water stains darkened the stone beneath each tall, narrow window, giving the ghastly illusion that the house had been crying. I shivered at the thought. Beyond the house, a sheer cliff tumbled raggedly down to the sea. I could see the black water churning in the distance, and I could hear the breakers smashing against the rocky shore.

And still Jameson drove his small black car farther. He turned off the drive and drove through the brush, and as we went, it seemed a path opened out where none had been visible before. We drove deep into a tunnel made of briars and brush so dense it was impossible to see outside it. Impossible, I realized, to see *inside* it, as well. Ingenious.

And then Jameson shut off the engine. But he left the keys in the switch. For a fast getaway, I guessed. "Now," he said, looking at me in the darkness, seeing me just as clearly as I could see him, with his velvety brown, tiger-striped eyes, "you can get out."

Obeying this man made me cringe, but it seemed there was little else I could do. I opened the car door and got out. He was beside me so quickly I gasped in surprise. And again, he took hold of my wrist. I looked down at his hand, wrapped around me, and I knew he could break that small narrow wrist of mine with one simple twist. And at that same moment, it occurred to me that he hadn't once hurt me. Though he could have, and though it had seemed as if he'd very much like to on more than one occasion, he had yet to cause me any pain. His grip, when he found it necessary to hold me, was tight. Firm. Even unshakable. But not painful.

I thought of the careless cruelty of the one who'd taken me in the alley. He had hurt me. Time and again, without a thought.

It would be a mistake, though, to believe the two were so different. They were the same, both damned, both monsters, demons, servants of Satan himself. I would not let his deceptive gentleness lull me into complacency. I must escape him. And I would.

He led me still deeper into this tunnel of undergrowth, to a wall of the stuff at the very end, and then he pushed some of the branches aside, and stepped forward, and down, pulling me with him.

A staircase...cut into the very earth, and spiraling downward. For just an instant I envisioned the fires of hell awaiting me at the bottom, and I pulled against him.

He turned then, eyes narrow. "It's all right, Angelica. There's nothing here to be afraid of. I know all of this seems absurd, but believe me it's necessary. For our safety. Come."

Swallowing my fears, I went with him, down into the depths of the earth, and then along a narrow underground passage. We finally emerged from it, passing through a sturdy door and into a larger room, and it was then that I blinked in utter astonishment.

This was not at all what I had expected. A tomblike dungeon, yes. But not this.

The room was large and beautiful. With a stone fireplace at the farthest side, and kindling lying ready on the grate. A fragrant stack of cherry wood stood beside it. The walls had been painted a muted shade of rose, and paintings lined them. Lovely works, and I noticed then that many of them included a fiery sun's loving rays bathing various land and seascapes. Oriental rugs covered the floors, and a velvet settee, heaped with pillows and throws, stood in one corner. An antique cherry rocker in another. A marble-topped table littered with objets d'art in a third. There were oil lamps everywhere, and doors. More doors like the one through which we'd entered.

He closed the huge door through which we'd come, and for the first time, I saw the digital panel on this side of it. He punched some buttons, and a red light came on. It was true, then, what he'd said. I was trapped here, with him.

"You see," he said, facing me again. "Nothing to fear. Through there is a fully functional bathroom, and you'll find plenty of clothing in various sizes stocked in the closets. You'll be able to bathe and put on some real clothes. That ought to feel pretty good after all those months in nothing but this thing." As he said it, he touched the thin white gown I wore, brushing his hand over my shoulder. And I shivered.

He let his hand fall to his side again, averting his eyes. "Everything you need is right here. There are exits from each room. Tunnels like the one we came through. They each open onto various parts of the property, so if we need to escape, we can. And here—" he nodded at the small appliance built into the wall, a minuscule refrigerator "—is enough sustenance to keep us going."

I stared at the little door, aghast. "What…what do you mean?"

He opened the door with a little flourish. I'm not certain what I expected. A long narrow vault holding the bodies of his victims or something equally horrendous, I suppose. But instead, I saw stacks of plastic bags like those used in blood banks and hospitals. My shock must have shown in my eyes, because he tilted his head, and sent me a look as if he knew exactly what I'd been thinking. "You see how little you know, Angelica? We don't feed on the living. That comes straight out of Sunday afternoon monster movies. Why the hell would we prey on innocent humans, when there's blood readily available elsewhere?" And he slammed the door, shaking his head in disgust. "I suggest you feed. I'm going to shower and change. Don't try to leave. The doors will not open without the proper codes. Even if you happened on them by chance, an alarm would sound. And if all of that somehow failed and you did escape, you'd only find yourself out in the open with no shelter in reach and daylight approaching. You'd toast in the sun." He turned as if to leave me alone there.

"And the sun would kill me?" I asked. I couldn't stop myself from asking. For nine months I'd existed without knowing the first thing about myself. He'd made me realize, in his crude way, how very little I knew. Not even what things might kill me. And these were things I had to understand. The questions that had been boiling inside me at first—the ones I'd buried and ignored in my foolish certainty that none of it mattered, since I'd be human again one day—came bubbling back to the surface with a new urgency.

I was a member of a race I knew nothing about. Like a newborn, unfamiliar with her own body. I wanted to know.

His back went stiff, but when he turned to face me once more, his stern expression had softened. His brows rose in bewilderment. "Yes. Of course it would. My God, Angelica, you don't even know that much?"

I lowered my head and turned away from those knowing eyes. I'd revealed too much already. Anything I told this creature would be turned against me, I knew that.

He stared at my back for a long moment, awaiting an answer. An answer I dared not give. So instead, I attempted to change the subject entirely. "Where will I sleep?" I asked.

"Ah, yet another of Eric's marvels. I'll show you." He moved past me to yet another door and pushed it open. Then waved a hand so that I would precede him inside. "Not my first choice, of course," he was saying as I walked into the room. "But when you see the safety of these, you'll understand. Eric is a genius about these things. He's installed…Angelica?"

I could not move. I stood rooted to the floor, staring in horror at the two caskets, gleaming at me in the darkness. I could not breathe, I was so terror-stricken. Even looking at them, I could feel myself trapped inside, feel the cramped space closing in on me, hear my own screams and feel my hands beating against the lid, to no avail.

Jameson touched my shoulder, and all my pride left me in a rush. I spun around to face him, falling to my knees and gripping his hands in mine, not caring that I knelt at the feet of a demon. Lowering my head to hide my tears did nothing to keep the sobs from breaking my words into fragmented bits. "I…beg of y-you…" I said, choking on the words. "Do not put me into that box. Please…"

Jameson's heart tripped to a stop as he saw what his thoughtlessness had reduced this fierce woman to. Kneeling on the floor, clutching his hands and shaking. She was cold as ice. Damn. How could he have been so cruel as to forget where he'd found her?

Sealed in a tiny box and left there for God only knew how long. Left there to die.

He bent down, closing his hands around her small waist and lifting her until she stood again. When he tilted up her chin, he saw the tears staining her cheeks, and he swore. "Jesus, Angel, of course not. I wasn't thinking...." Keeping one arm anchored around her waist, he moved her out of that room as quickly as possible. She was still shaking like a frightened rabbit. "No," he told her. "God, you truly do think I'm a monster, don't you? You honestly thought I'd force you into one of those coffins, seal you inside the way those bastards at DPI did? How could you think that?"

She closed her eyes, and he could see her battling the panic that had overwhelmed her, fighting for control. "What else would I think? You said I was your prisoner. You said you'd keep me here until we found her."

"I was thinking of our safety. Eric has those coffins equipped with all sorts of...never mind, it doesn't matter. I should have thought before I ushered you in there. I didn't mean to frighten you like that."

He turned, crossing the first room again to open a door on the opposite side. And this time he entered first, leaving her to follow at her own pace. He went to the nightstand and bent to light an oil lamp. They didn't need it to see by, but he thought the amber glow made things seem warmer. Less frightening.

She came in, slowly, warily. God, she mistrusted him. He stood where he was and watched her examine the very normal-looking bedroom. A huge canopy bed held state like a royal personage. Rhiannon's doing, of course. She preferred luxury to caution. Always had.

"Is this more to your liking?" he asked.

She stepped farther inside, turning her head, taking in her surroundings.

"Look," he said, pointing. "The bathroom is through there."

She looked, nodded, but her glance returned to the bed. When her violet gaze had first fallen there, it had seemed to Jameson that her muscles relaxed a bit. She sniffed and brushed at her eyes.

Her breath escaped her in a trembling sigh as she closed her eyes. "Yes," she breathed at last. "This is much better."

Jameson stepped away from the bed, shaking his head in puzzlement as she came forward, tugged the plump satin comforter down and nodded in approval at the way the bed looked.

"You'd better feed now, Angelica," he said, his voice taking on the tone of a parent instructing an innocent child. "Dawn is only a short while away, and you need the sustenance before you sleep."

She nodded, absorbing that information. "Yes, all right." And she moved past him into the front room again. He heard her open the refrigerator, heard the chink of glass as she located the crystal stored in the cabinet above it. Heard her pouring.

How in the world, he wondered, was he going to manage to hate a woman who needed him so desperately? She knew nothing. Nothing about her strength, nothing about her psychic abilities. Not even how to feed, or what could kill her! It was uncanny. He needed her help to find his daughter, but first she needed his help. To know what she was now, what she had become.

There was no way he could hate a woman who needed him the way this one did.

So he'd try to help her, instead. But the next question on his ever-growing list was how the hell could he manage to help a woman who detested him? She hated him, and his kind. She hated herself, by all appearances. She hated what she was. She didn't want to learn about her new nature, didn't want to explore it, didn't want his help.

Yet she'd taken it when he'd ignored her objections and given it to her. She'd erected the mental barrier around her mind as he'd instructed. She'd fed when he'd advised her to. She'd even asked him a question or two.

Perhaps he could help her. And perhaps she'd realize that he and his kind were no more monstrous than mortals were. Much less so in most cases. And maybe she'd give up her ridiculous notion of taking his daughter away from him. Maybe she'd realize that his own child did not need to be protected from its father.

Or maybe she wouldn't realize it.

There was so much to think about. But not now. He'd drive himself insane if he tried to solve the puzzle of Angelica now. For now, he'd simply light the fire, and see that she'd fed enough to sustain her, but not enough to make her ill. And then he'd let her rest, while he planned what to do tomorrow.

Tomorrow. When she would awaken stronger, and likely more determined to escape him than ever. Not to mention more able. How would he deal with her then?

One thing, at least. It ought to be easier to hate her when she no longer appeared so helpless.

And that was a good thing. Right now, he was realizing just how dangerous not hating this woman could be. Because when he wasn't hating her, he was wanting her. And the sooner he rid himself of that particular longing, the better.

Chapter Seven

Jameson never did get around to showering in the wee hours of that morning. He watched her far too long, lost himself somewhere in the long locks of her satinlike hair, or perhaps it was among the glittering facets of her eyes. Nonetheless, he put it off too long, and the day sleep crept over him with the dawn. She'd fed, and then crawled into the oversize bed and fallen asleep instantly, and still he was watching her.

And finally, he managed to pull himself away in time to get to the settee in the front room before he fell asleep at the foot of her bed. Like a devoted servant sleeping at the feet of the mistress he'd die for.

Right.

When the sun went down again, he rose before she did. He headed for the bathroom before even giving her a passing glance. While he was washing beneath the spray, he reminded himself several times that he hated her. And that she hated him. And that the sharing of their blood was what made him crave her so. Dream of her, when the day sleep should be too deep for dreams.

Having convinced himself of that, he emerged from the small bathroom wrapped in a terry robe and rubbing his wet hair with a towel. But he stilled in the doorway when he saw the utter confusion on Angelica's face. She stood staring into the closet, her brows drawn together, head tilted to one side as her graceful hands flitted over the clothes that hung there. Her skin had more color this evening. The day rest had done its magic in rejuvenating her. She seemed stronger. And the bones no longer protruded from her face. Instead of sharp and angular it was gently oval now, with cheekbones an actress would die for.

"Something wrong?" he asked her, snapping his attention back to the matter at hand.

And she jerked as if surprised by his presence. She really did need to tune in to her newly heightened senses and learn how to use them. She should have sensed him there, felt his eyes on her. Instead, she reacted like a mortal.

"These…these are all very…normal."

"You were expecting…what? Black satin capes with stand-up collars and scarlet lining?" He tossed the towel onto the foot of the bed as he passed, then stood just behind her, looking over her shoulder at the clothes.

"Of course not."

"Sure you weren't. Hell, I only know of one vampire who still wears a cloak, and I think he just does it for the dramatic effect." He moved past her to pull a violet cashmere sweater from the rack. One of Tamara's old ones. Modest and demure and sweet, like her. It would fit this woman…in size, if nothing else. And the color nearly matched her eyes, although no man-made dye could ever equal those sparkling amethysts of hers. Jameson blinked and shook himself. "Here. This will do you for tonight." Then he continued flipping the hangers. "And a pair of jeans to go with it. What size are you?"

"Size?"

"In jeans," he said, pausing with a pair of black Levi's in his hands. When she didn't answer, he turned to look at her. "Well?"

"I'm…not sure."

Jameson frowned at her. "How can anyone not know what size jeans they wear?" Then he narrowed his eyes. "Don't tell me you're one of those women who refuses to tell a man her size."

"That would be the height of vanity," she said, and she averted her eyes. "It's simply been quite some time since I've worn blue jeans."

Aha, he thought. A clue to who this mysterious woman had been. "Why is that, Angelica?"

Her head came up sharply, eyes wary.

"I mean, what kind of things *did* you wear? Perhaps I can find something like what you're accustomed to."

And it seemed to him in that moment that she came as close to smiling as he'd ever seen her do. Not that she actually smiled. Not at all, but there was a hint of mirth in her eyes. "Nothing you're likely to find in a vampire's closet," she said. "The jeans will be fine."

But Jameson wasn't as willing to change the subject as she seemed to think he'd be. "You were wearing a dress of some sort when I saw you that first time. Though...I didn't have preternatural night vision, then. And it was quite dark. I seem to recall it as black and loose fitting. Kind of like a—"

"I'm going to bathe now," she said, interrupting him, and leaving him with no illusions that it had been unintentional. "I really care very little what I wear. I just want to hurry and begin the search for my child." And she tugged the jeans from the hanger, turned and quickly crossed the room, closing the bathroom door behind her.

And for the first time, Jameson thought back to that night when she'd nearly killed him. *Really* thought back. Oh, he'd thought about it before. Far more often than he'd like to admit, actually. But he'd always focused on the way she'd felt, pressing tight to him while her avaricious little mouth fed at his throat. The way he'd felt...

Now he needed to get past that madness, and focus on something else. Details. Senses besides the one flaring to life in his libido. He went to the bed, sat down on its edge and mentally replayed all of it, from his first glimpse of her. Her tangled hair. Her dirty face. The sunken cheeks and hollow violet eyes. And the tattered black...dress...or was it a dress?

There had been beads of some sort, clutched in her bony hands.

Beads she'd been worrying or playing with, and that she'd dropped abruptly when he'd spoken to her. Beads...and she'd held them, one by one, between her fingers. Held each one, caressing it, and muttering before she moved on to the next. And they were...

My God. Rosary beads? And the black dress could have been...a habit. Jesus, was it possible? Had Angelica been some kind of...of nun in life? In life, yes, even up to the very moment when she'd been brought over, or she wouldn't likely have still been wearing the habit.

She'd called him a heretic. She'd spoken of vanity. And she was so damned concerned about God and Satan and good and evil, and being damned. It made sense. Lifting his head very slowly, Jameson stared at the closed bathroom door. Beyond it he could hear water running, and the nearly inaudible sound of singing, her singing, very softly so he wouldn't hear. "Amazing Grace." And then the sound of Tamara's hair dryer drowned out her song.

He was still sitting there when she came out, wearing the jeans and the sweater he'd given her, sometime later. And he was still reeling from what he thought he had learned about her. And more determined than ever to know the truth. And yet part of him tried to get in the way of his curiosity. It was the part of him that knew full well she wore nothing beneath the sweater. He hadn't given her a bra, wasn't even sure Tamara kept such things around down here, and wouldn't have known what size to choose if he'd found a cache of them in the closet. His eyes were drawn to her breasts, and the cashmere clung to them because of their dampness. And he could see her shape very clearly underneath. Her nipples poking out into the fabric in reaction to its rough, yet soft texture rubbing against them.

He licked his lips.

She stopped halfway across the room, and froze there, waiting. And when he realized she was looking at him, looking at her, he forced his gaze upward and met her eyes. And he knew she was only pretending to be offended over where he'd been staring. Because he could see the awareness flaring in the violet depths. The arousal. The hunger.

He licked his lips again, and told himself to get to the matter at hand. Was she…had she been…what he thought she had?

He cleared his throat. "I was wondering, Angelica…if perhaps I should be addressing you as *Sister* Angelica?"

She took the question well, he thought. The swift intake of breath and slight widening of those eyes the only clue she'd been dealt some kind of blow. "If I had taken my solemn vows, I would have been Sister Mary Elizabeth. Since that day never came for me, I'm still simply Angelica."

"If not exactly angelic." He quipped. Then he saw her wince and almost regretted it. "So you were a novitiate?"

"Something like that." She came forward, and finally resumed pulling the brush through her now gleaming and utterly glorious hair. It was incredible, that mane of hers. Thick and wild and long. The hair of a goddess. Or an Angel. A dark angel. "Of what order?"

She turned, still brushing. "Why is it you ask so many questions about me, Vampire? You hate me, blame me for all that's happened. So why do you want to know?"

"You…bore my child. Isn't it natural for me to be curious?"

"Nothing about you is natural."

"And you know that for sure, do you? Are you sure you were just a novice nun and not God Almighty Himself?"

Her head snapped toward him. "How dare you!"

"Well, you certainly pass judgment as if you were, as much as you try to deny it. I was merely checking."

She got up, paced away from him in quick, angry strides. She was stronger now. Maybe just a little bit more herself. Having sustenance had helped even further to restore the shape of her face, and the gleam to her hair. And the sparkle to her eyes. And the spring to her step.

With her hair flying wild, and her eyes flashing, wearing sinfully tight-fitting jeans, and an equally revealing sweater, it was easier to imagine she'd been a centerfold than a sister.

Jesus, he wanted her.

"I want to go now. I want to find my baby. I'm tired of you and your prying. What will we do to find her? Where will we begin?"

He stared at her for a long moment. It should be easier to hate her now that she was strong and well. It should be. Why wasn't it?

Before he'd been distracted by the way she looked, and then by who she might have been in the other life, he'd been trying to decide how best to warn her about the possible nature of their child. He hadn't come to any perfect conclusion, but he knew he had to say something. Give her some kind of preparation, just in case.

"Before we begin," he said, slowly, "there's something...I'm not certain you're aware of. Something you need to prepare yourself for, Angelica."

Her brows furrowed. "You're frightening me, Vampire. Whatever it is, just tell me and let's be on our way."

Jameson licked his lips, averting his gaze. He'd been wrestling with the possible nature of his child for days. It had been a blow when he'd first realized the implications. But he'd been among friends. People who loved him and explained it gently, and who would be there for him no matter what.

It would be far worse for her. She was alone, except for a man she despised more with every breath she drew.

Bracing himself, he met her eyes. Brilliant now, glowing like amethysts in candlelight. Breathtaking. "There has never been a child born to a vampiress before. None...that I'm aware of, at least." She blinked. That was all. "Angelica, we have no way of knowing...what we'll find, when we find our baby."

"What...we'll find?"

"Whether she'll be mortal...or immortal. Or some cross between the two. Whether—"

"No." She took two staggering steps backward, then gripped the back of a chair, her fingertips digging into the fabric.

"I hope to God she'll be a normal child, Angelica, but we can't be certain until we see her. It would be tragic if—"

"Your kind," she whispered. "They never grow older?"

Again, she confirmed his suspicion that she knew nothing about her own race. "No. Our kind never grow older."

"She'd be trapped inside the body of a newborn for all of her life?" She shook her head from side to side, rapidly. "No, it's too horrible. It can't be."

"It might not be. I only...I only wanted to warn you. In case..."

She lifted her chin, and met his eyes, her own wide and clear and filled with fierce determination. "God won't do this. Not to her. It's enough...sweet Jesus, it's enough to punish me. But not my baby. She is a healthy, normal little girl. She is. I know it."

Had he thought her weak? Physically, perhaps. But never in any other way. Not her. She looked like an avenging angel just now. And he found himself nodding in agreement with her. "You're right. She's fine. I'm sure of it. I've been worrying for nothing."

And in that very brief moment, when their eyes met and held, something passed between them. A connection was made. They touched on some level. And then she looked away and the feeling vanished.

"Do you have any sort of plan?" she asked him.

"Just a starting point. This woman who contacted my friend Tamara to tell her about the child...Hilary Garner. She works for DPI, but apparently even she couldn't stomach them using a child this way. I have her address. We'll go there tonight, talk to her. She might know where they've taken the baby...and she might be willing to tell us."

"And if she isn't?"

Jameson gritted his teeth. "Then we'll convince her."

Hope surged in my heart as we neared the building where the woman lived. I sought with every part of me for some sense that my daughter was near, but felt nothing. Still, I clung to that hope. This woman would know something. And she would help us.

Surely that had been her intent all along, or she never would have contacted Jameson's friend. Jameson…

He was not living up to my expectations of him. He'd taken me from that horrible place. Fed me from his own body. Even…oddly enough…tried to comfort me when I'd been terrorized at the sight of those coffins. And he seemed as determined as I was to rescue our child.

Our child. It was wrong to keep referring to her in that way. "She needs a name," I whispered, half to myself.

Jameson turned to stare at me, brows lifted, then lowering as he understood. "Yes, she does. Do you have something in mind?"

I tilted my head. "When I was alone, chained to the walls of my cell, or trapped in that box waiting for my guards to feel the urge to release me, I talked to her. I sang to her and cradled my belly in my arms and pretended to hold her. I called her Lily. That's the way I envisioned her. As perfect and flawless as a beautiful lily. And Amber, because she was a mystery as old as time. A child born to a vir—" I bit my lip, then. But too late. My loose tongue had given away yet another of my secrets.

"Born to a virgin?" His eyes widened in disbelief. And then he smiled. "It's almost…holy. The first child born to a vampire…is born of a virgin."

"There is nothing holy about what they did to me," I said, and again wished I would learn to keep quiet and not blurt my every thought to this man.

"No. Of course there isn't." He was silent for a moment. Then, "I know what it's like, Angelica. I was held by them, too. And more than once."

"Perhaps you know what captivity is like, Vampire. But you cannot know how it feels to have your living child taken from your womb by your enemies. Taken away from you while you're told that you will never set eyes on her again." Tears welled in my eyes then. That pain was still fresh and sharp. It cut to my very soul, if indeed, I still possessed one.

"No. I can't know that. It must have nearly killed you."

"I'd have preferred they cut out my heart." I averted my face to hide my tears from him.

"You can tell me, Angelica. There's no need for embarrassment between us."

I looked at him, and knew it was true. We were linked, somehow. Bonded by blood, and by the child we shared. Much as we might dislike each other, that bond was not going to be easily broken. Perhaps not broken at all.

"I was drugged. Weak. I should have been able to help her...but I couldn't. I couldn't move. It was like a nightmare, where you try and try to make yourself wake up, but you can't. It was horrible."

I lowered my head, only to feel his hand cover mine gently. Warmth and comfort in his touch. It surprised me. "We'll find her," he said, and his voice was firm and sure. "Amber Lily will be all right."

For a moment, I felt reassured. Imagine, reassured by a man I knew was a monster. A demon. An abhorrence to God.

But then he reverted to his true nature. "And when we have her safe, I'll make them pay. I'll kill them. One by one...all of them. They deserve worse than death for what they've done."

"Only God can say who deserves death, Jameson," I told him.

"God is too slow." The anger I saw in his eyes frightened me. It was there in those black tiger stripes that split the brown velvet apart, a jet-black flame, leaping and crackling with rage. "Vengeance is mine, sayeth the vampire." He stopped the car, and looked up at the towering apartment building's myriad lighted windows. "And it begins with this one right here, unless she tells me what I want to know."

Hilary Garner's apartment had been ransacked. Thoroughly, and recklessly. Jameson knew DPI's tactics, and he knew their searches were usually conducted with such care that few people would even notice they'd taken place. This time, it had been different. They must be very angry with this woman.

Or they had been. She wasn't here, and he wondered whether

she were even still alive. DPI did not deal lightly with agents who wanted out. Or who betrayed the organization.

He heard Angelica's gasp, and whirled to see her staring at a photograph in a silver frame. One of Hilary Garner and a friend, arm in arm, smiling at the camera. "What is it?"

"This woman," she said, pointing. "She was with me when I gave birth. She...I could see in her eyes that she was suffering.... She bent close to me, and told me that the baby was a girl."

"But did nothing to keep those bastards from taking her away."

"I pled with her to help Amber Lily. And she nodded. Very slightly, she nodded."

"Trying to ease her own guilt." Jameson swung his arm and sent the photograph crashing to the floor.

Angelica stared at him, wide-eyed. "She got word to you. She tried to help."

"She worked for them, Angelica. For years, she served the devil himself. One token act now doesn't exonerate that."

"Even the worst sinners can repent," she whispered.

"The hell with repentance. I want her to pay. I want them all to pay. Dammit!" He slammed his fist onto the table where the photo had been, and the wood split in two. Tears burned in his eyes. The disappointment did likewise in his gut. Damn, he'd been so sure he'd find something here. Some clue. Angelica could afford to be charitable. She probably didn't have a clue what those bastards might be doing to that helpless baby right now. But he did. He did, and the nightmarish images would not go away.

And then she was standing very close to him, head tilted to one side as she stared into his eyes. "You...you're *crying?*"

He turned away abruptly, not wanting her or anyone to see the torment inside him.

"I didn't know," she whispered from behind him. "I didn't know you...you care as much for Amber Lily as I do, don't you, Jameson?"

He sighed. "Jesus Christ, Angelica, why do you think I'm here? What the hell do you think I'm doing if I don't care?" He faced her again, saw her shaking her head.

"But I thought...I thought..."

"I know what you thought. You thought I was a monster. An animal without feelings or emotions. Well, surprise, Angel. I'd cut off my arm if it would save Amber from those bastards. I'm every bit as human now as I was before, Angel, and so are you, whether you can see it or not. The differences are physical, not spiritual. Hell, if anything, I feel things more deeply than I did then. And you do, too. You know damn good and well you do."

She shook her head slowly from side to side, her gaze turned inward. Jameson sighed hard, frustrated with trying to make her understand. She was as bad as the rest of them.

"You're hurting," she whispered, searching his face with eyes that were wide with surprise and wonder.

He closed his eyes, tipped his head back as the pain overwhelmed him. "I just want to hold her in my arms. I just want to know she's safe and...and..."

His voice broke, and he was ashamed. Until he looked at her again and saw the tears flowing like rivers from those violet pools. "I know," she whispered. "Yes...I know...I don't know why I thought..."

"Let's get the hell out of here," he said.

"Do you love her?" she asked, and as she did she lifted a hand to touch his face.

"I love her more than my own life, Angel. I'd die for her here and now if I knew it would make things safe for her. And I know that I'll love her even more when I lay eyes on her. When I touch her for the first time..."

His tears ran down to her hand where it rested on his cheek. And she stepped closer, a tremulous smile dancing over her lips as she nodded. "Yes," she whispered. "Yes, you will. Oh, Jameson, she's so beautiful. Her hair is thick and satiny and dark as a raven's wing."

Like yours, he thought, and he touched a strand, ran it between his fingers.

"And her eyes are as black as midnight. So big, and innocent..."

And that was it. All she could take. She choked on a sob, and her face crumpled. She cried noisily, her entire body shaking as he pulled her close. Hell, he felt like crying, too. He might dislike the woman, but they shared something. This...this grief and worry and gut-wrenching fear for their little girl. And they always would share it. No matter what.

He held her close, rubbed her back and stroked her hair. "It's gonna be okay, Angel. We'll find her. I'm telling you, I haven't even begun."

"Aw, gee, isn't that touching?"

Jameson stiffened. The deep voice came from the doorway, and they both spun around to see its owner. The man stood there, pointing a weapon at them. A weapon Jameson knew contained the one most powerful tool in DPI's arsenal. The drug they'd developed that would render even the most powerful vampire helpless.

In a flash, Jameson had pushed Angelica behind him. That he'd done it instinctively and without forethought didn't matter. It was understandable. Protecting the mother of his child would come naturally to any man.

"You have no use for us," Jameson told the man calmly, slowly. "You've got what you wanted from us. Don't go risking your neck for nothing."

"Do I look like a fool to you?" the man asked, smiling slightly. "Now talk, Bryant. Where is the child?"

Jameson's blood went cold. "What the hell do you mean, where is the child? You're the ones..." He paused, narrowing his eyes. "You don't know where she is?"

"Stop playing games. We've had this place under surveillance for days in case Garner tried to come back, though I can't believe she'd be that stupid. Now where is she? Where is she hiding that kid?"

He felt Angelica's eyes on him. Felt some kind of foolish hope spring into his chest. "The child," he said slowly, "is in a place where you'll never get your filthy hands on her again. Guarded by a hundred vampires. A thousand by the end of the week. Tell your boss to give it up. It's over. We've won.''

The man's brows lowered. "You're lying."

Jameson only shrugged.

"Come on, you're coming back with me. We'll get the truth out of you lying scum, one way or another." He looked past Jameson at Angelica, and smiled just a little. "I'm gonna have a good time trying various ways to make you talk, sweet thing. I've heard your kind can't get enough. We'll find out, I promise."

"Touch her and I'll rip your heart out," Jameson growled, and he had no idea where the words came from, but knew he meant them.

The man's eyes flashed with anger, and he lifted the gun barrel, centered it on Jameson's chest.

"No, there's no need of that," Angelica said from behind him. "Please, don't...don't use that thing."

"That's a good she-dog," he said. "There, you see, Bryant? Your girlfriend wants to cooperate. Maybe she knows a real man when she sees one, eh?"

She was too upset to guard her thoughts. And she felt ill, physically ill at the thought of this pig laying his filthy hands on her. And yet, she'd submit, if it would keep her alive long enough to rescue her child.

Jesus, she had a core of solid steel in her.

"Fine," Jameson said. "We'll come along peacefully. You can put the gun down." And he took a step toward the man. The fellow looked surprised, then smug. He waggled the barrel of the gun, and Jameson moved forward.

No! Angelica's thoughts rang clearly in his mind. *Jameson, don't go over there! He'll shoot you!*

Easy, Angel, he told her without words. He knew damned well the bastard would drop him where he stood. It was Angelica he wanted alive, not him. And he'd be damned if he'd let the pig touch her. *This animal isn't going to lay a finger on you. Trust me. I just need to get a little closer.*

He sensed her start of surprise. She'd spoken, mentally, for the first time. And heard his reply in her mind as clearly as if he'd said the words aloud. She hadn't truly believed it possible, he thought. Well, now she knew.

Jameson moved a few more steps...and then he lunged with such speed he knew the mortal could see no more than a blur. He twisted the gun from the startled man's grip with one hand, hit him hard in the face with the other. And ended standing over his unconscious attacker. Looking down at the helpless bastard, he pointed the gun, knowing the drug contained in its dart would be lethal to a mortal.

And then Angelica gripped his arm. "You don't have to kill him. He's no threat to us now."

Jameson swallowed the bile in his throat. "You're right, I don't have to kill him. I'm killing him because I want to."

He closed his finger around the trigger. Angelica's hands swept in like the wind, and snatched the gun away. She couldn't have done that if he'd been expecting it. But he hadn't been. As he looked up in startled surprise she flung the weapon, and it sailed across the apartment, smashing the window and arcing into the night.

"Jesus Christ, Angelica!" he snapped. "Why the hell are you protecting this bastard? You know what he intended to do to you."

"Murder is a sin, Vampire, no matter what one's justification may be."

"And according to you, I'm already damned, so what the hell do I care about one more sin on my record? Hmm?"

He bent down, gripping the man by his lapels, lifting him off the floor, intent on doing him in with or without the dart.

"No," she cried, and gripped his shoulders. "No, Jameson. I...I might have been wrong about that. What if I was wrong?"

He turned, looked down into her pleading violet eyes.

"Please," she whispered. "Please, don't kill this man when you don't have to."

And he couldn't. Not now. For some reason, her eyes did him in, and he let the worthless lump of flesh thud to the floor. "No doubt he didn't come here alone," he said. "Come on."

He led her over the body and into the hall, but not to the elevators or the main stairs. Instead he went the opposite direction. He found a service elevator, and hit the button marked Roof. And once inside, he allowed himself a hint of hope. Just a bit of happiness, and relief.

"Jameson, where are we…what…"

"Did you hear what that bastard said, Angelica? They don't have her. They don't have our little girl."

He looked down into her eyes, and saw his own excitement reflected there. "I heard."

"Garner," he muttered, thinking out loud. "It had to be Garner. She must have taken her. I can't imagine why, but…"

Angelica closed her eyes and a soft sigh escaped her parted lips. "She has kind eyes, this Hilary Garner. She's trying to help. She won't hurt her."

"She'd damned well better not." The car jarred to a halt, and its doors opened. Jameson stepped out, and up the short flight of stairs to the door at the top. Then through it. And he was on the roof, beneath the stars. Hurrying to the edge, he peered down to the street below. Cars were parked helter-skelter, at cockeyed angles, and men were hurrying from them into the building as more vehicles screeched in behind them.

"This place is swarming."

"There's a fire escape, down this side of the building," she called, drawing his gaze. And for just a second, he stopped, and just looked at her. She was silhouetted by a starlit night sky, and her hair blew in the wind like a shining ebony flag. And when she turned and looked at him, some of that starlight danced in her eyes.

"Jameson? The fire escape?"

He shook himself. "They'll be expecting that. They'll have it covered." He turned and glanced at the building next door. Separated by an alley no more than ten feet wide. "We're gonna have to jump for it, Angel."

On legs that seemed unsteady, she crossed the roof to stand

beside him, and her eyes widened as she looked down, then up at him. "We can't...we'll fall and—"

"You don't know the half of what you can do. This is a short hop for you, now. You're strong. Stronger than ten of them," he said, nodding toward the men below.

"I'm not."

"You are," he insisted. "You want to know our best-kept secret, Angel?"

She stared into his eyes, obviously frightened. "Yes," she said.

"The truly ancient ones...can even fly."

She shook her head. Then stopped, stared at him, and her eyes went even rounder.

"They'll laugh us out of immortality if we can't make this little leap. Come on, Angel. Trust me, I've been around vampires all my life." He took her hand, led her back to the other side. "We run, and we jump. Don't hesitate, or you'll put us both in some pretty intense misery."

"The fall would kill us."

"No. But it would probably hurt like hell."

She looked doubtful. He squeezed her hand. "Our baby is safe. She's not in their filthy hands anymore, Angelica. Doesn't that make you feel like you could fly?"

She nodded, still shaky though.

"If we don't get out of here, we won't get her back. For her, Angel. For our Amber Lily."

The fear in those violet eyes vanished. She nodded once, firmly. "All right."

"Good girl." Clinging to her hand, Jameson ran, and she matched him, step for step. She didn't falter, didn't hesitate, poured every bit of her effort into it. As one they pushed off, and as one they sailed into the night, arching high. He felt the rush he'd felt each time Roland had challenged him to push his abilities to their limits, only to find they truly had none. The wind whistling in his ears, riffling through his hair. And then they landed, hard, on the next building, and he pulled her close to him on impact to keep her from falling forward and smashing her face.

His arms linked around her waist, her body pressed to his, he looked down to see her...smiling. Her eyes glittering up at him. "We did it!"

"I told you." That smile of hers. That was what got to him. Seeing her smile, when she'd been in such agony such a short time ago. An agony they'd shared. There was hope now. Real hope, and they were sharing that as well. He lowered his head, and he kissed her. And it was lunacy. Madness. But her lips were full and moist and chilled from the night air. And they felt good beneath his, ripe and succulent, and he drew on them, traced them with his tongue, parted them and slipped his tongue between them.

The lust hit him hard, like a freight train, and he felt it running her down as well. She shuddered and clung to him, parted her lips and tipped her head back. He bowed over her, and plunged his tongue deep into her mouth, and thought about plunging himself deeply into her body.

A thought he forgot to guard.

She heard it loud and clear, and went stiff. Then gently, she pulled free of him and turned away. She was breathless. And so was he.

"I'm..." He pushed a hand through his hair. Christ, he'd just kissed the hell out of an almost nun. And thought about doing one hell of a lot more to her. Which was nothing new, and nothing she hadn't been thinking as well. But... "I'm sorry."

"We have to go, Vampire," she said, but her voice was coarse and shaky. "They'll find us here soon enough."

"Yeah." He let her lead this time, and he followed, wondering what the hell kind of insanity had just had hold of him.

When we reached the ground again, Jameson and I crept through the shadows of the night. I could hear very clearly the crackling of their radios as they spoke to one another. As they searched for us. It was obvious that we were a high priority to them. No, that wasn't exactly right. It was our daughter they wanted. A tiny babe who didn't even know why so many people should be hunting for her.

And I would die before I would let them have her.

I looked sideways at the man who stood close to me, and I realized that he would likely do the same. Give his life to protect the baby. Already, he'd risked it, and more than once. Perhaps... he was not exactly the monster I'd believed him to be.

Or perhaps he was. I'd seen the rage in his eyes. I'd watched him stand over a helpless man, perfectly willing to take his life. No hesitation. No compunction. No morality. Perhaps it was only in regard to his child that he showed any sense of honor or nobility. Perhaps.

He had kissed me.

I still marveled over how that had come about. But it was easy enough to understand. We'd both been exhilarated at the knowledge that perhaps our child was safe, somewhere. Carried away in the moment. He'd never have laid a finger on me otherwise, I had no doubts about that. He hated me. Had told me as much. Even blamed me for this entire predicament. Held me solely responsible for the danger Amber Lily was in right now. And yet I responded to him like a lust-starved lover. And I did not understand why.

As for his judgment of me, I, for the most part, agreed with it. I'd been a fool. An utter fool. And he was right, it was my fault our child had been taken. But I hadn't known, then, the horrors that I knew now.

I only knew that I should have listened to him as he lay on the floor near death, telling me not to go, not to trust the DPI agent who'd come for me. I should have listened.

We stood now in an alley, peering through the night at the men who surrounded the building. The vampire's squat black car waited like a deadly spider, only a few yards away from us. But those men were only a few yards beyond it. They stood facing the building, in case we came out, no doubt. Their backs were to us.

We can make it to the car, I heard him say. And then realized that he hadn't *said* it at all. This silent way of speaking made me dizzy. He took my hand, an act that seemed to be becoming his habit, and led me forward. Then he opened the driver's side door, which was nearest us, and crouching low, I crawled over his seat and into my own. When I was there, I kept my head down.

Jameson was beside me in no time at all, and he pulled the door very gently shut. And then he turned the key.

Immediately, those men spun around. Jameson jerked the shifting lever, and the car lurched into motion. But not before those men began firing their weapons at us. Such a horrific scene I'd never imagined. Men, firing guns at us. The black barrels spitting fire in the night. The window beside me shattered, and I heard Jameson swearing as he yanked hard on the wheel. Only seconds later, those other vehicles came to life, and roared in pursuit.

But the chase they gave was not my main source of concern. A searing pain, like a red-hot blade, screamed through my mind, enveloping my entire body. I'd never known such pain. The labor had torn through me like this, yes, but I'd been drugged, and it had been duller. Distant. This was immediate and agonizing. And yet it was not my own. Not my own.

"Don't worry," he said, maneuvering the vehicle at dizzying speeds. "They'll never catch us. This car goes like hell, and I have the advantage. I can run without lights." He looked toward me, and tried to keep the pain from his eyes. But when his gaze met mine, he saw the agony in my gaze. "Angelica?"

"Tell me, Vampire," I said softly, "is it only the sun that can kill us? Or would their bullets do the job as well?" And as I spoke, I lifted my hand and laid it against his waist, and I felt the blood there, dampening my palm.

"We'll worry about that later," he said, but I knew he was in terrible pain. He spoke through gritted teeth, and his flesh was white, eyes sparking with anguish. "First we have to get the hell out of here." He took a corner so fast that I was flung against him. I cried out when his pain grew worse, and he looked at me sharply.

"Angelica? You're not hurt, too, are you?"

"No," I whispered, staring down at the blood that pooled on

the seat around him in horror. "No, it's your pain I feel, Vampire. As if it were my own. Why? Is this normal?"

He shook his head slowly, grating his teeth. "I don't know."

"You're weakening!" I said, because I knew it. "You'll bleed to death, won't you?"

"Put pressure on the wound," he instructed, and he caught my hand and drew it to his side, pressing my palm to the blood-soaked injury. "Don't let it bleed, Angel. We can bleed to death in no time flat. It's deadly to us." Another corner, and I did as he said, but my hand was shaking, and I was afraid my efforts were doing little to stanch the flow. But the pain began to fade as well. And then his head fell sideways, and his eyes closed.

"Stay awake, dammit," I ordered, my voice harsh as I took the steering wheel when his hands dropped to his sides. "Don't you die on me. Hold on!"

But I don't think he heard me. He just lay there, and the pain went away. I steered the car off the road, pulled him out from behind the wheel and took over the driving myself. We were almost back to the house near the sea, so that was where I took us. But I was terrified. Terrified he was going to die and leave me to face this challenge alone. And though he'd called himself my captor, I found that the thought of his death gave me no pleasure. In fact, it filled me with a horrible dread. I'd become dependent on him to some extent. And I needed his help. Those things were true. But they were not the source of my anguish.

I simply didn't want this man, this enigma I'd only begun to understand, to die. I didn't want him to leave me. Not yet. Not like this.

And that feeling frightened me almost as much as the blood oozing from his side did.

Chapter Eight

Their luck seemed to be nothing but bad. Dammit, the bastards had shot him. He shouldn't have risked it. Should have just left the damned car and taken off on foot. He'd been an idiot, thinking like a mortal, a habit he'd thought Rhiannon's constant chiding had cured him of.

As he blinked his eyes clear of the pain-induced haze, he realized Angelica was driving. She'd pulled him from behind the wheel at some point—though he had no memory of it—and now she was speeding over the highway as if the devil were on her tail. He hadn't even realized she knew how to drive. Had never bothered to ask her. But she was driving, and burning the pavement right off the damned roads in her wake.

Only several miles and hair-raising turns later, when she apparently thought she'd lost her pursuers, did she slow down. Her gaze kept dancing over him, and her violet eyes were alive with worry. Glancing nervously into the mirror first, she pulled the car off the road, and turned to him where he lay slumped in the seat, clinging to consciousness with everything in him. He'd passed out once or twice already. He was sorely afraid that if he did it again, he wouldn't wake up.

Her pretty eyes widened when he thought that. "You're getting better at it," he managed. "Reading my thoughts."

"You're too weak to prevent it," she said, and she tore his shirt open, and he recalled dreaming of her doing something very similar. Only under radically different circumstances.

She sucked air through her teeth, and that made him look down. The wound was a jagged tear in his side, an inch or so above his hipbone, which pulsed with blood at an alarming rate. A flesh wound that would barely threaten a mortal.

"Why does it bleed like that?" Angelica whispered. "It isn't that bad. Why won't it stop?" And as she spoke she began searching the car, looking in the glove compartment and leaning over into the back seat.

"Any wound can kill a vampire," he told her. Her teacher, that's what he'd become. Someone older and wiser, whom she needed in order to survive. And that was why she was so worried about him right now. Wouldn't do to let himself go thinking anything else. "We tend to bleed like hemophiliacs when our flesh is torn deeply. I'm afraid, sweet Angel, that I'll be dead within minutes unless we can stop the flow."

Apparently, Angelica had already reached the same conclusion. Because before he finished speaking, she yanked his shirt off him, tearing the fabric in the process. She tore off a sleeve with her teeth, and balled it up, pressing it into the wound. The rest of the shirt, she twisted into one long band, then wrapped it around his middle, so tightly he could barely inhale. She pulled it hard to apply pressure to the wound, and he moaned. Pain. She was causing him intense pain, and she knew that. And she was feeling it, too, an oddity he still hadn't figured out. Maybe Roland could explain it.

As for the pain, it couldn't be helped. Though he had thought she'd be a bit more squeamish about inflicting it on him. She hadn't been, though. Hadn't even flinched, and it was probably a good thing. He'd die otherwise. When she'd finished the job, she waited, watching the makeshift bandage.

"Don't bleed," she muttered, half to herself and half to the wound in his side. "Don't bleed, don't bleed, don't bleed...."

"It doesn't dare," he told her. Then he leaned back in the seat and closed his eyes.

"Don't leave me," she told him.

He looked at her, frowning. But she said no more. She started the car again without looking at him—at his face, anyway. The wound, she perused often. She popped the clutch, then, and sped back to Eric's house as fast as Jameson's high-performance engine could take her there. And then she put her luscious arms around him, and struggled to pull him from the car. He tried to help her, even got his feet out the door and onto the ground. She anchored one of his arms over her shoulders, and helped him inside. No doubt she could have carried him if she'd had to. She had the strength, though he wasn't certain she was aware of it yet. Still, he hadn't been a vampire long enough not to feel a bit odd at the prospect of being picked up and carried by a female, so he told her he could walk, and then he managed to do so. Barely. She took him down through the passage, and then inside, and she activated the locks after she closed the door.

"Jesus, Angel," he said, pausing for a few shallow breaths before going on. "That was stupid." She eased him into the bedroom, and then gently onto the bed.

"What was?"

"The locks. You don't know the code. How the hell will you get out if I die?"

"You'll just have to stay alive, Vampire. If you don't, I'll be stuck. So buck up and tell me what to do." And then, as he felt himself starting to slip away, she was leaning over him, shaking his shoulders. "Dammit, Jameson, what should I do?" And he saw tears standing in her eyes.

She was, once again, the woman he could not hate. The woman who needed him. He'd always had a weak spot for women in need. Tamara, first. He remembered trying once to take on a grown man in a bare-knuckle fight when he'd been no more than a scrawny twelve-year-old, to protect her. Even Rhiannon, the strongest woman he'd ever known, had her weak moments, and Jameson would have taken on the world to protect her.

And now, this one. This dark angel who seemed to need him more than any of them ever had. He didn't want to feel protective of her, but it was unavoidable. He felt it. He couldn't do otherwise. Even though he was the one lying here at death's very door, he felt her need. He wasn't going to drop dead and leave her on her own. He was going to fight, so that he could stay alive. He wanted to be with her when they found their daughter again. He wanted to see those violet eyes when they were alight with joy. He never had.

Hell, he was actually beginning to like the woman.

He stroked her hair away from her beautiful face. "Any wound will heal during the day sleep," he told her. "All you have to do is keep me alive until then."

"How?"

He tried to smile. "Stop the bleeding. Replace what I've lost. You manage that, I'll be just fine." He struggled to keep his eyes open.

She blinked. "What if I can't?"

"Look in the bathroom, Angel. There should be some supplies in there for…this sort of emergency."

She touched his face, checked the wound and then, biting her lip, went into the bathroom in search of supplies. Jameson had no doubt she'd find what she needed there. Eric kept this place stocked with everything anyone might conceivably need. And his friend didn't let him down. Angelica returned with an armful of bandages, and even needles and silk thread. The bandages would have to do. No way was he lying still while she stuck that needle into him. And she wouldn't have time, anyway. It would be dawn soon.

She returned to the bed, removed his makeshift tourniquet and watched with horror in her eyes as the bleeding began all over again. With one hand pressed to the wound, she tore strips of bandage with the other, and her teeth. Pinching the jagged edges of his torn flesh together, she taped them there. Bit by bit, closing the wound. And when she finished, and blood still seeped through, she made a clean, new bandage from a roll of gauze, knotting it tightly around his middle. And then she sighed in relief, nodding. He assumed that meant the bleeding had stopped.

While he lay there, thinking this was going to be all right after all, the woman picked up a needle and some of that silk thread.

"No," he said, his voice a raw whisper. "That's not necessary."

"I didn't think so either, at first," she told him, unerringly spearing the needle's eye with her thread. "But I see now that I was wrong. If you so much as move the bleeding is going to start again," she told him. "You could die, Vampire." She finished threading the needle, and loosened his bandages again. "Hold on," she told him. "This is going to hurt like hell."

He passed out from the intense pain when I sewed up the gash in his side. That and the blood loss. I hadn't realized pain was different in all of us, not just in me. Everything that hurt me, hurt me more since the change. Now I knew it was part of this new nature of mine. Pain was magnified, just as every other sensation was. And for some reason, I could feel his pain. I hadn't felt the pain of those other vampires, who'd been held captive in the cells alongside my own. Nor that of my maker, when I'd set him afire and watched him burn. But I felt Jameson's pain.

It didn't seem so odd. The man was in my blood, in my soul. He was like a virus I could not cure. Slowly growing stronger and spreading throughout my system, until he affected my every thought and feeling.

In a very short time, I'd somehow become quite attached to this man who claimed to be my captor. It had begun, of course, with the physical sensations I'd experienced when I'd taken him. And then the longing. The craving for more of that. It had deepened, I believed, because of the child we'd shared. I'd carried his very flesh and blood within me for months, nurtured it. Loved it.

How could I not be attached to him? Even…even fond of him, despite his being an unrepentant monster, and despite his violent hatred for DPI. He'd spared the man's life tonight. Because I asked it of him, he'd spared it. Surely, he was not quite as horrible as I'd believed him to be at first. Certainly not the same as the beast who made me. No, I'd been wrong about that as well. Jameson would never force himself on me that way.

Though there was, deep inside, a small part of me that wished he would. For then I would be able to experience the fulfillment I craved with him, and suffer none of the guilt of making the choice to do so.

The thought heated my face, and made me sweat. I pushed it aside and focused on the matter at hand. I sewed the wound very well, and then cleaned and wrapped it. And then I just looked at him, lying there, soaked in his own blood. The bleeding was stopped. It would stay stopped. And if what he had told me about the regenerative qualities of the day sleep were true, he would survive. Maybe.

But he needed to feed, to replenish what he'd lost. And then to rest. The wound, according to the vampire, would be healed when he woke. I needed only be sure it didn't break open again before then.

The sweater I wore was soaked in Jameson's blood. Ruined. The jeans, too, had absorbed a great deal of blood. His were in worse shape than my own, though. And I knew I would have to clean him up. There was no one else here to do it. And the task excited me. I know it is shameful, but there it is. I was aroused at the thought of undressing him, of bathing him.

I first shed my own clothing. What good would it do me to hold him and wash him if I were only soiling him again in the process? I dived beneath the shower spray very briefly, just long enough to rinse the blood away from my skin. I donned the robe he'd worn earlier, and hurried back to his side. All told, I wasn't away from him for more than three minutes. And he was still all right.

Lifting him gently, I peeled what remained of his shirt over his head and dropped it to the floor. As I turned back to him, I went completely still. Naked from the waist up, he was…he was beautiful.

I had never looked upon a man's form before. Not this way. He was firm. Muscular, yet lean, and somehow very graceful. His skin lay taut and supple and I longed to touch it. To run my hands over his chest, and flat belly, and feel him beneath my palms.

It was a foreign longing, and yet I was growing used to it. I'd never experienced such attacks of lust before. My curiosity had been answered by the sisters, who simply told me that such things were sinful and unsuitable for a young woman to be thinking about. Nothing more. I was forbidden to touch my ripening body, forbidden to explore it, and learn the secrets of its pleasure. But now, they were secrets I longed to know. Never before had I been so absorbed with physical desire. Only with him. His body held my eyes prisoner. And while I was embarrassed and ashamed, I could not stop myself from looking my fill. His chest intrigued me most, I think, with its hard nipples tempting me to touch.

I licked my lips, pulling my eyes away. But they were drawn back again. And again.

He needed my help right now, not my passion, I reminded myself. But my hands trembled as I unfastened his jeans. And my entire body shook as I stood over him, and worked the denim down over his hips, and thighs, and finally worked it free of his feet. I wouldn't look. I told myself that I would not look at him anymore, and forcibly, I kept my gaze away from him, rushing back to the bathroom for a basin of warm water and a clean, soft cloth. But there was no helping it. I had to look at him as I gently washed the blood away. I washed his arms and his chest as my eyes feasted on the smooth taut skin of his belly. And I washed his hard, rippling abdomen, and the narrow curve of his hip as I stared down at those powerful thighs and the dark curls between them. And the root of him, at rest now, but beautiful and filled with erotic promises I couldn't even begin to understand. Dark. Mysterious. And I wanted to touch him. To awaken that organ and see it come to life in response to my touch. I wanted to feel it, explore it. Learn the secrets of his pleasure as well as my own.

This was so unlike me, these wanton thoughts. I bit my lip, and chased them away. It was wrong, I knew, to look at him this way while he was unable to prevent it. Wrong. And it would be even more wrong to touch him while he rested. Because perhaps if he could object, he would. I knew all too well that he held no tender feelings for me. Hated me, in fact. Given all of that, he might resent my taking liberties with him.

Carefully, I washed the blood from his legs, but even this was a sensual pleasure; running my hands over him again and again, with only the soft cloth between his flesh and my own. My hands tingled where I had touched him. And I felt good. Sinfully, wantonly good.

When I finished, I was hot. I was breathing too rapidly, and beads of sweat dampened my face and my neck. My pulse fluttered in my throat, and my stomach clenched. And I knew why. I wanted him. I was hungry for him. I told myself that it was ridiculous, that I didn't even like him. That he detested me in return. That I could very easily have been his murderess one night long ago, and that it wasn't something a man like him was likely to forget...much less forgive.

But it didn't matter that he hated me. That minor detail did nothing to dampen this desire that blazed to life inside me. I wanted him. How could any woman not want him, when he was laid out before her, naked and beautiful and utterly helpless? Even a virgin, even a nun, even a saint, would have been stirred to a sensual awareness. And I was none of those things, right now. I was none other than a vampiress. A creature of pure sensuality. A creature in whom every sensation was heightened and magnified a thousand times. And for the first time, the very first time, I realized that I was relishing this new nature of mine. Delighting in the sensual awareness. Wanting more of it.

What would it be like, I wondered, to make love to this man?

Foolish notion, of course. Oh, I could look on him, even touch him without his consent and perhaps without his knowledge. But I certainly couldn't make love to him. It was impossible.

And I was getting waylaid by my newfound fascination with the male form. Because he was still in danger from the blood loss he'd suffered, and I mustn't forget that.

He needed to feed. And there was plenty of sustenance in neat little bags just in the next room. I rose, dropping my washcloth into the basin and turning to go and get him some. But then I stopped as I realized how difficult it would be to feed him. I had only glasses. He was unconscious. I might be able to rouse him enough to make him drink, but...

But I didn't want to bring it to him in a glass, cold and stale and weak. I knew the difference between that and warm, living blood. And I also knew the sinful delight of drinking from him. And that it had left him shuddering with desire as much as it had me. And I wanted to feed him myself. I wanted his mouth on me, his teeth sinking into my flesh, his lips drawing my very essence into him. It would stir the desire in me even higher. I knew that, sensed it, because of what had happened to me each time we'd shared blood before. But it would also give me such intense pleasure that I could not resist.

This craving for his touch had driven me to madness long enough. I would explore it a bit now, while he was unconscious, and unable to ridicule my longing with those knowing eyes. I would let him take from me, because I wanted to know what it felt like. And because I was feeling free and uninhibited with him lying there completely unaware.

Boldly, I stretched out on the bed beside his naked body. Wearing only his robe, I lay there, and I pulled him, gently, onto his side, and then lower, so that his head and shoulders lay across my chest. Oh, and I closed my eyes, delighting in the feel of his masculine weight pressing me down into the mattress. And then I sighed in anguish at the feel of my breasts being crushed beneath his bare chest. These were feelings I'd long ago decided that I would never know. The weight of a man on top of me. It was forbidden me. So I relished each sensation, one by one, enjoying it thoroughly before moving on to the next. I parted the robe I wore, baring my breasts so they could feel his chest against them. And it was good. I ran my hands up and down his spine, closing my eyes as I learned his shape. I cupped his buttocks. They were so perfect and small and firm in my hands as I pulled at them, arching my hips so that his erection pushed against me.

Yes, erection. He was hard now. Not even conscious yet, but

responding to my touch as if he were. I'd sensed this desire ran both ways between us. Now I knew it was true.

I moved one hand upward, sliding it over the perfect curve of his muscled back, cupping the back of his head, and gently guiding his face to my chest. With my mind, I reached out to his, in just the way he had shown me. *Feed now, Vampire. Take what you need...what you crave...take it from me.*

And he did. His mouth moved over my skin, and I closed my eyes. He kissed my breast, and then his lips parted, and his teeth pierced that tender skin. I cried out in pleasure and pain and he drank from me, took from me, as I had taken from him. His movements were slow, and clumsy. He suckled me slowly, very slowly, and gently. Too gently. His hands fumbled upward, like the hands of a sleepwalker, and they found my hair, and stroked it, like stroking a cat, over and over as he fed. And lust for him raged and burned inside me, growing more powerful each time he swallowed.

I could feel him growing stronger. Feel him regaining his power. Soon his hands were in motion, finding mine, and sliding up my arms to settle on my shoulders. And then he lifted his head, opened his eyes. Hungry eyes, glazed with passion, heavy lidded. They met mine for only a moment, and there was no inhibition in them. No resistance. No hesitance. Just desire.

And a jolt of fear surged inside me, as I wondered what sort of beast I had roused to life. I should end this, right now, I thought. I should gently move him off me, and give him the chance to come fully awake.

He licked his lips slowly, and then lowered his head again, and all of my good intentions dissolved. His fevered lips traced a path to the roundest part of my shoulder, and then he nipped at me there. Sharp, strong teeth drawing blood, and I tipped my head back, gasping in delight. And then he moved again, down over my chest. Pausing and making me gasp again. He sampled each of my breasts, and the skin over my rib cage, and my belly, and my hip, and then he buried his face between my legs, licking and biting at me even there. By the time he began working his way back up my body again I was in agony. My facial muscles contorted into a grimace of longing and restraint. My breaths rasping in and out of my chest. My skin dampened by his mouth, and dotted with tiny, erotic wounds.

He stretched his nude body atop mine, and lowered his mouth toward my lips, and I caught him, framing his face with my hands and I whispered, "Wait."

God, the look in those tiger-striped eyes of his. He was a creature driven sheerly by sensation right now. And I was very close to joining him in that state. Very close.

"Wait for what, Angel," he whispered, from somewhere deep in his throat. And he pressed his mouth to mine, caught my lower lip between his teeth and snapped at it.

I twisted my head to one side. Perhaps I never should have started this. I hadn't intended for it to go this far. I hadn't been fair to him. He likely had no idea what he was doing. I hadn't thought it through, hadn't planned on what would happen if he should awaken. "You're losing yourself to the bloodlust," I managed, though I didn't want to talk right now. Didn't want to explain things to him or warn him away. I simply wanted him to take me. Now, before I had time to think it through. I wanted him inside me. Fast and hard and deep.

"Yes," he said. "Yes, fast and hard and deep, Angel."

Oh, God, I'd forgotten to guard my thoughts.

"Oh, Christ, Angel...touch me. Touch me like you want to." And he took my hand, and brought it down between us. And I did. I ran my fingertips up and down him, encircled him and squeezed him. And I read every one of his thoughts as they passed through his mind. He wasn't blocking them. Not at all. All Jameson could think about was how every single sensation was magnified a thousand times since he'd been brought over. And how Rhiannon had told him that with sex it was more like a million times, and how he hadn't experienced that yet. And how he wanted to. How he'd been wanting to since he'd first felt the touch of my lips on his skin. How he'd dreamed of doing this with me.

Knowing it drove me to lunacy, I think. I pressed against him, arching my hips, and then his lips trailed down my jaw to my throat, and he sucked at the skin there. And St. Francis of Assisi couldn't have resisted. I wrapped my arms around him and held him tight, and he brought his head up and kissed me. Deeply, the way I'd been wanting him to. Pushing his tongue into my mouth and feeding on mine in turn. Kneading my buttocks with his hands and lifting my hips toward his in a fury of need as well as promise.

Frantically, he pushed at my robe and I lifted my upper body from the bed to help him peel it from me. Between the two of us, we managed to remove the robe completely without breaking apart at all. His heart hammered against my chest. He was panting, and his skin was hot to the touch. He muttered, and I kissed him and clawed at his skin, nearly incoherent with the need burning in me.

He knew how overwhelming it could be, I sensed it. He was kicking himself for it. It had all been patiently explained to him. He'd been warned, so he knew what to expect, he told himself. While I did not. All I knew was that every cell in me was screaming for release. He was weak from the pain of that bullet, and still, I was certain, not fully aware of what he was doing. But I couldn't stop it now. I couldn't.

Ah, but dammit, he was coming aware, and he was thinking he should stop.

"Angelica..."

I lifted him away, rose just a little, parting my thighs wider, positioning myself beneath him. His passion-glazed eyes held mine as he lowered his body, slipping inside me. I arched against him, tilting to receive him as he pushed deeper. I took more of him. And I closed my eyes and moaned. And that sound seemed to take the last of his resistance, and grind it to dust. He grasped my buttocks and pulled me tight to him, plunging himself all the way into my body. And I tipped my head back and cried out in pleasure. He began to move inside me. And I rode him, clung to him, felt like a warrior goddess as I took all he could give and demanded still more.

When I began to tremble and shake, and when my eyes flew open wide, he knew. I hadn't erected any shields around my mind either. Not just now, and he knew exactly what I was feeling. Even *felt* exactly what I was feeling. I was shocked at the pleasure of this. Shocked at the delicious tightening going on at the very hub of my body. I'd never felt it before, didn't know what the pinnacle was, but strained toward it all the same.

And when it came, he bent his head and sank his teeth into my throat, and sucked hard at me. And the orgasm doubled, and trebled, and went on and on and on. I felt shattered by its power, and I screamed, and my nails scratched bloody trails down his chest, as I arched like a cat, pressing my hips to take his erection all the way into me, and pressing my throat to take his teeth all the way into me. And he came too, his shuddering release seeming to spill more than his seed into my body, seeming to draw more than the slick fluids from my core, and from my throat. It seemed his soul was drawn from him as well, and it seemed mine was drawn from me. And the two tangled and twisted and mingled together, even as our body fluids were doing, and became one. The ecstasy was so intense I thought I would die. I honestly thought I would die. Waves and waves of it washed over me, sweeping me away into a world of insane sensations, pure, undiluted physical ecstasy. No pleasure this incredible could come without a price.

But I didn't die. I came back to myself, very slowly, and when I did, I felt disconnected, dizzy, as if my brain were still floating out there somewhere.

And Jameson was collapsed on top of me. Arms twined around me, his head on my chest. Utterly relaxed and already, I thought, sinking in a pool of velvety sleep.

When he woke...

I drew a deep breath and let it out very slowly. When he woke there was going to be hell to pay. I doubted he'd forgive me for this latest transgression any more easily than he had when I'd attempted to murder him. This had been very close to rape.

I reached down for the comforter, and pulled it up to cover us both. And then I lay there, and wished that this fevered coupling had assuaged the hunger I had for him. But it hadn't. It still burned inside me. Still grew. If anything, this had only made it stronger. Deepened and empowered it to demanding new levels.

Lord help me, I craved the man like never before. And I was damned if I had a clue what to do to change it.

I was ruled, for that brief interlude, by nothing but feeling. Sensation. Lust. Desire. Sin. And I took him like a true harlot. No seasoned streetwalker could have seemed more thorough, I'm certain, than I was that night.

Out of my mind. Overwhelmed by my own heightened passions. I must have been.

But then I woke, to find myself naked as the day I was born, and twined around the vampire like a vine that would wither without him. And I was mortified.

Worse than anything else for me then was that I remembered every second of it. Every guttural sound I'd made, and every shameless thing I'd done. I even remembered the climax that had seemed to shatter my soul into a thousand glimmering bits.

Very carefully, I pulled myself out of his arms, and sat up…and then I gasped in horror at what I had done, for it was even worse than I had realized. I'd scratched his chest with my long nails, and he was covered in tiny bite marks. And he was naked, and sleeping, and easily as beautiful as a god. A dark pagan god. My temptation. My downfall. My Satan.

God help me, but desire stirred in me anew as I looked down at him there. I pressed my hands to my face in shame. And then I cried. For I did not know this creature I had become. I did not know her at all. And I was not at all certain I wanted to.

"Angelica," he whispered, and I felt movement as he sat up. His hands touched my shoulders as if he would slip his arms around me and pull me close. Comfort me.

But I could not bear his touch. Not now. Not when I wanted it so.

"How could I have done it?" I whispered.

"Ah, Christ, Angelica—"

"You should have warned me. You knew what would happen to me if I were ever to let you drink from me. Because it was the same when I drank from you. You knew, didn't you? Didn't you, Vampire?''

Lowering his beautiful striped eyes from mine, he nodded. ''Yes. I knew what kind of lust would hit you if I drank from you, Angel.'' He lifted his head and looked me in the eye. ''I just had no reason to think you would do it. Why would I warn you against something I thought you'd never do?''

''You should have. Don't you see what you've done? What you've taken from me? What you've made me?'' I turned my face away, snatching at the blankets to cover myself.

''I didn't *make* you into anything, Angelica. You are what you are, and you did to me exactly what you wanted to do. You were the aggressor, Angel. I was barely in my right mind. Hell, if I'd done to you what you did to me you'd be screaming rape.''

I turned my face away in shame, unable to deny that he was right. He was so right.

''You wanted it as badly as I did, Angelica. We're both adults. Why are you so mortified?''

''You made me want it,'' I whispered, but I knew, even then, that he spoke the truth. I'd felt desire for him from that first night. It had been a large part of what made me take him then, that first time. It hadn't been hunger alone, but lust. Even then, though I had denied it with everything in me.

''I tried to stop you,'' he muttered, as I climbed out of the bed, dragging the covers with me. ''But, Angel, you drove me....''

I gritted my teeth and, battling tears, turned away from him.

''You're disgusted by what you did, aren't you?'' he asked. ''You're ashamed. Aren't you, Angel?''

''Of course I'm ashamed!'' I all but shouted.

''Yes. Yes, of course you're ashamed. Disgusted. You gave in to physical desires and made love to a monster. A man you despise and the very thought of it makes you want to throw up.''

I shook my head in denial. He had it all wrong. I had decided he wasn't a monster, that I'd been wrong about him. It was my own lasciviousness that shocked and appalled me. Not him. Lord, I was so ashamed.

"Come back to bed, Angelica," he said very softly. "Look at you, you're teetering on your feet. The sun is coming up outside. You can't stay awake any longer."

But I ignored him, and made my way into the adjoining room, wrapping myself in the blankets and sinking onto the settee. My limbs felt heavy. My brain, foggy and dim. I knew it was dawn. My body sensed the sunrise as it had since I'd been made over into this creature I now was. A creature of immoral appetites and uncontrollable hungers. A creature of sin, surely.

He stood in the doorway, looking at me, and he, too, was weakening.

"Leave me alone, Vampire," I whispered. "I won't shame myself further by sleeping in your arms."

I saw the anger flash in his eyes. "Sleeping in the arms of a monster, you mean? I'm no more monster than you, Angelica. But have it your way. I won't touch you again. I wouldn't have done so this time, if I hadn't been half-delirious with blood loss. Believe me, I'm no more thrilled by the notion of sex with a person I detest than you are." And he turned, stepping out of my sight, returning to the bed we'd so recently shared.

So he detested me. I was about to tell him that his assumptions were wrong. That I was ashamed of my sinful nature, and not of having given myself to him. Not of wanting him. For if I were to desire anyone, it seemed quite natural that it should be him. No other man had ever even begun to stir me this way. No, I was ashamed of the desire itself, not the object of it.

But it was just as well I hadn't told him, for now I knew that he detested me, and resented my taking him the way I had.

It only shamed me more to feel a desperate yearning to go into that room with him, to feel his nude body pressed to mine once again. I still hungered for him. More now than before. The coupling had done that, I knew it instinctively. It was as if our souls had joined. The sensation had hit me before, when I'd drunk from him. But now it was greater and more intense. And if I lay with him again, I sensed this link between us would become still stronger. Each time I surrendered to this need, it would have more power over me. It would grow harder and harder to resist. And resist I must, if there were to be any hope at all for my stained soul.

"Come, get dressed. It's night."
I stirred awake, only to find his hand clasping my shoulder. I pushed him away, shoving him at the very spot where the bandages were before I realized what I was doing, and then I winced and drew away, an automatic response.
"The day sleep is regenerative," he reminded me. "It heals us."
I sat up, holding a blanket to my chest, and examined his waist, where I fully expected to see a gaping, bloody hole. But there was none. And then I looked up at him. He stood there, wearing a fresh pair of jeans, slowly buttoning a clean shirt. And the marks I'd put on him with my nails and my teeth, had vanished as well.
"You see," he said. "You didn't lose so much to me after all. You're a virgin again by now."
"You bastard."
His response to that was a bitter smile. He buttoned his sleeves and turned away from me. "You might want to dress, Angelica. We'll have company before long."
I lifted my brows, and forced myself to look at him again. His gaze had been fixed to my bared neck and shoulders, and gleaming with that need I still felt. I was not flattered by his desire. For I knew that in him it was only physical, and that he hated me. He quickly averted his eyes. "Go on, they're coming even now."
"Who?" I asked, getting to my feet with the blankets wrapped around me. Fear churned to life in my stomach. Surely if those DPI men had discovered our hideaway he wouldn't be so calm.
"Some friends of mine. Monsters, like me." He stepped closer, reaching up to stroke my face in a mocking gesture. "Don't be so skittish, Angel. They might want to rip your pretty throat out for the way you left me to die, but I won't let them."
I know my eyes widened. And then, without warning, the door burst open, and I came face-to-face with a woman who must

surely be the queen of all of them. Tall, and regal, with long, perfectly straight raven hair that nearly reached the floor, and black eyes that gleamed with anger. I backed away slowly, my heart racing.

"Jameson!" she snapped in a deep, rich voice. "What reason could you possibly have to frighten her that way? Look at her, she's shaking."

He did look at me, his mouth twisting in a mocking smile. "It's no more than she deserves, Rhiannon."

But another woman had entered behind her, a small, gentle-looking creature, with masses of ebony curls. She smiled at me, and came to where I stood. "It's all right," she said softly. "We're friends. We're here to help, honest."

"Don't be so quick to comfort her, Tamara," Jameson said, as two men came in as well, one of them wearing a cloak that reached to the floor. "But I'm lax in my duties. Eric, Roland, ladies, I'd like to introduce Angelica. The vampiress who attacked me less than a year ago, and then left me to die."

They all stared at me. All those dark eyes, and probing minds. And I turned, and fled into the bedroom, closing the door and turning the locks, even knowing that could not keep them out if they wanted to come for me.

I stood there, trembling, watching that closed door, and waiting. Fully expecting one of them to come crashing through it at any moment. My God, these were his friends. His vampiric protectors. The ones who had saved his life when I'd left him for dead. They'd kill me, surely!

Trembling, I fumbled for some clothing, never taking my eyes from the door. What I ended up pulling over my head was some sort of dress, black gauzy fabric that brushed my shins, and straps that crossed my chest, surrounded my neck and crossed again at my back.

At least I was decently covered now. I wouldn't die naked.

Chapter Nine

"Really, Jameson," Roland sighed. He turned from staring at the door Angelica had just closed, to face Jameson, his black satin cloak swirling theatrically. "Was that really called for?"

Jameson closed his eyes and shook his head. "She thinks we're all monsters. Worse than the devil himself," he said, but he was tired. And putting a scare into the holier-than-thou Angelica hadn't given him the pleasure he'd half hoped it would. Acting as if sex with him were going to damn her soul hadn't exactly endeared her to him. She'd been so hungry for him, so wonderfully passionate in his arms...and then, she'd been disgusted by her own actions. Disgusted by him.

It infuriated him!

"Was it really her who attacked you that night?" Tamara asked, her delicate brows lifting.

"Yes."

"But why, Jameson? Has she told you why?"

He paced to the settee, and sank onto it, sighing. "She hasn't. But I have a pretty good idea." They were all waiting, expectant eyes on him. "Look, I'll explain it all later. Right now, we need to find Amber Lily and—"

"Amber Lily?" Tamara said, her eyes widening, her lips softening in a tremulous smile. "Oh, Jamey, that's beautiful."

And he couldn't help smiling back. "Yes, and so is she," he said. "Angel says that her eyes are wide and round and dark, and that her hair is curly."

"Angel?" Tamara frowned. "That's an odd thing to call a woman you seem so...angry with."

Jameson averted his eyes. Unusual, indeed. It was a damned term of endearment. When had he slipped into the habit of calling her that? It had begun as a sarcastic barb. But it had become more.

"Jamey?" Tamara said, searching his face. "Are you sure there isn't something more going on betwe—"

"Enough of this sentimental nonsense." Rhiannon's voice filled the room with its tone of command, and Tamara cut herself off. "I do believe we have a situation here that needs attention. That *woman* in the next room attempted to murder one of us. Our own Jameson. And I, for one, am not about to let such a crime go unpunished."

She took a step toward the bedroom. Jameson's stomach clenched. Jesus, what had he done? He'd been furious with Angelica, yes, but why had he run his mouth the way he had? Rhiannon's temper was nothing less than explosive...especially when someone she cared about was hurt. He jumped from his seat and stepped into her path, holding his hands up. "Rhiannon, no! Wait—"

"Wait?" she said, lifting her brows. "That creature fed on you. Tried to murder you, and you tell me to wait?"

Jameson looked past her, searching Roland's eyes for assistance. Roland only shrugged. "She does have a point."

"Of course I do. I'll never forget the way we found you, Jameson, lying there near death in that crumbling ruin! The woman must pay. Now step aside and let me deal with her."

"Dammit, Rhiannon, it wasn't like you think!"

She narrowed her eyes. "Move on your own, darling, or I'll do it for you."

"No. Listen to me, dammit. She'd only just been brought over, and she thought that made her some kind of monster. She refused to feed, thinking it was a sin."

Rhiannon lifted her brows. "Surely the one who made her could have clarified—"

"She was alone, Rhiannon, and scared to death. By the time I found her she was half-starved and two thirds out of her mind. I don't think she even knew what she was doing."

"Make all the excuses you want for her, Jameson. She attacked you, and now she's going to regret it." Rhiannon put one hand on his shoulder and shoved him aside.

Jameson caught himself, and stepped into her path again. "You're not laying a finger on her, dammit! She's the mother of my child, Rhiannon, and if you want her you'll have to go through me."

Rhiannon tilted her head to one side, folded her arms across her chest and gave him a very small, very smug smile. "That's about what I thought," she said. "Well now, perhaps you'd best remember this little episode, Jameson dear, before you go terrorizing the poor creature again." She poked him in the center of the chest with a long, dagger-sharp nail. "Because if you don't, you'll answer to *me*." And then she turned to Roland, and winked. "Thank you, darling, for not interfering."

"I knew you were pulling Jameson's chain, Rhiannon. And I was certain you had a point to make."

Eric lowered his head, shaking it slowly and sighing. "You had me worried," he admitted. "I thought blood was about to be shed."

Tamara laughed aloud. "And *I* thought you were going to step in and ruin everything," she said to Eric.

Jameson just shook his head as his tense muscles finally uncoiled. He'd thought Rhiannon seriously meant to do Angelica harm. He should have known better. The witch was just tormenting him, trying to prove some obscure point or other. "Damn you for that, Rhiannon."

"You'll thank me for it someday," she told him. "Now step aside so Tamara and I can attempt to speak with the woman you were so willing to risk your life for."

"I wouldn't call that risking my life," he said, but he moved.

Now that he knew Rhiannon wasn't going to hurt Angelica, he was more than willing to let her pass.

Rhiannon lifted her regal brows. "Then you don't know me very well." Then she sailed past him. With a penetrating glance at the door, which released the locks, she walked into the bedroom, Tamara close on her heels.

"Now, Jameson," Roland said, stepping to the minirefrigerator and opening it. "Where are they keeping this daughter of yours?"

Rhiannon was like an ancient queen. She wore a skintight, scarlet dress that swept the floor at her feet, with a dramatically plunging neckline. Her nails were long and sharp and painted bloodred.

Tamara looked like an ordinary young woman. She wore jeans, as Jameson seemed always to wear, too, and a turquoise sweater with pale flowers embroidered all over it. She was petite, softspoken, and had a warm, easy smile. Of the two, she was the more approachable, or the one I feared least, anyway.

"Don't look so afraid," Rhiannon said in her deep, rich tones, and she even smiled a little. "Jameson explained everything. You heard, did you not?"

I nodded, though I was still shaking. "It surprised me...that he'd bother to defend me at all."

"Why does that surprise you, fledgling?" Rhiannon asked.

"B-because...he hates me."

Rhiannon slanted a dark glance at Tamara. Tamara winked. "No doubt he'd like you to keep right on thinking that," she said. "But now you know better, right?"

I closed my eyes, lowered my head and battled the tears that seemed always to be trembling near the surface. "I don't know anything anymore. Not who I am...or *what* I am. Or what I feel."

"Oh..." Tamara came close to me, sliding her arms around my shoulders, hugging me like a sister. "Oh, Angelica, you're crying! There, now, please. It's going to be all right. I promise you."

I sniffed and lifted my eyes to hers. Beyond her, I saw Rhiannon roll her eyes, and begin to pace. "How can you not know *what* you are, dear? You're immortal! All this blubbering is no more than a waste of time. You should be reveling in your new nature. *Relishing* it!''

"Rhiannon, it's harder for some. Be patient." Tamara turned again to me, her eyes very large and very kind. I was surprised to see such things in the eyes of one of the damned. "It takes time, Angelica. But soon you'll realize that you're the same woman you were before. The changes are only physical. So your diet has changed, and you're stronger now. Your senses are heightened, and you'll never die of those bothersome 'natural causes' that take so many mortals. You won't age. But deep down, inside, where it counts, you're just the same."

I faced this sweet-faced vampiress, more ashamed than I'd ever been, and I shook my head. "But I'm *not.*"

"Sure you are. I'll prove it to you. Tell me, what did you do before you were brought over?"

I blinked away my tears. "I was...I was studying with the Solemn Order of the Sisters of Mercy. In another week, I'd have taken my solemn vows, and..." I broke off there as the two women looked at each other, eyes wide.

"You were..." Rhiannon whispered, "a *nun?*"

"Almost," I said.

"Good God, no wonder you're so thoroughly distraught!" Rhiannon paced across the floor. "Certainly not a candidate for immortality," she ranted. "Not this kind, at least. Who brought you over? He took you by force, didn't he? You certainly didn't ask for this! Tell me his name and I'll teach him a lesson about—"

"He's...he's dead."

Rhiannon seemed to skid to a halt in the center of the bedroom. I lifted my chin and met her astounded eyes, ready to take whatever punishment she'd attempt to dole out, as I confessed my dark secret. Not only had I attacked her friend and left him for dead, I had actually murdered another of her kind. But I wasn't going to deny it. "He killed an innocent man, right in front of me," I said. "And then he tried to force me to do the same, to a boy. Just a frightened boy. And I couldn't. So I..." I closed my eyes, swallowed the lump that came into my throat, nearly choking me.

Rhiannon came closer, staring down into my face. "You killed him, didn't you?"

I opened my eyes, but was unable to face her. Looking at my hands in my lap, I nodded once. Only silence came from the two, and when I got up the nerve to look at them again, Rhiannon's lips had curved very slightly at the corners in a mysterious, Mona Lisa smile.

"My, my," she said. "You might just be made of sterner stuff than is at first apparent."

"He deserved what he got," Tamara said softly. "You mustn't blame yourself, Angelica. It's not a sin to kill in defense of another."

"I wasn't defending anyone when I nearly killed Jameson, though, was I?" I turned and paced away from the two of them, miserable and disgusted with myself. They seemed so good, and so sure of themselves. Graceful and wise, and somehow quite comfortable with what they were. Why couldn't I be like them? I wondered.

"Well," Rhiannon said, "there might have been a bit more involved there."

"Yes," I said. "I was hungry. Such a selfish reason to hurt someone."

"Somehow I doubt you hurt him much." Rhiannon's eyes met Tamara's, and it seemed to me they twinkled. "The taking of blood from a living being is more than simply feeding, darling. As I'm certain you learned that night. It's quite sexual, actually. At least, it is if there is already an attraction there."

I know I blushed. I averted my eyes.

"Don't be embarrassed," Tamara said. "It takes some getting used to, Angelica. This must be very hard on you. But believe me, if you're still having...*feelings* for Jameson, it's only natural. Once you drink from a man, any existing attraction sort of...well, gets magnified."

"Magnified, hell, it explodes," Rhiannon added. "But it should

be a comfort to you to know that it works the same way on him.''
She smiled more fully now. ''And from the way he stepped in
front of me to protect you, fledgling, I suspect you two have exchanged a bit more than blood by now.''

''Please, I can't bear to talk about this anymore!'' I turned my
back to them both, covering my face with my hands.

''*Rhiannon,*'' Tamara scolded. ''Can't you see she's mortified
by all of this? She was a nun, for heaven's sake. They're celibate,
you know.''

''Well then I'd say she had a narrow escape. She's obviously
not cut out for that sort of...chastity.'' She grimaced when she
said the last word. ''The sooner she gets beyond that, the better.
It's such a mortal response! We're *vampires,* fledgling. We *feel*
as no other creature can feel. It's the best part of being what we
are, don't you see that? A gift. A blessing, really.''

I whirled on her, then, horrified by her heresy. ''How can you
talk about blessings and gifts? Don't you know that you're
damned now? We all are!''

Rhiannon stared right into my eyes, blinking in surprise. ''First,
little one—and you might want to file this away in that righteous
little brain of yours for future reference—*never* shout at me.
Never. I am older than ten of your lifetimes. I am Rhiannon, of
Egypt....''

''Here we go,'' Tamara muttered.

''Daughter of Pharaoh, princess of the Nile,'' Rhiannon went
on. ''Worshiped by men. A goddess among women. Envied by
all—''

''Enough, already, Rhiannon. She gets the picture. You want to
move on to point number two, now?''

Rhiannon scowled at Tamara, but it was a playful scowl. ''Just
making sure she has the facts,'' she said, then turned to me once
more. ''Secondly, who are you to say who is damned? Do you
pretend to know the mind of the Almighty? How do you know it
wasn't He who created us? Would a loving God damn one simply
for being different?''

I blinked in shock. But Tamara picked up the conversation from there, and I ended up staring at her. "You're so sure we're evil, Angelica. But how do you know? Because that's the way horror films have painted us? Surely that isn't enough to go by." She took my hand. "There are good and bad among us, just as there are among any race of people. So look at us, Angelica. Look at who we are. What is it about us that would make us evil? We don't hurt anyone. We don't kill—"

"Well, not unless someone really asks for it," Rhiannon said. Then she offered me a wink.

"Why should we be damned just because we drink blood, and exist by night? Mortals eat meat, don't they?"

I tilted my head and studied them. Two, kind, beautiful women. Vampires. Telling me that they were not servants of Satan. But just people. Just people, like anyone else.

"I don't know what to say." I shook my head slowly as I tried to look at them that way. As just people. "I hadn't thought of it this way. All I've thought of since the night I was changed, was finding a way to go back to what I was before."

"You still are what you were before," Rhiannon said. "Only better."

"Angelica," Tamara said, "we came here to help you get your baby back. But…but I'd like to do more than that. I'd like to be your friend…if you'll let me."

I saw nothing but sincerity in Tamara's eyes. And then I glanced toward Rhiannon, to see if she felt the same.

Rhiannon shook her head. "This is beginning to resemble a scene from *Steel Magnolias,*" she said in a sarcastic tone. "Accept our offer of friendship, Angelica, before she starts weeping."

But beyond the flippant words, I could see that she, too, wished to help me. Why, I did not know. I had done nothing but judge and condemn them both. Truly they were showing more godlike qualities than I had.

"I accept," I said. "And I'm sorry for what I said before. That you were damned. You're right, I'm not God. It's wrong of me to sit in judgment."

Tamara smiled and started forward, opening her arms to Rhiannon and to me.

Rhiannon held up a hand. "I do not do group hugs," she said softly. "And I believe we've wasted enough time. There is a child out there in need of our help. And if any of those bastards has done a thing to harm her, then I doubt even God Himself can protect him from Jameson's wrath." She lowered her head. "And if He does, He should probably worry about mine, next."

"I think Amber Lily is safe...for now, at least."

Both women turned to me, brows lifting in question.

"Your friend," I said to Tamara. "The woman, Hilary Garner. We think she's taken the baby and gone into hiding, somewhere."

Tamara sighed hard. "If she has, then you're right. The child couldn't be safer. Hilary is a good person." Rhiannon narrowed her eyes. "She *is*," Tamara insisted.

"We'll get her back, fledgling. Make no mistake about that," Rhiannon said. "Now perhaps you ought to put on some shoes." This with a sheepish glance at my bare feet.

It was Tamara who dived into the closet and emerged with a pair of dainty black flats. "These will look great with that dress." She handed them to me. "And the dress is fabulous on you. Jamey's eyes will pop out."

"Jamey," I whispered, half-smiling at the cute nickname his friends had given him. How he must hate it. "He could not possibly care less what I look like."

"You're mistaken about that, young one," Rhiannon told me. But of course, she was wrong.

There was a tap on the door, and then it opened. Jameson stood there, and when his gaze met mine I sensed something that could almost have been concern in his eyes.

"Is everything all right in here?" he asked, pulling his gaze from mine and looking from Tamara to Rhiannon.

"Being born in this century, Jameson," Rhiannon said, walking past him and pausing at his side, "you obviously know very little about honor and chivalry. I'd strongly suggest you learn it." She stared hard into his eyes. "Soon."

"And I'd strongly suggest, Rhiannon, goddess among women, that you learn a little something about minding your own business."

She lifted a hand, and I held my breath, half-expecting her to strike him. Instead, she gently patted his cheek. "You're lucky I adore you," she told him.

"Enough wasting time," the cloaked man said, coming forward to slip a possessive arm around Rhiannon. When he did, she rubbed herself against his side almost like a cat. "Jameson has reason to believe Hilary Garner has run off somewhere with the child. We have to track her down immediately. She won't be able to hide from DPI for very long."

"Yes, Angelica told us." Tamara paced into the other room. "Hilary had relatives up north. She used to talk about visiting there. Some cabin in the mountains."

"That's too vague," I said. "How will we find it? And even if we do, what if that isn't where she's gone?"

"If you know about this cabin, Tamara," the other man, Eric, said, "then chances are, DPI knows as well."

"If they do, it will be in Hilary's file. Eric, if we could get to a computer…"

"We could tap into the DPI information banks, get everything they have on Hilary and go from there," Eric said, nodding hard.

As they discussed their plan, speaking rapidly, I felt my heart sinking in my chest, so rapidly that it left me dizzy. Pressing my palm to my breast I sank against the wall, all my breath rushing out of my lungs.

"What is it, Angel?" Jameson—the only one of them who seemed to detest me—stood close to my side. "What is it?" he demanded, searching my face.

"I don't know. I just feel…we have to go to her. Now. We can't wait."

He stared hard into my eyes. Not looking away, he said, "She feels…there's a connection to the baby. She senses things. We should start north, right now." Finally, he broke eye contact, turning to Tamara. "Can you give me anything else to go on, anything at all?"

Closing her eyes, Tamara seemed to search her memory. "Hilary used to take the train north to someplace called Petersville. I think she'd rent a car and drive from there."

"Then that's where we'll go," Jameson said. He took my arm and pulled me upright again, none too gently.

"Perhaps Tamara and I should start north with Angelica," Rhiannon said, and to my surprise, I detected a note of concern for me in her voice. "You men can work on getting more information and then join us there."

"Not on your life," Jameson snapped.

Tamara and Rhiannon exchanged amused glances.

"Forget what you're thinking. I don't suppose my dark angel told you her plans, did she?" He scowled at me. "No, I didn't think so. She wants to run from me, monster that I am, at the first opportunity. Use this psychic link to find Amber Lily and then take her away where I'll never have the chance to put my godforsaken, cursed hands on her. Isn't that right, Angelica?"

"If you still believe that, then you truly are a monster," I whispered at the hate I saw in his eyes. "I'm only just now beginning to realize that it has nothing to do with the fact that you're a vampire. You must have been just as monstrous as a mortal man." I tugged my arm free of his hateful grip and stalked back into the bedroom for the shoes I'd left lying on the bed.

"She doesn't set foot out of my sight," I heard him saying, his tone commanding and harsh. "Not for a minute. I don't trust her as far as I can throw her."

"Jameson, for heaven's sakes," Roland said.

"Lad, you have a great deal to learn," Eric put in with a sigh. "I thought we'd taught you better. Will you listen to yourself?"

"Oh, let him be," Rhiannon interrupted him. "Can't you see, Eric, darling? He thinks he's fooling someone—besides himself, I mean."

"Damn it, Rhiannon—"

"Oh, do shut up," Rhiannon replied. "Take your fledgling and go north, Jameson. We'll find out what we can here, and then we'll join you.'' And then she lowered her voice to a conspiratorial whisper. Why she bothered, I did not know. She must have known I could still hear her very clearly. Perhaps it was only for effect. ''And take good care of her, Jameson. Take very good care of her. If harm comes to her, you'll have to answer to me for it.''

''What's this?'' he said, astonished. ''You her best friend all of a sudden?''

''I...like her,'' Rhiannon replied. And she said nothing more. I heard her soft steps coming closer. She came into the bedroom, where I was sitting on the bed's edge contemplating the pretty shoes Tamara had found in the closet. ''Don't take any nonsense from him, Angelica. Never forget, you're of the superior gender.''

''It's difficult to feel superior, when I've somehow become his prisoner.'' I knew Jameson could hear me if he cared to listen. But I didn't care.

''Prisoner, posh!'' Rhiannon said. ''Have you tried to escape him yet?''

I shook my head. ''No, of course not.''

''I doubt he could keep you here against your will, Angelica. In our kind strength comes largely with age. And he's no older than you. Younger, in fact, if only by a few days.''

I tilted my head, my eyes widening in wonder. ''You mean...I'm as strong as he is?''

''Quite possibly so, darling. Keep that in mind when he gets bossy. And remember, if you're not trying to escape, you're here of your own free will. No matter what he tells you.''

My chin rose a bit. ''Thank you, Rhiannon.''

She smiled slightly, then turned and strode from the room. As she passed Jameson, she whispered, ''Prisoner, indeed. Did we teach you nothing at all?'' But she never slowed her pace. She marched right out the door, and the other three followed seconds later, leaving me alone, once again, with the man I wished I could detest.

He stared at me for a long moment, in silence.

"They...are not at all what I expected," I said, unsure what it was he was waiting for.

"No," he said. "Because you were expecting a band of monsters like something out of an old horror film."

I shook my head. "Maybe. I'm not really sure what I was expecting."

He nodded. "They are the finest beings I've ever known, human or otherwise," he said, turning to stare at the door they'd just exited. "They've saved my life more than once, risked their own safety for me often, been like family to me."

"And made you one of them when I had left you for dead," I whispered.

"Yes."

"And yet they don't hate me for that."

He shrugged, and reached out as if to take my arm. But still stinging from his earlier biting remarks, I shrugged away from his touch.

"I forgot," he said, his eyes boring holes into mine. "My touch repulses you...even when you're the one to ask for it. I'll try to remember that from now on, Angelica."

"That isn't fair," I said. "You don't understand—"

"I understand, my dear, that I won't sample your charms again even if you beg me to. Or...should I say, when you beg?"

"I would never—"

"Save it," he said. "Only time will tell, Angel. I'm just letting you know in advance that I won't stain your snow-white flesh by putting my cursed hands on you again. So don't hold your breath waiting."

My anger flared as it seldom had before. I hadn't been repulsed by him, as he seemed to think. But I was now. "Has it even occurred to you, Vampire, that I saved your worthless life by doing what I did?"

"And you have my undying gratitude," he said, his eyes flashing with sarcasm. "Next time I find you dying for lack of blood, honey, I'll return the favor. Give you a little of mine and screw you senseless while I'm at it. You'd like that, wouldn't you?"

I lashed out with my hand, hitting him hard across the face. So hard his head snapped around sideways, and an angry red welt appeared on his cheek.

He snagged my hand in a cruel grip, and pulled me tight to his body. His hard chest pressed to my breasts, and his warm, angry breaths fanned my face as his eyes blazed down at me. And though I hated him at that moment with everything in me, I wanted him, too. And he knew it. Damn him to hell, he knew it.

"Yeah," he whispered. "You'd like that." And then he released me abruptly, turned away and left me there alone. He headed out through the exit that led to the car in its hiding place of brush and briars. And I watched his powerful strides, his magnificent grace, his tightly leashed control.

The bastard knew it, he knew that I wanted him. And I would have been humiliated by his obvious knowledge of my wanton desire for him.

Would have been...but I wasn't. Because I wasn't alone in my misery of need. He might see my hidden desires, but I could see his just as clearly. I had seen what flashed in his eyes, in spite of himself, before he turned away from me.

He wanted me, too.

Chapter Ten

Jameson had been driving in silence for several hours, with no real idea of his ultimate destination, aside from Tamara's vague reference to Petersville. Once there, he had no idea what to do next. But he'd worry about that when he got there. For now, he had other things on his mind.

Angelica.

She sat beside him, pensively silent, and he knew she was worrying about Amber Lily. She'd spoken little since getting into the passenger seat. But her skills at guarding her thoughts were still not quite what they should be—what they *would* be, with a little more practice—and he could read them. He suspected that even when she became adept at building the wall to guard her mind, *he'd* be able to see inside. Because there was something between them. Something powerful and potent, and he was beginning to suspect that all his explanations for it were no more than nonsense. Because he was beginning to think that this was something that had been between them from the very first. It was what had allowed his mortal ears to hear her preternatural sobs. What had drawn him to that building in the first place. It was what had made her lose control when she'd taken from him that first time.

He didn't know *what* it was. But there had been something there. And he was a fool. A thousand times a fool. Because he thought she was the most beautiful, passionate, fiery, strong woman he'd ever known. And he wanted her more every time he looked at her.

And she was disgusted by him.

And knowing it didn't stop his stupid mind from wandering into forbidden territory. All it did was wound his pride, and his pride, when wounded, was more deadly than an injured grizzly.

He knew she wouldn't want him sharing her thoughts, invading her mind, as she called it. But he couldn't stop himself. He even tried. But it wasn't working. It was as if each feeling that flitted through her mind was flitting through his as well.

The sex had deepened the link between them. He'd known it would. Just hadn't been certain how it *could.* Now he knew.

He didn't hear her thoughts word for word, as he'd been able to do at first. But the feelings came through. Fear. Gut-wrenching, soul-wringing fear. She was sick with it. Utterly ill with it. It was killing her, slowly, and by cruel degrees, that she didn't know where their baby daughter was.

And he'd been unmercifully tough on her. He was regretting it, now, though he really shouldn't be, because she'd deserved it, and then some. Looking down at him as if he were some lower life form. Thinking of him as a demon, a monster. Believing him unfit to be a father to his own child. She deserved his anger for that. What did she expect, that he'd be thrilled with her condemnation of his kind?

Her kind?

He glanced across the car at her. And he knew above all that it was his pride she'd hurt. He wanted her to be as completely engrossed in him as he…

Scratch that.

She sat stiffly, concentrating very hard on trying to get a sense of the child. But he didn't think she was having much success at it. They'd been driving for hours, and she'd been doing this the whole time. Searching, striving, reaching with her mind. He could see the lines of tension at the corners of her lush lips, and in her forehead. And he was overcome with the ridiculous urge to ease them.

"We have no reason to believe she's not safe and sound with the Garner woman," he said. He couldn't believe he was trying to comfort her. Couldn't imagine what would make him even give a damn how much she was suffering right now. Dammit, if he couldn't *feel* her pain, he might be able to ignore it.

"I know," she said, her voice gruff.

"Tamara says Hilary is a good person. We have to believe that."

She nodded. "Yes."

And then she went right back to worrying again. Her head was throbbing with a pain that reached all the way down the back of her neck. He could feel that. And the pain was weakening her, as pain tended to do to their kind.

"You're making yourself sick, Angelica."

She blinked, and turned to look at him. So much pain in those eyes of hers. So much...ah, God help him...*need*.

"I can't help it."

"You have to help it. Try not to think the worst. You'll be so worn down by the time we find them that you'll be no help at all."

She tilted her head. "Worrying can weaken me?"

"No, but the headache it's causing could damn well do it."

Her brows drew together in a frown. "You're poking around in my mind again? Reading my thoughts?"

"Not voluntarily, I'm not."

Her curious gaze scanned his face. "What do you mean?"

Jameson drew a deep breath. He had not wanted to bring up the subject with her. Not when just thinking about it reduced him to a mass of unfulfilled yearning. But he supposed he owed her an explanation. "We shared blood, Angelica, and that was enough to forge this bond. We had a child together, and I think we both know that strengthened it. And then we...we had sex." He saw the flare of memory in her eyes. It seared him before she quickly turned away. "That forged an even more powerful link between us. Kind of like the link between you and Amber Lily." He shook his head, sighing hard, knowing she'd likely be even more repulsed when she realized how much a part of her he had become. How much a part of him she had grown to be. "Whether I like it or not," he said, "I know when you're hurting. I can feel your pain, and I imagine you could probably feel mine as well."

"Yes."

Not disgust in her voice. Not that at all. Just affirmation. He looked at her quickly, but she wasn't grimacing.

"I felt it even before we made love," she whispered.

Made love?

"I felt it when you were shot. Knew you'd been hit even before I saw the wound. I thought at first the bullet had torn through *my* side, but then I looked, and there was no wound in me. It was in you, instead."

"And you felt it?" he asked her, amazed.

"Yes, I did."

He blinked, thinking this through. "Then the tie between us— whatever the hell it is—was already very strong. The sex...well, that would only serve to make it even more powerful. Very strange."

"It's disturbing," she said. He looked at her. Not disgusting, but disturbing.

"How so?" he asked her. "What do you feel from me now, Angelica? There's no pain, nothing to upset you."

"All I feel from you now, Vampire, is rage. It's frightening in its intensity. Huge and black and potent." She lifted her head, staring straight ahead of them, as if she could see his anger. "And I would hazard a guess that the rage inside you can be as debilitating to you as this worry might be to me."

Jameson felt his lips thin. "You'd probably be right."

"Why do you hate them so?"

"They have our daughter, Angelica. How can you ask me why I hate them?"

She shook her head slowly. "No. That isn't all of it. You hated them before then. That night...that night when I stupidly went away with that agent, believing all his promises, you hated them then. It was in your mind when you tried to warn me.''

''But you went anyway.''

''Yes. And you can't forgive me for that, can you? You can't forget that it's my fault they have our child. My fault, for believing their lies.'' She fell sideways until her head rested against the window glass. ''I don't blame you,'' she whispered. ''You're right to hate me for letting them take her. But you can't possibly hate me for it any more than I hate myself.''

Jameson looked at her, saw the twin tracks of tears slowly moving down her face. She was wrong. He might have blamed her for this once, but not anymore. Not since he'd realized the hell she'd been suffering in that ruined building where she'd gone to hide. Gone to starve.

''So tell me,'' she said. ''Why did you hate them so?''

He lifted his chin, swallowed hard. ''Years ago, they held Rhiannon prisoner. Had her strapped to a table while they took samples from her flesh. This was before they'd developed their nasty little tranquilizer. Their only method for keeping us too weak to fight them was starvation. There was nothing to ease the pain of their experiments. Those bastards tortured her nearly out of her mind. But she escaped. Killed one of their top scientists in the process. Broke his neck, she did.''

''I can believe that.''

Jameson looked at her as he drove, saw her shudder in response to his words. ''When Tamara was a small child, her parents died of a rare virus. And a doctor who'd sort of taken her under his wing offered to be her guardian. There was no one else, and his petition was approved.''

Angelica's lips were parted, eyes wide with interest.

''Turned out the doc was really with DPI, and the parents' exposure to that virus was all part of a well-laid plan. They knew Tam had the belladonna antigen—that rare blood type that enables a human to become a vampire. And they also knew that people with that blood type often have a special bond to one particular vampire, who tends to watch over them.''

She gasped softly. "Is that true? I had no idea."

"Yes, it's true," he told her. "A vampire feels a special affinity for a given mortal, feels drawn to them, senses when they're in danger. And often steps in to protect them, though most of the time, the mortal never knows any of it. Eric had been Tamara's protector. Saved her life once when she was just a little girl. And DPI knew it, knew he'd come back someday. So they wanted to hold Tamara as bait. And they stopped at nothing to do it."

Angelica was shaking her head, her eyes filled with sympathy for the child Tamara had been. "They killed her parents...my God. It's horrible." And then she turned those big round eyes on him, and he almost forgot to be angry with her. "And what about you, Jameson? When did you get involved with them?"

"I met Tamara when she worked for DPI."

"She—?"

He nodded. "Yes. Well, remember, she was raised by one of them. He brought her into the organization largely so that he could keep tabs on her. But she wasn't in on any of the really sensitive stuff that went on there. They gave her milk-toast cases. Like working to discover the alleged psychic powers of a twelve-year-old boy."

"You?" she asked.

"Yeah. Only the psychic stuff was a ruse. They wanted me under surveillance because I had the antigen. The whole damned cycle was gearing up to start all over again. But Tam figured it out. The bastards kidnapped me to get to her and Eric. Roland saved my ass, for the first of many times. When it was over, my mother and I had to get the hell out of the area. Roland took us to France with him, gave my mother a job, sent me to private school."

"And you knew...you knew they were...vampires?"

"Sure I knew. I was young, but not blind."

"And it didn't frighten you?"

"It was those DPI bastards who frightened me."

She nodded, and it seemed to Jameson that she was truly interested in what he was saying as they drove the many miles that separated them from their child. "Where's your mother now?"

"Died a couple of years later. Roland took care of me, though, until later when those DPI bastards tracked us down again. After that he got to thinking I might be better off with my birth father. Hired a PI to track him down, and I ended up in San Diego living with Dad until he passed on two years ago. And my old pals at DPI didn't catch up with me again until last year. They bundled me into one of those inconspicuous gray vans and took me to their 'research center,' for 'testing.' In fact, the others had only busted me out of that hellhole a few nights before I found you in the condemned building."

She nodded slowly. "So DPI has been a thorn in your side for most of your life."

"They've been one step behind me all the way. Same as the others. No one should have to live looking over their shoulder."

"And you're going to be the one to end it."

"Someone has to." He felt his jaw clench, and tried to relax it. "Jesus, Angelica, when I came for you, there were others. Those freaking cells were all full. Some dead, some dying, some just being kept alive long enough for those animals to finish their experiments on them. It can't go on. It just can't go on."

"But can one man stop them?"

"This one can." He slanted a sideways glance at her. "I have motivation, Angelica." She lifted her brows, waiting. "Our daughter," he explained. "I'm not going to let her grow up with the constant threat of those bastards looming over her. I can't."

She blinked twice, and nodded. As if she...maybe...understood.

"So now you know what makes me such a monster," he said. "I hate them. I want them all to pay. And I fully intend to extract their penance with my own two hands. Just as soon as my daughter is safe."

She lowered her head, shook it. "You're letting your anger control you," she said. "You could die in this feeble attempt."

"Then I'd die for a cause," he said. "Better than dying in a stone sarcophagus, helpless and sheeplike."

She lowered her head quickly, stung by his words. And dammit, he should have thought before he'd spoken. "You'll never be able to forgive me for turning myself over to them," she said.

He shrugged, tried to find words to tell her that he did now. Wondered why he couldn't just blurt it, and knew the culprit was his pride. "You thought I was a monster. You thought that DPI agent was safer than me."

"I did think that. I did, it's the truth. The one who...who changed me..." Shaking her head, she let her voice trail into silence.

"What about him?" He could feel her reaction to even thinking of that one. Terror. "You never told me, Angelica. What happened to you to bring you to this?"

She looked at him, really looked at him. And then she sighed. "I can't believe it will make any difference to you."

He sighed. He wasn't going to beg her to tell him. Hell, he'd told her his entire life history, and she couldn't tell him one little bit about her own past? Fine. Let her close herself off from him if that were what she wanted. She was so resistant to him. So...almost afraid of him it seemed. It made him angry all over again.

He was quiet after that, for several miles, and I was, too. He'd given me a great deal to think about. I could even understand his irrational hatred of DPI. But I still disapproved of his intention to destroy everyone involved in the organization. There were good among every group.

Even vampires, as I was rapidly learning. "I never told you so, Vampire," I said, after a long period of silence between us. "But I'm sorry for what I did to you that night when we first met."

"I'm not."

I looked at him, and my surprise must have shown very clearly.

"Oh, I didn't think I was ready for the change," he said, and I sensed he was being as honest as he'd ever been with me. "But I'm better than I was before. Stronger, and smarter. I'm experiencing life now in a way I never could have then. Ironic, isn't it? Only when my mortal life ended could I truly savor all it was."

I nodded mutely, waiting for him to continue.

"When you...when you drank from me that night...God, I had no idea it would be like that. I didn't even fight you, Angelica. You remember that?"

"You did," I told him. "At the very last."

"It was ecstasy," he whispered. "I didn't want it to end."

I remembered. How well I remembered the erotic thrill that shot through me as I suckled at his throat like a babe. It had frightened me and thrilled me and confused me, all at once. I hadn't understood it then. I still wasn't certain I did. That he would confess he'd felt the same way, amazed me. Surely he couldn't hate me when he'd been so eager to participate in his own draining.

"It's the allure of the vampire," he told her. "His victims give themselves willingly, and die in a storm of sensations that are beyond physical orgasm."

"Yes," I whispered, and I closed my eyes, recalling the way I'd felt when he'd brought me to a similar pinnacle the night before, in the wee hours before sunrise. A rapture beyond human endurance.

"That's why we don't drink from the living, Angelica. It would be too easy to get carried away. To hurt them by taking too much. We deny ourselves that rush, in order to protect them. But the craving is always there. Always."

I nodded my head. Because he was so right. The craving was here, now. Burning inside me. Whispering that while we couldn't take from the living, we could take from each other. Whispering that if he could truly feel my pain, he could surely feel this ache that was gnawing inside me, yearning for his touch, for his teeth, for his taste, once again.

Rhiannon had warned me of this. And if we gave in to this lust again, it would only become stronger the next time, and the next. I knew for the first time the power of drugs over the addicts I'd helped care for in the city's shelters. But this was worse. Far worse.

Jameson cleared his throat, drawing my gaze. His jaw was tight.

His eyes, bright with passion. "That sign," he said in a rusty voice. "Petersville, five miles."

"Good," I said. "We're nearly there."

"We'll need to find shelter," he went on. "We've been driving all night. It will be dawn not too long from now."

I met his eyes, stared into them, and I knew he saw my hunger, because I saw its reflection looking back at me. I would not shame myself again, I vowed. He disliked me, and I him. Oh, yes, I'd come to believe that perhaps all of his kind were not damned, after all. But he was damning himself with anger and hate. And I was so afraid of what I felt for him. So afraid he'd keep his earlier vow to throw it back in my face should I admit how much I wanted his touch again.

And though he'd conceded that the passion was mutual—a conclusion I had already reached on my own—it was still very clear that he disliked me. Distrusted me. And I could not have sex with a man who didn't even like me! I would not let animalistic urges overwhelm me to that shameful extent. Not again.

And I know he saw my firm decision in my eyes. Because his darkened with renewed anger, and his jaw went tighter.

He stopped at a dilapidated, abandoned house, a mile past the cluster of neat country homes that made up the town of Petersville. The place had been modest, a two-story farmhouse, perfectly square. And it wasn't sagging or rotten. But the windows were mostly broken out, and the wood stood gray and peeling and sadly in need of paint. He drove the car around the back, out of sight from the road. And when he cut the engine, we sat there in the darkness, silent, for a long, tense moment.

"I suppose we should go inside," he said at last, and I heard the tightness of his voice. "To make sure there's a place safe from sunlight, where we can rest."

"Yes." I opened my door and got out, stepping into the dry brittle grasses that rasped over my bare calves and brushed the hem of the black dress I wore. I didn't want to go into the house with him. I didn't want to lie down beside him. Not yet, while there was still more than an hour before sunrise would lull me to sleep. He saw too much of what went on in my mind.

"You're afraid," he said, coming up to stand beside me where I'd stopped, just outside a boarded-up rear window. "You don't trust me, do you, Angelica?"

How could I tell him that it was myself I didn't trust?

"Don't worry," he snapped when I didn't reply or even look at him. "I'm not going to touch you again. I already told you that, didn't I?"

I closed my eyes to try to block my thoughts. But they raced around in my brain anyway. And I strained to keep him from hearing them as well. I wanted him to touch me. I wanted him to make me lose my mind the way I'd lost it before. So the decision would be taken out of my hands, and I'd be left with little cause to feel the guilt or shame I knew I should feel. I wanted him to force me, so that I could assuage this burning hunger inside and leave my conscience clear.

I was ashamed of these thoughts, and lowered my head to follow him inside.

"There's a basement. It would be the safest place," he said, his voice stiff and formal. "The floor is concrete. Not comfortable, but better than damp earth."

He stood at the mouth of a blackened doorway, looking down. And I moved as close to him as I dared, peering past him. There were no stairs. Had been once, but only a few rotted boards remained. Without a word, Jameson jumped down and forward, landing on his feet on the floor. Then he turned, hands busy brushing the dust from his jeans. "Coming?"

I drew a breath and swallowed. Rhiannon said I was as strong as he was. Difficult adjusting to the idea. Even more difficult for a woman who still felt very much mortal, to pitch herself down from the top of a nonexistent stairway, to the concrete floor below. Gritting my teeth, I closed my eyes and pushed myself away.

He'd stepped backward, but I hit him anyway. My body crashed into his and sent him sprawling. I landed on top of him. My body was pressed hard against his, just as it had been that night. And

I could smell the masculine, exotic scent of his flesh, and I could hear the thrum of blood rushing in the veins just beneath it. My own pulse pounded harder. The steady beat in my throat growing stronger, more demanding.

His hands came to my shoulders, and gently lifted me, as he slid himself out from under me. He cleared his throat, but didn't look my way. I couldn't have looked him in the eye even if he had. "You need more practice."

Practice was not even close to what I needed. What I needed was escape. I needed to be away from him. I'd be awake for another hour, and this burning for his touch would surely drive me insane.

"I think," I said, recognizing the coarseness in my voice, hearing the slight tremor in my words, "that we should split up."

"Do you, now?"

I nodded, forcing myself to look him in the eye. "We could cover more ground. Find Amber Lily that much sooner."

"You mean you'd find her sooner. You're the one with the link to her. And then what, Angelica? You disappear with the only child I'll ever have?"

I lifted my chin. "I give you my word, Vampire. I won't run away."

"Ah, but you're just one of the damned now, aren't you, Angel? A monster like me, without a soul or a shred of morality. What is your word worth?"

"I won't run away," I said again. "Besides, you say there's a...a connection between us, now. Surely, even if I ran, you could find me." I was testing him.

"I'd find you," he said softly. "If I had to search to the ends of the earth, dark Angel, I'd find you. Make no mistake about that."

"Then why not let me go on my own?"

"Because I don't want to *have* to find you. And because I don't trust you. You have to admit, your judgment has been rather flawed to this point. I don't want you making a mistake that would get my daughter killed."

I lowered my head, closed my eyes and sat down on the concrete floor. "So the things you said in the car were only lies. I should have known."

He came closer and sat down beside me. "Let's talk about lies, shall we, my dark Angel? Hmm?"

I lifted my head and looked at him. Saw the anger in his eyes. "I haven't lied to you," I said.

"Oh, but you have. You don't want to get away from me for the baby's sake. It's for your own. You can't stand it, can you, Angel? A saint like you. It makes you sick to your stomach to be so hot for a monster like me. Doesn't it?" I turned my face away but he pressed his palm to my cheek, turning me to face him again. "You think I can't see it, Angel? You want me. You're burning up inside for me. You can't stop thinking about it, can you? My hands on you. My mouth on you." He smiled bitterly, and shook his head. "Poor little Angel's spirit is at war with her flesh, and she's disgusted by it."

"You're wrong," I told him. "I don't want you! I don't even want you in the same room with me! I hate you!"

"I know you hate me," he whispered. "But it doesn't matter, does it?"

Shaking my head in denial, I clambered to my feet, turning my back to him. But he was right there behind me, standing so close I could feel the heat of his flesh. And then his breath fanned my neck, and his body brushed up against the back of mine. I couldn't move, couldn't breathe. With one hand, he swept my hair aside, and lowered his head, his lips hovering close to my throat, but not touching. I trembled all over, from head to toe, I shuddered. And inside I was screaming for his touch.

He moved his hips, and his hard arousal pushed against my backside. And then he bent lower, and his lips brushed my throat. All the fight went out of me in a long, shivering sigh, and I let my head fall back, and to the side, baring my neck in blatant offering to him.

His breaths on my skin were coming in hot gusts now. "I

thought you didn't want me in the same room with you," he whispered, but it was a breathless whisper, and strained.

"Please," I moaned, from deep in my throat.

And he wrenched himself from me, turning away, pushing his hands backward through his hair. "So who's the liar now, Angel?" he growled.

I wrapped my arms around myself, hugging tight, and slowly sank to my knees. My head bowed, and I wept in bitter frustration.

He stood there, looking at me. "Believe me," he said, "it's every bit as distasteful to me, wanting someone I can't stand the sight of. But at least I'm not so goddamned self-righteous that I lie about it. You're not going anywhere, so we're both going to have to live with this situation."

And I rose, anger and indignation giving me the strength his nearness had robbed me of only seconds before. I turned, and looked him in the eye. "The hell we are," I told him, and I turned toward the doorway at the top of the stairs, bent my knees and pushed off. Amazingly, I sailed upward as easily as I'd once stepped over a crack in the sidewalk, and landed on the floor above. And then I ran, out of the house and into the night.

The wind whispered in my hair and my ears, as I ran. I knew he was coming after me, but I didn't turn around to confirm it. I just ran, and in seconds, I'd forgotten about my pursuer, my demon. There was a new thrill in running this fast, so fast everything around me became a blur. I didn't run into anything, though I was going far too quickly to see clearly. Some kind of inner guidance system I hadn't been aware of before, kicked in, to steer me around obstacles and over dangers in the path. I raced through the forest, for miles. Miles I ran.

And then I stopped. And I wasn't even breathless. Amazing. My blood was surging in my veins, my heart beating strong and sure in my chest. I felt strong. Stronger than I had ever felt in my life. And I thought I understood what Jameson had said before, about not fully savoring his life, until it ended.

Oh, but that fool understood very little else. I wasn't disgusted by him! I yearned for him. Why did he have to be so cruel?

"Dammit, Angelica, what the hell do you think you're doing?"

Ah, yes, my Lucifer had caught up to me at last. I turned to face him. "You can't keep me against my will," I said. "I'm every bit as strong as you are."

He rolled his eyes. "Remind me to thank Rhiannon for telling you that, will you?"

His sarcasm was not mean. Not biting. And I almost smiled at it. Almost. Perhaps the exertion was what we'd both needed to break the tension between us.

No. It wasn't what we'd needed. But it was better than nothing. And then I heard something. A cry, very distant. The cry...of a child. My heart tripped to a stop in my chest. But the wailing sounds grew louder, more insistent.

"The baby," I whispered. And Jameson stared into my eyes, every bit of animosity gone. As one we turned and raced as fast as we could, in the direction of that sound. Down a wooded hillside we flew, crashing through dense undergrowth and thorny briars, and all but tumbling onto the gravel-topped road that wound along at its base.

"There," Jameson shouted. And I turned to see a woman, lying still on the ground. The wailing was louder now than ever. In a single leap, I was crouching at the woman's side, lifting her head and shoulders from the ground, shaking her.

"Wake up, woman! Where is she! Tell me, where is the baby!"

Groggy eyes opened, then widened. A look of panic came into them as she scanned the area around her. And then she screamed, clasping her face between her palms. She screamed and screamed and screamed.

I turned my eyes to where she was staring, and saw it then. The car, flipped over and lying on its top. The child, trapped inside, hanging upside down and howling in fear. The flames licking up into the night sky from the base of the automobile, where the gas tank would be, unless I were sadly mistaken.

"My baby!" the woman screamed, over and over again. "Please, save my baby!"

Her baby. Not mine. The cries I had heard had been the cries of this woman's child. The result of a car accident.

"Hurry!" she shouted, struggling to her feet. "Hurry, for the love of God, the gas tank!" And then she collapsed in a heap of unintelligible sobs.

I could not believe what I was seeing. Jameson was clambering over the vehicle to reach the door nearest the child. The flames—and I had seen firsthand the explosive effects of flames on a vampire—were licking up around him. So close to him...

I got to my feet, leaving the woman, hurrying forward. The vampire wrenched the door free and sent it flying into the night. If daylight had allowed the young mother to see his strength, she'd have fainted dead away. I nearly did, when I saw how far that scrap of metal sailed. And then Jameson was inside, crawling, tearing at the belts that held the child prisoner. He paused no less than three times to beat at flames that lapped at his clothes. But each time went right back to the child.

I ran closer, reaching the car just as he emerged with the baby cradled in his arms. He raced toward me, pushing the child at me, dropping to his knees, and it was only then that I realized his delicate vampire's skin was smoldering. Thin spirals of smoke rose from it like specters reaching to the night sky. His black eyes held mine for only an instant, and I saw the agony there. And then I felt it, the hot brands searing his skin, as if it were my own. He rose, staggered away from us, and I saw the stream gurgling in the distance. I heard the splash as he reached it, and the heat on my skin faded, but the pain remained.

The baby cooed and chirped at me, drawing my gaze. I looked down at her, and hugged her gently to my breast. But my heart was slowly breaking. Her lush hair wasn't raven, but red. Her eyes, not jet, but baby-blue. And the plumpness to her cheeks and triple chin, her drooling mouth gave me to know she was a good deal older than my Amber Lily. Cutting teeth already, perhaps.

One chubby, questing hand reached up to grip a handful of my hair and tug almost playfully.

"Please..."

I lifted my gaze. The woman. She'd managed to get to her feet again, and she stood before me now. Her face already bruising, her hair tangled and her lip bleeding. She stretched out her arms toward her child, tears streaming down her face.

Closing my eyes, I swallowed hard. Her child. Her precious child, not mine. I bent to kiss the infant's silky-soft cheek, and then I placed it in its mother's loving arms.

She hugged the baby close, bowing her head as sobs wrenched her slender frame. Sirens in the distance, then. Another vehicle pulling off the road. White headlights illuminating the darkness, contaminating its preternatural purity with artificial light. Light that didn't belong in the night, I thought. It was an intruder.

I took one last look at the mother and child, embracing and sobbing. And then I slipped away into the shadows, where I belonged.

Chapter Eleven

Jameson lay neck-deep in the icy waters of a fast-running stream, and let the chill sink in. Its cold seemed to work into his pores, easing the horrible searing sensation. Stopping the blistering and popping of his skin. It slowed the burning. Even numbed the pain a little. Not nearly enough.

Dammit, he was hurting.

He closed his eyes, wishing the cold would anesthetize him to it, but he knew better. The best he could do was find shelter and let the day sleep do its work. At least he wouldn't have to suffer long.

And as soon as the sun set tonight, he'd go after Angelica. No doubt she was long gone by now. He just hoped she didn't find his baby and take her off to parts unknown before he caught up with her. He wanted to see Amber Lily. He wanted to hold her just once in his arms, snuggle her close, before he returned to take DPI down. He needed to feel her, to know she was real.

He didn't really blame Angelica for seeing him as an unfit father. An unrepentant vampire must seem like a pretty strange being to her. One who loved what he'd become. One who relished it, and wouldn't go back to being mortal if it were as simple as swallowing a pill. When it was all she longed for in her heart of hearts. And besides all that, there was his violent nature. His hatred for DPI, and his determination to destroy it. She didn't really think he'd expose his daughter to that dark side of him, did she? He only wanted to love her. Just for a short time, before he did what he had to do.

But thanks to some cruel twist of fate he might never get the chance now. Angelica would be far away by the time he'd recovered enough from the burns to go after her. But he would find her again. He didn't think there was a force on earth that could keep him from finding her.

Soft splashing sounds made him jerk his head up fast. And then he blinked and squinted to be sure he wasn't seeing an illusion. Angelica, sloshing through the water, soaking the sexy black dress she wore clear to her hips as she made her way to him. She stopped beside him. And he looked into her eyes and was thinking of making some smart remark about how he'd expected her to be gone by now.

But he couldn't. Because what he saw in her eyes was devastation. And she looked at him, and her lips pulled away from her teeth in an expression of pure heartbreak. Her back bowed forward and her shoulders shuddered and her eyes squeezed shut tight. But she didn't burst into tears. She battled them back. Fought them valiantly. And won.

Ah, hell, he knew that bitter anguish. He'd felt it, too. At first, when he'd heard that baby's cries, he'd thought...

He'd thought he'd finally found his daughter. And when he'd held the baby in his arms, even knowing by then that she wasn't his own...it had been heaven and hell all rolled into one.

Angelica drew a shaking breath and stiffened her spine, slowly standing straight and strong again. A water goddess, rising from the waves, taming them. A phoenix bird, full of fire, rising from the ashes. Pulling herself upright, despite the pain. "Can you stand?" she asked him. "Walk?"

Her voice was brittle. Like it would snap right in two in a stiff breeze. She hated him. He didn't blame her, either, after that little fiasco in the basement. But for Christ's sake, he was half out of his mind wanting her. Craving her. Fantasizing about the things he wanted to do to her. Knowing full well she felt the same…and all the time knowing she was repulsed by wanting him that way. He repulsed her. It was a lot for a man's pride to take.

And he'd been hot as hell and frustrated and furious over the entire situation. Who better to take it out on than her? She who was disgusted by his very touch. Who better?

Her hands slid over his shoulders and she pulled him to his feet. "I asked if you could walk, Vampire. Answer me."

"I can walk," he said. Then he stood up to prove it.

"Then you'd better do so. And fast. It will be dawn soon."

He narrowed his eyes, tilted his head. "I thought you'd decided to go off on your own, Angel? Thought you'd be halfway to Timbuktu by now."

"Well, I'm not." She walked close beside him, one hand poised near his elbow, as if she'd catch him should he fall. She walked slowly, her dress dragging through the swift-running dark waters. And he remained at her side, and wondered why she hadn't left him. Why she was helping him. Why it made him so damned angry to know her true feelings. The emotional ones, not the physical.

To his horror, he stumbled the second he stepped out of the water. Without the stream's icy touch, the pain was back, full force, and it hit him like a mallet.

But his Angel was right there, living up to his sarcastic nickname for her. She stood close, pulling his arm around her shoulders, and slipping hers around his waist. She held him so close it was almost as if she truly cared. And she winced each time the pain flared hotter, and he knew she was feeling it, too.

He couldn't move very far. He knew that. He hadn't the strength, and he'd never make it all the way back to that abandoned farmhouse they'd planned to spend the day in. Maybe, if he had strength enough for speed. But not like this. He'd never make it before dawn. She ought to go on alone. He ought to tell her.…

But he needn't have worried. It was only minutes before she found shelter, a miniature cave cut into the rocky hillside. She helped him inside, moving all the way to the farthest reaches of the place, and then easing him down onto the cool, rocky floor. She hurried outside, leaving him alone.

He didn't suspect her of abandoning him this time. No, he was beginning to know her a bit too well to think she'd leave him in this sorry state. She might hate him, but she was a woman of ethics. He didn't imagine she could leave her worst enemy in this kind of agony.

She returned, moments later, her arms loaded down with pine boughs. Half a tree's worth, by the looks. She wove a solid wall of them, and braced them at the mouth of the cave to keep out the sun. And then she came back inside, kneeling before him, sharp black eyes racing over his body, narrowing on every angry red burn mark that she spotted.

"I could make a fire, to dry our clothes," she said.

"I'd rather not look at another fire for a while." The burns were small brands, up and down his calves mostly, but a few patches on his forearms and back had taken some heat as well.

"Will this kill you?" she whispered, her eyes meeting his.

"You couldn't be so lucky," he told her, and he saw her lips thin. The pain in her eyes intensified.

"You're in agony."

"So are you," he said, sitting up a little, searching her face. She averted it quickly, but not quickly enough. He'd seen the tears. "My pain will be gone with the night, Angel. It's only a few more minutes until dawn. But yours is going to follow you into your dreams, isn't it?"

Her shoulders quaked, and when she turned to face him again, her cheeks were wet, her body trembling. "I thought it was her," she whispered. "When I heard that baby crying, I thought...."

"I know." His own throat tightened. "I know, Angel. I thought so, too."

Her head bowed as the tears overwhelmed her, and he couldn't help himself. He wrapped his arms around her shuddering frame and pulled her close to him. And he held her, choking back his own anguished tears. He hated this woman, he told himself. He hated her because she was disgusted by him.

The hell with it. He'd get back to hating her later. He didn't hate her now. Not at all. He stroked her silken hair, and caressed her trembling shoulders, and he rocked her in his arms until the pine needles at the entrance began to lighten with the rising sun. And then he cradled her as she slipped into sleep. A few moments later, he followed her there.

He was not a monster. I stirred awake, still nestled in his arms, my head resting upon his chest. And I knew that I had misjudged him so thoroughly that I could not have been more wrong. Of course I had. I'd put him on the defensive right from the start, attacked him and accused him, and he'd shown me his worst in return. If he despised me, I realized, I'd given him reason.

He had known that the screaming child was not his own. He had known it *before* he'd gone to the overturned car. There was no doubt of that. And yet he'd gone, all the same. He'd burned himself, and I knew enough of my kind to realize that a single false move or stray breeze or misstep could have sent him up in a blinding conflagration. At any moment, he could have suffered the same agonizing death as that creature I'd killed. But he risked it, to save the child of a stranger. And a mortal stranger, at that.

I had known mortal men, Christian men, who would not have done what this dark demon had done. He was not the embodiment of evil. He was not a devil sent to tempt me into sin. He was just a man, I realized, lifting my head and allowing my eyes to roam his face. A man filled with anger and in search of vengeance, yes. But also a man with a good heart, and boundless courage, and unselfish valor.

And beautiful velvet-brown eyes with stripes of ebony that glittered in the moonlight.

And a well-deserved dislike for me.

His eyes opened, searched mine. "You're awake before me," he said, still sounding sleepy. "That's unusual."

"The burns must have weakened you more than you realized." I sat up slowly, hating to pull my body from the wonderful nest of his. His chest made a fine pillow, and his arms had remained around me even as he'd rested.

"You're probably right. I still feel a little fuzzy."

My head came around, my eyes locking with his. "Perhaps you need…"

His gaze dipped to the hollow of my throat only briefly, before he slammed his eyes closed and turned his head away. "What I need is to get the hell out of this cave." He lunged to his feet and hurried to the doorway, a single swipe of his powerful arm sending my pine-bough door sailing into the night. Then he stepped outside, tipped his head back and inhaled, expanded his marvelous chest and stretched his arms overhead. I remained in the doorway, simply watching him. Fully appreciating—not for the first time—the utter beauty of the man. And I realized that perhaps I had been unable to see such things before. Clinging to my mortal ways of thinking.

It was high time I got used to the idea that I was not a mortal woman anymore.

The thought sent a shiver of what might have been fear—or might have been excitement—up the base of my neck. And I realized there was something else tickling my senses as well. Something bright and shining.

And then I recognized it. My child…she was near. And she was well. Content and safe. Warm, and comfortable, and unafraid. I was slowly infused with a new sense of hope, and a certainty that I would hold that tiny blessing in my arms before this night ended. The knowledge—and it was that. Knowledge—certainty—left me nearly giddy with excitement.

I left the cave, and went out to stand behind him. "She's all right," I said to him, and he turned very slowly, frowning at me. "Amber Lily is well, and safe, and we're close to her, Jameson. I can feel her."

He smiled, fully smiled. And if I'd seen his smile before, I did not remember it. The flash of his white teeth in the darkness was a thing of rare beauty. He came close to me, took both my hands in his. "You're sure?"

"Yes," I told him. "Yes, we're very close. We'll find her soon. I know it."

He closed his eyes in relief, releasing the night air he'd inhaled, and letting my hands fall from his grasp as he did. "Good. The others should be coming along any time now," he said. "We'll meet them at that abandoned house where we left the car."

I tipped my head sideways. "How do you know that?"

He laughed, a sultry, sensual sound that came from deep in his chest. "Angelica, we're not the only two vampires who can communicate without words. Though…it does seem much more powerful between you and me."

I didn't look away when he stared down into my eyes.

"Close those amethyst eyes, Angel," he said softly, speaking to me as gently as if he were speaking to a lover. "And think of the others. Speak to them."

"But they're not even here yet."

"Try," he coaxed.

So I did. I closed my eyes and put Tamara's gentle face firmly in my mind. My thoughts were slow and deliberate and I concentrated fiercely. *Tamara? Are you there? Can you hear me?*

I'll be seeing you within the hour, Angelica. Very clearly and as soft as her spoken words, the voice of Tamara's thoughts sang out to me.

My eyes opened wide in surprise. *Did you find out anything?* I thought rapidly, hope surging in my chest.

We have a location for the cabin. By the time you two get back to Jamey's car, we'll be there. I promise, Angelica.

I frowned and looked at the vampire, who'd been watching me intently. "She calls you Jamey," I said, brows lifting. "I've been meaning to ask about it."

"It's what I was called when I was just a boy. Tamara seems to have trouble breaking old habits." He shook his head in exasperation. "Sometimes she has a hard time remembering that I'm not a child any longer."

How anyone could look at this strong, tall, handsome man with the anger in his soul and think of him as a child, I did not know.

He had the build of a god. A dark, dangerous pagan god, with erotic promises gleaming in his eyes. And the more time I spent with him, the more desperately I wanted him to fulfill those promises for me.

His head snapped toward me, eyes flaring wider.

"What?" I asked him, startled.

He blinked, and shook his head. "Nothing. Never mind. Come on, we'd better start back."

"There is no hurry," I told him, joining him stride for stride all the same. "I can run just like the wind."

He looked at me a little strangely. "Yes, that's true enough."

"I didn't realize it before." I turned to look up at him as we walked. "What else can I do, Vampire?"

His brows rose, jaw twitching now and again. And he seemed unable to look into my eyes for very long. "Well, you know already about the jumping."

"Almost like flying," I said, and I tipped my head back, eyeing the tall, broad limb of a hard maple tree. "I wonder how high I can go?"

"Angelica, not now—"

But I was off, bending low and springing skyward and sailing high into the night. I didn't clear the limb, but caught hold of it with my hands, and dangled there. They couldn't keep my daughter from me, I mused as I swung back and forth. No one could. I was stronger. More powerful. And for the first time I was allowing myself to feel that strength surging inside me.

I glanced down at the vampire, who stared up at me as if very puzzled. And then I let go, and pirouetted as I plunged downward. I fell when I landed, in an ungraceful tangle at his feet. He only stared down at me, shaking his head.

"Are you all right, Angelica? You haven't gone a little nuts on me, have you?"

I got to my feet, brushing twigs and dried-out leaves from my dress. "We're going to find her. I can feel it."

He nodded at me. "I believe you."

I looked skyward. "And I spoke to Tamara. Miles away still,

and I spoke to her with my mind, Jameson. Do you know how incredible that is?''

One corner of his mouth quirked upward. ''Yeah. I know.''

''What else is there?'' I stood before him, looking up into his eyes. ''What other things have I failed to notice about this new nature of mine?''

His brows drew together, and he studied my face for a long moment. ''Listen,'' he said softly. I parted my lips to speak, but he held up a finger for silence. So I was quiet, and I listened. At first I heard only the normal forest sounds. A breeze teasing the pine needles, and the song of a night bird here and there. But then, slowly, more sounds joined in the chorus. The creaking of a bough, and then of several of them. The sound of a squirrel's feet as he scampered through the fallen leaves. A distant woodpecker's drilling. The gurgling laughter of that stream. Each sound was distinct, and clear. Not a jumbled mix as I might have heard before. They were amplified, yes, but so individual. I heard a deer leaping. The beat of a bird's wings. A pinecone fall to the forest floor from a tree that was miles away.

''It's amazing,'' I whispered.

''Yes.''

I sighed and looked up at him. ''You know what's even more amazing than this?'' I asked him. ''It's that I'm a mother.'' Lowering my head, shaking it sadly, I went on. ''It wasn't in my plan, you know. It was the farthest thing from my mind, but I was all wrong. And I'm beginning to think maybe...maybe that bastard did me a favor that night.'' I trembled when I said it, a chill-evoking memory slipping through my brain. But I shook it off at once. ''I'm a mother, now, and I can't imagine not being one.''

He took my shoulders in his hands, searching my face. ''You're...different, Angelica.''

I nodded. ''Yes. Very different. And it's about time I quit whining and dealt with it, don't you think?''

I didn't pull free of him, just stared up into his eyes.

''You never told me,'' he said, turning me and beginning our trek through the woods, slipping my arm through his as if it were the natural thing to do.

"About what?"

"About you." He turned to look down at me. "I gave up all of my secrets, Angel. But I still know nothing about you. So tell me."

And I nodded. It was time. Perhaps what this man and I needed was to start over again. Perhaps if I treated him as just a man, and not a monster, we could come to some sort of understanding. Maybe even a truce.

"I was nine when my mother left me at St. Christopher's," I told him.

"And why did she do that?"

I shrugged. "I'm told she was very poor, unmarried and possibly addicted to heroin, but of course, I don't remember. I should, I suppose. Maybe I've blocked it out. I recall her face. Reed-thin, and pale, with dark circles around her eyes, and hair like mine, only cut short. I remember her voice. Harsh. Never gentle. Never tender. I remember crying and crying and crying for her, for weeks after she left me there. But it did little good."

He pushed a pine bough out of my path, and I walked past it, leaning a little closer to him than I needed to. But relishing his warmth.

"So the sisters took care of you?"

"Yes. They raised me. I got the notion that I'd done something bad to make my mother give me up. And decided then and there that if I could only be good enough, she'd come back for me one day."

"But she didn't," he said, and when I met his eyes, they seemed sad. For me. Was he feeling my pain, then? Or just feeling for the knowledge that I felt it?

"No. She didn't. And I must admit, I wasn't very good at being good."

"No," he said, feigning disbelief.

"I was somewhat adventurous. Used to sneak out after dark

and roam the streets. Explore the belfry. Swing from the ropes there.''

''You must have given the poor nuns heart failure.''

''They said so often enough.''

''And yet you wanted to join them?''

''Yes.'' I thought back, thought back hard, really searching my soul. ''I think perhaps I never quite got rid of the notion that my mother had found me not good enough. That I had to be good. I couldn't think of a better way to prove I was good than to join the order.''

''I suppose that makes some kind of sense.''

''But I was never truly content there. All I ever wanted to do was get out. And our excursions from abbey walls were extremely limited. So when it was my turn to work with Sister Rebecca in the homeless shelter, I was always very eager to go.'' I looked up at him, and his eyes darkened as if he knew my fear as I remembered. ''That last night in particular. It was snowing, you see. And I've always loved the snow.''

He stopped walking, stared intently at me. ''And what happened, Angel?''

I lowered my head. ''Rebecca was ill. I broke the rules and went anyway, alone. And I missed the bus, and decided to walk.''

''Alone?'' he asked, eyes widening. ''At night?''

I only nodded.

''And that's when it happened?'' he said, urging me to continue.

''He was waiting for me.'' I shivered a little, and hugged myself. ''He dragged me down among the garbage. I thought...well, I thought everything but the truth. There was nothing I could do to fight him. He was a vampire, with strength like I have now. I was just a mortal woman. Oh, I tried, of course. I beat him bloody, but it didn't even faze him.''

''He...he forced the dark gift on you?''

I nodded, unable to look Jameson in the eye.

''And then left you alone, not teaching you anything about yourself?''

"No. No, he wanted to teach me. You told me once that there is some special bond each vampire has with a chosen human. I think, perhaps, I was his. He said he'd been watching me all my life. But he was sick...twisted, somehow. My first lesson was to be the murder of a young homeless boy. He demonstrated the technique first, of course, by taking a frightened old man. And then he chose my victim for me." I lifted my head then, and faced him. "I took a burning length of wood from a barrel fire, and I hit him as hard as I could. The blow put him on his knees, but it was the fire that killed him."

"You killed him," he muttered, staring down at me in disbelief. Then he shook his head. "Good. Saves me the trouble."

"I thought," I said, starting forward once more, "that God had cursed me. I thought the only way I could survive was by killing, and I vowed not to do that. So I hid myself away, and waited for death. I had no idea the bloodlust would become so overwhelming."

"You had no idea about much of anything at all," he said.

I nodded my agreement. "But I've decided to learn."

"I can see that."

"It's because I know she's safe," I told him. "I know she's all right, and for the first time since that horrible night, I...I feel good."

That was a lie. It wasn't the first time. I had felt good once before. He'd made me feel...utter ecstasy.

I averted my face, because I could feel him trying to read my thoughts. And then I walked faster, back toward the abandoned house where we'd left Jameson's car. He caught up to me in short order, and when he reached my side, he walked just fast enough so he pulled ahead of me. So I quickened my pace to pull ahead of him, and then he did likewise.

I slid him a sidelong glance, saw the twinkle in his eyes and sprinted as fast as I could go. He took up my unspoken challenge, and we raced all the way back to that tumbledown house.

And there I collapsed on my back in the grass, staring up at the stars, and thinking that I had never truly appreciated the night's ethereal beauty before. Never once.

He stood there looking down at her. Yes, she was damned near giddy because of this feeling that had come over her in her sleep. The sixth sense that assured her their daughter was fine and safe, and very nearby. But Jameson sensed that there was more to it than that. That perhaps she was beginning to come to grips with her new nature. To see her new reality and to deal with it.

And as her fears and insecurities were slowly, methodically, stripped away, the woman she'd been before was beginning to emerge. He sensed it, knew it, the way he knew so many things about her. Even with the sisters, she'd been a hellion. Always tempting fate, and playing jokes and causing mischief. A child at heart, always. He'd seen it all so clearly when she'd told him her story.

The frightened, desperate woman he'd known wasn't even a shadow of the real Angelica. Lord, he'd been thinking that was all she was. The truth was a revelation.

She lay in the grass now, with her lustrous dark hair spread all around her, and the stars twinkling their reflection in her eyes. And he almost groaned with the force of his desire for her. Almost lay right down upon her, right there, and...

"Ahem," Roland said pointedly.

Jameson turned to see his friend standing behind him, and then he wondered just how much of his errant thoughts Roland had been able to read. "You're here. Good."

Rhiannon walked up next to Angelica, lifted her arms out at her sides and let herself fall backward to the ground. Angelica laughed.

It was, Jameson realized with a small start, the first time he had heard her laughter.

"You're looking better, fledgling," Rhiannon said, sprawled on the ground beside her.

Angelica sat up, smiling. "She's near us. I can feel it. We'll find her soon."

"And?" Rhiannon prompted.

"And...and knowing she's all right, safe and happy at this very moment, has given me...I don't know. A respite, I guess, from all the worrying about her. And I did what you said, Rhiannon. I let myself...enjoy,...what I've become."

"As well you should, young one."

Jameson tore his eyes from her beautiful face, and turned to Roland. "Where are Eric and Tamara?"

"Staking the place out, and waiting for us to arrive. We thought it best to get someone into position as soon as possible, in case the child is moved again."

Jameson nodded. "Where is this place?"

"Only a few miles from here," Roland told him.

Angelica came between them. "Let's hurry, Vampire," she said, her eyes pleading, making Jameson's heart trip over itself in his chest. Dammit, why couldn't he accept the friendship she seemed to be offering him, and leave it at that? Why did he have to hunger for so much more? "I want her in my arms," she rushed on. "I want to hold her close to me. Please."

He nodded, averting his eyes because he didn't like seeing the love gleaming from hers. Love for her child. It lit up her entire face. He started toward the car with Angelica at his side, then stopped when he realized Roland wasn't following.

"What are you waiting for?"

Roland nodded toward Jameson's car. "You know how I feel about those things," he said. "The trip up here was unnerving enough. Rhiannon and I will come along under our own steam. We can cut through the forest, and probably get there before you, too."

Angelica tilted her head, eyeing Roland. "You're faster than a car?" Roland nodded. "You must be very old, then," she said.

Jameson's dearest friend smiled broadly. "Milady, I am ancient. And yet my darling mate is several centuries older."

"When I said I was a daughter of Pharaoh, child, I was not joking," Rhiannon said, moving forward to take Roland by the arm. "I was alive when the pyramids were built."

Jameson watched Angelica's angel-eyes widen in awed wonder.

"I'll tell you about it sometime," Rhiannon said with a wink.

"I'll hold you to that," Angelica replied, and then she turned and hurried to the car. Roland had given Jameson the directions, so he bid his friends farewell and jumped behind the wheel.

"Hurry," she whispered, turning those excited violet eyes on him one more time. She meant what she said. She felt something. Felt it strongly. It showed.

"I will."

We parked some distance away, and then crept through the night-shaded woods to the cabin. It rested on a hilltop amid stands of virgin pines that filled the air with their scent and whispered secrets to one another when the breeze moved through their needles.

Jameson kept one hand cupped around my elbow as we moved silently through the forest, creeping up on the cabin. I saw the glow of oil lamps in the windows, and the soft gray spiral of smoke floating from the chimney. I smelled burning wood.

But something felt...wrong.

Jameson turned to me, brows furrowed. "Tamara and Eric aren't here," he said.

I blinked, closing my eyes and trying hard to home in on that sense of my daughter. The calmness, the safety of her environment and her comfort still reached me. As did her nearness.

But not as near as she should be.

My heart plummeted to my feet. All that exuberance rushed out of me like air rushing from a punctured balloon, leaving me weak and devastated. "She isn't in that cabin," I whispered. "Jameson, we're too late. We've missed them."

He looked into my eyes, shaking his head hard and fast. "No. Look, maybe Hilary just went out for supplies or something. Eric and Tam probably followed her."

Hope seemed to run from his eyes to mine, filling my heart. "You think so?"

"My best guess, Angel. Let's go in for a closer look, okay?"

I nodded, drying my tears, and we crept closer, out of the cover of the trees and into the open. The house seemed devoid of life, utterly deserted.

Until a blinding spotlight glared into our eyes, and a loud voice boomed, ''Take another step, and we'll kill the child!''

Panic rooted my feet to the very ground. But not Jameson's. He quickly stepped in front of me, pushing my body behind his in a gesture that was so protective it left me breathless with amazement.

''Back up slowly,'' he whispered.

I did exactly as he said, knowing it was the protection of the trees he sought. But I clung to his waist, pulling him with me as I backed toward shelter.

''I said stand still. Don't move, or the child dies!''

''Liar!'' I shouted. ''You don't have my baby!'' But despite my brave words, I stopped moving, doubting my own instincts.

''Not here,'' the voice replied. ''But we have her. Go ahead and run, and you'll find out.''

Only by squinting into the blinding light could I make out the shapes of several men standing just beyond it. And then one of them stepped forward, and I cried out. Because he was holding sweet Tamara in his arms. Her head hung limply forward, and it seemed it was her captor rather than her own legs keeping her upright.

''Tam!'' Jameson shouted, lunging forward, but freezing again when the man lifted a blade to her throat.

''Stay still, or watch her bleed like a pig!''

He did as he was told, and I felt his anguish. Shared it. ''Don't hurt her,'' Jameson said, his voice strong and clear. I was convinced only I could detect the waver that lingered beneath his words. He adored Tamara. I'd known they were friends, but not the extent of their closeness. Not until now. He would die for her. Gladly, he would. ''Let her go,'' he went on, taking a wary step forward, holding his arms out at his sides in a nonthreatening posture. ''Let her go, dammit, and take me instead.''

I gasped in horror. Then bit my lip. *Please, Jameson, don't!*

''We'll be taking all of you.'' The DPI thug lifted a gun, one

I recognized, and my stomach lurched in fear of the tranquilizer I knew the weapon held. And I could see now, from where I stood, better than I had before. I could see the slumped forms of Eric and Roland lying on the ground. Unconscious...or perhaps dead. And just beyond them, Rhiannon, that most regal of all vampires, as several men slung her limp body onto the back of a truck.

I took a single step forward, as an unbelievable fury rose in me.

Run, Angelica! Jameson's mind screamed out to mine. *You can get away. Go, find the baby and take her as far away from them as you can get!*

"I can't leave you like this," I whispered, automatically speaking aloud, too frightened to think clearly enough to do otherwise. "I can't—"

Go! You're the only chance our daughter has now! If they catch all of us, she'll be theirs forever, Angel. Do this. Run!

Trembling from head to toe, I turned and started for the trees. I heard the shot, and glanced behind me in time to see Jameson, the man I'd once thought of as a monster, leap into the path of the dart that was flying toward me. I saw it plunge into his chest, and saw him sink to the ground. I screamed.

Run.... His thoughts were weakening as the drug did its work. *Run, for the love of Christ, run....*

And I ran.

I raced through the forest, heedless of my direction. Limbs slapping my face and tearing at my clothes and hair. I ran, pouring all of my vampiric strength into getting away from them. Jameson was right. I had to stay free, I had to find Amber Lily, and take her from those beasts! But there was another thought, too, whirling in my terrified brain as I plunged through the wilds of the forest. I had to stay free so that I could go back. For him. I had to go back for that arrogant vampire. I couldn't go on if he died at their hands. And the others, as well. I'd go back for all of them.

Chapter Twelve

Hilary Garner ran. She'd seen them coming, seen them surrounding the cabin that had been the only safe haven she could think of for the child. And God help her, she'd stolen the tiny baby right from under their noses back in White Plains. She'd had no idea if the child's mother was still alive. But her father was. Tamara had received Hilary's cryptic message, and told her Jameson was on the way.

But it had been impossible to wait for him.

Every day, Hilary had checked in on the newborn. Those big dark eyes, and tiny hands, and satin hair, had enchanted her. And she couldn't wait. DPI's roster of experiments had been finalized, and the first of them had been put on Rose Sversky's schedule. And dammit, Hilary couldn't wait.

So she'd taken her, and she'd brought her here. And the bastards had found her. One of them must have realized she'd slipped away from the cabin, too, because she could hear them coming. Heavy footfalls, crushing the leaves and twigs as they ran toward her.

She hugged the bundled-up baby tight in her arms. "Don't worry, honey," she whispered. "Hilary's going to take care of you, baby. I promised your mama. And I promised myself. I said

I'd watch over you, sweetie, until your daddy came for you, and that's what I'm gonna do. I swear, I will.''

She ran faster, weaving and ducking through the trees. But the footsteps came closer, louder, and then someone shouted.

"No. Please, God, help me keep my promise!''

Shots rang out in the night, and searing hot hammers seemed to pound her in the back, slamming her body forward.

"Jesus Christ,'' a man yelled. "You'll hit the freaking kid, you idiot!''

She tried to keep going, tried to keep moving. But she lost all the feeling in her legs. They buckled, and she fell to her knees. And then slipped lower. And her arms cradled the baby, and she bent her head to kiss the plump cheek. "I'll keep my promise,'' she whispered.

And even before she finished, the men were looming over her, taking the child from her arms. The one man passed the baby to the other. "Here. Whaley said to radio in when we had her, and then get her into a vehicle headed straight back to headquarters. No stopping. No detours. Got it?''

Hilary weakly turned her head, to see the other one nod once and turn to go. She watched the baby disappearing from her sight. "He'll...never...make it back there with her,'' she managed. "I won't let him.''

"You aren't going to be much help to anyone for much longer, Garner.''

"I have to,'' she whispered. "I promised.''

He shook his head, his eyes dipping down to her torso, then turning away in disgust. He left her there, shouting to some of the others as he did. "It's all over here. Let's get back to the house and transport the others to The Pit.''

"But one is still at large, sir.''

"One, we can handle,'' he said. "Later. Let's be sure the others are taken care of first.''

And she listened to them tromping away, their footsteps growing fainter, and then fading entirely. Hilary closed her eyes, and let her head rest against a hunk of moss-covered deadfall. "Please,

God," she whispered. "It's been so long since I've come to you...I know that. But...but I'm sorry." She gritted her teeth in pain, and drew a breath, forcing herself to go on. "I don't know if you can forgive me for...for all the time I spent working for those monsters. But I didn't know, God. I didn't know."

The wind seemed to whisper through the pine boughs. It seemed to be calling her name.

"Forgive me, Lord," she went on. "And help me. I need help to keep my promise." She opened her eyes and looked up at the dark sky. "Send me a sign," she whispered. "Send me an angel, and I'll know I'm forgiven. I'll know you're hearing me now, if you'll just send me an angel."

Jameson woke in chains. His mind was groggy, and weak from the drug, but he fought the debilitating effects, blinked his vision clear and tried to survey his surroundings.

He was underground. The smell of the earth surrounded him, even beyond the circular wall made of huge concrete blocks. Jesus, he was in some sort of round dungeon. He was slumped on a hard floor, his legs shackled to the wall behind him, his arms chained up and outspread. Clenching his jaw, he tugged at those chains, but they only rattled in response. He was too weak. Damn, he was too weak to break free.

A soft moan drew his gaze, and he saw the others, chained just as he was. Eric and Roland, Tamara and Rhiannon, her dark hair hanging over her face. But not Angelica. There were other chains dangling from the walls. Empty of prisoners, hanging alone. Angelica occupied none of them.

Thank God. Thank God, she'd gotten away.

Roland staggered to his feet as Jameson looked on. He lifted his head, and their gazes locked.

"Where the hell are we?" Jameson asked, though he was certain Roland had no more clue than he did.

"I can't be sure. Probably one of the safe houses the bastards have scattered all over the country. They'll bring in reinforcements before they try to move us back to White Plains, I imagine."

Jameson could believe it. Armored trucks and armed guards.

And perhaps there was another reason they hadn't been moved just yet. "They want all of us," he said, realizing his speech sounded drunken and slurred. Roland's brows came up. "Angelica got away. And she's the only one left who'll keep trying to rescue the baby."

"Yes," Roland said, nodding slowly. "They'll want to eliminate every possible threat to their keeping that child. She must be considered their most valuable prisoner."

"I don't believe they have her."

Eric was stirring awake now. And then Tamara and Rhiannon as well.

"What makes you think so, Jamey?" Tam whispered.

"Angelica," he said. "I'm not sure what might have happened since, but right up until the moment we were ambushed, Angelica was convinced the child was still safe. She didn't believe them when they said they had her, and I have to cling to that. She senses things about the baby. And she was feeling...almost exuberant. So sure our Amber Lily was in safe hands."

"Maybe," Tam whispered, her head nodding once before she pulled her chin up once more. "Maybe Hilary got away before they found the cabin. Maybe the baby is still safe with her."

"Yes," Eric put in, sounding weak. "They knew we'd come after her at the cabin, so even if they had missed catching her there, they'd have lain in wait for us."

"With all of us in captivity, they'll be sure we don't reach the child before they do," Roland said.

Rhiannon lifted her head, her eyes flashing with anger. "Captivity, my love, is not at all what they have in mind for us. They know better. They won't risk it." She lifted her head, then slowly closed her eyes. "Look above us," she whispered.

And one by one the others tipped their heads back. Jameson did likewise, and then felt as if he'd been kicked in the stomach. There was no floor above them. This was no basement, no dungeon, but a pit, with its circular stone walls rising high all around them. An arching ceiling towered high above. A ceiling entirely made of glass.

Jameson tugged at the chains with renewed vigor. Damn the drug! He was as weak as a mortal! Weaker. He pulled until the iron cuffs cut into his wrists, and still didn't loosen their hold on him.

"God, no," Tamara whispered, and then Jameson heard her soft crying, saw her tears. Her eyes sought Eric's, and her hands strained against their bonds to reach his, but too much space separated them. "I love you, my darling," she whispered between sobs. "You've given me so much happiness. So much joy..."

"Tamara..." Eric moaned, straining against his bonds.

Rhiannon's eyes narrowed. "Stop it! Stop with the dying declarations of love. We are far from finished!" But her voice didn't quite ring with its usual conviction.

Because she knew, as they all did, that when the sun rose and filled this hole with its golden light, it would be the end. For all of them.

"Dammit," Jameson shouted. "Dammit, I shouldn't have let you get involved in this. I knew better. I knew I'd just bring trouble to all of you."

"We're family, Jameson," Roland said, his voice level and low. "We couldn't not get involved."

"At least there's still a chance for your child, Jamey," Tamara whispered. "Angelica will find her, take her away to safety."

"There will never be a chance for my child," he said, his rage rising up to envelop his entire being, "Until DPI is brought to ruin. Dammit, when will the rest of you see that? We should have destroyed them long ago. They won't rest until all of our race is annihilated, I know it. And you do as well."

They said nothing. But there was guilt in their eyes as they looked at one another. He didn't need to hear them say he was right. Maybe they still didn't believe he was. But Jameson knew. One day, someone would rise up. Someone would lead them in revolt, and DPI would be laid to waste. He'd planned to be that someone. But now it looked as if the job would fall to another.

To his own daughter, perhaps.

Jameson lowered his head, closed his eyes, and focused every fiber of his being on Angelica. *Find her, Angel. My beautiful, dark Angel. Find her and keep her safe. I can't be there for her. It's over for me. But you can. You must. Save her, Angel, and tell her about me. Tell her about her father. Tell her...that he loved her.*

I stopped running. I was not certain what made me stop, but something did. Some sense. Some feeling. And then Jameson's voice flooded my mind. His farewell. His goodbye. And my heart twisted and tore and bled. "No!" I cried out, shaking my fists at the night. "Don't do this, Vampire! Don't leave me!"

But there was no further reply. I tried to get a sense of where he was, using my mind, but I found nothing. And I sobbed, great heaving sobs that tore through me and left me weak.

I had to find him. And my daughter. And I would. Dammit, I would! I raced through the woods, sending my senses out before me, searching, seeking.

Someone was near.

I halted in my panicked race, and turned in a slow circle. And then I heard it. A soft moan, guttural and pain-racked. And for just a moment, I recalled the night that seemed a lifetime ago. That night when a similar sound had drawn me into an alley, where a nightmare awaited me.

Every nerve in me jangled to life. I came fully alert, and turned toward the source of the sound. I saw only a mass of deadfall. But the moan came again.

Closing my eyes, I sent out my senses, *feeling* the very air around me. But there was no one else. Only one person. One very weak, pain-racked mortal. Moving silently, I stepped closer. And then I saw her. She lay very still among the brush, and the scent of blood was strong around her.

My hesitation vanished, and I hurried forward. Brown eyes opened when I crouched beside her, and I knew her. This was the dark-skinned woman with the kindness in her eyes. The one who had been with me when my daughter was born. The one who'd promised, without a word, that she would help my innocent baby.

Hilary Garner. She lay still, and very near death. Her body

riddled with bullet holes, and blood flowing slowly from each of them.

"You," she whispered, and it was a tremendous effort for her even to speak.

"I'm here," I said, stroking her hair away from her face. "Don't try to talk. I'll help you. It will be all right."

"No." Weakly, she shook her head. "Nothing…you can do. It's enough…that you're here."

And yet I pressed my hands to the wounds in her chest, attempting to slow the ebb of life from this woman.

"I asked…" she rasped, "God…to send me an angel. And…he sent you."

I blinked in shock, and looked down at her. Angel. It was what Jameson called me. But surely God wasn't still having a hand in my life. Surely he hadn't guided my steps. Surely it wasn't possible that I was still a part of his plan.

Was it?

"They…they took her. They took…the baby…."

"I'll get her back," I said, and I tore strips of cloth from my dress and packed them into her wounds.

"He'll…protect her," she said softly. "He promised…*I* promised."

"I owe you more than I can ever repay, Hilary Garner," I whispered.

"White Plains," she said, and she was weakening rapidly. "They're going to try…to take her back…there."

"I'll go for her. Don't worry, I'll find her."

A soft hand came up to grip my wrist as I worked to pack another wound with cloth. "The…others…first."

I frowned down at her.

"Route…Ten," she gasped and bit her lip. "Twelve miles north. An old…l-logging road…veers east."

"And what is there, Hilary? Is that where the others are being held?"

She nodded, her eyes falling closed. But then popping open

again, blazing with urgency. "The Pit," she whispered. "Dead...
by dawn...all of them..."

My hands stilled as an icy chill swept through me. "By dawn?"
My God, how could I do this? How could I, alone, rescue the
others before sunrise? I couldn't.

"I...I didn't know," the weakened woman went on. "All those
years...worked for them...didn't know...I swear..."

"I know that. You're a good woman, Hilary. A kind, caring
woman."

"P-pray for me...Sister...pray...for me...."

I closed my eyes in anguish over this woman's pain. And over
what she asked of me. "I can't..."

"Yes. You can. God sent you to...find me. He...still hears
you."

Tears burned in my eyes, because I did so want to believe it
was true. Whether I did or not, though, I couldn't deny her this
one small comfort. Bowing my head, I gathered her hands in mine.
"Our Father," I whispered, "Who art in heaven..."

She mouthed the words along with me for a time, but stopped
before the end. A soft smile played at her lips then, and her eyes
opened, wide and clear and bright. "Thank you," she said to me.
And then looked beyond me, lifting a hand toward something I
could not see. "Yes," she whispered. "Yes...I'll keep my promise now." Her face relaxed, and her eyes fell gently closed. Her
hand dropped to the ground at her side. And for just an instant, it
seemed a soft white glow emanated from her still form. A glow
that seemed to rise like mist from rain-damp ground. I blinked,
rubbing my eyes. But there was nothing there, when I looked
again. Only a still, empty body. And I thought of the abandoned
farmhouse not far from here.

I buried Hilary Garner in a shallow grave, which I scraped from
the earth with my hands. I gathered what stones I could find
nearby to build a cairn atop her. And I knew it was enough. Nothing would disturb this grave. I sensed it, knew it with my heart.

And then I rose on wobbly legs, and turned in the direction that
would lead me to the road.

* * *

Stiles drove while Special Agent Keller—the rookie who'd come running out of the woods looking spooked with the infant in his arms—rode shotgun in the back seat. He sat beside the kid, gun drawn, wide eyes skimming the dark woods they passed. He was scared. Stiles knew scared when he saw it, and the rookie had all the symptoms.

Figured he'd get saddled with a spooky recruit on a job this important. It just figured. If he lost the kid again, Whaley would have his hide.

They were almost to the town of Petersville now. Stiles automatically glanced into his rearview mirror to check on his passengers, and then he did a double-take, because he could see the little one very clearly in the mirror. And she was kicking her blankets away from her and smacking on her fist like any normal baby might do.

His stomach clenched a little as his conscience whispered in his brain. What if the kid was…was normal? What if she didn't turn out to be like those animals who'd spawned her?

He looked at her again, and the tiny fist lowered from her bow-shaped mouth. Her huge, dark eyes seemed to stare straight into his, in the mirror. His throat went dry. He had to look away.

Stiles forcibly tore his gaze from the baby's, and when he did, he shouted an expletive and jerked the steering wheel. The car went into a skid, sliding sideways, throwing dirt and gravel as it scraped the road's shoulders, and finally coming to a jerky stop halfway to the ditch.

"What the hell are you doing?" Keller shouted, righting himself and retrieving his gun from the floor. "Trying to get us killed?"

Stiles blinked and stared at the road. "There was something…" he muttered. He got out of the car and walked a few steps from it onto the dirt road, and stood there looking left and right.

Keller came up behind him, gun back in his hand. "Did you see something?"

"Yeah," Stiles whispered. "But..." He gave his head a shake, and turned to Keller. "I don't suppose you saw it, did you?"

"I didn't see anything," Keller said. "What was it? A deer? Or...hey, Stiles, it wasn't one of them, was it?"

Stiles shook his head slowly. "No. Damn, Keller, you can't tell anyone about this, okay? Anyone sees us sitting here, we say we had a flat tire. You got that?"

Keller nodded. "Sure. So long as you're gonna tell me what you saw."

"What I *thought* I saw," Stiles corrected him. "Because it wasn't real."

"So what did you *think* you saw?" Keller asked, shoving his gun back into his pocket.

Stiles shook his head, looking at his feet. "There was this light. And then we got closer, and it looked like..."

"Looked like what?" Keller prompted.

Stiles sighed. "An angel. White gown and wings and the works. All glowing with this white light, and standing right in the middle of the damned road." Again, he shook his head, this time with a nervous laugh. "And then it was gone. Stupid, huh? I think I need to get more sleep, maybe take some time off..."

"Or...m-m-maybe not," Keller said.

Stiles lifted his head and saw the rookie's ashen face. His wide eyes and trembling forefinger were both aimed at the car, and when Stiles looked, it was to see that same eerie white glow spilling from every window in the vehicle. It glowed brighter than any man-made light could possibly do, just for a moment, and then the light faded away.

He gave his head a shake, as if he could somehow clear it, and then forced himself to move forward. But he had a pretty good idea already what he was going to find when he reached the car.

He leaned over the vehicle, peered inside, and then straightened and looked back at Keller, who was still rooted to the spot where he stood.

"The baby?" Keller asked.

Stiles blinked, feeling dazzled and shell-shocked. And then he just shook his head. Gone. The kid was gone as if she'd never been there.

Keller was breathing hard all of a sudden. "We gotta get out of here," he muttered, hurrying back to the car. "It might come back here...for us, this time."

Stiles gripped his shoulder and pulled him up short. "Listen, Keller, and listen good. No one is to hear about what we saw here tonight, got that? We talk about this, we're gonna get locked up in a rubber room somewhere. Hell, we might even end up subjects for DPI study."

Keller gasped at that statement. "We had a flat," he said slowly. "We got out to change the tire, and someone grabbed the kid. We didn't see a thing."

Stiles nodded, swallowed hard, and, with frequent nervous glances over his shoulder, made his way back to the car.

It had been a miracle, Susan Jennings thought, over and over again. Only twenty-four hours ago, she'd swerved her car to miss a deer, and lost control. God, in heaven, she'd never forget the fear that had taken hold of her as the wheel had been wrenched from her hands and the car somersaulted down the side of that embankment.

Or the utter horror of pulling herself from the ground and realizing that little Alicia had still been inside.

And then, just like angels, those two strangers had appeared, as if out of nowhere. Just like angels, she thought again, smiling as she pushed the rocker into motion, cradling Alicia in her arms and holding her bottle to her lips. They'd saved her baby's life. And then vanished in the night before she'd even had a chance to thank them.

Alicia's gentle sucking slowed, and then stopped as her blue, blue eyes fell closed. Susan got up carefully, and tiptoed across the room to lower the baby into her bed. Then gently tucked the covers around her.

A soft knock sounded at the front door.

Susan turned, frowning hard, and sending a quick glance toward the clock on the wall. Who in the world would be calling at this time of night? She went to the door, opened it a crack and stared out into the kindest brown eyes she'd ever seen.

I raced north on Route 10, driving Jameson's car, which I had located right where he left it, concealed by a stand of pines off the roadside a few miles beyond the now-abandoned cabin. And I did as he had so wisely done then. Hid it from DPI's vigilant eyes. I saw the log road that veered to the east, but drove past it, pulling the car into a grove off the roadside, and then turning back on foot.

And when I found the logging trail again, I did not travel upon it, but cloaked in the shadows of the trees that lined its edges. The darkness was my friend tonight, as it had never been before. And as I drew nearer, black clouds skittered across the face of the low-hanging moon, painting it with velvet brush strokes, and deepening the night still more.

I saw a bubble in the ground, like a clear glass dome. And around it, four men stood like sentries guarding some coveted treasure. All of them armed, I knew. I could not hope to take them on all at once. One of them would be bound to shoot me with his deadly little darts.

What should I do?

Lure them away, I thought. One by one, if necessary. But Lord, the sun would not be long in rising. And I saw now why that would spell death for the four who must be trapped beneath that clear bubble.

I gripped the lowest bough of the pine under which I stood, and with a twist of my hand, snapped the branch in two. It made a startling sound in the night, and all four guards went stiff and alert.

"What was that?" one demanded. "Who's there?" He lifted his weapon.

"Probably just an animal," said a second.

"I don't think so."

"So go check it out."

The first man shook his head. "Whaley said to do everything in pairs. You know how tricky their kind is."

"Come on, then. We'll both go."

The two men turned toward me, and started forward, moving slowly, weapons aimed. One drew a flashlight into his free hand, pointed it my way and clicked a button. I pushed myself off the ground quickly, landing in the safety of the pine tree's arms before that beam of light fell on me. One at a time had been my plan. Not two at once. No matter. I wouldn't give up. Couldn't. Jameson, that vengeful vampire, was trapped like a rat, and when the sun rose...

I shuddered as I thought of the agonizing way in which he would die. Felt a peculiar emptiness growing inside me at the very thought of it, and my stomach tied itself up in knots. And then I stilled myself, and waited. The two did not walk close together as I'd hoped they would. But not far enough apart to suit me either. One of them stopped directly beneath me.

The other stood, perhaps four feet away, his back to me now. I would have to be quick, and smart. Quicker and smarter than the men were. It shouldn't be hard, I told myself. I was a vampire.

I let myself fall from the tree, landing squarely atop the man who stood there. He emitted a loud grunt before my fists crashed down onto his skull, rendering him unconscious...at least. The other one whirled at the sound and leveled his weapon at me. Using all my speed, I dived to the side, and the dart his gun fired skimmed over my arm, cutting, but not embedding itself in my skin. Its tip sank into the tree beside me. I prayed it hadn't discharged any of that drug into my flesh. In the split second it took for the man to find me again with his sights, I'd plucked the dart from the tree and hurled it at him.

It drove itself deeply into my attacker's throat. His gun clattered to the ground, and his eyes rolled back in his head. Then he fell forward, and did not move again.

But I had not been as quiet at I would have liked. The two remaining at the dome were aware of the commotion, and one lifted a radio to his mouth. I snatched the gun from the ground, pointed it and pulled the trigger. But only a muted "click" came in reply. The gun hadn't been reloaded. "Something's going down,'' a guard shouted at his radio. And I threw the empty weapon at him with all my strength. "Get us some back— unnnnnhhhh—'' The metal dart gun hit him squarely in the face, and he was flung backward so hard he crashed through the glass dome behind him. I heard him hit the bottom, far below, and then I heard no more.

I stood, without shelter, my eyes holding those of the one remaining man. He held his hands toward me, shaking his head from side to side. "Please…just take them, okay? Just—''

I must have been quite a frightening sight to this poor mortal. My hair in tangles, and no doubt littered with pine needles and stray leaves. My hands scraped raw and dirty from digging a grave for Hilary. My dress torn from my mad race through the forest, and my arms and chest spattered and smeared with Hilary's blood as well as my own.

Perhaps she'd been right. Perhaps God was directing my steps. Somehow.

I nodded to the gun in the remaining guard's hand, and he dropped it to the ground. I lifted a hand and pointed to the radio attached to his belt, and he tossed that aside as well. And then I moved toward him. The fear in his eyes reached me, and I almost felt sorry for him. He began to back away, but I didn't want him falling through the shattered dome and dying, so I pushed off with a burst of speed, and before he could have seen me move, I had him by the front of his shirt.

"D-d-don't kill me,'' he whispered. "P-please…''

I put my arms firmly around him, and jumped through the break in the glass bubble. He howled aloud as we plummeted, but I held him tight when we hit, not falling on my backside as I was so prone to do.

Around me I sensed the stunned expressions on the faces of the others. But I only glanced away from my captive long enough to assure myself they were all there, and all alive. My eyes locked with Jameson's for a long moment. He pulled uselessly against the chains that bound his wrists to the wall, and I felt anger such as I had never known at those who had put him here, left him here to die. But I pulled my gaze free, forcibly so.

"Where is my child?" I demanded, giving the guard a shake.

"I...I don't know...I s-swear—" His wide eyes danced around the room, fear-filled as he saw the fury of each captive vampire, and then horrified still more as he saw the prone form of the other guard, the one who'd fallen through the glass dome. The man's body lay broken in the center of the floor.

I shook him again, snapping his head back and forth with the force of it. "Pay attention to me, you little liar," I said to him. "Where is she? Where is my baby?"

"They were taking her back...to headquarters," he stammered. "B-but they had a flat. Th-they got out to change the tire and—and—and—"

"And what, mortal!"

"The kid was gone!" he blurted, sobbing now. His nose was running and tears pooled in his eyes. "Just g-gone. S-someone took her right outta the c-car. A radio alert went out—w-we thought it was you!"

I believe the man was telling me the truth, or as much of the truth as he knew. Of course, what he said could not have been what had truly happened. The only ones who could have rescued my baby were here, with me. Except for Hilary, of course, but sweet Hilary was dead. I'd buried her among the pine needles, beneath the pungent, sentrylike trees in the forest.

"But I thought...I thought Hilary had the child," Tamara's soft voice asked, filling this dark pit with warmth.

I turned to face her, meeting her wounded eyes. "I'm sorry, Tamara. They...they killed Hilary."

She cried out when I said it, then let her head fall until her chin touched her chest, and her tears fell in silence.

"I found her in the forest. Dying. And she told me where you all were being held, that you'd be dead by dawn unless I found a way to help you."

"Thank God for her," Tamara whispered.

"I have," I replied. "I buried her there in the forest. It's a beautiful place, Tamara. She's at peace there.'' She nodded, thanking me with her eyes, if not with her lips.

"And now DPI has my daughter again.''

"They don't,'' the guard piped up. "I told you—''

"No doubt they've told you this as a ruse,'' I said. "A ploy, in case I came here and forced you to talk.'' I looked at the others, the chains that bound them to the walls, and then glanced above me at the sky. Paling, already. Paling. I gave him another shake. "The keys.''

"R-right front p-p-pocket.''

I snatched the keys from the man's pocket and pulled him with me to where Jameson stood, bleary eyed, and pale. Holding the guard with one hand, I unlocked the Vampire's shackles with the other. Jameson stared at me. "You shouldn't be here, Angelica. Dammit, can't you ever do what you're told?''

"I'm saving your life, Vampire,'' I snapped. "Or hadn't you noticed that yet?''

Jameson stepped away from the wall, and I slammed my prisoner up against it and snapped the vacant shackles around his wrists. Then I raced to each of the others, freeing them in turn.

Rhiannon rubbed her wrists, and gave me a weak imitation of her almost smile. "That was very good, Angelica. I might just make a goddess-among-women of you yet.''

"Thank you,'' Tamara said, rushing into my arms and hugging me as hard as her strength would allow. "I thought this was the end. Thank you, Angelica!''

"Some people seem to have more difficulty showing gratitude than others,'' Eric intoned. "But I, too, thank you, my dear.'' This he said with a pointed glance at Jameson. And then he took Tamara into his arms and held her hard, closing his eyes tight, kissing her hair.

"Don't be so quick with your gratitude, Eric. We're not out of here, yet.'' As he said it, Jameson looked upward. "None of us is strong enough to climb, or jump, out of this pit.''

"None but me, you mean.'' I tapped Tamara's shoulder, and when she turned to me, I wrapped my arms tightly around her, bent at the knees, and jumped with all my might. And we sailed past the shattered dome, landing safely on the ground. "Hide," I whispered. "One of them managed to use his radio before I got to him. More might be coming." Then I went back down for the others, and one by one, brought each of them out in the same manner.

Jameson insisted I take the others before him. Rhiannon reluctantly stepped into my embrace. "Imagine," she said. "I'm reduced to depending on a mere fledgling for salvation."

"Even worse," I told her. "You're being forced into a hug."

She scowled at me as we soared upward. But I saw her deep affection for me hiding there beyond the scowl. And I wondered how I could come to love a woman more truly than if she were my own sister, in so short a time.

At last only my nemesis remained. We faced each other for a moment. "You shouldn't have come," he said. "I told you to go after the baby."

"I'll stand a far better chance of reaching her with your help," I told him.

"You're stubborn and foolish!"

"You're an arrogant, overbearing jerk," I spit back.

"You could have been killed, coming back for us," he said to me.

"And you would have died if I hadn't," I whispered. "I had to try, Jameson. I couldn't bear the thought." I slipped my arms around his waist. "Hold on to me."

He gripped my shoulders in his hands, and I looked up, into his eyes. "No," I said, and my voice trembled now. "Hold me *close.*"

He stared down into my eyes for a long moment, and then he pulled me tight to him, bowed his head and kissed my mouth. Feverishly, he kissed me. Desperately. And I clung to him, and kissed him back with the same unrestrained fierceness. When at last, he lifted his head away, I was shuddering with longing for this man I knew felt nothing for me except contempt. But it didn't fill me with disgust and self-loathing as he probably thought it did. I refused to let it. I wasn't yearning for the touch of a monster, or even of a sinful man whom I hated. I yearned for this man, whom I had come to care for, somehow. And I saw no terrible sin in that.

We bent our knees and jumped together, though he was still too weakened by the drug to be of much help, and we landed on the ground, still clinging to each other. He stood, pulled me to my feet and, for some reason I did not understand, he clung to my hand as we ran off into the forest, in the direction the others had taken. We didn't speak again. I saw lights in the distance, heard mortal voices as DPI troops fanned into the woods like soldiers, searching for us. No doubt intent on killing us all, on sight. We went quickly, and quietly, and when we reached the car, we piled inside. Even Roland, though he protested at riding in the thing.

The sky became lighter, paling to purple, as I sped back to the only shelter I could think of. The abandoned house where Jameson and I had planned to stay that first night. But when I stopped the car and got out, Jameson touched my arm.

"We'll leave the car here. If they find it, they'll think we're trapped inside the house, and it might distract them. But I think we should head for that cave of yours."

"There's no time," I said, searching his eyes.

"It's darker in the forest," Rhiannon said quickly. "There will be time, if we hurry."

We did hurry, though the others were far slower than I. Twice Tamara told me to run ahead, to leave them and wait for them at the cave, but I refused to leave these newfound friends. I had come, in a very short time, to care for them very deeply. They'd become the family I had never had. The reward I'd always dreamed my goodness would earn for me, as a child. They were all risking their lives to help my baby daughter. And I would lay down my life for any one of them.

But even if it hadn't been for the love I felt for Tamara and Rhiannon, I could not have brought myself to leave Jameson. If the sun rose and began to blister my skin that very moment, I could not have gone on without him.

It was because he was the father of my child, I told myself, as I walked beside him through the gathering light. I was linked to him through the baby. That must be the explanation.

He turned and looked into my eyes then, and something inside me seemed to rouse from a heavy slumber. And I knew that my theory held no water. There was a bond between us. But for my part, at least, it wasn't our daughter alone that had created it.

There was something more. Something I could not begin to understand.

You're in love with him, fledgling, Rhiannon's voice whispered in my mind.

I swung my gaze to meet hers, startled, realizing I'd forgotten to guard my thoughts.

She smiled at me, sent me a wink. And I sensed she spoke to me alone, and kept her thoughts between us, so Jameson couldn't hear them. Yet another trick I'd like to learn. *Of course, I knew it from the first time he spoke of you. You'll be good for him, Angelica. Exactly what our arrogant young Jameson needs.* Her smile grew larger as she slanted a glance at him. Then she looked at me again, mischief in her eyes. *Don't tell him just yet, young one. He needs to suffer a bit longer, I think.*

Suffer? Oh, Rhiannon might be wise, but she had no clue about Jameson. He wasn't suffering at all on my account. His only torment came of his longing for our child, and of his craving for revenge against DPI. He might want me with the passion of a madman. But there was nothing beyond that. And as for me, well, I most certainly was not in love with him.

It would be a very foolish woman, indeed, who would let herself love a man who despised her.

Chapter Thirteen

Jameson came awake slowly, the scents of the night gradually filling his lungs and coaxing him away from the heavenly arms that held him in his dream. When he was half-awake, at just about the point where he'd decided he'd rather not wake up, he realized those arms were Angelica's. And those were her lips, and her soft moans he'd been playing in his mind all day. It made him angry that he couldn't control his mind while he slept. He wouldn't dream of her that way if he had a choice in the matter. Because it was too disappointing to wake to the harsh realization that she would never whisper the things to him in the realm of reality, that she did in the dreamworld.

He'd been resting against the cool stone wall. And he'd fallen asleep with Angelica close beside him. But as he wrestled himself more fully awake and turned to look at her, just to assure himself she wasn't truly as beautiful as his dream had painted her—though he knew full well she was—he didn't find her there. She was gone. A tiny trill of alarm shivered up his spine, and he sat up straighter, blinking the sleep haze from his eyes.

"Good, you're awake," Roland said. "We need to get an early start if we're going to catch up to them before they have the child firmly installed in that building in White Plains."

The others were up as well, Rhiannon brushing her long hair, Tamara snuggling sleepily in Eric's arms.

"Not we," Jameson said softly. "I."

"Jamey—" Tamara began, sitting up straighter, but he cut her off.

"No, Tamara. I'm not willing to have you risking your lives for me anymore. You could have been killed. And the risk is even greater now. They'll be furious that we escaped, and more determined than ever to kill us all." As he spoke his gaze kept darting toward the cave's entrance, but no sign of Angelica appeared there.

"Worried about her?" Rhiannon asked.

Jameson snapped his head around, met her mischievous black eyes. "Where is she?"

"She went out to scout the area. Said she wanted to be sure it was safe for us to emerge."

"She shouldn't be out there alone," Jameson said, and he started toward the entrance.

"Just what is going on between the two of you?" Tamara asked, and her tone suggested she might be thinking there was considerably more between them than there was.

"Don't start, Tamara," he said. "There's nothing between Angelica and me."

"Nothing but a baby," she countered.

"Oh, there's more than a baby," Rhiannon said, lifting her brows. "There's passion. The air practically crackles with it when they're close. And the way they *look* at each other." She smiled softly. "I think you love the girl, Jameson."

"Rhiannon," Roland warned, but she only smiled at him, and sent her knowing gaze right back to Jameson.

Hearing it stated aloud like that made him feel more miserable than ever. "Of course I don't love her," he snapped. He'd be a damned fool if he did, wouldn't he? Since he knew perfectly well she felt nothing for him. Nothing beyond the physical at least. "I feel nothing for the woman," he said.

A sound near the entrance brought his head around. Angelica's eyes met his, but she quickly looked away. There was no doubt in his mind she'd heard what he'd said. And for some reason, he sensed a shimmer of pain in her gaze. Ridiculous.

"I don't see any DPI men hiding in the trees," she said softly. A little too softly, in fact. "I think it's safe to venture out."

"Next time wait for me," Jameson told her.

Her violet eyes fixed on him, flashing with rebellion. "That's right. I'm still your prisoner, aren't I? Forgive me for not asking permission before I went out of your sight. Foolish of me to think that saving your life would change things, wasn't it?"

"That's not what I meant—Angelica!" But she'd turned and hurried out of the cave again, leaving him there to wonder why she was so angry.

"Well done," Rhiannon said, clapping him on the shoulder. "Well done."

He shrugged free of her touch and hurried out of the cave, stepping gratefully into the bracing coolness of the night. A chill autumn breeze snaked up his neck, eliciting a shiver. The moon was completely invisible tonight, obliterated by dark clouds that filled the entire sky. And the wind moaned and whistled in the pine boughs. He didn't see her at first. And then he spotted her, standing with her back to the cave, staring off into the forest. Her hair danced in the wind, long satiny fingers waving, crooking. As if to draw an unwary traveler close. As if to draw him close.

Stiffening his spine, he went to join her there, knowing full well he was letting himself fall victim to her silent allure. But then, that was what he'd been doing all along, wasn't it? Hell, he'd never been a man who found it easy to admit defeat. He stepped up behind her, standing very close. But she didn't acknowledge his presence. Didn't even look at him. It was a revelation, to know a woman who detested him so thoroughly. A new experience for him.

"I didn't mean that you needed to ask permission before leaving my side, Angelica. You know that. It's just that going out alone could be dangerous. I was concerned for your safety. That's all." And as he spoke he stepped up beside her. Still not touching her, though everything in him wanted to.

She slanted him a brief glance, but quickly returned to her contemplation of the forest. "Well I appreciate your concern, Vampire, but it's unwarranted. You may not have noticed, but I'm becoming quite adept at taking care of myself."

"I have noticed," he said. He scanned the surrounding trees, hoping to see what she found so interesting. Seeing nothing unusual, he concluded she simply didn't want to look at him.

"I must have seemed like a pathetic wretch of a vampire to you," she said, her tone musing. "I've no idea why it took me so long to find myself again. But I assure you, Jameson, when I was mortal, I was never so needy or weak."

"I never thought you were weak."

She turned to him, facing him fully for the first time. "But I'm still your prisoner. Tell me, Vampire, do you really think it is still my intention to steal our daughter and take her away where you'll never find her?"

Her eyes were a pale lilac color in the centers, deepening to dark purple at the edges, glittering everywhere. "I don't know," he said, unable to look away. "Is it?"

She blew air through clenched teeth, an exasperated sound, and turned away. "If it was, then why would I have come back for you? I could have left you there to die, and had my daughter all to myself when I found her."

"If you found her," he said. "As you pointed out, you'll have a far greater chance of getting her back with my help."

"And you believe that's the only reason I came back for you." She stated it flatly, neither confirming nor denying it.

"What else would you have me believe?" He leaned one shoulder against a sticky pine, folded his arms across his chest, and eyed her. She didn't care for him. Detested him. Had told him as much. It hurt that her desire for him disgusted her. It hurt far more than it should. "The lust between us is strong, Angelica, but I can't believe you risked your pretty neck just for the chance to have me again."

"You're an arrogant fool."

"Not so arrogant," he told her. "It runs both ways. You know that."

He reached out, stroked the slender column of her throat with the backs of his fingers. Maybe...he just needed to make sure. Glutton for punishment, wasn't he? She slapped his hand away, but not before he'd felt the gentle shudder that worked through her. Yes, she still wanted him. And yes, she was still repulsed by it. He had his answer.

"Come along, lovebirds," Rhiannon called with barely concealed laughter in her voice. Jameson felt certain she'd witnessed that little slap. And it angered him all the more. "We need to get moving."

He leaned in close to Angelica, and even before he spoke he knew that wounded pride was a dangerous thing. "It doesn't matter that my touch disgusts you, does it, Angel? We both know you crave it."

"Remind me of that when you touch me again and I'll tear the fingers from your hand, Vampire." And with those scathing words, she turned to join the others as they hiked through the forest.

No DPI forces surrounded the abandoned house where they'd left the car. So once again they all piled inside and started south. Their destination was DPI headquarters in White Plains. They knew that was where the bastards would have taken Amber Lily, and if it cost Jameson his life, he'd get the child back.

And once she was out of harm's way, he'd return there. To make the world a safe place for her.

They'd only traveled a bit more than ten miles, though, when they spotted a DPI van, and then several other cars with the familiar government emblem on their doors, all parked along the roadside, practically lining the tiny village of Petersville. Men in suits were knocking on doors, talking to people.

"What the hell is this?" Jameson whispered, as he slowed to a crawl, and drove carefully along the town's main street.

"Either they've decided to sell cosmetics as a sideline," Tamara said, "or they're doing a house-to-house search."

"For us?" Angelica asked, eyes widening.

"No." Rhiannon's comment drew all eyes, except for Jameson's. He kept his hopping between the road and the men who had apparently invaded the town. "We've never made a habit of seeking refuge in a mortal household," Rhiannon went on. "What earthly reason would they have to think we'd start now?"

Jameson blinked. In the seat beside him, Angelica drew a trembling breath.

"The baby?" she whispered.

"Perhaps that guard wasn't lying when he said she'd disappeared," Roland offered.

"But that's impossible. Who would take her? And why, for God's sake?" Angelica's voice rose an octave, and Jameson knew panic when he heard it. "What kind of person would steal a baby from a parked car, while its drivers were busy changing a tire? What kind of sick, twisted person would—"

"Angel." Jameson put his hand over hers, closed his around it, felt it trembling. It was odd the way he forgot his anger and frustration with the woman when he saw her upset. "Don't think the worst. We don't even know that's what this is. They might very well be searching for us."

"Keep driving, Jameson. We'll find out what's going on here in short order," Eric said. So Jameson drove. But he couldn't quite bring himself to release his hold on Angelica's hand. Before they got to the edge of town, though, he could see the roadblock set up farther along the road. A battered pickup truck ahead of him was stopped and then searched, its driver questioned.

Jameson looked around for another way out of town, but saw none. Stopping in the middle of the road would draw suspicion, and pulling a U-turn would likely get them all killed.

The hand he still held exerted gentle pressure, and when he looked at Angelica, she was nodding toward an oversize, modern log cabin at the very edge of town. It stood atop a small hill, with a long driveway leading up to it, and seemed set apart from the village proper. "There," Angelica said. "It looks empty. Pull in the driveway and act as if we belong here."

"And what if it's not empty?" Why was it, he wondered, that he felt compelled to disagree with everything she said?

"Look, those scaffolds on the far side. And the roof. It's only partly shingled."

"She's right," Eric put in. "The place is still under construction. Pull in, Jameson, we don't have much of a choice in the matter."

Nodding his agreement, Jameson turned the car into the driveway, drove all the way to the house and then cut the engine. They sat silently at the cabin's feet, an elevated redwood deck stretching out above them.

"It's a beautiful house," Tamara said.

"It's nearly all windows," Rhiannon returned. "Foolish mortals and their damnable love of glass."

"We should go inside." Angelica sent a worried glance at the cars still blocking the road just south of town. "It will look suspicious if we just sit here."

"If we go all at once, and they see us..." Jameson bit his lip, to stop himself from disagreeing with her yet again.

"It's dark, Jameson," Rhiannon pointed out. "The moon is covered by clouds. They can barely see their own noses, let alone count heads from way down there." And since she was sitting beside one of the rear doors she opened it and got out. Roland and Tamara followed, and then Eric got out the passenger side in the front, extending a hand to Angelica. Always the gentleman, Jameson thought rather unkindly. But he got out as well. They trooped around the deck to the broad steps, mounted them, and entered the house from the deck through sliding glass doors. They'd been locked, but mortals had yet to develop a lock that could keep a vampire out.

Inside they were met by a broad cobblestone fireplace, with a glass face, a gleaming hardwood bar, wall-to-wall plush carpeting and a sofa, love seat and chairs that resembled fat brown teddy bears.

"This place is fabulous," Tamara said, sinking into one of the chairs. The thing seemed to hug her. "I wonder if the plumbing is finished? What I wouldn't give for a hot bath about now."

Jameson stiffened. "You won't be staying that long." Tamara lifted her head, and eyebrows at the same time. "What do you mean? We can't very well go on, Jamey, with them blocking the road."

"You know damned well you can," he told her. "You just take to the woods, and skirt around them. Borrow another vehicle south of town and continue from there."

Roland tilted his head to one side. Eric crooked a brow. "What about you?"

"I'm staying," he said. "I'll stick around just long enough to find out what they're looking for. If it isn't my daughter, then I'll move on exactly the way you did."

"And go back to White Plains?" Eric asked.

He only nodded.

Tamara got up, pacing, running her hands over the crocheted afghan that was draped over the back of the sofa. "We'll all stay," she said, though it was obvious she knew he'd argue. "And then we'll leave together."

"Tam—"

"Jameson is right." It was Angelica who spoke, and they all turned to face her, with surprise in their eyes. "You're good friends, but you were already nearly killed in this search. I know you want to help us. But think of what it would do to Jameson if one of you lost your life in the process. Think of how he would feel."

Grating his teeth, Eric nodded. Roland lowered his head. Even Rhiannon seemed resigned.

"There's time enough left tonight for you to get out of here," Jameson said. "I don't want you trapped in this town with DPI agents milling around like flies. I won't be here myself any longer than I have to."

He saw Tamara's eyes moisten. But she nodded. "All right,"

she said. "I...I guess I'd feel the same way if I were in your place."

"You know damn well you would." He turned to Angelica, then, knowing the toughest battle would be this one.

"Don't even suggest it," she said.

He drew a deep breath. "I can find out what we need to know by myself," he said. "There's no need for us both to take the risk. Go with them. Meet me back in White Plains."

"And if Amber Lily is here? What then, Jameson? You might pass by her and not even realize it. No. No, if you want me to leave you'll have to drag me out of here. Otherwise, I'm staying."

"Angelica—"

"I'm her mother," she said, staring at him with so much determination and fire in her eyes that he knew the fight was lost. "I have every right to be here. And here is where I'm staying."

He closed his eyes, lowered his head.

Tamara came to him then, hugged him hard. "I love you, Jamey. Be careful. Please."

He hugged her back. Then said his goodbyes to each of the others. He noticed, not for the first time, that they seemed just as reluctant to leave Angelica as they were to leave him. She had a way about her. Worked right into a person's soul before he knew what the hell had hit him. Obviously, he wasn't the only one so beguiled by her magic.

Finally, the others slipped out the back and vanished into the forest's sheltering arms. Jameson watched them go, and then he paced. He needed a plan. He needed a solid, safe plan whereby he could find out what the hell was going on in this town without being seen. And without putting Angelica in danger.

But he was damned if he could think of any way to do it.

She sat on the sofa, her fingers absently toying with the afghan on its back. And he didn't like looking at her there, because he wanted her so much it was painful.

So he stalked into what would no doubt be the kitchen when finished. It was now no more than stark white wallboard with blotches of spackling compound in regular patterns. A stepladder stood in the room's center, with a painter's apron tossed over one rung.

He turned when Angelica came in behind him, knowing she was there even before he saw her.

"We can't just sit here," she told him. "We have to find out what they're searching for."

"And how do you suggest we do that, Angelica? Walk up to one of them and ask?"

"Not one of them, but one of the residents of the town. It should be a simple enough mission." She had the crocheted throw in her hands now. As he watched, she wrapped it around her like a shawl, complete with a hood that hid her hair.

"You're not going out there," he told her.

"They've seen you a lot more recently than they've seen me, Vampire. In fact, when I was held there, very few people ever saw me. Most of them wouldn't recognize me even without my little disguise. I'll walk back to that little shop we passed, on the pretense of buying something. It will be simple."

"No."

She came closer to him, put her hands on his upper arms. "Jameson, please. We have to do something. I can't just sit here, it's driving me crazy."

Jameson saw the desperation in her eyes. Dammit, he couldn't refuse her when she looked at him that way. What was wrong with him, anyway, that he found even the smudges on her face endearing? He sighed hard. "All right, if you insist on this, then I'll go with you."

She rolled her eyes. "You shouldn't. You'd be too easily recognized, Vampire," she told him. "You told me yourself how often you've dealt with them."

But for once he was ready for her arguments. "I'll follow you. I'll keep to the shadows. No one will see me."

"And if they do, they'll think nothing of some dark stranger stalking a lone woman in the middle of the night," she said.

"My way or no way, Angel. I go with you or you don't go at all."

"While we argue over this, our daughter could be..." She closed her eyes, not finishing. "All right," she said. "You win." And she lifted her head to search his face.

He restrained himself from wiping a smear of dirt from her cheek. It wouldn't be wise to touch her just now, when she was looking so vulnerable...so beautiful. "Go on, got get cleaned up," he told her. "You're sure to attract notice like that."

She looked down at her clothes as if shc'd forgotten the state she was in. "Okay."

He watched her go in search of a bathroom, listened to the sounds she made, the water splashing over her skin. She was quick, back in minutes, looking cleaner, but no less worried.

Not waiting for his permission, she walked past him, going back through the living room to the door they'd entered.

"Wait, Angelica," he said, hurrying after her, putting a hand on her shoulder. "If you're going on the pretense of buying something, you'll need cash. Here." He pressed several bills into her warm hand. Felt it shaking with anticipation of what she was about to learn. "Go slow," he warned, "and keep your head down. Be careful, Angelica. I'll be close by if you need me."

She met his eyes, held them for one long moment, and he thought she might have wanted to say something. But then she seemed to change her mind. She turned, and hurried out the door.

Jameson turned in a slow circle, pushing his hands through his hair. He didn't like what he was feeling. Didn't like it a bit, and didn't want to think about it. Not now, when he had to focus everything in him on finding his daughter. But soon. Soon he was going to have to come to grips with this thing that seemed to have taken possession of his very being.

Soon. Right now, he had an angel to follow.

I knew he'd kept his promise to follow me. I could feel the infuriating man, close to me, wherever I went, though I never once saw him. I glanced behind me often. I felt him close. But he seemed invisible.

The store was not far away. I found it easily, and thanked my stars that it was still open. Though nearly deserted. It seemed most people in this town had taken to their homes early tonight. Likely these troops of inquisitive government agents had frightened them half to death. The place was one large room, cluttered with bric-a-brac and snack foods. A bell over the door tinkled merrily as I stepped in from beneath an old-fashioned red-and-white-striped awning.

"Hello," a friendly, male voice said, and I looked up, startled. But it was only the man who stood behind the counter, and his eyes held no malice. His head was shiny pink, with not a hair to be found, and he wore rectangular bifocals low on his nose. "Can I help you find something?"

"Do you have postcards?" I asked, trying to keep any hint of fear from my voice. The shop smelled of fresh coffee, and peppermint sticks.

"Sure do." He came around the counter and led me to a rotating rack filled to overflowing with scenic postcards. "Lookin' for anything in particular?"

"I'll know it when I see it," I said with a tight-lipped smile. And I began scanning the cards as if in search of just the right one.

"So you're a tourist. Didn't think I recognized you."

"Yes, just passing through." I pulled a card with a photo of trees and mountains and blue sky. "Seems I picked a bad time to visit here," I said. "Judging by the roadblocks and those men roaming the town. Was there a prison break or something nearby?"

The man shook his head, clucking like a hen as I handed him the card and he headed back to the register. "Crying shame, is what it is. What the world's coming to, I'll never know." He punched buttons and the register chimed. The drawer slid open. I handed him a dollar bill.

"What happened?" I ventured.

He shook his head again. "Kidnapping," he said. "Some young couple was traveling just north of town, and had a flat. Got out to change the tire, and when they got back in, their little baby daughter was gone. Someone snatched her, right outta that car."

I lost my breath. My God, could what that guard have said been true? My baby had been stolen from me by DPI, and then stolen from them by…by whom?

"I know," he said, shaking his head. "It's a terrible thing. Can't believe it could happen right here in Petersville. Never had anything like this happen around here before. Goddamn perverts oughtta be shot."

I caught my breath, tried to speak. "What are they doing to find the baby?"

"Well, they've got a roadblock set up south of town. Checking every vehicle that passes. They got search parties goin' through the woods, and more men going door to door askin' questions. Personally, I don't think it's gonna do 'em any good. One of those kind gets hold of a child…well, they rarely find 'em. Alive, anyway."

I braced my hands on the counter to keep my knees from buckling. "Alive?"

"Them kind usually go for the older kids. Can't imagine what they'd want with a little one like that. Sick sons-a-bitches." He dug for change and closed the drawer. "Here you are, miss."

I held out my hand for the chilled coins. "Thank you," I muttered and turned to go.

"Don't forget your postcard," he called, and I turned back again. The card still lay on the counter. I picked it up, but I knew my hands were shaking badly. "You have a nice trip, now," he called as I left the shop. I only nodded, and stepped outside.

Chapter Fourteen

She was shaken. More than shaken, when she came out the door with the bells that chimed with every movement. She stepped under the striped awning onto the broken sidewalk, stood perfectly still for a moment, closing her eyes. And then she shivered visibly, and she turned and she ran.

Jameson was so startled by it that he didn't react at first. Just stood there dumbfounded and watched her go, watched the blanket shawl fly from her shoulders unnoticed as she disappeared, ducking around the corner of a building.

He shook himself and went after her, all thoughts of remaining hidden fleeing his mind. He paused where the blanket had fallen, picked it up and pressed its woolen softness to his hands. Damn. Something was wrong. Whatever she'd learned in that store had hit her hard.

For just a moment he wondered why a more obvious explanation for her flight didn't occur to him. Shouldn't he be assuming she'd run away, not from what she'd heard in the shop, but from him? Shouldn't he be thinking that she'd fled as she'd promised she would, intent on finding his child and taking her far from the reach of a monster like him?

Probably. If he truly believed the things he'd been telling himself about Angelica from the start, he would, no doubt, have been thinking those thoughts. If he'd truly accepted his own rash judgment of the woman—that she saw them all as some lesser species, as animals, saw herself as somehow better than the rest of them, the things he'd been chanting like a mantra in his mind—then he'd have been furious with her right now.

But he wasn't furious. He was worried. And there was, for some reason he could not explain, no question in his mind that she had not run from him. Why?

Because she'd risked her life to save the lives of his dearest friends. To save *his* life. Because he'd seen the way she'd hugged Tamara and the affection in her eyes when she bantered with Rhiannon. Because he'd seen her slowly become aware of her newfound strength, and watched her explore it and test it. Running beside him like a mischievous wood nymph. Leaping to see how high she could go. Reveling in the beauty of the night. Marveling at her psychic powers. Taking on four armed men like a lioness protecting her cub, and frightening one of them nearly to death as she questioned him about her child.

Angelica was none of the things he'd believed her to be. Least of all, selfish. And she would not deny him his child. Not when she knew how much that baby meant to him. And she did know. Because she couldn't help but know. They were connected, the two of them. She felt what he did. And he felt...

He closed his eyes, sought for her with his mind. Anguish! Tears! Sobs that were painful in their intensity. And fear, a sickening, gut-churning fear. Those were what he felt right now, and the sensations came clearly, from her. From Angelica.

Jameson walked to the edge of the building, and looked down the wide lane that ran along its side, twisting up a hill and then vanishing into the forest. She'd gone this way. And he would find her.

She might still detest him. Hell, part of him couldn't even blame her for that. He'd condemned her for a fool from the night he'd taken her from her cell. He'd made her his prisoner, threatened her, and then given in to the physical urges he knew she could not control—because, dammit, he couldn't control them either.

Yes, she probably had more reason than ever to think of him as a monster, and to hate him. But he realized slowly that he'd lied when he'd said he hated her.

He'd never hated her. Not even on that long-ago night when she'd nearly taken his life.

Jameson turned and walked along the road she'd taken, searching for her with his mind. And it wasn't long before he found her.

Just inside the edge of the forest, she lay facedown on the moss-covered ground, her entire body shaking with the force of her sobs. He stood there for a moment, wondering at the pain he felt seeing her like this. Not her pain, though he felt that too. But his own. Why did it tie his stomach in knots to see her crying? Why did his throat close up tight? Why did his eyes burn?

"Angel," he whispered.

She drew a shuddering breath, and pushed herself up on her hands, lifting her head, looking at him. Her face was wet with tears, her eyes swollen and stricken. Some force compelled him to move forward, and he dropped to his knees in front of her, his hands sliding beneath her arms and closing around her as he pulled her tight to his chest. "Angel," he whispered again, though speaking was agony. "Don't cry. Please, it kills me to see you cry." His fingers tangled in her hair, as if of their own will, and he cupped the back of her head. Her damp face pressed to his neck, where his skin absorbed her tears. Her arms encircled his waist.

"It's t-true," she sobbed. "Someone has taken her, Jameson. They don't know who has our baby. They don't know where she is. What if—"

"Shh." He stroked her hair, her shoulders, her back, willing the spasms to stop wreaking havoc on her slender body. "She's away from them, Angel. She's away from DPI. They can't hurt her now."

"But what kind of person would take her? What if it's some horrible, demented—"

"No." He clasped her shoulders and set her away from him, just a little. Just enough so he could look into her eyes as he spoke to her, enough so she could see the conviction in his eyes. "You'd feel it if she were in pain or distress. You know you would. And you don't. You don't.''

She blinked at the tears that pooled in her amethyst eyes, and stared so deeply into his that he felt she could see everything he'd ever been, or ever would be. "No," she said softly. "No, I don't."

"Then she's safe. We have to believe that, Angel. She's safe for now. And away from those bastards who held her. We'll find her before they do. I swear to Christ, Angel, we'll find our daughter.''

He saw her lips tremble, and impulsively he pressed his lips to them, his only thoughts at that moment of stilling their tremors. Of soothing and calming this woman. He tasted her tears. When he lifted his head away, she searched his face.

"I'm so afraid for her, Jameson."

"I know. I am, too." He forced himself to let his arms fall away from her. Because he knew that in a few more moments, he wouldn't be able to.

"No," she said. Jameson looked at her, let her see his confusion. "I need..." she began, but her voice trailed into silence.

"What, Angel?"

"You. Your strength. Please, just hold me. Don't let me go, not now. I've never felt so alone. I've never needed this way before, and I can't...''

He'd sworn he'd refuse her the next time she came to him this way. He'd sworn...ah, but he'd been a fool. He could never refuse her. If she came to him a million times, he'd accept her a million times. He...

No. It wasn't that.

He pulled her into his arms again, holding her close, and she clung to him as if she'd shatter should he let her go. She turned her face up to his, and he kissed her. No questions, no worrying over the repercussions. The guilt she'd feel when it was over. The revulsion that would swamp her when she realized that she'd given herself, once again, to a man she despised. It would come. He didn't doubt that. But he didn't care. She needed him. She'd said so. And Jameson needed her, right now, too. She was the only person in the world who truly understood his anguish over their missing daughter. The only one who could. It was the one thing they shared, this agony. And it seemed only fitting they share the comforting as well.

He kissed her, and her lips parted when he nudged them with his tongue. He tasted her mouth, knew its sweetness was his addiction. He'd never get enough of this...never get enough of her. Her hands became feverish, tugging his shirt open, tearing its buttons and scattering them on the forest floor. And then her mouth drew away from his, and she kissed his neck, and his chest, and his belly as he knelt there in the pine needles. Each touch of her mouth on his skin made him tremble, and he reached down to grip her tattered dress by the hem, and pulled it over her head.

Her naked breasts tantalized him, rubbing against his chest as she kissed his lips once more, their nipples hardening and pressing into him. His hands on her shoulders, he pushed her backward, until she lay down, and then he fell on her, feeding on her breasts like a man possessed. He suckled her hard, fiercely, bit at those distended nipples while her hands clasped his head to her.

This was madness. Sheer madness. But he couldn't fight it. Didn't want to fight it.

He rose, and pulled her to her feet. And then giving a gentle shove, he pressed her back against the stringy trunk of a pine. She stood braced there, panting, eyes half-closed, lips wet from his kisses, nipples erect and pulsing. And he released the button and the zipper on his jeans, and pushed them down until he could step out of them. Then he knelt, and kissed the sable curls between her legs. His tongue slipped between her lips, tasting the salty moistness there, and she gasped. He pressed his hands to her thighs, parting them, and then he pushed his face into her, licking up inside her, growing more frenzied with each taste of her, and driving deeper with his tongue. To devour her wasn't enough, though he tried. He used his teeth and his mouth, heard her cries and felt her hands tugging at his hair.

And then he rose once more, sliding his mouth up over her

belly, tasting her breasts on the way, and then taking her mouth again, holding her to the tree with his body while his hands worked to make her as crazy for him as he was for her.

"Take me, Vampire," she whispered and she laid her head back against the pine, tilting her chin up and offering her luscious throat. Offering him everything. All of her. "Make it good. Make me forget..."

Gripping the back of her thighs and lifting, parting, he plunged himself inside her. She cried out in pleasure, and he thrust deeper, withdrawing and sinking himself to the root again and again. He felt her body responding, felt the tightening around him. Her hands at the back of his head again, guiding his mouth to her throat. "Do it," she moaned. And he did. He opened his mouth over her soft flesh, and then he bit down, piercing her skin, and then her jugular. He thrust his hips forward, burying himself inside her even as he was drinking from her. And when she came, every part of her vibrated. Her legs locked around his waist and jerked tight, pulling him deeper. Her head tipped back farther pressing his fangs more deeply into her throat. Her back arched as she pressed herself open to take him all the way. Her arms clenched around him, and she screamed. His seed shot into her, and he held her there to receive it. All of it. And then he held her still longer, until the madness receded, and his body relaxed, and they sank to the ground as one.

And he didn't want it to be over. He wasn't ready for her guilt and revulsion. Her hatred of him and his kind. As he held her, he caught her chin, tipped her head up, and he lowered his, and he kissed her. Their passion was spent, and they were, for the moment at least, sated. Even drowsy. But he kissed her all the same. And it was a tender kiss, long and slow and gentle.

When he lifted his head, she opened her eyes, searching his face, her expression one of confusion.

"You're not my prisoner, Angelica. You never really were," he told her. "Whenever you feel you want to strike out on your own, you're free to go."

"I don't want to leave you," she whispered, and for just an

instant, there was something in her eyes that took his breath away. "Not ev..." She bit her lip, averted her gaze. "Not until we find Amber Lily."

He only nodded. And then he released her, though to his surprise she seemed in no hurry for him to do so. He got to his feet and gathered up their clothes. And before he put his on, he went to her with the poor misused dress that had seen better days. And he slipped it over her head, and gently helped her put her arms through the sleeves, relishing every instant he could spend touching her.

She sat there on the ground, staring up at him, watching as he put his own clothes on. And she said, "I've been so wrong... about...so many things."

He didn't want to misunderstand her. He didn't dare jump to conclusions, because it would destroy him. "About what, Angelica?"

She closed her eyes. The breeze came very gently, lifting her hair, making it dance. And then her head came up, and her eyes opened wide. "Listen," she said.

Frowning, Jameson listened. But he didn't hear a thing, apart from the usual myriad forest sounds. "What is it, Angel?"

"Don't you hear them?" She tilted her head. "Bells, Vampire. Church bells."

He felt a little shiver race up his spine, because there were no bells. My God, had his poor dark Angel been pushed too far? Had she slipped over the edge, to the black bottomless pit of insanity?

"Angel," he whispered, taking her hand. But she was already getting to her feet, turning toward her imaginary sound, looking as if she were mesmerized or worse. And she started walking.

"Angel, wait. Where are you going?"

"To church," she whispered, and then she turned to face him, her eyes perfectly sane. "It's been too long, Jameson. I accused God of turning His back on me, but I was wrong. I was the one who turned my back on Him. Don't you see? Hilary...she made it all so clear to me. When she was dying there in the woods...she told me God was still with me, guiding my steps. She told me that He would help her keep her promise, to watch over Amber Lily until she was safe in our arms again. And now...now those bells.''

He saw the relief in her eyes, wished to Christ these imaginary bells of hers were real.

"It has to mean something, Jameson. It has to. I'm not damned by God. I might have come close to damning myself by believing it, but not anymore. It's going to be all right.''

"Yes," he told her. "It is. I promise.''

She touched his face. "Come with me.''

And he nodded, because he didn't have the heart to tell her she was imagining things. She took his hand, and started walking through the pines, higher and higher up a thickly forested slope. And then the wind picked up, just briefly, and for the slightest instant, Jameson thought he heard...bells.

I followed the sound of those bells, because I felt as if I had to. I had to go into the house of God, and fall to my knees, and tell Him that I was sorry. That I understood now. All that had happened to me had happened for a reason, and who was I to pretend to know why? I didn't know. I only knew God still had a plan for me. I wasn't estranged from Him at all. I'd only thought I was.

When we reached the top of the hill, I heard the vampire mutter under his breath. The bells had stopped now, but I no longer needed them. The tiny chapel sat alone amid the deep green pines. We'd come to it through the forest, but I saw the narrow, winding road that led to it from the town below. Its spire was nothing spectacular. Plain glass, rather than brilliantly stained panes filled its windows. A small red door stood at the front.

I sighed in relief, feeling as if I'd come home. And I climbed the steps. Jameson came along beside me, clinging to my hand, searching my face often. The door was unlocked as I'd known it would be.

The place was filled with yellow candlelight that danced and flickered on the hard wooden pews, and on the altar. A single worshiper sat there. A woman, who sat in the front pew, rocking the baby carriage she'd parked before her. And I recognized her.

"Look," I whispered to Jameson. "It's her."

He nodded. "Yeah, the woman who had the car accident."

"The one whose child you risked your life to save," I said, and I squeezed his hand.

I moved on past. Jameson sat down in the front pew, and let me go forward on my own. And I did. I crossed myself and knelt before the wooden crucifix that stood alone on the altar, and in silence there, I prayed.

Jameson watched Angelica kneeling there. She seemed so serene, all of the sudden. And he knew this meant a lot to her, to make her peace with God. He sat beside the woman whose name he didn't recall, and she looked up at him. Her eyes widened and then she smiled.

"You!" she whispered to him.

"Yes. Quite a coincidence, isn't it? How is the little one?"

"Alicia is fine," the woman whispered, but she was shaking her head.

Jameson frowned, sensing her turmoil. "Is something wrong?"

"No. No, not wrong. Just...so many odd happenings. Seeing you again is the least of them, I suppose." She closed her eyes. "Two miracles, in such a short space of time. First you and that...that beautiful girl, saving my baby from the car. And then..."

He tilted his head. She rocked the baby carriage that sat in front of her gently. "And then?"

"And then...I don't know, exactly. But I think I was visited by an angel."

Lord, but why must religion make so many people so very crazy? he wondered.

"She was beautiful, too. A dark-skinned angel, with the kindest brown eyes I'd ever seen. All dressed in white, and sort of...sort of glowing."

Jameson saw Angelica stiffen. But she didn't turn around. Just knelt there, rigid, listening.

"And...what did this *angel* want?" he asked.

"It was incredible." The woman shook her blond head. "She said I owed a debt. That my baby had been saved for me, and that now I must save someone else's. She had a little girl in her arms. A newborn. And she just handed her to me, and said that I should keep her safe, until her mother came for her."

A soft, wounded cry was wrung from Angelica. She stood up, turned slowly. And her eyes were so wide, and so hopeful that he thought he would probably wring this woman's neck if she were making up stories.

"The angel said," the woman went on, her words coming slowly now as she met and held Angelica's eyes, "she said I'd know her when I saw her." And then she smiled. "It's you, isn't it?"

But Angelica couldn't seem to speak. Her lips parted, but no sound came out. Big fat tears filled her eyes and spilled over.

"Yes," Jameson said. "If you've found a missing baby, she's ours. Please..."

"Something told me to come here. Just come to church, and wait. And sure enough..." She shook her head again, getting up, bending over the carriage, and pulling the blankets away.

Jameson looked. Angelica didn't. She stood rooted where she was, almost as if she were afraid to look. Afraid to see that her baby daughter wasn't there.

The fat-cheeked, carrot-topped baby, Alicia, lay sound asleep in the carriage. And tucked close beside her, a tinier infant, with raven's-wing curls, and wide ebony eyes that stared right up at him.

And his heart seemed to swell until he thought it would burst. He bent over that carriage, reaching his big hands down to gather up the fragile bundle. He gathered her close, very close, and he closed his eyes and held her to him.

"Amber Lily," he breathed, because he couldn't seem to speak any louder than that. His face was wet. And he opened his eyes again, and lifted his head, and saw Angelica standing there, blinking and dazed, her beautiful violet eyes fixed on the child. She drew a gulp of air, and blinked, and fell to the floor. Her legs seemed to melt into puddles beneath her.

Jameson moved closer to her, and knelt down. And then he very gently eased his daughter into her mother's arms. Angelica's entire body shook, and she was smiling and crying and trembling all at once. She bent to kiss the baby's forehead, and a tiny hand clutched a handful of Angel's hair, and tugged.

Angelica looked up at him from watery eyes. And he knew, right then, that he loved her. He loved her. And he loved the child they'd created together. And he always would. No matter what. And part of him, a very large part of him, wanted to bundle the two of them up in his arms, and run away to a secluded cabin somewhere, and just live there in ecstasy forever.

But there was another part of him that knew that was impossible. And not only because Angelica could never feel for him what he felt for her. But because there would be no peace, no happiness for her, or for her child, until DPI was annihilated.

No one else would do it, he thought, and as he looked at the woman he loved cradling his daughter in her arms, he knew why. No one else had as much reason.

He reached forward, stroked his hand slowly over Angelica's tearstained cheek. "Wait here, Angel," he told her. "I'll go back into town and get the car, and then we'll make our way out of here."

"Yes." She didn't look at him as she spoke. Her eyes were only on her daughter, and so filled with love he thought he would die from the sheer beauty of it.

He bent to kiss his child, and then turned and hurried out of the chapel. He took only enough time to be sure no one was around, and that no one noticed him cutting through the woods that lay along the back of the town, angling down so he emerged on the hillside just beyond the vacant cabin where he'd left the car.

He hurried now. Got into the car, and backed down the long driveway, cutting around into the narrow road, shifting into drive. He didn't speed through town. That would be asking for notice.

Although, now that he was back, he didn't see the official-looking cars and vans lining the streets as he had before. And there were no men in dark suits or trench coats knocking on doors or questioning passersby, either.

What the hell was going on? They couldn't have given up, could they? Not so soon...

A tiny shiver of apprehension raced up his spine as he turned the car easily onto the well-worn dirt road that would take him back to the chapel on the hillside.

And that was when heard Angelica screaming.

It wasn't with his ears that he heard her cries. It was in his mind. And it wasn't the telepathy coming into play. She wasn't speaking to him directly or deliberately. But she was horribly afraid...or in pain. Or both.

And then her cries stopped and Jameson heard nothing at all. He pushed the accelerator to the floor, his wheels churning up clouds of dust as he sped over the narrow road. He took hairpin curves far too fast, nearly fishtailing out of control and jerking hard on the steering wheel to right himself again. But he never slowed down, and he never lost the horrible, gut-wrenching feeling that he shouldn't have left them. Angel and Amber. He shouldn't have left them even for a minute.

The sky glowed up ahead. Black smoke billowed up into the clouds like the breath of the devil. He careened around a corner and skidded to a stop in front of the church, but it wasn't a church any longer. It was a nightmare. The tiny building was nearly burned to the ground already. Nothing identifiable remained. It was just a misshapen mass of fire and smoke, a heap of flaming rubble.

He wrenched his door open and got out, running forward, shielding his face with a bent arm when he felt his flesh start to blister.

"Come back," a voice cried, barely audible over the roar of the flames. "You're too close."

His mind was numb, his body chilled to the core, despite the heat. He turned and saw the blond woman, cradling her child in her arms and sobbing, stretching one hand out toward him. And he went to her, shaking his head, demanding answers.

"Angelica! My daughter, where are they!"

But the woman only sobbed and shook her head.

He stopped when he stood right in front of her. "What the hell happened here, woman! Tell me, dammit!"

"I don't know," she said, her words broken and weak. "I'd just left, when the place...it was like a bomb went off inside! God, it was terrible. Terrible!"

No. No, his mind whispered. "Angelica and the baby were still inside?" Turning, he started toward the burning ruin once more, but her hand gripped his arm, stopping him.

"They never had a chance, God bless them. I'm so sorry."

"No!" He stared at the fire, the pile of debris, and he knew that if they had been inside when the explosion had happened, they were dead now. Both of them. Dead. Burning-hot tears blinded him. He clenched his fists. "No," he yelled again, and then he tipped back his head and howled in anguish and grief and helpless fury. And his preternatural voice rose into the night like a cry to the heavens, and its power reverberated through the skies and the forest, causing the towering pines to tremble.

They heard an odd cry that night in the town of Petersville. One so loud and anguished that it rolled like thunder, and echoed endlessly as it faded away. It was a blood-chilling kind of a sound. The kind of thing that could break a heart and give a man goose bumps all at the same time. Some said it was the cry of a wounded beast of some kind, though none speculated too loudly on what sort of beast could make a sound like that one. But most were of the opinion that they'd heard the voice of the devil himself.

Chapter Fifteen

My daughter was beautiful. And healthy.

And mortal.

I wasn't so overwhelmed that I didn't understand what it meant when the woman, Susan her name was, told me how good Amber Lily had been about sleeping the night through. And about her healthy appetite. She'd been feeding my daughter the same formula she fed to her own. And she claimed Amber Lily had gained two pounds already, and that her hair was getting curlier all the time.

She was mortal. She was growing and changing like a mortal child would do. I didn't know what vampiric traits she might have inherited from me, if any. But I was so relieved to know she needn't feed the way her parents must, and that she would not be trapped for eternity inside the body of a newborn. And those things alone gave me hope.

Things were going to be all right. Finally, at long last, everything was going to be fine. I couldn't wait for Jameson to come back so that I could tell him.

Susan, the woman I knew I'd never be able to repay, said she had to get her own child back home now, and gave me her good wishes.

"Thank you," I said to her. "It's not enough, but—"

"There's no need," she said, and she looked deeply into my eyes. "We're even now."

I nodded, and I know my smile was bright as I held Amber Lily in my arms, and she squirmed and kicked.

I watched Susan and Alicia go. It was only as the door closed behind them that I felt the presence. And I whirled, to see several men coming into the tiny chapel, invading its sanctity, from a rear entrance.

"Don't move," one said, and he held a rifle. "Don't even wiggle. My sights are on the baby, and if you so much as twitch I'll blow her right in half. We're through playing games with you, lady."

I didn't move. I couldn't, because I knew he wasn't lying. He'd kill my child without a second thought. The pig!

The others closed in around me, and then one jabbed me with a needle and I felt myself weakening. It was only when a third took my daughter from my arms that I panicked. But I needn't. Jameson would come, he would come for us!

They half dragged, half carried me out the back door as the drug quickly did its work, turning my body into a disobedient mass of limp flesh. Hurry, Jameson, I thought. He would come, and he would know what had happened. He would know we'd been taken. He would know where to look for us.

They tossed me into the back seat of a car, and then one of them turned and glanced down at his watch. He stood there, waiting, and I frowned.

And then the chapel exploded in a white-hot blast that shook the ground beneath the car. I cried out, horrified, wondering if Susan and little Alicia had gotten far enough away to be safe before it had happened. And then the man smiled and got behind the wheel, and I knew. I knew what they intended. For Jameson to believe we were dead, killed in that chapel. So he'd never look any further for us. And as long as they kept me drugged, I thought, slipping closer and closer to that horrible black sleep this drug would induce, I'd be unable to tell him any differently. Two men were in the front of the car, and two others came around to get into the back, with me. One of them was holding my daughter.

Barely able to move, I nonetheless managed to push one of my shoes off my heel until it dangled on my toe. As the man bent to get into the car, I let the shoe fall to the ground. And then he shut the door, and the car pulled away. I kept my gaze on my baby's wide ebony eyes, until I couldn't do so any longer.

He sat there on the ground, and eventually the woman left. And other mortals showed up. A shiny red fire truck with local men manning hoses that soaked the blazing wreckage and turned it to a pile of smoldering blackened beams and charred ground and piles of ash. He sat there, never moving. And he wouldn't, he wouldn't move, not ever again. He'd sit there until the sun rose, and he'd greet it with gratitude.

He'd lost them. Lost them both. And dammit, he'd barely had a chance to know his child!

But he'd known Angelica. Known her laughter, the light in her violet eyes. He'd known her touch. He'd loved her. Dammit, he'd loved her with everything in him, and he'd never even told her.

How could she be gone so suddenly? Torn from him without warning. How?

And why for the love of Christ?

"Son, why don't you let the medics have a look at you?"

"His wife and baby were in that church," said another strange voice. "So someone said, anyway."

"Merciful heavens, no wonder he looks like that!"

"Think he can hear us?"

"No. I'm afraid the man's gone plumb out of his mind."

"Son, come on. Get up, now."

He didn't speak, but he did rise. He didn't want to be bothered by the well-meaning mortals. He wanted to go away and be alone and remember her while he awaited the dawn. His feet scuffed the ground as he wandered away from all of them, heading around the wreckage that used to be the chapel, circling it like a planet circling the sun. It was as if some force pulled at him, and kept him from leaving this orbit. His heart...his heart was in that mess of rubble. His soul. His child....

Or...*was she?*

DPI had called Amber their most valuable research subject ever. Would they really have destroyed her?

"No...."

He tripped over something, and he glanced down at it, irritated. "Oh, Jesus," he whispered, because the pain that came then was almost more than he could bear. "Oh sweet Jesus, it's Angelica's shoe." He dropped to his knees, and scooped it up as carefully as if he were handling a fragile treasure, and then he hugged it to his chest, and let the tears come. His back bowed with them, and he choked on powerful sobs that nearly split him in half. Because he knew that while DPI might balk at murdering Amber Lily, they wouldn't have hesitated to kill her mother. Angelica. And he didn't think he could go on without her—and yet he had to find a way. For their baby.

When he grew too weak to remain sitting up, he fell, facedown on the dusty road, and his bitter tears wet the tire tracks in the dust, and he couldn't breathe, and he didn't care.

It came to him slowly. Very slowly. But when it did, it was enough to stir him out of the well of mindless agony. Enough to make him reach, one last time, for cognizance, and perhaps... perhaps hope. He pushed himself into a sitting position again with one hand, and stared at the shoe in his other. It wasn't burned. Wasn't even singed. Or torn or damaged.

He turned his head, and saw that there was a hell of a lot of distance between the wet, smoke-belching remains of the church and this spot. And as he examined the ground here, he saw no other debris. Nothing else was thrown this far in the explosion. And the tire tracks...

This was the area in back of the chapel. And, yes, the small dirt driveway circled around behind the building, but all the townsfolk had stopped out front. None had driven back here.

Jameson got to his feet, and scanned the ground, walking slowly toward the church. And sure as all hell, he found footprints. Men's shoes. Several men. And the uneven marks between them that suggested something being dragged. Or someone.

"She's alive," he whispered. He held the shoe tight in one hand, and fell to his knees right where he stood. He bowed his head, closed his eyes. "She's alive...she has to be. Thank God," he whispered.

Jameson stood alone just outside the fenced-in perimeter of DPI headquarters in White Plains. Angelica was inside. He knew it as well as he knew his own name. And things were ready. He'd met with the others just north of the city, and explained all that had happened. Tamara had contacted Susan Jennings, and offered her more money than she'd ever seen in her life to come back with them, and care for Amber by day. No one had explained why it was necessary. She hadn't asked. Jameson trusted her.

He'd had his short, precious time with his sweet, wonderful daughter. And now it was over. He'd get no more time with her. But he'd save her from these bastards. And then he'd make sure she never had to worry about this damnable persecution from them again. He'd bring this place to ruin...tonight. He'd make the world safe for her. And he would very likely die in the process, but not until he'd accomplished what he'd come here to do. And it would be well worth the sacrifice. He'd see to it that Angel and Amber had the life they deserved. And to hell with the consequences. They were worth this, worth anything to him.

He leaped the fence, and started forward. He'd do this, because it needed doing. And he'd do it alone.

And then he stopped, because someone had hit the ground beside him. "Not alone!" a voice called, and Jameson turned in surprise. Eric stood at his side. He smiled and winked. "Not by a long shot, my friend."

And even before he finished speaking, others came forward, stepping out of the shadows one by one, to stand beside him. Tamara was there, and Roland and Rhiannon. Even Rhiannon's cat had joined them. And there were others. One in particular. A man who seemed as though he must be a king.

He was taller than anyone there, and darker, too, with huge, haunting eyes and a voice like thunder. "I am Damien," he said, extending a hand to Jameson. And Jameson blinked in shock as he took it. This was the oldest...the first, of all of them. "And I'm grateful to you for stirring us to action."

"But I didn't..." he began.

"No. No, your Angelica did. But on your behalf."

Jameson turned toward the building that held her, dumbfounded.

"Seems she finally mastered those psychic skills," Rhiannon said softly. "And though weakened and drugged, she managed to call out to us. She knew you would come, Jameson. And she begged us not to let you do this on your own. She said she'd rather die here than to know you'd given your life attempting to save her."

"She told us what you intended to do tonight, shamed us, really, for not being here to back you up," Damien added. "So here we are." He nodded to the people who surrounded him, vampires, all of them. "My bride, Shannon. Former DPI agent Ramsey Bachman and his wife, Cuyler Jade. And every other vampire who was within range of Angelica's rousing mental wake-up call." He put a hand on Jameson's shoulder. "We're in this together," he said. "Your Amber Lily is not just your child, Jameson. She is our child, our miracle, the first of a new generation, be she mortal or otherwise. And she is going to be the most cherished being we've ever had the privilege to love."

"You'll need help caring for her," the pixielike woman named Cuyler Jade said softly. "It will be difficult, sleeping by day. But there is a place, far to the north, where darkness lasts so very much longer than light for part of the year. And I want you to take your child there, so that she, and not the sun, can decide when you should sleep."

"Yes," the man beside her said. "And we should establish another home in the southern reaches, for the other part of the year."

"We'll all help you," the pixie said.

Eric nodded. "For now, we have a warm, safe haven waiting,

and Susan, your mortal friend, is there, ready to care for Amber through the daylight hours."

Jameson nodded, seeing now that this thing was possible. That everything would be taken care of for Angel and the baby. "You might end up taking them there yourself, Eric. I have no intention of leaving this place until all that remains is rubble."

"That's understood," Eric told him, and he glanced sideways at Damien.

Damien nodded. "It needs doing. We all know it, and we're here to see that it's done."

Jameson looked up and down the length of the mesh fence, blinking in wonder. There were hundreds, perhaps a thousand of them. And before his eyes, they began linking arms, all the way around the building. A chain of the living dead, moving slowly forward, intent on reclaiming their right to exist.

Jameson focused his mind on Angelica's as he began to move along with them. And a hand closed around his left one, and another around his right. As one living wall of justice, they closed in on the heart of their persecutors.

I did not know whether my pleas had been heard by any others. But I knew Jameson was coming. I sensed it with everything in me. My efforts at contacting others, begging them to help him tonight, combined with the effects of the drug, left me weak, and barely conscious. I'd hoped to have enough strength left to contact Jameson...to tell him the enormity of what I now realized I felt for him, just in case it was the last chance I had. But I had no power left in me. I was conscious, barely conscious. But I was alert enough to know that night was nearly over. Dawn would come within the hour. Jameson might well be overwhelmed by the sun before the DPI forces could murder him. The odds against his success were staggering. And yet I prayed, with everything in me, that God would protect him, and protect my daughter. For I loved them both with every cell in my body.

They hadn't had us here for very long at all. Amber and I had been sealed in a cell in one of the lower levels, while guards stood outside our impenetrable door, awaiting their leader's arrival, and his orders. I wondered what those orders would be. How would they attempt to kill me this time, and what would become of my precious little girl?

They'd left me unchained, apparently confident that I was too groggy to cause them any trouble. I sat on the floor in the corner and hugged her close, and I sang to her as I had done in those lonely months before her birth. And she smiled. She smiled at me as I sang.

It was not pretty, but Jameson had known it wouldn't be. It was war, and needed to be treated as such. These people were intent on murdering his own. As soon as they were sighted, guards emerged, armed guards firing weapons filled with conventional bullets for the most part, though a few managed to get their hands on the dreaded tranquilizer guns as well. But they really didn't stand a chance against so many.

They were immortal. They could move faster than the human eye could see, becoming blurs of shapeless color in motion. They could leap out of the paths of the bullets fired at them, and with a single swipe of a single preternatural hand, render the shooter unconscious. Or worse.

And Damien...

Jameson paused only once to witness in stunned awe the sheer power of the oldest of all immortals. The way he would focus those intent eyes on something until it burst into flames. The way he could whirl until he vanished in the night.

But even the wonder of seeing firsthand the legendary abilities of the man couldn't distract him for more than an instant. The first lines of defense were nearly broken, and Jameson was the first vampire to cross them, smashing a door from its hinges in his rage, and lunging inside.

Those who approached him found themselves sailing bodily through the air, crashing into walls and sliding to the floor, bloodied and immobile. Someone yelled from behind, and he whirled, only to see Pandora's sleek black form spring upon a guard who'd been about to shoot him in the back.

The guard's cry was chilling, but brief.

All around Jameson people were shouting, guns were going off, explosions were rocking the ground. He made his way to the back, fighting through the armed men who rushed forward to join the battle. And then through the others, the cowards, who knew what was happening—who had, perhaps, known all along that this day of reckoning would come—and whose only goal now was escape. Like rats fleeing a burning ship they raced for the rear exits. Jameson passed the research lab just as its barred windows were smashed to bits, and hordes of vampires surged inside, intent on destroying every trace of information these bastards had gathered. He heard the computers being hurled to the floor, smelled the smoke as the files were set aflame. But he didn't stop. He kept moving onward, finding the stairs, not trusting the elevators. And his instincts were good, because halfway down, the lights went out. Someone was using his head. Vampires could see perfectly in the dark. Humans, on the other hand...

He collared a white-coated fool who was whimpering for mercy, and slammed him against the wall. "Where are they?" And when the man didn't answer he slammed him again, and his wire-rimmed glasses fell to the floor.

"D-d-d-down...th-that way...p-p-please—"

Jameson released the man, and raced in the direction he'd pointed. And then he skidded to a stop in the dark, cold hall of the lower level. Because...he heard her.

She was singing. Her voice was wavering, weak...but she was singing, and it was the most beautiful sound he'd ever heard in his life.

"Angel..." His knees nearly buckled in relief, but he forced them steady and ran to the door that was all that remained between them. And growling with the effort, he tore the thing away and hurled it back down the hall.

She sat there, on the floor, and she lifted her head, met his eyes. "You came," she whispered, and tears flooded her face.

"You knew I would," he said, and he ran forward, fell to his knees, his hands cupping her head, his eyes searching her face.

"Are you all right? Tell me you're all right, Angel, because I can't quite believe—"

"I'm all right. It's...the drug. That's all."

He closed his eyes in relief, then opened them again when a small hand smacked him in the chin, and looked down at his child, warm and safe in her mother's arms. "And you're all right, too, aren't you, my love?"

She cooed and chirped at him like a small bird just testing its voice.

"She's more than all right," Angelica whispered. "She's mortal, Jameson. She eats and sleeps and grows...just like any other child."

"Not like any other child," he told her. "No, not my Amber. She's far from normal. She's the daughter of an Angel."

He leaned forward, pressed his lips to Angelica's and saw her close her eyes and absorb his kiss. And when he straightened, he slipped his arms beneath her and scooped her up. "Hold Amber Lily tight, sweet Angel. I'm taking the two of you out of here."

She blinked up at him. "Yes...but Jameson, there are others. Other prisoners, suffering here, and I—"

"That, my dear, is being taken care of," said a regal, familiar voice from near the doorway. He turned with Angelica in his arms, to see Rhiannon, her cat at her side, and a barely conscious, reed-thin vampire in her arms. "Now come, I want that precious little one out of all this."

Jameson hurried forward, and made his way to the stairs again. He carried Angelica up them, back through to the front entrance, dodging smoke and fires and debris, but very few bullets now. This battle was already waning. He raced outside, carried Angelica and Amber Lily to the mesh fence and lowered them to the ground in the shelter of some bushes near it.

He straightened, looking back toward the building.

Angelica grabbed his arm. "You're not going back."

"I have to."

"You could be killed," she cried.

And he stared down into her eyes. "It doesn't matter now. You and the baby are safe. It doesn't matter."

"No, Jameson. I'm not going to let you go back there. It does matter, don't you see? It matters more than ever."

He looked down at her, frowning, saw fresh tears brimming in her eyes. "But—"

"But nothing. Dammit, Vampire, if I've only survived all of this to lose you now…" Her voice trailed off and she bit her lip.

Jameson's heart leaped, but he didn't dare think…no, she was drugged and grateful and overwhelmed. "Angelica," he said, kneeling beside her. "You and Amber Lily are safe now. And free. And I've got no more excuses to coerce you into staying with me, the way I've been doing for the past few days. You…" He sighed hard. "You can go, if you want to. But Angel, I don't…I don't think I want to live long enough to hear you say goodbye."

"You're immortal," she said softly. "And even with that, you'll never live that long."

He looked down at her. "What are you saying, Angel?"

"I'm saying that I love you, Jameson." She stared up at him through her tears. "I love you."

He blinked down at her, his jaw dropping, his heart squeezing into a knot. "Angelica…" He couldn't go on, couldn't speak.

She lowered her head. "I was hoping…you might feel something for me, too. Maybe…maybe I was wrong.…"

Jameson gathered her into his arms, with their daughter between them, and lowered his head and kissed her deeply and passionately, as his heart swelled to bursting.

He lifted his head away. "I've loved you all along, Angel. Even that first night, I felt something…something I couldn't explain. I told myself I hated you, but I didn't. I couldn't. You…you're everything to me, Angel. Everything."

She smiled weakly, and he kissed her again. He held her there, in his arms, and he caressed her face, and reveled in her closeness, her love. And as they embraced, the others surged out of the building, crowds of them, all that had gone inside and still more. Other captives, free now, some weak, some near death, but all rejoicing. And when everyone was safely outside, Damien stepped forward, focusing his gaze on the building before them for long, tense moments. And suddenly, it exploded in a blinding ball of energy. Every brick crumbled. The percussion rocked the ground, and the flames lit the night like a torch of hope. A deafening roar of triumph went up from the crowd of vampires.

Epilogue

No one would have guessed that most of the adult chaperons at the junior prom were vampires.

Jameson held his wife pressed close to him in his arms. They swayed slowly in time to the music played by suited youths on the stage in the center of the decorated gymnasium. He and Angelica lingered in the shadows, as did most of their friends. Rhiannon and Roland sat at a candlelit table, watching the festivities. Eric and Tamara were dancing near the rear exit. It wouldn't do to draw too much attention to themselves. They'd promised their little girl they wouldn't, after all. And besides, this was her night.

"Go ahead," said a young man several yards away to another one who stood nervously beside him. "Ask her."

"No way. She'll shoot me down and I'll have to go jump off a bridge."

"Maybe she'll say yes," said the first.

Both of them were watching the most strikingly beautiful girl at the prom. She was tall and slender, with hair as black as a raven's wings that danced around her waist when she moved. And haunting ebony eyes that seemed to hold countless secrets. She stood near the punch bowl with her best friend in the world, Alicia. Both of them swaying a little in time to the music.

Clearing his throat, the nervous teenage boy approached her. "Hi, Amber," he said.

And she smiled. "Hi, Jimmy."

"Would you...um...would you like to dance?"

"I'd love to."

The boy's face split in a delighted smile, and he took her into his arms.

Amber looked across the dance floor and caught her father's eye. *I love you, Daddy.*

I love you, too, Amber Lily. He sent his thoughts out to his daughter without a word, and then added a wink. *Just see the young man doesn't hold you too close.*

Amber smiled and rolled her eyes ceilingward as her partner whirled her around the floor.

"Have we done it, do you think?" Jameson asked his Angel, pulling her still closer, nuzzling her ear with his lips.

"Made her happy? Yes, Jameson. I think we have."

"Maybe we shouldn't have come," he said. "Maybe we're overprotective."

"She doesn't mind at all," Angelica whispered. "She loves us, Jameson. Don't you know that?"

He nodded thoughtfully, but still feared he might have offended his daughter by volunteering to chaperon her prom. He loved her so much, it was hard to know when he was overstepping, and when he was only being reasonable. "She's so beautiful," he said. Then he bent lower, and kissed the neck that so tempted him. "Like her mother."

"And every bit as stubborn as her father," she replied.

Frowning, Jameson glanced back at the dance floor. "So what do you think of this Jimmy?"

"I think he's cute."

He grumbled, and Angel kissed his nose.

"I also think we should let Amber Lily decide about Jimmy. She's inherited her father's brains, as well, you know."

Jameson closed his eyes and sighed. "She's really all right."

"You still having trouble believing it?" she asked him. "Even after you made Eric repeat those blood tests five times to be sure? The belladonna antigen is different in her,'' she reminded him, repeating what Eric's tests had proven time and time again. ''The gene that causes premature death in mortals who have the antigen is missing.''

He nodded. ''And yet she has psychic powers as strong as ours—and her physical strength is getting more amazing every day.''

''Rhiannon likes to think she inherited her preternatural abilities from her aunt, the princess,'' Angelica mused.

''It's a miracle,'' he said. ''*She's* a miracle.'' He smiled and looked into her eyes. ''Have I told you lately, my Angel, how very much I adore you?''

''Yes,'' she said. ''But feel free to tell me again.''

Just as he was about to kiss her, he felt a tap on his shoulder, and turned to see his little girl holding hands with her young man.

He straightened up, clearing his throat.

''Dad, Mom, I want you to meet Jimmy.''

''Hello,'' they said in unison.

Jimmy gawked at them for a moment, then looked at Amber again. ''You gotta be kidding me. That's your mom?''

''Looks great for her age, doesn't she?'' Amber sent her mother a knowing glance that probably only made her seem more mysterious to the smitten young man.

''Yes. I mean…um, nice to meet you…both.''

''Likewise,'' Jameson said.

Amber looked up at her father. ''It's almost the last dance,'' she told him. ''I saved it for you.''

Jameson felt his throat go tight, and his eyes begin to burn. But he managed to blink them clear as he took his daughter's hand, and walked with her onto the floor. As he held her in his arms, he met Angel's eyes across the room, and he saw the sparkle of happy tears there that matched his own.

''I'm glad you're here tonight, Daddy,'' Amber whispered.

''I'll always be here for you, Amber Lily,'' he promised. ''Always.''

* * * * *

BEYOND TWILIGHT

To Lisa, my littlest angel

Chapter One

He twisted away, but her hands were still there. Burning him. Whispering across his chest like wind over water. He shivered. He sweat. He gasped for air but inhaled only her scent. He reached for sanity and found his fingers entangled in short, satiny hair. He opened his eyes and found them captured by hers. Huge, dark, innocent. Imploring, hot, sexy eyes, staring down at him as he lay trembling with desire on his bed. And he knew he was lost. He lifted his arms, slid them around her small body to pull her down to his chest. Parted his lips to taste her succulent mouth...

And there was nothing there. He lay panting and alone, his torso and face coated in a slick sheen, his arms wrapped around themselves. He sat up fast, blinking in the gathering dusk, grabbing the first thing his fist closed on and hurling it into the opposite wall. Both hands pushed through his hair. Dammit, he was still shaking, still hotter than hell for some fantasy woman; a dreamworld pixie who looked more like Peter Pan's Tinkerbell than a swimsuit-issue cover girl. What the hell was the matter with him?

"Pressure." He muttered the word to himself and slid naked from the bed for his ritual cold shower. The dreams had been coming for months on a regular basis. "Stress," he added, stomping into the hotel bathroom, flicking the light, twisting the knobs.

It was the job. Hell, it would get to anyone. He'd failed his last mission, damned near got himself killed while he was at it.

His latest assignment had been handed down eight months ago, and he still hadn't had any success. So many close calls, so many near misses. Every time he thought he had her, she pulled some trick out of her sleeve and slipped right through his fingers. And *almost* didn't cut the mustard with DPI. An agent for the CIA's secretive Division of Paranormal Investigations had to deliver the goods. He was closer than he'd ever been to doing just that. She was here, in this small, middle-of-nowhere town in northern Maine.

Stephen ''Ramsey'' Bachman was a hunter of sorts, but his quarry wasn't human. She was a vampire.

It was her house and she had finally come home to roost. The place was like something out of an old Vincent Price movie. Big and gothic and sadly in need of a coat of paint. The front door was unlocked. It was just before dusk.

Finally, he had her cornered, right in her own backyard. She'd been on DPI's Most Wanted List for more than a decade. He didn't know why. It wasn't his business to know why, just to bring her in. And he had a feeling he was about to do it.

He gripped a small leather satchel in his right hand. Inside were three syringes, each containing a dose of tranquilizer developed by legendary DPI researcher Curtis Rogers. His original formula had been lost when he had been killed, probably by one of *them*, though no one had ever proven it. But Bachman didn't need proof. They were all the same, ruthless killers who preyed on the innocent.

DPI's scientists had been painstakingly working to recreate Rogers's tranquilizer and they thought they'd finally succeeded. He swallowed hard. Tonight would be its first actual test.

The huge, darkly stained door groaned when he pushed it open. His steps echoed on the dusty, time-dulled parquet. He ignored the baroque furnishings, the dark woodwork, the cobwebs, the dust, and he headed straight for the spiral staircase. It creaked with every step.

He'd cased this house early on, as soon as he'd learned she owned it. He knew the basement was prone to flooding and that there was only one room in the place with no windows. That room was where he was heading right now. It had been empty the first time he'd seen it, but he had a strong feeling it wouldn't be vacant tonight.

He reached the top of the stairs and started down the tall, narrow corridor, moving right past the rows of closed doors. He knew which door hid his nemesis. When he reached it he paused with his hand on the knob.

His first inkling that something wasn't quite right came when he turned the knob and it gave without resistance. His feet planted, he stood still a moment, listened, *feeling* the very air around him for a warning, a sound.

Nothing.

He pushed the door inward and stepped slowly inside. Night-marish candlelight illuminated the entire room. A hundred tapers danced and flickered, casting lively shadows on the walls, the ceiling, the floor. And there was music. The melodramatic chords of a ghostly pipe organ floated softly on the air. A little chill raced up his spine. Not one of fear, induced by the music and candles. But one of foreboding, as he wondered just what in hell she was up to this time.

The coffin gleamed black with shining brass trim from atop a flower-strewn bier. He stepped forward, noting the dead roses at the head and foot. Nice touch. If he found her, he thought he'd choke her before he ever took her in. He was tired of this, tired of her games and jokes, all of them seemingly designed to make him look like a fool.

He approached the coffin, glancing over his shoulder every second or two, just in case.

A thick curtain of cobwebs stuck to his face and he swept it aside with an angry gesture. The music swelled a little louder, he thought as he put his hands on the lid.

Jaw clenching, he opened it.

Then he stood there, blinking in shock as he stared down at the most horrendous creature he'd ever seen. She had hair like a matted rat's nest, tight facial skin tinted blue, with black rings encircling the sunken, closed eyes. The cheeks were hollow, gaunt. The lips were pulled back in an almost snarl, baring the pointy tips of yellowed incisors. He could count the bones in the narrow hands that lay crossed upon her chest. The gruesome image, along with his own, was reflected in a mirror on the inside of the lid.

Ramsey poked a finger into the skin of her arm, then let his chin fall to his chest as he blew every bit of air from his lungs. She'd done it to him again, damn her. The body in the coffin was made of wax. And Cuyler Jade was probably a hundred miles away from here by now.

Soft laughter, like crystal water bubbling over smooth stones, filled the room. He stiffened and spun around. The woman stood in the doorway, her hand over her mouth, her mischievous eyes twinkling with candlelight and mirth.

"If you could have seen your face..." She laughed some more, closing her eyes and tipping her head back.

She was tiny. Her gleaming black hair was cut short, with spiky bangs on her forehead and jagged ends laying on her neck. She brought her head level and tilted it slightly as she studied him. She looked like a pixie, like Peter Pan's Tinkerbell.

Impossible. It's your imagination, dammit. She's not the woman in your dreams.

He said nothing. She stepped into the room, bold as brass. "I'm kinda tired of this endless chase, Ramsey."

He blinked. "What did you call me?"

"Ramsey. Isn't that what all the guys in military school dubbed you? Stephen Bachman from Ramsey, Indiana, became Ramsey in the tenth grade, if I remember correctly." She smiled and moved closer. "Don't look so surprised. Isn't the first rule of all you secret agent types to know your enemy?"

He watched her approach until she stood only inches away from him. She wasn't the one he was after. She couldn't be. She was the imp from his dreams. The erotic, sexy, innocent-eyed devil that smiled as she touched him. The one that drove him half out of his head with pure animal lust. She wasn't a monster.

She offered a tiny hand, and as he closed his huge one around it she told him the last thing he wanted to hear. "I'm Cuyler Jade. The one you've been chasing all over the country for the past eight months."

He swallowed the sand-covered rock that seemed to have lodged in his throat, and quickly dropped her hand.

"So here I am," she told him. The impish light in her eyes was tempered with a hint of uncertainty. The brazen smile on her lips, a little unsteady. "Question is, Ramscy, now that you've got me, what are you gonna do with me?"

He stiffened his back. Okay, so she was a vampire. And he'd had recurring, wildly erotic dreams about her for the past several months. Almost as long as he'd been after her. So what? He had a job to do, and that was his priority—not his unruly libido.

"I'm going to arrest you." His voice sounded cold, harsh. Good. "You're now a federal prisoner, Ms. Jade. I'm taking you back to New York, to our headquarters in White Plains."

"Are you?"

God, her eyes were big. And dark. And those thick lashes made him think of Bambi, made him feel like the heartless hunter.

"Afraid so."

"And what if I won't go with you? You going to overpower me?"

She knew he couldn't do that. Remarkably, she stood still while he opened the satchel and brought out one of the syringes. "I could tranquilize you."

She frowned at the hypodermic. "That stuff work?"

He shrugged. "One way to find out."

He reached for her arm, but she danced away from him before he could grip it. Tapping her chin with a coral-tipped finger, she faced him once again. "Suppose I was to come along peacefully?"

He studied her through narrowed eyes, all too aware of her knack for tricks and pranks. "Why would you do that?"

Her black eyes narrowed. She came back to him, leaned in so close her breath fanned his throat. One of her small hands came up and her fingertips danced over his nape. "'Cause you're not going to go through with it, Ramsey."

He swallowed again, hoping she wouldn't press any closer and accidentally discover the effect she was having on him. He shifted his stance and tried to remind himself what she was. She only looked like a woman. Beads of sweat popped out on his forehead, and he tried to summon the will to jab the needle into her arm before she could slip away again.

Instead he only managed, "What makes you think so?" His voice sounded coarse. Not at all as intimidating as it ought to.

Her lips curved upward just a little. "I know about the dreams," she whispered.

He didn't let it shake him. All right, it shook him, but he didn't let it show. "Because you caused them? Another one of your tricks?"

She shook her head. "I don't know *what* caused them, Ramsey. But I've been having them, too."

Chapter Two

She watched him, waited to see his reaction to her words. She truly believed what she'd told him, that he wouldn't be able to take her into custody. But she didn't think he was fully aware of it. Not yet, anyway. Ramsey Bachman had a thing or two to learn about himself. And Cuyler had decided she was the only one who could teach him.

He was speechless for a long moment. Then he shook his head, staring at her from wary, deep gray eyes. "You're a good liar, Cuyler. But not that good. You haven't had any dreams about me."

"No? Want me to describe them to you?"

"No." He said it too quickly.

She smiled. "I get to you, Ramsey. You know I do. It's not a big surprise, really. You get to me, too. I'm not afraid to admit it."

"Dream on, Cuyler." Still holding the syringe in one hand, he clasped her arm with the other and turned her toward the door. "Come on, if you're so eager to surrender. My car's out front. You want to pack a bag?"

"Not just yet." She resisted the urge to pull her arm away yet again. She couldn't do that, couldn't let him think she was up to something. But the big boys from DPI were getting restless waiting for Ramsey to bring her in. Much longer and they'd come for her themselves, and she'd rather take her chances with Ramsey than with them. She had to play her cards fast and well.

The wariness had never left his eyes. It only intensified. "You're trying to pull something on me."

"I have a deal to offer you. Take it or leave it, it's up to you."

"No deals. You're coming with me. Now."

"No. I'll come in with you in a few days. Without a peep. No tricks, no struggles, no fuss. I promise."

"And I'm supposed to believe you?"

"You want me to write it in blood?"

He released her arm, let his own hang loosely at his side, and stared at her so hard she could feel the touch of those eyes. More than that, she could feel the anger behind them, and the pain. And her arm still tingled where he'd held it. It still baffled her, this awareness between the two of them. This attraction. She'd felt it before she'd even laid eyes on him.

"What do you want in return?"

"Hmm, a hunk with a brain. You're a rare specimen, Ramsey."

"What do you want?" he repeated, impatience giving an edge to his voice.

She tilted her head, shrugging delicately, walking in a small circle with a happy bounce in her steps. He was faltering. He wouldn't even have asked unless he was considering giving in. "Nothing much. Just a little bit of your time. Three nights of it should be enough."

"Three—"

She stopped, spinning on her heel and pointing at him. "You spend three nights with me. At dusk on the fourth, I'll be ready and willing to head off to Nazi headquarters with you. Okay?"

He shook his head slowly. "Three nights...doing *what* with you?"

She rolled her eyes, threw her palms up. "Not that, for crying out loud. Crimey, if *that* was all I wanted from you, I could have had it months ago!"

"The hell you could."

"Forget it, Ramsey. I'm right and you know it. Picture it. You wake from one of those hot and heavy dreams to find the real thing naked in your arms. You tellin' me you'd roll over and go back to sleep?" She moved closer as she spoke, leaned into him, stood on tiptoe until her nose nearly touched his chin. "I don't think so."

"I don't give a damn *what* you think."

She shrugged, but backed down and resumed her circular pacing.

"So if you don't want me sleeping with you, then what are the three nights for?"

"I *sleep* during the day." She ruffled the short layers of her hair with both hands. He was exasperating. She hadn't expected it to be this difficult. She turned away from him, picked a slender white candle from its holder and tilted the flame to an incense dish, igniting the cone in its center. She inhaled the sweet fragrance. Just because she hadn't expected difficulty didn't mean she hadn't prepared for it.

"Look, Ramsey, I need to spend some time with you if I'm going to figure this out, that's all. I just want to get to the bottom of this...this *thing*."

"What thing?"

She made two fists, held them near her temples and squeezed her eyes tight. She was going to hit him if he didn't stop acting so obtuse. She took a step backward, and he very logically advanced an equal distance. He stood near the incense. A spiral of scented smoke rose around his head.

"You know I could have killed you months ago, or hurt you so badly you would have been off my case for a long time," she told him. "I could have closed my eyes and given one good mental scream and had half a dozen older, stronger ones here to get rid of you for me."

"Then why the hell didn't you?"

"*I don't know!* That's the *thing* I want to get to the bottom of! I can't even think about hurting you. Hell, I've got this off-the-wall notion that I ought to be looking out for you, but—"

"*You?* Looking out for *me?* That's a laugh."

"Damn straight, when I know you're planning to haul me off to a death camp."

"It's not—"

"Don't bother, Ramsey. DPI's research techniques are well documented. Look, I made you an offer. What's your answer?"

He shook his head slowly, then pinched the bridge of his nose with two fingers and shook it again. Glancing down at the syringe in his hand, he straightened a little. "Sorry, Cuyler. I've been the butt of too many of your tricks. I don't believe you for a minute, and whether it's three nights from now or not, I'm still taking you in. Why delay the inevitable?"

She lowered her head, looked at the floor. "Well, I'm sorry, too. But I'm afraid you don't have a choice in the matter."

He lunged toward her, but she'd known he would. She was ready. Before he could blink, she snatched the offensive little hypodermic from his hand. She snapped the needle with her thumb, dropped it on the floor and crushed it under her foot. Facing him, she lifted her palms. "Try again?"

"Damn you…" His voice trailed off. He squeezed his eyes tight, opened them, closed them again.

She stepped closer to him.

"What…what did you…" He swayed backward.

Cuyler gripped his shoulders, held him steady. "You'd better sit down, Ramsey."

He did. His legs folded and he hit the floor hard, but remained upright, one palm pressed to his right temple. He lifted his head to look at her, the gleam of anger in his eyes dulling. "I knew…I couldn't…trust one of you."

"You can, Ramsey. I promise, you can." She knelt beside him as his eyes closed. His body fell backward, but she caught him and eased his shoulders and head to the floor. She bent close to his ear and whispered, "You'll see." She stood and snuffed out the drugged incense.

He opened his eyes slowly, warily, and registered surprise that he was still able to do so. The throbbing in his head was enough proof that he was still alive. So she'd only drugged him. But for what purpose?

He struggled to sit up, only to feel her hands on his shoulders pressing him back down. "Lie still for a while. Here, this will help." She laid a hot cloth across his forehead.

He blinked her into focus, then looked beyond her. The room was dim, but he knew with a glance that they weren't in her tumbledown house. He'd been all through it. There'd been no canopy bed surrounded by sheer black curtains. No stone walls. No fireplace snapping and crackling with red-orange heat.

"Where the hell am I?"

She pursed her lips. "My hideaway. I can't tell you where, exactly. Just in case I'm wrong about your inherent sense of decency. I wouldn't want you running back to DPI with directions to my one and only haven."

He grated his teeth. He'd strangle her as soon as he got his strength back. He didn't think he could stop himself. With an angry snarl he sat up, brushing her hands away. His feet swung to the floor and he got up, swayed a little, caught himself. Then he walked unevenly toward the arched window cut into the thick stone wall. He braced himself against the cold sill and stared through the thick, tinted glass.

All he saw was snow. Gentle hills and valleys of it, without end, unrolling like a lumpy sheet beneath a starry sky.

He turned toward her again, dazed with disbelief. "Where the hell am I?" he repeated.

"North. You are definitely north."

"North of what?"

"Just about everything." She ended with a little laugh, those eyes of hers glittering with mischief.

"Dammit, Cuyler—"

"Look, all you need to know is that you're miles from another human being. There are no roads, no transportation, and no phones. Nothing. Just you and me, together for the next three nights. Just like I told you."

Letting his head fall backward, he stared up at the vaulted ceiling, the gaslights glowing in the chandelier.

"Don't look so upset. I'll take you back when I know what I need to know."

He shook his head, met her gaze. "If there's no transportation, then how the hell did we get here?"

"That doesn't really matter."

He pushed one hand through his hair, scanned the room, spotted the open door and left her standing there. She followed him. He heard her steps on the ceramic-tiled floors as he moved quickly through the corridor, glancing into rooms furnished as if for some fairy-tale princess. Satins and ruffles and lace. Trinkets he didn't take time to examine littered every surface.

He found the stairway, broad and stone with a gleaming hardwood banister, and he hurried down it. Another fireplace. More gaslights, more stone. More expensive-looking antique furniture.

The front doors were huge, and double, with stained-glass panes in starburst patterns centering each of them. And they were unlocked. He flung them wide and stepped out into the biting wind, bitter cold. There was nothing. As far as he could see, there was just nothing. A sense of doom settled on his shoulders like a thousand-pound pillar.

She touched him again. Her small hands closed around his upper arm and tugged at him. "Come back inside, Ramsey. It's going to be all right, I promise you."

He lowered his head. The wind stung his face, his ears. He let her pull him back inside, but he was shaking his head. "It isn't."

"It will." She closed the doors, turned to face him.

"There are things I need..."

"I know. The insulin."

His head came up fast. "How do you—"

"I brought everything from your hotel room. Your clothes, the medicine, everything. The only thing I didn't bring was that nasty drug you were planning to inject me with." She closed her eyes, shook her head slowly. "That really disappointed me, Ramsey. I didn't think you'd do it to me, but you were going to."

"Immoral bastard that I am, right? I notice you didn't hesitate to do the same to me."

Her brows rose, then she smiled a little and gave a shrug. "Guess you have me on that one. But, honestly, the incense is harmless. It just lasts a few hours and the only side effect is a bad headache."

He rubbed one throbbing temple with his forefinger. "Tell me about it."

"You want something for it? Aspirin or—"

"I don't want anything except to get the hell out of here." He was angry. He hated feeling trapped, forced into a situation he didn't like. And he sure as hell didn't like this. Being locked away in a miniature castle with the object of his most vivid, graphic fantasies. Knowing he couldn't lay a hand on her. Hell. That's what this was. Hell on earth.

"And you will. Soon. But, Ramsey, there are things I have to know."

"If you think you can pry any DPI secrets out of me—"

"Not about your precious organization. About you." She reached out to him, took his hand, drew him into the huge room, and pressed him into a chair near the fire. "Relax, Ramsey. Please, just try to accept that you're going to be here for a few days, so we can get on with this. Think of it as a minivacation."

He looked up into her innocent eyes, marveling that they could hide so much deceit. "A vacation?"

"It's warm and safe. There's plenty of food. I have wine, too. Your favorite kind. You want some?"

"So you can knock me out again?"

"I don't need to knock you out again."

She turned and walked away from him, fishing a bottle of white zinfandel from an ice bucket on a nearby pedestal table. She poured some into a glittering cut-crystal glass and brought it to him, pressing it into his hand. He'd had time to get up and run, but what was the use? There was nowhere to go.

She knelt down in front of his chair, her hands resting on his knees, and stared up at him with more intensity in her eyes than he'd ever seen. He braced himself against that look. He wasn't going to believe a word that fell from those full, moist lips. And he wasn't going to entertain a single erotic thought about her current position.

"I want to tell you something, and I want you to listen to me. I'm out of tricks and tired of games. Everything I say to you from here on will be nothing but the truth. I'd like for you to return the favor."

She paused, waiting. He said nothing.

"Ramsey, if you take me to that research lab in White Plains, I'll die. And I won't be the first."

"That's bull. DPI isn't in the habit of murdering—"

"But they are."

Ramsey shook his head hard. "They're scientists. They want to learn all about you—"

"They want to eradicate us from the planet."

"Yes." He sighed, admitting that much. "Yes, but not by killing you. By finding a cure."

Her eyes flashed with anger and for just a second he felt the force of her rage. "A cure. Where do you get this stuff, Ramsey? It's not a disease. We don't need a cure for what we are any more than you need one for being tall or for having gray eyes."

He was skeptical. "You wouldn't like to be human again, to *feel* again?"

"I'm as human as you are, dammit. And what makes you think I don't feel?"

She stared up into his eyes, her own brimming with so much emotion he almost wondered if she might somehow be an exception to the rule. But her eyes narrowed and she looked at the floor.

"The good ol' DPI handbook, right, Ramsey? We're all animals. Emotionless, cold-blooded killers."

He swallowed the lump in his throat. "Aren't you?" He wasn't asking. Not really. He knew what they were.

She bit her lower lip, blinked fast. "No. But they are. Do you have any idea how many of us have died at their hands, in the name of their so-called research?"

"And yet you promised to go there with me, willingly, after these three nights." If he sounded skeptical, then he was. He wasn't as gullible as she apparently thought he was.

"Yes. If you still want to take me there."

"Why?"

"Because I know that you won't. I'm as sure of that as I am of my own name, Ramsey. I don't know why, but I am."

He shook his head slowly. "That doesn't make any more sense than dragging me up here."

"I think it does." She closed her hand around his, held it there, and he felt the warmth of her flowing into him, through him. A tingling awareness skittered along his nape, up his spine. Something odd happened to him. He felt invaded, as if her very soul was seeping into him, or his into her, or something.

"Do you feel it?" she whispered. "There's something between us, Ramsey. You know there is."

He shook his head in denial and tugged his hand away from hers. It was no more than another of her tricks.

"It's more powerful than the connection I feel with one of the Chosen." She said it softly, eyes downcast.

"The Chosen...that's your term for humans with that rare belladonna antigen in their blood?" He sat forward a little, thinking maybe he'd get something out of this forced incarceration, some kernel of knowledge to take back with him. If he ever *got* back.

She nodded. "They're the only ones who can be transformed. We all had that antigen as mortals. But you don't have it. I'd have known right away if you did."

"How?"

She rose, chewing her full lower lip with even, white teeth. "We sense them. I can't explain it, but we always know. We have an instinctive need to watch over them, protect them—"

"Make them into what you are?"

She shook her head. "No. Never, unless they want it and we're sure they can handle it. Most couldn't deal with it, I think."

He leaned back in the chair, studying her face for a long time. She was telling him things she didn't have to tell him. And she was being honest. He'd read up on the connections between certain humans and vampires. What she said matched the research DPI had done on the subject. So, was she serious about not lying to him, or was she just trying to gain his confidence?

Stupid to even consider that she was sincere. She was just baiting her trap.

"There's usually one person in particular to whom a vampire feels the strongest connection," he said, quoting almost verbatim from the studies he'd read. "Is that right?"

She paced away from him, nodding as she went.

"So, who's your pet mortal?"

She stood right in front of the fire, her back to him. "You are."

Ramsey blinked, then forced the shock into submission and tried to keep a logical, analytical mindset. "That doesn't make any sense, Cuyler. I don't have the antigen."

"You think I don't *know* that?" She shouted it as she whirled to face him.

He stood and slowly moved toward her, searching her face for a sign she was lying. He saw only turmoil and frustration in her eyes, as real as if she were honestly experiencing those feelings. She had him completely confused, and he didn't like it.

"Then why do you think—"

"I dream about you, Ramsey. I think about you when I'm awake. I know when you're angry, when you're sick, when you're in pain."

She grasped his shoulders, and he couldn't believe that there was moisture in her eyes.

"I want you to the point of madness, but it's more than that."

She wanted him. And that should scare the hell out of him, because he knew that with her kind, sexual desire was so closely entwined with the bloodlust that the two became inseparable. If she wanted him, then she not only wanted him in bed. She probably wanted to drain him dry, too.

Another reason to keep his mounting desire under control. Hell, if he gave in to it, he'd end up dead.

"You're out to destroy me," she went on, her voice catching

in her throat. "I ought to be running away from you as fast as I can go. But all I feel is this longing to be as close to you as I can get."

She released him, looked at the floor, and he saw the way her lips trembled.

"My rest is torment. I wake up frustrated and confused instead of rested and strong. It's driving me crazy, Ramsey. All I want to do is figure out why. Can you really blame me for that?"

Ramsey had trouble swallowing when a single tear spilled onto her cheek. Not a manufactured one. She quickly turned away from him, brushing the back of one hand over her face to wipe it away. For some reason he had the urge to wrap his arms around this suffering pixie and make it all right for her. He grated his teeth, stiffened himself against the softening that seemed to be happening inside him. She was the enemy. She was a master of lies. She had murder on her mind; his murder. He had to remember that. He didn't know what she could possibly have to gain by convincing him of all this bull, but there had to be something.

In a private office on the fifth floor of a building in White Plains, N.Y., three men stared at a small, lighted screen, watching the little red blip flash on and off incessantly.

"It has to be a malfunction," Stiles said.

"No. No, it makes perfect sense. It's dark there eighteen hours straight, this time of year," Whaley argued. "Perfect for one of them."

"But why would she take him there?"

The third man hadn't spoken yet. He removed a pipe from his teeth and tapped spent tobacco into a plastic ashtray on his desk. "I knew he'd turn on us. Hell, it was a given. A matter of time. I'm just glad we planted the tracking device in his suitcase."

"A matter of time?" Stiles frowned, puzzled. "You sound as if you were expecting this."

"I was," Fuller said.

"But, Mr. Fuller, I don't—"

"Until you need to know, don't bother asking."

Stiles sighed hard, but nodded his acceptance. "So, what do we do?"

Wes Fuller paced the room for a moment, his bulk making his steps fall heavily. Then he calmly began refilling his pipe. "We get some maps, some more information, some equipment, and we go up there. Get ourselves two research subjects for the price of one."

Chapter Three

It wasn't the castle it at first appeared to be. It was actually no bigger than an average house, all made of stone, blocks of it two feet in depth. Deep gray here, lighter there. Sometimes nearly white. It had the huge rooms and high ceilings of a mansion. But the place wasn't what it seemed. The ground floor consisted of only three rooms. The palatial front one with the fireplace, a dining room fit for a king, and a tiny cubbyhole of a kitchen with a fridge and stove that appeared to be gas-powered, like the lights. He tried the faucets, found they worked. Hot and cold. The place had every comfort.

It was a whimsical place. Made him think of the castles and enchanted cottages in fairy tales. Everywhere he looked there were crystals. Huge blocks of quartz with jagged points like countless fingers, sparkling at him. Glittering purple amethysts. Lapis lazuli, so blue it hurt your eyes to look at it too long. Tiger's eye, flashing and winking yellow and gold at him as he passed. And a hundred others he couldn't identify. Tiny pewter statuettes peered up at him from every inch of space not occupied by a stone. There were fairies, unicorns, dragons, wizards, castles on high. My God, there were hundreds of them. And the art that adorned her walls held similar themes. No pastels, though. Grim colors, grays and browns and dull blues. Lots of charcoal sketches. Pegasus. Pan. An ugly creature that might have been a troll.

Interesting.

"Looked your fill yet?" She sat on a beanbag chair near the fire—a beanbag!—with her legs curled beneath her. She hadn't followed him, seeming content to let him explore the house on his own. More evidence there was really no way out. If there was a chance he could escape, she wouldn't have let him out of her sight.

"I haven't looked upstairs yet."

"Three bedrooms, with a bathroom between two of them. No big deal. Can we sit down and talk now?"

"The place is smaller than it looks. The size of the room is deceptive."

"Astute observation. Please, Ramsey, I have so much I want to know." She sat a little straighter, pleading with those big, round eyes that seemed to want to suck him into their depths.

"How'd you ever find this place?" He poured himself some more wine, his back to her. He had to avoid looking at her if he was going to manage to remain in control, maybe get her to let something slip, like how the hell he could get out of here.

"I had it built. Always wanted a castle all my own. Ever since I was a little girl."

That tidbit made him turn to face her. His next question was impulsive and not at all what he'd intended to ask. "How old are you, Cuyler?"

"Ninety-nine." She smiled fully when she said it. Her smile was something to see. Made her eyes crinkle at the corners and sparkle with mischief. "Pretty spry for my age, huh?"

"How long have you been—"

"Didn't do much research on me, did you, Ramsey?"

He shook his head. "Research isn't my job."

"Right. I forgot. You just hunt us down and bring us in."

"I'm not going to apologize for it."

"Who asked you to? I just wondered why you suddenly wanted to know about me." She turned to stare into the firelight. It made her eyes glow, and gleamed its reflection on her multilayered ebony hair.

"I'm curious."

"Is that all?" She didn't look at him. Just sighed softly before she went on. "I was twenty-five. My sister and I danced at a gin joint in Chicago during the height of Prohibition."

He stopped with his wine halfway to his lips and just stared at her with his mouth gaping. "You were a flapper?"

She shrugged, looking at him, grinning. "I was young and I needed the money."

He laughed. He couldn't help it, she was funny. She'd always been funny. Every time she'd pulled one of her pranks on him and slipped out of his reach, she'd done it with a stroke of humor that couldn't be ignored. More than once he'd been in the midst of anger and frustration, only to find himself smiling and shaking his head at her wit. That dummy in the coffin at her house had been just one more example of her impish streak.

He stared at her, tilted his head a little. He could see her very clearly in his imagination, wearing a fringe-covered sac dress and a headband with a feather. Then his laugh died. He wasn't sure he wanted to hear any more. Seeing her as a real person with a life and a past would only make this harder.

"Honestly, I loved to dance. We both did. And we were good at it."

"I'll bet you were." It slipped out before he thought about it. He averted his eyes, cleared his throat. "So, what happened?" He could have kicked himself. Hadn't he just decided he didn't want to know?

"There was this woman, the most beautiful woman I'd ever seen in my life. She was elegant. No, regal is a better word. But she was fun, too. She used to come in all the time, bugged us to teach her the dances. One night she came in dressed as a flapper and joined us on stage." Cuyler shook her head slowly, smiling, the movement drawing his gaze against his will. "She was something. Every man there wanted her, but she never seemed interested. And when the lushes got a little out of hand with us, she'd step in and scare the hell out of them.''

Ramsey wondered what man in his right mind would be interested in any other woman when Cuyler was in the room, then frowned and reminded himself what he was doing here. ''Who was she?''

Cuyler only leaned back in her beanbag, drew her knees up to her chest and wrapped her arms around them. She ignored his question. ''One night there was a raid. FBI. G-men as we called 'em back then. The owners fought back, naturally. The rest of us got caught between machine guns.''

She released her legs and rolled to her feet with a little bounce. She walked toward him, stopped when she stood right in front of him, then caught the hem of her blouse and lifted it.

Ramsey licked his lips and tried to deny his instant reaction to the sight of that taut skin, her flat belly, the curve of her waist, the dark well of her navel. He stiffened when she took his hand and pulled it toward her, but he didn't pull away. And then his palm was pressing to her warm flesh and he felt odd puckers that shouldn't be there. They barely showed, but he could feel them.

He frowned, moving his hand over her waist, feeling more of the puckers, and more on her rib cage. Slowly, it dawned on him just what these scars had to be, and for some reason his stomach convulsed, twisting into a knot, and a hot fury came to life in its center. He set the wine on a stand and stood, both hands on her warm skin now. Clasping her waist, he turned her slowly and ran his palms over the small of her back, as well, then higher, slipping them beneath her blouse and up to her shoulder blades.

He tried to swallow as he felt the scars left on her smooth flesh where the bullets had passed through her body. But he couldn't. His throat had closed off. He had a sudden image of her, with her short ruffly hair held in place by a feathered headband, her fringed dress filled with holes, her small pixie's body riddled by bullets.

His hands stilled on her skin. He closed his eyes, trying to block out the image.

She leaned back just slightly, pressing herself closer to his touch. "My sister was killed, and I wasn't far behind her. But that woman found me in the chaos. She took me out of there while the bullets were still flying. I don't know how, but she did. She laid me down in the alley and she asked me if I wanted to live."

"And you said yes."

She turned to face him and somehow his hands ended up on her shoulders. He ought to move them away. He really ought to.

"What would you have said?"

He shook his head slowly. It wasn't a clear decision between good and evil. It wasn't an easy question to answer. Not the way he'd always thought it would be. He couldn't get the image of it out of his mind, her small body jerking like a marionette's as bullets tore hot paths right through her. Her lying still, the life seeping away from her. Why was this so vivid to him? Why did he feel as if he'd witnessed the whole thing? His hands tightened a little on her shoulders, a natural reaction to the sensation of her life slipping away. "I don't know."

Her hands rose in slow motion, came to rest lightly on his chest. "I probably wouldn't have known, either, if she'd asked me while I was strong and alive. But I was bleeding. I was dying. I couldn't even feel the pain by then. And I said yes."

He couldn't blame her. He couldn't imagine himself in the same situation doing anything differently. But the decision, that single moment in time, was only the beginning. And he found himself wanting to know more. "What about afterward? When you were changed, a completely different being? Did you regret your choice?"

She closed her eyes, smiled softly. "But I wasn't a different being. Ramsey, the changes were physical. I was the same person inside. A little flaky, maybe. A believer in fairy tales. A practical joker. I was the same. I still am."

His stomach clenched. For a second he wondered what right he had to drag this woman off to DPI's research center. He stared down at her wide eyes, her moist lips, and felt her lean toward him. His hands tightened on her shoulders. She rose on tiptoe and tilted her head up, fit her mouth to his...

The hiss of resin seeping from the firewood got louder just as he caught her lips, began sucking at them, tracing their shape with his tongue. A loud snap worked like an electric shock, jarring him out of the spell she'd woven around them. He wouldn't have fallen so easily unless she had. He deliberately called up the image of his mother's lifeless body and unseeing eyes, focused on it to remind himself of why he'd joined DPI in the first place.

He lifted his head and pushed her away. Dammit, she was playing with his mind, making him feel things he had no business feeling. Those dreams he'd had of her, these pictures she was drawing for him, it was all part of her plan.

He looked at her. She was biting her lip, shaking her head, looking everywhere except at him. "I'm sorry. I didn't mean to—" She spun in a circle, pushing both hands through her dark hair, ruffling it until its short layers resembled the feathers of a flustered raven. "It won't happen again. That's not why I brought you here."

She was apologizing. He gave his head a shake. Why the hell was she apologizing?

"Look, Ramsey, I'm not trying to seduce you into anything. If we can come to an understanding, I want it to be because you've thought things through and listened, and you believe me. Not because your libido was too strong to resist."

He blinked twice, more confused than ever. Seduction would be her best weapon here. Did she mean to tell him she wasn't even going to try? And why did that idea feel like such a letdown? Hell, he ought to be relieved. At least he wouldn't have to worry about her passions taking over and him ending up dead.

Glancing at the grandfather clock in the corner, he felt his eyes widen. They'd been talking for a couple of hours, yet it hadn't seemed more than a few minutes.

She followed his gaze, shook her head. "You ought to eat, Ramsey. And take your insulin before you get sick."

He frowned, glancing through the windows where the pale winter darkness still reigned. "Just how far north are we, Cuyler? Shouldn't it be light by now?"

She shook her head. "Dawn around 9:00 a.m. Dusk again by three this afternoon. That's part of what I like about this place in the winter."

"Don't you get tired on so little rest?"

"Hell, Ramsey, since you've been on my tail my rest hasn't been very restful, anyway."

He knew she was referring to the dreams. Maybe she really *had* experienced them. He doubted it, but there was probably a slight chance. And there was also a slight chance, he conceded at last, that she was being straight with him about her reasons for bringing him here. For, even though he couldn't admit it to her, she'd been haunting his life the same way she claimed he'd been haunting hers. Only difference was, he hadn't known who she was. Just the pixie with the big sexy eyes that seduced him in his dreams. So maybe she did want to understand this thing, and maybe she would let him go when she had her answers. Maybe she was telling the truth.

But he doubted it.

Wes Fuller held the lighter to the tobacco in the bowl and inhaled until it caught. He puffed appreciatively, then held the pipe in his hand and blew smoke rings as he studied the maps tacked to the wall.

"Only way in will be by helicopter. And then they'll hear us coming." It was Stiles, his chief aide. Stiles, always the cautious one, always wary. "We could land a few miles away, though, and hike in. But we'll want to be sure we can get in and out by daylight. We want to be well out of there before dark."

"What's the matter, Stiles? Afraid the three of us can't handle her?" And that was Whaley, the intrepid. He wanted a battle. It gleamed from his eyes like a fever.

"Stiles is right in this case," Wes said slowly. "We have no way of knowing whether she's alone up there or not. There might be half a dozen others with her."

Stiles's eyes widened. "I hadn't thought of that. My God, do you supposed Bachman is still alive? I mean, what if they just took him up there to—"

"He's alive."

"But, sir, how can you—"

"He's alive. There's not one of them who'd hurt Bachman. If there was, he'd have been long dead by now. God knows, I've given him the riskiest assignments, sent him up against the worst of them. But he's never been hurt beyond repair, and he's never brought one in."

Stiles blinked.

Whaley frowned. "You telling me you've deliberately put Bachman in high-risk situations with them? Including this one?"

Fuller nodded. Whaley wanted to hit him. Fuller could see it in his flashing eyes. But he wouldn't. He was a subordinate and he knew his place. "You'll understand in time, Whaley. Till then, you'll just have to trust my judgment. Bachman's been one long experiment. And his usefulness to us has just about run out. Don't trust him, whatever you do. He's never really been one of us. He just didn't know it."

Chapter Four

He'd eaten, injected his insulin, and searched the house from top to bottom. For what it had been worth. The most interesting thing he'd found had been a sled in the basement and some harnesses hanging on the wall. No dogs, though. No outbuildings where any might be kept. So the sled was useless. Everything he'd found had been useless.

Interesting, but useless. He'd left her bedroom for last. He figured the longer he waited, the more deeply she'd rest. Now he stood at the foot of the fanciful bed and stared at her through the sheer red bed curtains. She lay uncovered, curled on her side, hugging her pillow. A gossamer bit of a nightgown hid very little. Her legs were not long, but so shapely he caught his eyes roaming them from her exposed slender hip to her small toes.

He blinked fast and forced himself to look somewhere else. He'd come to see if she had secrets hidden in her bedroom, hadn't he? Well, he ought to be looking for them, not gawking at her perfect little body and wondering if she would wake up if he went over there for a better look. He hadn't expected this. He didn't know what he'd expected. Maybe that she'd seem like a corpse as she rested, lying flat on her back, hands folded over her chest, not breathing, cold, white. Instead she looked just like any other woman. Relaxed. Warm. Breathing deeply and steadily. No, not like any other woman. Much better. Almost irresistibly innocent and vulnerable right now.

He swallowed hard and walked to the dresser against the stone wall. There were three black-and-white framed snapshots of Cuyler and another young woman in full flapper regalia. He didn't like looking at her that way. He knew she'd been mortal when the photo had been taken. Vampires didn't show up in photographs. But, honestly, he couldn't spot a single difference in her. Mischievous grin, sparkling black eyes, innocence and sex appeal all wrapped up in the most appealing package imaginable.

He turned from the photos to examine the books. There were at least a hundred of them lining the shelves that stood against the wall, and as he scanned the titles, he noted they were all high fantasies. Sword and sorcery stories, with knights and dragons and magic. She was really into that stuff.

He gave up on the bedroom, because no matter what he chose to investigate, he found his gaze drawn back to her again and again. He couldn't stay in that room with her. It was dangerous. God, could she weave spells even in her sleep?

He headed back downstairs into the dining room. He hadn't examined the books on the shelf there, but as he did, he noted they were the same. Fantasy stories about other worlds where good always won over evil. Ironic.

Then he spotted a few that were different. He pulled one out, frowning. He grinned as he scanned the blurb. It was about vampires, of all things! He slipped the book back into its place, wishing he had time to read a little of it, see what the latest fiction writer had dreamed up and whether it compared with the real McCoy. But he had to catch a few hours' sleep while he had the chance. From the looks of things, there wasn't much else he could do right now.

She writhed in her bed, knowing all of this was just a dream, but dying of sheer, tormented pleasure all the same. He was kissing her. His mouth was warm, wet, eager as it moved from her fingertips over her wrist, along the inside of her arm and into the hollow of her elbow. He tickled the sensitive skin there with his tongue, then moved higher, up to her shoulder, over it to her neck. She tipped her head back, closed her eyes, moaned softly. Her fingers buried themselves in his hair as he pushed the nightgown from her shoulders. Then he moved to her breasts, taking one in his hungry mouth, feeding on it like a starving man while he tormented the other with his fingers. His knee moved between her thighs, nudging them apart.

She touched his unclothed chest, raked her nails lightly over his nipples until he panted. Then her hand slipped lower, finding the smooth, rigid core of him, encircling it, squeezing, running her fingers over the tip.

He stared down at her, saying nothing, just watching. Then he closed his eyes, and she knew his need was almost painful. She opened to him, and he settled himself on top of her, nudged against her slick opening. She lifted her knees, desperate for him, for fulfillment. She needed this, needed him. No one else could fill the emptiness inside her. And she knew that he needed her just as desperately. Only she could soothe his wounded heart, erase the pain that darkened his soul, replace his anger and hatred with tenderness and love.

Her hands reached for him, to pull him to her...

But there was only air. Her eyes flew wide and she screamed in frustration, tugging at her hair. She punched the pillow, threw it, knocking half a dozen pewter figurines from the stand beside the bed, then pressed balled-up fists to her eyes and moaned like a wounded animal.

Her door banged open and he stood there, staring at her. His face was flushed, beads of sweat stood on his brow. His breathing was uneven. He looked at her, and when their eyes met she knew he'd had the same dream. Every image she remembered was reflected in his eyes. He must know it, because he averted them, as if that would stop her from seeing.

"You cried out. Are you okay?"

She drew three open-mouthed breaths, closed her eyes, and finally shook her head. Her palms rose to her face and she lowered her head. "I can't take this anymore, Ramsey. I can't. I'm gonna go stark raving—"

His weight made the mattress sink, and then his hands gripped her shoulders. "You think I don't know? It's driving me to the edge, too, Cuyler."

She sobbed, and he drew her head to his chest. She felt the warm skin, the muscle, smelled him, wanted him. She slipped her arms around his waist and clung tighter.

"Dammit, Ramsey, why'd you come in here? You're only making it worse." She turned her face to his chest, pressed her mouth to his skin and tasted it. She kneaded his shoulders with her nails as her pulse thundered in her temples.

One of his hands lowered to her waist. The other crept over her nape, up into her hair, and he tipped her head back. Then his mouth came to hers. She parted her lips, and his tongue dug into her, stroking deep and pulling back in an erotic pattern. She fell backward on the bed, and he came down on top of her, feeding on her mouth, crushing her body to his. She felt his arousal pressing hard between her legs, and she arched against it.

Then he stiffened and rolled off her. Sitting on the edge of the bed with his back to her, he pushed both hands into his hair, clenching fistfuls of it, and swore in a voice rougher than tree bark.

"Damn you, Ramsey...." She rolled onto her side to face the other way and tried to stop the flow of frustrated tears.

"I can't. I can't do this."

"Then why did you—"

"I didn't mean to. Hell, Cuyler, I was still half-asleep, probably having the same dream you just had."

He got up and paced away from the bed, the front of his jeans poking out like a tent.

"This is crazy. It's crazy."

She blinked, sitting up and fighting the tears into submission. "Maybe if we just did it, the dreams would stop..."

He turned slowly to face her and his eyes were hard, cold. "No."

The finality in his tone cut to the quick, and for a second she thought she saw the reason. "You're afraid of me, aren't you? You're afraid I'll take more than just your body."

He faced her head-on, not flinching. "Wouldn't you?"

Cuyler closed her eyes, grated her teeth. As much as she wanted him, who was to say she wouldn't lose control of her deepest desires in the heights of passion? Bracing her shoulders, she forced herself to be honest. "Maybe I would. But I'd never hurt you, Ramsey. You have to know that. I couldn't if I wanted to."

He searched her eyes for a long moment, and she felt as if her very soul were being scoured. "If you'd been capable of hurting me, I doubt I'd still be breathing. So I guess I have to believe that."

"Then why—"

"Look, I told you, I can't. It'd be unnatural for..." He stopped midsentence, maybe due to the shock and pain that must have shown on her face, or perhaps it was the involuntary cry she uttered. "That isn't what I meant. Wait—"

"Go to hell, Ramsey!" She was on her feet and through the bathroom door almost before he could blink. She slammed it so hard she loosened the hinges, then she turned the locks.

She didn't say a word to him when she came out, freshly showered, dressed in dark gray stirrup pants and a long, fuzzy, white sweater. She didn't have to say anything. He could see the hurt in her eyes. He felt like an assassin's bullet, like a cobra's venom. He felt like the lowest, meanest form of being in the universe for blurting what he had. Worst of all, he hadn't meant it. It had been his own voice of self-preservation trying to convince *him* to keep his hands off her. It had been desperation, searching for any excuse that would pull his hormones off the scent and tame his libido. Hell, he'd been holding himself back by believing she'd do him some kind of harm if he took her. But he hadn't believed it. Not really, and once his conscious mind admitted that, he'd had to come up with another reason to abstain from the erotic feast he imagined every time he looked at her.

Unnatural. He'd blurted it and she'd looked as if he'd just

kicked her right in the gut. It hadn't been what he really thought. And that was kind of odd, when he considered it. Because it *used to be* what he really thought. When had his spin on things undergone such a radical change?

She plopped down onto the bed and leaned over to pull on slouchy white socks. He walked over and sat down beside her. The second his backside touched the mattress she shot to her feet as if she'd forgotten something in the bathroom.

"Cuyler, listen for a—" The whir of a battery-powered hair dryer cut him off.

Ramsey blew air through his teeth and went into the bathroom with her. She sat on the vanity's padded stool, hair flying all over the place as she whipped the dryer through it. There was no mirror. He wanted to say something. He just wasn't sure what. He didn't want to make amends, exactly. Hell, she was still his enemy. The fact that he was burning up inside for her didn't change that. But he'd hurt her. And despite his years of learning that vampires had no feelings, he regretted it.

Opening the cabinet, for want of anything better to do, he found his kit right where she'd left it. He unwrapped a fresh needle and took out a color-coded strip. With a quick, practiced flick of his wrist, he poked the forefinger of his left hand, squeezed a fat drop of blood out, and smeared it on the strip. Then he watched for the color change. He was moving like a robot, doing the things that came automatically, without really giving any thought to them.

He felt her gaze on him, heard the hair dryer flick off, and looked at her.

"Are you sick?" If her eyes got any bigger, they'd swallow him whole.

"Just checking the blood sugar." He glanced at the strip again.

"And how is it?"

"Fine." He put the used needle and strip back into the container. He'd dispose of them properly when he got back to civilization.

"Do you have to do that every day?"

He nodded as he held his finger under the cold water tap for a second or two.

"Has it ever been out of whack?"

"My sugar level? No. It's always within normal range. I have a good doctor who keeps me in great shape. Hell, I'm the healthiest diabetic I know."

Her eyes narrowed to slits as she studied him. "And who is this Marcus Welby of the nineties?"

"Just one of the best hematologists in the country."

"Don't tell me. A DPI staffer."

Ramsey shrugged, wondering about her line of questioning, but relieved she'd apparently forgotten his earlier slam. "Yup. One of the perks of being an agent."

"Kind of balances out against having to work around us animals, doesn't it?" She got up and brushed past him, going back into the bedroom, yanking a pair of huge, fluffy slippers with unicorn heads on them from under her bed.

"Look, I didn't mean that."

"Sure you didn't." She lifted one foot, put a slipper on it. "Ramsey, if you didn't mean it, then why are we both dressed and vertical?" She never even looked at him. Just hopped on the slippered foot and dressed the other one.

It came out before he could order it not to. "Because I know damned well it'll do me in. Cuyler, once wouldn't be enough. I'd be addicted, and I know, as sure as I'm standing here, that I could OD on you. You really think I could take you to bed and then take you in? If I had you once, I..."

He glanced up at her, saw her blinking rapidly, staring at him in something like childish wonder. "What?"

Her lips curved upward a little. "I just didn't know you wanted me that much."

And she shouldn't have known. It didn't do any good tipping his hand to the enemy. But he'd been honest, if nothing else. He was determined to take her in, and he knew he couldn't do it if he ever made love to her. He lowered his head, refusing to meet her eyes. "I didn't say I did—"

"Sure you did, Ramsey. Don't try and take it back now." She
took his arm in her warm hand and tugged him along beside her
back into the bathroom. "Come on downstairs after you've had
your shower," she told him softly. "I'll get you some breakfast.
I don't want you getting sick."

Then she left him. And he had to wonder when he'd stopped
seeing her as something abnormal, something frightening, and
started seeing her as a woman with a few special needs. One of
which he'd really love to fulfill for her.

Chapter Five

"I'll keep this impersonal, Ramsey."

"What?" He finished the whole-wheat muffin, washed it down with a gulp of remarkably good coffee.

"As long as you find the idea of laying a finger on me so frightening—tempting, but still frightening—I'll try and make it as easy on you as I can. But we have to talk."

"We *talked* last night. I don't see that it's helped matters any." He wanted to correct her, tell her he didn't find the idea frightening at all, anything but, in fact. But it was probably better to let her hurt a little, let her hate him. And he wasn't satisfied with what he'd gotten out of her last night. He wanted to know more.

"I talked, you didn't."

He stiffened a little, watching her. "What do you want to know?"

"How you wound up working for DPI. When did they approach you, Ramsey?"

"My senior year at military school." It was a lie, but he figured the less she knew about the truth, the better off he'd be.

"And don't you find that a little odd? DPI's a secret organization. Even most of the CIA's top dogs don't know about its existence. They obviously don't make a habit of announcing their presence, or drafting high school students. So why you?"

He took another sip of the coffee. "How do you know so much about DPI?"

"Their exploits are well documented. I probably know more about them than you do."

"How? Where is all this documentation you keep mentioning? Where's the proof that they're guilty of all the crimes you accuse them of?"

She sighed and got up from her seat. Walking to the bookshelf he'd so closely examined last night, she pulled several titles from it, brought them to the table and set them in front of him.

The vampire books. He frowned up at her. "You call this proof? It's *fiction.*"

"The world in general seems to believe that. Those of us who know better have good reasons to let them keep believing it."

He glanced down again at the books, shaking his head in disbelief. He picked one up.

"You ought to read them, Ramsey. See the whole hunt through the eyes of the prey for a change, instead of the predator."

He riffled the pages, scanned a few, felt his blood chill. "There's classified information in here! Hell, this is a blow-by-blow account of a DPI investigation!"

She only shrugged. "Like I said, the world thinks it's fiction."

He slammed the book down on the table and stood, facing the bookshelves. "What about the rest of them?"

She smiled slightly, lifted her eyebrows. "What, my fairy stories? Who knows?" She turned to a shelf lined with pewter figurines, picked up a winged dragon and lovingly stroked its fierce-looking head. "I like to think they could be real, that there could be some other world where fairies and magic exist. I mean, why not? Vampires are real, and most people consider us fantasy."

He should be angry. He had been for all too brief a time. Why, then, was he feeling so enchanted all of a sudden? Couldn't DPI have sent him after a monster? Why the hell did they have to pick a beautiful pixie who believed in fairy tales? He cleared his throat and tried to focus on business.

"Does DPI know about these books?"

She shrugged. "I don't know. Are you going to tell them?" She looked at him with those huge dark eyes, all innocence and beauty.

He lowered his head. "I have to, Cuyler."

She was standing in front of him before he knew she'd moved. Her small hand lifted his chin a little, and she stared up into his eyes. "Why are you so dedicated to them? What did we ever do to you to make you hate us so much?"

He only shook his head. He couldn't tell her. It was bad enough that these traitorous feelings for her assaulted him with every breath he drew. His betrayal stung, and if he spent much more time with her, it would be complete.

"Tell me about your childhood, Ramsey. What was your family like?"

He stiffened. Was she reading something in his eyes, his thoughts? "There's not much to tell. I was my mother's only child. Never knew my father."

She lowered her head, walked slowly away from him, then reached for a battery-powered boom box on a low shelf. She pushed a button and soft, hauntingly beautiful music filled the room. A woman's voice, like a gossamer strand wavering in a slight breeze, singing in what sounded like Gaelic. New Age stuff.

Cuyler closed her eyes for a second, listening. Softly, she prompted him. "Tell me about your mother."

Hot blades ran through his chest. "She died when I was twelve." He turned his back to her, walking into the front room and sitting down in a chair near the fireplace. He stared into the flames, remembering.

Her hands closed on his shoulders. "She was all you had, and you lost her. No wonder I see so much pain in your eyes."

He said nothing, and tried not to feel her soothing touch as she began a rhythmic massage.

"How did she die?"

"I don't remember." His eyes wanted to close. He hadn't slept much, and when he did, he didn't rest. He only dreamed about making frantic, hot, imaginative love to Cuyler.

"Why are you lying to me, Ramsey?"

Her fingers kneaded the sides of his neck. He let his head fall sideways to give her more access. "I'm not going to talk to you about my mother," he said, but his voice lacked conviction. He sighed as the image of her danced through his memory. "She was beautiful, all carrot-colored curls and pale blue eyes. And she'd sing... Sometimes, right before I fell asleep at night, I can still hear her singing to me. *Wild Irish Rose,* that was her favorite." For a few seconds his mother's lilting voice played in his memory. Then he felt Cuyler's lips on his head. She bent and pressed her cheek to his, and he felt the dampness on her skin.

"I'd take the pain away, if I knew how."

"I know you would." Why did he say that? And why did it sound so true? He swallowed and tried to regain his strength. "We all have pain, Cuyler. Just part of life. You must have hurt, too, when you lost your sister."

She sniffed, and her hands slid down his chest to rest near his heart. "For a while I wanted to die. Then I wanted vengeance. I thought about hunting down every man involved in that raid. But it wouldn't have eased the pain. It wouldn't have brought Cindy back."

"Might have stopped them from snuffing out another life, though."

She straightened, came around the chair and knelt in front of him. He shouldn't have been surprised at the tears on her cheeks, but he was. Her kind wasn't supposed to have human emotions, wasn't supposed to care. Wasn't that what he'd been taught? And hadn't that particular bit of DPI doctrine been losing validity with every second he'd spent near Cuyler?

"What happened to you then?"

"A military school. Some benevolent organization foot the bill. I lived there, stayed with relatives who'd rather not have had me during vacations. Then the DPI academy, for training."

"And indoctrination."

He shook his head slowly, staring down into her beautiful face. "It wasn't like that."

But it was. Since he'd been twelve years old, he'd been edu-
cated under the organization's watchful eye, beginning with the
debriefing right after his mother's murder. They were the ones
who'd paid for his education, who'd provided a private tutor to
teach him the things he wouldn't learn in any school. He'd been
filled with hatred already, and that hatred found validation in his
secret lessons, the ones he'd been warned not to talk about. He
supposed now, that they'd seen him as the perfect candidate. He'd
had a score to settle. He'd been seeking vengeance all his life.
They'd known that, and offered him the means to achieve it.

And now he was sitting here with one of those he'd spent his
life hating. He was sitting here wanting her with every cell in his
body, talking to her like a cherished friend, finding a kind of
understanding he'd never expected shining from her teary eyes.

But it was all a lie. It had to be.

"I don't want to be here with you, Cuyler. You're too damned
convincing." He pushed her hands away from him and got to his
feet. Leaning against the hearth, he closed his eyes.

"Why do you hate me so much?"

Lifting his head, he looked down at her, still kneeling in front
of the chair. "My mother was killed by a vampire. One of you.
Someone that feeds on the innocent without a hint of remorse. A
killer." He hoped his words would rekindle the hatred in his soul,
reinforce his resistance to Cuyler and her wiles.

Her eyes widened and for a moment she only stared at him in
stunned silence. Finally she shook her head. "It wasn't me."

"You're all the same." He looked away from her. Dammit, he
couldn't spout DPI policy while he was looking into those eyes.
"So now you know. Nothing you can say is going to change it.
You can pretend to be just like us all you want, Cuyler, but I *know*
what you are. And I'll never stop hating you."

She rose slowly, anger beginning to simmer in her eyes.
"You're lying. You don't hate me. If anything, you hate yourself
for not being able to—"

He lifted a hand, cutting her off. "Don't bother. You're only
trying to convince yourself."

"But it's so stupid! Ramsey, one of *your* kind murdered my sister and pumped enough bullets through my body to kill an elephant. But I don't hate *you* for it. I don't lump all mortals in with the few truly evil ones. I don't go out hunting them down like animals to exact vengeance."

"Don't you?"

She flinched as if he'd slapped her. "How can you ask me that?"

God, the hurt in her eyes... He looked at the floor, at the bean-bag, at the fire. Anything but at that pain he'd caused. "Look, you got what you wanted. We've talked. Do you think we can get the hell out of here now?"

She stood so still, stunned maybe. "I don't have what I wanted. I still don't know why there's this connection between us. I still don't know what misguided force makes me give a damn about a man like you."

"Let's chalk it up to physical attraction and call it even."

"It's more than that and you know it!"

He faced her, forced his expression to remain hard as stone. "Maybe for you it is, but not for me, Cuyler." He strode to the stairway, started up it. "I'm packing my things. You line up whatever means of transportation got us here, and have it ready."

"I won't."

He never broke his stride. "Then I'll go on foot."

"I won't let you!" She came up the stairs behind him.

"You have to sleep sometime, Cuyler. One way or another, I'm out of here." He went into the bedroom, slammed the door and turned the lock. He couldn't look at her, listen to her, for one more second or he'd break. It was all a game, some mind game she was playing to win his trust, and it had been working all too well. Until he'd brought the memory of his mother's death back to burning life, anyway. Damn Cuyler for making him talk about his mother, for stirring up that old pain, and especially for acting as if she cared. Damn her.

Chapter Six

Like a potent corrosive, his rejection burned through her. But he didn't hate her. She knew better. It was in his eyes, in his voice. She was so attuned to his feelings that it was impossible to be fooled by his stubborn resistance. He liked her, in spite of his determination not to. He wanted her, though it went against everything he'd ever believed in. But she also knew that the conflicting emotions were slowly tearing his soul apart. She sensed his every emotion, even the ones he denied; frustration, confusion, anger, desire. Bringing him here, forcing him to see her as she was, instead of as DPI had painted her, was the same as torturing him. It was cruel to put him through this, especially now that she knew where his hatred originated. To see Cuyler as a woman and not a monster was, in Ramsey's mind, to betray his mother. To side with her murderer.

Maybe she ought to just take him back, let him go.

She twisted the doorknob, freeing the lock with her mind the way Rhiannon had taught her. Ramsey was asleep. He reclined on the bed, his back against the headboard, his head cocked to one side until his ear touched his shoulder. He looked as if he'd sat down there with no intention of going to sleep.

Cuyler walked softly to him. Even in sleep, he seemed strained. A slight frown puckered his brows. His lips were tight. His pain showed in his face, a pain he'd felt for a very long time. For a moment, as she looked at him there, she saw the image of the boy he'd been. A boy whose innocence and mischief had been stolen from him along with his mother. A boy forced to become a man before his time, a man who'd forgotten how to love.

She stared at him, sending silent, soothing messages from her mind to his. She focused her energy on relaxing him into a deeper sleep and chasing his worries from his mind the way an autumn wind chases fallen leaves. Then she leaned closer, clasping his sturdy shoulders and easing him lower until his head rested on the soft pillows and his back wasn't bent so severely. She tugged a blanket from the foot of the bed to cover him. Then she bent and brushed her lips across his, a whisper of a kiss.

When she straightened away from him, his hand reached toward her. He whispered her name.

She ran a hand over his cheek, into his hair. "I'm here. Rest now. Just rest."

His body relaxed again, and he sank back into his deep slumber. Cuyler sighed softly, shaking her head in remorse. She couldn't let him go. Not now. DPI had targeted Ramsey for their vile organization from the second his mother had been killed, she was sure of it. They must have known of his anger, his fury and feelings of helplessness. The guilt even a boy of that age would suffer; that he hadn't been there, hadn't been able to help her. Those ruthless men had stoked the fire of Ramsey's anger, built it into the blazing inferno that was rapidly devouring his soul. They were using a young boy's pain as a weapon against Cuyler and her kind. And she couldn't shake the feeling that they intended to use it against Ramsey, as well. DPI would see both of them destroyed unless she could find a way to fight them.

She understood so much more now. But still not enough. There was no explanation for the connection between her and Ramsey. She sensed the solution to all of this hinged on her discovering the cause of that emotional, mental link. And until she did that, despite the pain it caused him, she had to keep Ramsey here, with her.

* * *

Ramsey trudged through the snow, half-blinded by the brilliant sun flashing from its pristine surface into his eyes. He had to find a way out of this mess. He was desperate, and this was his last-ditch effort. There had to be some means of transportation, somewhere. A plane, a snowmobile, something. Clever as she was, Cuyler had probably hidden it a distance from the house to keep him from escaping. He didn't know why he hadn't thought of the possibility sooner.

He hadn't meant to fall asleep. He supposed the stress and sleepless nights were beginning to wear on him. It was only when he woke to see bright winter sunlight slanting through the window that he'd realized just how tired he'd been. Oddly, he felt rested, refreshed even. No dreams, for a change.

But that wasn't right, was it? There had been dreams, just not the usual wildly erotic ones that left him exhausted. He'd dreamed of Cuyler. She'd been leaning over the bed, touching his face, stroking his hair and whispering softly to him. Her touch had been soothing, her voice like a salve on his oldest wounds. He hadn't wanted her to leave.

He stopped walking and closed his eyes as a shaft of pain bisected his chest. There'd been a blanket over him when he woke. He didn't remember putting it there. Had Cuyler really come to stand over him, touched him that way, whispered so lovingly, so gently, as he'd slept?

She'd kissed him. Her soft, moist mouth had touched his for the barest instant, and he'd wanted to pull her into his arms, into his bed. He'd wanted to feel her smiling lips caress every inch of him, and then he'd wanted to do the same to her. The hell with the danger that she might go too far. The hell with the fact that they were sworn enemies. He wanted her with a passion above and beyond all of that. Above and beyond everything.

He opened his eyes and drew a deep breath, steadying himself. He had to get away from her. She was bewitching him, using her mental powers to make him forget his life's work, driving him so mad with desire he'd gladly exchange his every principle for a night in her arms. He was in danger with her, and he had to get out or lose his mind.

But now that he had, he almost wished he hadn't. He'd trudged a couple of miles, he figured, and the scenery hadn't changed in the least. Nothing but white. No trees. No vegetation of any kind. Hardly any hills. He was pretty sure what he was looking at could be described as tundra. He hoped to God he found some form of aid soon. He wasn't exactly dressed for long periods of exposure. Only thin rubbers separated his shoes from the hard-packed snow. His ski jacket was hardly sufficient, and he didn't even have a hat with him. The wind whipped hard out here with nothing to break its progress.

He walked a little farther, then frowned and tilted his head. What was that sound? A motor of some sort growled in the distance. He turned slowly, trying to gauge the source, then realization dawned. A snowmobile. No, more than one. And the sound came from the direction of the house, though he couldn't see it anymore. His first thought was that Cuyler was coming after him, using a machine she'd had hidden somewhere.

But that thought was quickly banished. It was still daylight. She wouldn't even be awake yet.

He blinked slowly as that thought sunk in. She wouldn't be awake. She'd be lying in her bed, behind unlocked doors, thinking she was completely safe up here in the middle of nowhere.

The motors died abruptly. They didn't fade away, but simply cut out. The snowmobiles had stopped, and as near as he could guess, they'd stopped near the house. Someone was there, and with a churning in his gut, Ramsey thought he could guess who.

It made no sense to think DPI had somehow tracked them here. But it made less sense to think some harmless folks had just decided to take a snowmobile ride north of the Arctic circle and happened upon her house. Cuyler was there, alone and completely helpless. Her stories of torture and murder were utter fabrications. He knew that. But they were echoing through his soul all the same as Ramsey started walking back the way he'd come. Then he started running.

He followed his own tracks for several yards, hands shoved deep in his jacket pockets, shoulders hunched against the biting wind. But the tracks got harder and harder to see as he went. He frowned hard, and whispered a little prayer they wouldn't disappear entirely before the house came into view. Damn, he'd been an idiot not to take windblown snow into account. It had been filling his tracks behind him all the way out here.

And then he couldn't see them at all. Not even the tiny depressions he'd been following this far. Dammit to hell, he couldn't see the house. Everything looked the same in every direction. The wind was blowing harder, its bite sharper with every gust. It would be dark soon, and colder than ever. He tried not to think about what might be happening in the house right now, but images danced through his thoughts anyway. Cuyler's warnings about DPI's tactics rang in his ears, no matter how he tried to tune them out. He hadn't believed her. He'd told himself she was just trying to convince him not to take her in. But he now found himself wondering if there was even the slightest chance of truth in her horror stories. He didn't want to believe that, wouldn't let himself believe it. But the idea that anyone might deliberately hurt her...

Why the hell did it drive him to the brink of madness to consider it? Why?

The motor sounds came to life again. He was closer. He tried to run faster, but the frigid air burned his lungs and throat. They were moving, fast, in the opposite direction.

"Ah, God, no..." He tried for more speed, but he was out of breath. His muscles screamed in protest. His legs gave out just as the house came into view, and he dropped to his knees in the snow, scanning the horizon where the sun hovered, about to set.

And then he spotted them. Three snowmobiles zipping over the tundra in the distance. One pulled something behind it. Something long and narrow that looked like a box. He groaned in anguish as they moved out of sight.

He wasn't sure how long he knelt there. Emotions raced through him, so potent and confusing that he felt dizzy. Hadn't he been determined to take Cuyler in himself? Hadn't he vowed that he'd never stop hating her and everyone like her for what they'd done to his mother?

Why, for God's sake, was he racked with guilt that he hadn't been there to protect her? The frustration was as bad as what had consumed him as a result of not having been there to protect his mother. Why? Why was he kneeling in the snow, burning inside with the urge to go after them, to somehow get her away from them? He cursed softly at the thought of riding in like some knight on a charger to rescue his damsel from villains. It wasn't like that. *She* was the villain of this piece.

Wasn't she?

He got to his feet and made his way back to the house, not even bothering to stomp the snow from his shoes as he ran through it and up to her bedroom, already knowing he wouldn't find her there.

The empty bed was rumpled, the drawers and closet gaping wide, clothes strewn everywhere. When he went back downstairs, he found more of the same. The place had been searched, hurriedly and recklessly, before they'd taken her away. Her pewter figurines lay strewn everywhere. Her crystals had tumbled helter-skelter to the floor. The bookshelves had been emptied, her precious fairy-tale stories trampled beneath uncaring feet.

He bent to pick up the first of the vampire books she'd shown him, and bit his lip against the burning in his throat and eyes.

He couldn't hope to hike out of here tonight. He'd die of exposure before he reached help, and then Cuyler would be on her own. He had to wait, though it would damn near kill him to do it. At first light, he'd go, with as many provisions as he could carry. He'd get out of here, somehow. And he'd find her.

After that, he didn't have a clue what he'd do.

For now, though, he had to sit tight and await the cold dawn. He sank into a chair, weak from turmoil, and opened the book in his hands.

Chapter Seven

It took him two hours to read the entire book. And Cuyler had been right. The entirety of one of DPI's most disastrous investigations had been documented there, from the viewpoint of its subjects. It was quite a different take on things from the one in the official records. Oh, the facts were the same, but DPI's methods and motivations and the characteristics of the subjects of that investigation, couldn't have differed more. Ramsey had to believe it was all propaganda. Because if it were true...

He groaned in undisguised agony. If it were true, then Cuyler had been right about the torture involved in DPI's research. Even several deaths, all detailed here in these pages.

But it wasn't true. It couldn't be.

He knew, though, that it very well could be. He'd never been involved in the research end of things, never actually witnessed the so-called harmless studies performed on the subjects. He wasn't a scientist. And while he'd been told that the prisoners brought in would be kept for a week or two and then released, unharmed, he'd never actually seen that happen, either.

DPI believed Cuyler and her kind to be no better than animals. Beings without emotions, incapable of caring. Heartless, soulless beasts who preyed on the innocent with no sense of remorse. That much he knew. And it wasn't so farfetched to think that an organization who believed that about a group might want to annihilate that group. Was it? So why hadn't he known about it? And would it have made a difference to him if he had?

Up until a few days ago he'd believed everything DPI said about the undead. And he'd had a personal vendetta, to boot. But not against Cuyler. Everything he'd ever believed had been a lie, at least where she was concerned.

He got up, intending to go to the little kitchen and begin packing supplies for his trek out. He was no longer so certain he could wait for dawn to break. There was a new urgency eating at his soul. He had to get to her, just to prove to himself that she was all right and not being subjected to the torments described in the book. With every second that passed, those scenes embedded themselves more deeply in his mind, only the victim wore Cuyler's beautiful face.

He stopped halfway to the kitchen, stiffening at the scraping sounds coming from the front door.

"Cuyler?" Hope surged in his chest as he sprinted and yanked the door open.

A big, furry dog stood there, staring at him. It barked twice when he only stared back in confusion. Where the hell had it come from? More barking followed, and he looked up in amazement to see three other dogs, identical to the first, sitting patiently in the snow. Huskies, all of them. Silvery fur and ice blue eyes. Magnificent, wide chests.

Sled dogs?

The one at the door barked again. Ramsey frowned, thinking of the sled and harnesses he'd seen in the basement. Was this how Cuyler had brought him here? Were these dogs hers? But what were they doing here now? Where had they been?

It didn't matter. He saw the means to get out of there, and he knew he had to take it. Leaving the door wide, he ran into the basement and hauled the awkward sled up the stairs. He dragged it outside, and went back for the harnesses, praying he could figure out how to put them on properly, hoping the dogs would allow it.

Hell, he didn't know what good it would do. He had no idea which way to go, even with transportation.

When he brought the harnesses outside, the dogs surrounded him, barking excitedly, tails wagging. They seemed impatient as he stretched the straps out, trying to see which way they went. But they stood motionless when he draped the things around them, and he knew they were used to this procedure.

Once he got them hooked to the sled, he ran back inside long enough to get his coat. That was all. His thoughts of bringing provisions had fled. All that remained was his urgent need to get to Cuyler, to make sure she was all right.

He stood on the back of the sled and picked up the reins. The dogs were off like a shot the minute his feet touched the narrow platform, nearly jarring him off into the snow. He didn't try to guide them. They seemed to know exactly where they were going. All Ramsey could do was hang on and pray that they really did know.

He wasn't sure his prayers were answered until several hours later when the dogs stopped and stood barking like a raucous group of soldiers celebrating victory. A huge, barnlike structure stood in the middle of the perfectly flat, snowy plain. As Ramsey tried to adjust to the oddness of finding it here, a gruff voice called out to him.

"I expect you'll be wanting to fly out of here, after that other plane."

Ramsey turned and gave his head a shake. A grizzled old man, his face completely obliterated by a massive gray beard, came from the barn and bent to expertly release the dogs from their harnesses.

"Who are you?"

"Just call me Kirkland. Did they take Miss Jade?"

"How do you—"

"Miss Jade, she told me there might come some men someday to try and take her. Warned me not to tell a soul about her house out there. And *I* never did." His tone suggested he thought Ramsey might have.

He couldn't believe this old man knew the truth about Cuyler, couldn't imagine her entrusting him with it. "Did she tell you why they would want to?"

"Nope. And I never asked. Ain't my business." He slung the harnesses over his shoulder, absently stroking the heads of the dogs who milled and danced around his legs. "Knew there was trouble, though, soon as I spotted that other plane. Miss Jade's a good woman. Kind of heart. Nursed one o' my dogs after he'd tangled with a wolf. Took care of him as if he'd been her own. Even sat up all night with him, didn't she, Duke?" He ruffled the fur of the dog in question before turning his attention back to Ramsey. "So are you gonna help her?"

Ramsey could only nod mutely.

"Good, then." He walked into the barn and Ramsey followed, watching him hang the harnesses on the wall. A small plane sat like a giant bird at rest, taking up most of the space. The old man tugged a large, sliding door and Ramsey helped him open it.

"I don't get this. What are you doing up here?" Ramsey followed him, getting into the plane behind him. He ducked his head and settled into the seat beside Kirkland in the cockpit.

"Livin', mostly. I fly folks in and out for hunting and such. Transport supplies for the Inuit village a few miles off." He slanted a sideways glance at Ramsey. "Best buckle up. Takeoffs are rough."

"Do you know where they went?"

The old man nodded, but didn't say a word as the engines came to life and the craft rolled slowly out of the barn.

"Where is he?" The man blew his offensive tobacco smoke into her face, and Cuyler turned her head as much as she could. It wasn't much.

She was handcuffed to a chair in what she took to be a bedroom, with three cruel faces watching her every move. Ordinarily she'd have simply snapped free of the cuffs, knocked the men on their arrogant backsides, and made her escape. Unfortunately she'd had the extreme displeasure of proving their newly developed tranquilizer did, indeed, work. She'd been injected just as she'd begun to rouse with the sunset. And now she was as weak as a mortal. A tired mortal. Her mind was murky at best.

Not so murky that she couldn't wonder about Ramsey, though. At first she'd thought he might have been involved in her capture. The relief that filled her when they'd begun asking her for his whereabouts had made her weaker than she already was.

"Miss Jade, don't make us resort to drastic measures." The fat, white-haired man had cruel eyes, like two small blue buttons on his face. Emotionless, snake's eyes. "We all know how sensitive your kind is to physical pain. Don't make us hurt you."

When she averted her face, he caught her chin and forced her to look at him. Another gentle puff of smoke in her face. She coughed.

"Tell me where Bachman is."

"I told you already, I don't know what you're talking about. I was alone in the house."

The man—the others called him Fuller—smiled grimly and shook his head. "His suitcase was there. We know he was with you."

"I stole it," she lied. "He'd been hounding me for months. I thought I might find out why if I took his things and went through them." She tried to keep her chin up, defiantly. She forced her sagging spine stiffer. She had to be strong, but she couldn't help but wonder where Ramsey had gone. Maybe the dogs had come early. Maybe he'd found them and run away from her while she'd slept. God, she hoped that was the case. She'd arranged with old Kirkland to turn the dogs loose on the third day, knowing they'd make a beeline for her home. If Ramsey found them, if he knew how to use them, he'd be okay. They knew the way to Kirkland's hangar as well as they knew each other.

Fuller turned to the thin, dark one. "What do you think of that, Whaley?"

"I think she's lying."

"I'm not." She blinked and tried to think of a way to convince them, but only came up blank. "Why are you after him, anyway? I thought he was one of you."

"So did he—" Whaley began, but his reply was cut off by a swift look from Fuller.

The third man sat in a chair, silent. He didn't appear to have the same stomach for abuse his two colleagues shared.

"You're going to have to tell us, Miss Jade. We can't go back to headquarters without him."

She sagged inwardly. They were taking her there. And if they did, she'd die. She could have called mentally, begged others of her kind to come to her aid. But with this tranquilizer in DPI's arsenal, any who tried to help her might end up sharing her fate. She didn't want to die with that on her conscience. God, if only she knew Ramsey was all right.

Fuller's hand disappeared into his pocket. It came out with a big, shiny pair of pliers. He opened and closed their ridged teeth slowly, right in front of her face. Then he handed them to Whaley, who moved around behind her.

"Begin with the little finger of her left hand," Fuller said matter-of-factly. "Crush it."

She felt the cold instrument touch her finger. "Wait! All right. All right, I'll tell you the truth."

The tool moved away from her hand. Fuller looked down at her, smiling grimly. "That's more like it. Where is he?"

Kirkland brought the plane in expertly at a small airport.

"This is it? This is where they landed?"

"Nope."

Ramsey drew a sharp breath and waited. Kirkland had already explained that he'd been able to track the other plane with the sonar equipment back at his hangar. But the guy was a man of few words.

"Landed at Loring, not too far off. Couldn't very well take you to an air force base now, could I?"

Grating his teeth, Ramsey prayed for patience, and time. He kept telling himself that Cuyler was fine. They wouldn't hurt her. But more and more, his own voice of reason sounded like a liar.

Kirkland opened the hatch and Ramsey jumped to the ground. He took a look around, but apart from the runways and hangars and small planes, there was nothing to give him a clue. "Where the hell are we, Kirkland?"

"Northern part of Maine."

Northern Maine? Why the hell would they bring her here? Why not go straight on to White Plains? He scanned the place, sifting his mind for answers.

"Nearest city's Limestone," Kirkland continued. "Caribou's a little farther. You got any idea where they took her?"

"Limestone?" He almost sagged in relief. DPI had safehouses scattered all over the country, kept them at their agents' disposal. If an operative got into trouble, he could take refuge at one of them. They had security systems like Fort Knox, and direct phone and computer links to headquarters. Like the obedient, devoted agent he'd always been, Ramsey had memorized the addresses of every safehouse in the northeast. There was one just past Limestone.

He didn't know why they'd have taken her there. Capturing her had been their goal, and now that they'd done that, what could they have to gain by delaying their return?

Unless she wasn't their only goal? Maybe there was something else, something here, that they were after.

Ramsey faced the grizzled man beside him. "I need a car."

Chapter Eight

It was ridiculous to be going about it this way. He worked for DPI. He was one of them. He could punch in the code, walk right through the gates, up to the front door, and demand to see the prisoner.

But something held him back, made him cautious. Crazy, vague suspicions clouded his mind. He'd put them to rest when he saw that she was okay, but until then, he figured he'd be better off erring on the side of caution.

He'd had to argue with Kirkland to get him to stay behind. Hell, the guy had no idea what he'd be getting into if he came along. DPI was big. Powerful. It was dangerous to get on the wrong side of them. It was bad enough Kirkland was going to make the call.

Vaguely, she heard the phone and the low muttering from beyond the closed bedroom door. Two of the men remained with her. One, the one called Fuller, had gone out to answer it. Seconds later, he returned.

"We've got him."

Whaley rose from where he'd been comfy on the bed. "Bachman?"

Fuller nodded. "That was the hospital in Caribou. Seems Bachman was brought in, unconscious. They found this number on him.''

Cuyler bit her lip to keep from gasping. God, what had happened to Ramsey?

"What the hell was he doing in Caribou?'' Whaley asked.

"Probably trying to make his way here, to the safehouse. I still think you guys are wrong about him.'' That was Stiles, the most. gentle of the three. "How bad is he?''

"Doesn't look like he'll make it through the night. We'd better get over there.''

Pain tore through her heart. Dying? Ramsey was dying? She squeezed her eyes tighter to stop the tears that burned in them.

"What about her?''

Fuller glanced at Stiles, who stood unspeaking in the corner. "Can you handle her?''

The pale man nodded.

"She gets too lively, just give her another shot. We'll call in from the hospital.''

She didn't lift her head as the two walked out. Just let it hang. She'd be damned if she'd give them any reason to inject her with more of that awful, debilitating drug.

Ramsey crouched behind a shrub near the gate and waited. Two men came out of the house. Their car started up, headlights came on, and he cringed lower. An electronic hum, a metallic groan, and the gates swung open. The car rolled through, and they began to close again.

He watched the car accelerate as soon as it hit the road. The gates were still closing. Taillights disappeared around a bend, and Ramsey lunged to his feet and dove. The metal scraped his sides as he threw himself in, then banged solidly as his body hit the ground. Closing his eyes, he drew three steadying breaths. Night birds slowly resumed their nightly serenade. A few seconds later, frogs joined in. The wind rustled the trees again. Other than that, Ramsey heard nothing. He got to his feet, brushed himself off, and started toward the house.

The numbered panel beside the door stared at him, the System

Armed light glaring like an evil eye. If they'd changed the entry code and he punched in the wrong numbers, an alarm would tell anyone inside of his presence. And he was certain there *was* still someone inside. They wouldn't leave Cuyler unguarded.

His tongue darted out to moisten dry lips, and he tasted the sweat on his upper lip. There was no other way. If he opened a window or door without entering the code, the alarm would sound anyway. His hand rose slowly, hovering at the panel. He wiggled his fingers, grated his teeth, and entered the four-digit code he'd committed to memory.

The red light blinked out. A green one came on instead.

Ramsey pressed his ear to the door, listening. Only silence came from within. He gripped the knob and his hand slipped on its surface when he tried to turn it. Rubbing his palm against his pant leg, he tried again.

The door opened without a creak, and Ramsey ducked inside, closing it quickly and quietly behind him. He didn't hesitate, but went directly to the staircase and up it, straining every cell in his body to be quiet.

At the top, he froze as heavy footsteps sounded. Pressing his back to the wall, he waited and watched. A door opened down the hall. In the muted light he recognized the man who emerged. Ron Stiles. Ramsey had worked with him before. He'd personally thought the guy lacked the grit to be with DPI. Tonight, though, he was secretly relieved the mild-mannered agent was the one guarding Cuyler.

Stiles crossed the hall and ducked into a bathroom, never once glancing Ramsey's way. When the door closed, Ramsey hurried to the room Stiles had exited and slipped inside.

Cuyler sat in a hard chair, her arms pulled severely behind her. Her head leaned forward unnaturally. She wasn't moving, and Ramsey felt his pulse skid to a stop. Dropping to his knees in front of her, he caught her chin and lifted it.

Her eyes were tear-swollen and closed. A vivid purple bruise marred her cheek, and her lower lip was crusted with dried blood. He just stared at her, unable to form words.

Weakly, she tugged her chin away from his hand. "Leave me alone," she murmured. "Please, just leave me alone."

"Cuyler..."

Her eyes opened, but they were unfocused. She stared at him from somewhere behind that drugged haze. "Ramsey?"

The toilet across the hall flushed and a second later steps came toward him. Ramsey fell back a few steps, so he'd be behind the door when it opened. Stiles came inside.

"If you twitch, I'll have to shoot you, Ron." Big words, he thought, for a man with no gun.

Stiles's narrow back stiffened, but he didn't move. His hands rose slowly on either side of his head. "Bachman? I thought you were—"

"Never mind what you thought." Ramsey came closer, reached around Stiles and took his side arm. "Now get me the key to the handcuffs. Quick." He prodded the man's back with his own gun, glad Stiles had fallen for the bluff.

Stiles nodded hard, dipped into his pants pocket and brought out the key. He held it up, and Ramsey prodded him again. "Get those cuffs off her."

"Damn."

"Do it!"

Stiles moved slowly around to the back of Cuyler's chair, bent down and unlocked the cuffs. He stood again, dangling them from one crooked finger. "I didn't believe Fuller when he said you'd turn on us." He shook his head. "Guess he was right."

Ramsey moved forward, keeping the gun leveled on his former colleague. "Why did he think that?"

Stiles just shook his head. "I'm not saying any more. Kill me if you have to."

"Okay, if I have to." Ramsey nodded toward the man. "Snap one of those cuffs to your wrist, Stiles." He waited while the other man complied. "Good. Now turn around, hands behind your back. Come on, you know the drill." Stiles turned. "On your knees." When he complied, Ramsey moved quickly to slip one cuff through the foot of the bed, around the frame, and then snapped it around Stiles's other hand.

"You won't get far, Bachman. Fuller and Whaley will be back here just as soon as—"

"Fuller?" Ramsey gave his head a shake, stuffing the automatic into his waistband. Fuller was his immediate superior, a man he'd trusted. And Whaley was the cruelest s.o.b. ever to walk the planet.

Ramsey went around in front of Cuyler again, kneeling. She sat limply, rubbing her wrists. Ramsey's anger grew when he saw the way the cuffs had cut into her flesh. He grew still more angry when she lifted her head to look into his eyes and he saw the pain in hers.

"Which one of you did this to her, Stiles?"

Stiles only glared at him and shook his head.

"And why, for God's sake? It's pretty obvious the tranquilizer works. Why'd they have to hit her?"

Stiles swore viciously. "She wouldn't tell us where you were. You'd think she was human the way you're carrying on. Hell, Bachman, she's only one of them. An animal, like the rest." At Ramsey's glare, he lowered his head. "I forgot, though. You are, too, aren't you? Just like them."

"What the hell do you mean by that?" Ramsey rose, towering over the man on the floor, his fists opening and closing at his sides.

Stiles clamped his jaw and refused to say another word. Ramsey turned back to Cuyler, bent over her, gripping her shoulders. "Can you stand?"

She nodded, and tried to rise to her feet, only to have her knees buckle as she collapsed against him. Ramsey caught her, slipped one hand beneath her legs and lifted her. He carried her across the hall and into the bathroom. Propping her against the sink, he ran cold water onto a washcloth. Carefully, he bathed her bruised face, her swollen eyes. He dabbed the blood from her lip.

"Here, hold this to that bruise and I'll look for something to put on your wrists."

She took it, but shook her head. "We have to get out of here, Ramsey. Those other two..." Her words trailed off and she swayed a little.

Ramsey found a tube of ointment and some bandages in the cabinet and stuffed them into his pocket. Then he bent to scoop her up again. He carried her down the stairs, toward the front door.

Cuyler's eyes had fallen closed again. The damned drug. And God only knew what else they'd done to her. His fury was beyond anything he'd felt in his life. The closest he'd come was the rage he'd felt when his own mother had been murdered. But that had been a child's rage. It didn't compare to the full-blown tempest whirling inside him now. He wanted to kill the DPI bastards for hurting her this way.

He carried her out into the chilly autumn night, marveling at the way her small body fit in his arms. He cradled her to his chest as if she were something precious. Hell, she was! Why was that so hard for him to admit? Cuyler was special, no matter what else she might be, and she didn't deserve what they'd done to her.

His shoes ground over gravel as he ran to the gate, opening it. He didn't care that it set off alarms inside...it didn't matter now.

Ramsey reached the twisting, narrow road and started up the opposite direction from the one Whaley and Fuller had gone. The car sat off the roadside where he'd left it, surrounded by scraggly brush and branches. He managed to open the passenger door with one hand and lower Cuyler to the seat. He forced his hands to remain steady as he snapped the safety belt around her, but it wasn't easy. She looked bad, and he had no idea what to do for her. She might be dying for all he knew.

Gently he pushed her hair out of her eyes. Why had he left her the way he had? Why the hell hadn't he been there when those bastards had shown up? Why hadn't he believed what she'd told him about DPI?

Her eyes opened, mere slits fringed by damp black lashes. "Hurry."

Nodding, he slammed her door and raced around to the driver's side. Seconds later the car reversed out of its hiding place and onto the road. Grinding gears in his haste, Ramsey shifted, and spun tires as they sped away from the safehouse, away from DPI, away from everything Ramsey had known in his life.

Ron Stiles twisted and squirmed until he managed to work the extra key out of his back pocket. It took some maneuvering to fit it into the lock without being able to see what he was doing, but he did it. The cuffs sprang free and he automatically brought his hands around in front of him and rubbed his wrists.

Then he stopped and looked down at them. Cuyler Jade's wrists had been rubbed raw, bleeding. There'd been no reason for Fuller to put the handcuffs on so tightly. But he had, and it had pricked Stiles's conscience to see it. Still, he hadn't said anything.

And there'd really been no reason for Whaley to hit her. Not once, but twice. And they hadn't been slaps. The bruises on her face had come from Whaley's knuckles when she'd told them more lies about Ramsey's whereabouts. Once again, Stiles hadn't voiced his objections. If Ramsey cared about her at all, Stiles supposed it was little wonder he'd been furious to see her that way.

But that was the question, wasn't it? Why on earth did Ramsey care about her? How had he gotten so mixed up with her that he'd toss his career—his life—in the toilet by coming to her rescue that way? God, he knew she wasn't human. He *knew*. So what was going on in his head?

Stiles hadn't wanted to believe what he'd read in Ramsey's files. He'd balked against what Fuller had said. That Ramsey had turned on them. That he was the enemy now. But now that he'd seen the proof of it with his own eyes, he couldn't doubt anymore. He just wished he understood.

Stiles left the bedroom, jogged down the stairs, and picked up the phone.

Chapter Nine

She couldn't believe he'd done it. As Ramsey drove the car through the night, Cuyler forced her heavy eyes open and looked at him. His knuckles were white on the steering wheel. His jaw tensed as if he were grating his teeth. Perspiration made his forehead shiny in the glow of the dash lights, and dark stubble coated his face. Gray eyes, intense with concentration and maybe a little fear, darted her way every few seconds. And when he saw her gaze on him, one side of his mouth pulled upward slightly and briefly. An almost smile, meant to reassure her. No more.

"You really came for me."

"Don't tell me you're surprised." He shook his head, sighing. "You've been saying all along I wouldn't take you in."

She bit her lower lip, unable to take her eyes from his face, from the strength she saw in it. And the turmoil. "You risked everything..."

He turned onto a larger road and increased his speed. Then, licking his lips, he glanced her way again. One hand left the steering wheel and he brushed it lightly over her bruised cheek. His lips thinned. "I'm sorry, Cuyler."

"Sorry? You just saved my life—"

"If I'd listened to you in the first place, I wouldn't have had to. If I hadn't left you there, alone..." He blinked slowly, lowering his hand and focusing his vision on the road once again. "I tried to get back when I heard the snowmobiles, but—"

"It doesn't matter." She slid her hand over his on the wheel. "You came after me. You got me out of there."

He shook his head. "It's not over yet, Cuyler. They aren't going to let us go without a fight. And they're after both of us now."

"They were always after both of us."

He frowned, slanting her a sidelong glance.

"Ramsey, they kept asking me where you were. The fat one, Fuller, he told the others that you were never really one of them, that it was only a matter of time before you turned on them."

Ramsey blew all the air out of his lungs. "That doesn't make a damn bit of sense. Why would he say something like that? I've never given them any reason to question my loyalty."

"I don't know."

Ramsey swore under his breath and hit the brakes, snapping the headlights off as he pulled the car onto the shoulder. Cuyler followed his gaze and saw the flashing lights ahead, on the ramp to the highway. A roadblock.

"Do you think they're looking for *us?* Already?"

"DPI works fast." He pulled the car around in a U-turn and slowly drove back the other way, flicking the headlights back on when they were out of sight. "We'll have to take back roads out of here."

"To where? Ramsey, where can we go?"

He closed his eyes slowly. "I don't know." He turned onto a side road, and then another. "There's a map in the glove compartment."

She took out the map, unfolded it on her lap, and tried to keep her still-clouded mind focused on finding out where they were, and on discovering a safe route. "Okay, at the end of this road, turn left. That one runs parallel to the highway."

He followed her directions, but even before they reached the road she'd pointed out, Cuyler saw the glow of more flashing lights in the distance.

Ramsey swore. "They've got us boxed in." He stopped the car, shut it off, and turned to face her. "We're not gonna get by them in this car. How do you feel? You up to a walk?"

She lifted her chin and swallowed her fear. She had to be strong to help him through this, even though the pain they'd inflicted and the blood she'd lost made her weaker than she'd ever felt in her life. "I'm fine. Let's go."

With a nod, Ramsey shrugged out of his jacket, then used the sleeve to wipe the steering wheel and gearshift, the headlight button, and anything else he might have touched. "No sense leaving them any clues."

She nodded, taking the map with her as she got out of the car. Then he got out, and came around the car. He put his jacket around her shoulders, folded his big hand around hers, and led her into the woods at the roadside.

The darkness worked in their favor as they made their way from one small patch of woods to another, keeping the road in sight but staying far enough away from it to remain concealed by the trees.

She was exhausted. He knew she was. And frightened. Hell, he couldn't blame her. He was scared himself. DPI was not going to be easy to elude. Besides, he had other reasons to worry. He didn't have a drop of insulin on him. And if he didn't get some soon, he fully expected to start feeling the effects.

His watch told him there was an hour before dawn, when Cuyler suddenly stopped, clutched her stomach and doubled over. She fell to her knees, groaning and then retching violently.

Ramsey knelt beside her, held her shoulders. Fear made him shudder as he wondered what could be wrong. God, she was so weak, already.

She rose, unsteadily, leaning on him for support. "It's all right. I'm all right."

"No, you're not. Cuyler, what the hell is it?"

She sniffed, still not standing very steadily. "I don't know. Maybe the drug they injected me with. I don't know. It's all right now, though."

It wasn't. It was perfectly clear that she was anything but all right. She was pale, trembling, cold. She needed someplace warm to rest and... Hell, he didn't know what else she needed. But whatever, he was determined to get it for her. They were approaching a town, of sorts. A small grouping of neat little houses, with cars and the occasional bicycle in short, paved driveways. Supporting Cuyler with an arm around her shoulders, tucking her body close to his, he took her toward them, scanning for someplace, anyplace, where she might lie down for a while.

She stiffened when he pulled her out of the sheltering trees and toward clipped back lawns, all of them littered with colorful leaves. "It's all right," he whispered. "Come on, trust me."

She did, but hesitantly. They crossed three backyards before they found one with a prefab shed standing in it. Ramsey sighed in relief and started toward it, only to come to an abrupt halt when a huge dog lunged out of its doghouse and began barking loudly.

He took a single step backward, ready to duck back into the trees, but Cuyler caught his arm, stopping him. She didn't say a word. Just moved closer to the dog, staring at it with an intensity that was palpable. The dog stopped barking. It stared right back at her, ears pricked forward, head tilted to one side. Then its tail wagged. She bent forward to stroke his big head. Ramsey only stood, dumbfounded, watching.

She turned to face him, smiling weakly. "He'll keep quiet now."

Ramsey shook his head. "So, should I start calling you Dr. Doolittle?"

"It doesn't always work. But sometimes, I can let animals know I'm a friend."

He took her hand again and led her to the shed, thanking his lucky stars there was no lock on the door. It opened easily, without a creak, and he pulled her inside. When he closed the door behind him they were in total darkness. He held her close to his side as he moved to the back, tripping once over what felt like a lawn mower, knocking over a shovel. Against the back wall, he urged her to the floor, then went back, feeling his way. He found a tarp that covered some piece of small machinery, and tugged it away.

He returned and settled beside her, tucking the tarp around both of them for warmth.

"We could have gone farther." She snuggled close to him, resting her head on his shoulder.

"You're barely putting one foot in front of the other, Cuyler. You're sick and you know it." He ran one hand through her tousled hair. "What can I do to make it better?"

He felt her hesitation, could almost feel her deciding not to tell him. "Nothing. It'll pass."

"Funny how I can tell when you're lying." He drew a breath. "It's not just the drug, is it, Cuyler?"

She didn't answer.

"Cuyler, if there's something I can do to help you, I want to do it."

Her hand touched the side of his face. "No, you don't."

It was her tone, more than her words, that tripped the knowledge in his brain. "It's the blood loss, isn't it?" He felt her stiffen, knew he'd hit on it. "Your wrists bled, your lip. Quite a lot from the look of your blouse."

"The injuries aren't that bad, Ramsey. We tend to bleed a lot. That's all."

"So you need to replenish it."

"Tomorrow night. We'll find a blood bank somewhere or—"

"You could take some of mine."

"Ramsey, no—"

"You'd feel stronger, better, wouldn't you? Cuyler, it's all right. I trust you."

She sighed and sat up a little straighter. "That isn't the point. Look, Ramsey, it would make us even more connected than we already are. The link between us is already tearing you apart inside. I don't want to make it even stronger."

He sat up, too, gripped her shoulders and turned her toward him. "I don't go ten minutes without thinking about you, Cuyler. I've gone against everything I've ever believed in just to make sure you're all right. I don't see how it can get any stronger."

He felt her shake her head. "It's the situation. Ramsey, you'd made up your mind to get away from me. You struck out through the frozen wilderness on foot, you were so desperate to leave. And if those men hadn't shown up, I don't think you'd have come back. You'd have found a way out, gone back to your old life and stayed as far away from me as you could get. You still might want to do that, if we survive this.''

He closed his eyes and drew a steady breath. "I was still fighting what I felt. Dammit, you can understand that, can't you? One of you killed my mother, for God's sake. How could I—''

"One of us. You see? You still see it that way. An individual killed your mother, Ramsey. I had nothing to do with it.''

"I know that—''

"I could get help for us. I could summon others to help us out of this mess. We could stay with them until the danger passes. I could do it right now, Ramsey.''

He went utterly silent at her words. Others. Others like her. Vampires. The beings he'd been taught to hate for most of his life. He breathed deeply, and shook his head. He couldn't trust his life to them. Just because he'd finally realized that Cuyler wasn't a heartless predator, didn't mean the others weren't.

She sighed deeply, and he thought he heard sadness in the sound. "It's all right. I won't do it. I wasn't considering it, anyway. I wouldn't want to bring anyone else into DPI's sights. I only wanted to make a point.''

"Cuyler, you can't expect me to put my life in their hands.''

"No. And I don't. But, Ramsey, they're just people. We were all human once, just like you. There are good and bad in any group, and you can't just write off an entire race because of one incident. It's bigotry, can't you see that?''

"No, it's not. It's different—''

"It's different because *we're* different, right?'' She leaned against the wall, turning her back to him.

He knew he'd hurt her, angered her. But, dammit, it had been a major leap for him to see *her* as less than a monster, as a caring woman with thoughts and feelings like any other. Now she expected him to accept the entire race as just ordinary folks with a slight aversion to sunlight and solid food? They'd been different, even as humans. That damned antigen in their blood *made* them different.

No, dammit, he wasn't ready to concede that *everything* he'd ever learned had been wrong. DPI may have gone too far in their persecution, but they'd had reasons. Ramsey had reasons, too. His mother. She was his reason, and he couldn't let go of his old anger so easily.

Ramsey dozed, and it was full daylight when he woke. Cuyler slept in a corner, far away from him. It was the darkest spot in the shed, and while no sunlight touched her body, he covered her entirely with the tarp, just in case. There were no windows in the metal shed, but light spilled through seams in the tin here and there. He worried about the beams moving as the sun did.

Sounds of life—motors, air brakes—floated toward him. He opened the door a crack and peeked outside, checking first to make sure the light didn't touch Cuyler. A school bus rolled to a stop in front of the house. He couldn't see who boarded, since the house itself blocked his view, but a few seconds later it rolled away, followed closely by the two cars that had been in the driveway.

God, could he be so lucky? A two-career family with all the kids in school? He slipped out of the shed, glancing in both directions to be sure no one could see. He gave the dog a cursory glance, but the huge Newfoundland was busy devouring a fresh supply of kibble and didn't even look his way.

Swallowing a healthy dose of anxiety, Ramsey walked up to the back door and knocked as hard as he could. What better way to find out if anyone was home? He waited, rehearsing what he'd say if someone answered. He figured he could pretend he was at the wrong house. But no answer came. The lock was a snap for any government agent worth his salt. In a few seconds he was inside, carefully and quietly searching the place just to be sure no one was around. Sighing in relief when there wasn't.

It was too much to hope that one of the residents might be diabetic and have some insulin lying around. But he checked anyway. Not finding any, he was extremely careful when he raided the fridge. He had to eat, but God only knew what his system would do with whatever he put into it. He made do with a few stalks of celery and a sugar-free rice cake. There was a little coffee left in the pot, and he heated it in the microwave and gulped it down. Then he headed for the living room and snapped on the television, only to stumble a few steps backward when he saw his own face and a composite drawing of Cuyler's on the screen, with a 1-800 number beneath them.

He only heard the words ''Armed and extremely dangerous,'' before the picture changed and the reporter launched into another story.

His initial reaction was to head for the shed, gather Cuyler up, and run as fast as they could go. But he couldn't do that. He had to wait until sunset. There was no other way.

He got another rice cake, and sat down to work out the most immediate problem. Cuyler's condition. She was weak, sick. He knew what she needed to feel strong again. And he knew she wouldn't take it from him no matter how often he offered.

So he had to come up with some way to convince her. And there was only one that came to mind.

Chapter Ten

She woke to the warning vibrations skittering over her nerve endings. The tarp slipped from her shoulders as she sat up, calling out to Ramsey.

"Right here. I'm right here." There was a click, and then the beam of a flashlight bathed the space between them. One side of Ramsey's mouth curved upward before the other, but she got the feeling his smile was hiding some new turmoil. "Found a few treasures in the house."

She sat up straighter, but dizziness swamped her. He saw it, frowned at her, and she tried to change the subject. "You were in the house?"

"Yeah. No one was home." His smile died slowly. "I only took what we needed. They won't even notice it's missing."

Her breath escaped in a rush. "Just what did we need so badly you had to steal for it?"

His head came up fast, a look of surprise on his face.

"Didn't mean to shock you like that, Ramsey. I forgot, my kind isn't supposed to have any moral values at all. You're not going to faint on me, are you?"

His brows drew together. "You wake up cranky, anybody ever tell you that? You still don't feel very well, do you?" She refused to answer. Ramsey scanned her face. "You sure as hell don't look as if you do. Anyway, I didn't steal this stuff, exactly. I left some money. Stuffed it under the sofa cushion.''

She rolled her eyes. ''Wonderful. But it still wasn't worth the risk. You could have been seen.''

''But I wasn't. And I got us a much-needed flashlight. Ought to come in handy, since we can only travel by night.''

''I have excellent night vision.''

''A sleeping bag, so we don't catch pneumonia.''

''I *can't* catch pneumonia.''

''Some food—''

She crooked an eyebrow at him.

''Yeah, right. I forgot. How about this, then?'' He handed her some folded clothing, and she took it.

''What—''

''One pair of jeans, size six, petite. They must have a teenager about your size. And a warm sweater. Now put them on and quit griping. We have to move.''

She got to her feet, set the clothes aside, and grabbed the hem of her blouse. Then she paused. ''Well?''

Ramsey blinked, breaking his intense stare. ''Well, what?''

''You going to turn off that light?''

''Sure.'' There was a soft click, and the shed was once again bathed in darkness.

Cuyler heeled off her shoes, pulled her blouse over her head, then stepped out of her pants. She reached for the clothing she'd set aside, but Ramsey's hand closed over hers, stopping her.

She drew a quick breath, looking behind her. ''What is it?''

''Not dark enough in here, I guess.''

He stood closer, his shirt brushing her back. Then his hands crept around her waist, pulling her back against his strong chest. ''I still want you, Cuyler. I'm still having those damned dreams.''

She closed her eyes tightly, stiffening herself against the on-slaught of desire that rocked her. She couldn't let this happen, not now, not when her hunger was so strong. She hadn't fed in such a long time. Didn't he realize what would happen if they...

''I can't...''

"Why not?" His head bent over her shoulder, his lips finding and nuzzling her neck. The brush of his new whiskers scraped over her skin, and she shivered.

Any excuse would do. She had to stop this craziness. "You still see me...as... Stop, Ramsey." Her head tipped sideways as his mouth moved over her shoulder. Warm fingertips trailed upward, along her spine. "I don't want..." The words became a sigh.

"Yes, you do. And so do I. Hell, I'm tired of fighting it, Cuyler. I'm tired of trying to deny it, hoping it will go away. It won't. I think we both know that."

"But..." His palms came up beneath her breasts, cupped them, squeezed. "Ramsey," she breathed. "Ramsey, you still believe..."

"The hell with what I believe. This is physical. Beliefs don't enter into it." His fingertips closed on her nipples. She caught her breath. He applied more pressure and she sighed. In one quick motion he turned her around, caught her mouth beneath his, dug his tongue into her. She responded, sucking it, running her hands up his back, under his shirt.

He gripped her buttocks in his hands, lifting her as he sat down on the seat of a lawn tractor, pulling her onto his lap so she was straddling him. Then he attacked her breasts with his mouth, sucking, biting, licking at them until she writhed against the hardness she felt poking up through his jeans.

"This isn't fair," she whispered.

"It was your idea. You said back at the house that if we just did it once, we might get over it. Well, here we are, Cuyler. Let's test your theory."

He devoured her nipples again, one after the other, all the while holding her hard to his lap and moving his hips against her. Then his hands closed on her waist and he lifted her, higher, until her backside rested in the curve of the steering wheel.

"What—?"

"I did this in my dreams, Cuyler. I want to try it for real." His hands slipped up the insides of her thighs, and he pressed them open. Then he dropped kisses along them, moving higher, ever higher. Finally his mouth found its goal and he pressed his face to her. His tongue parted her and found its way inside. Cuyler's head fell backward as she felt him licking her, scraping her with his teeth, sucking at her until she trembled all over.

Her hands tangled into his hair and he lifted his head, staring up at her as his hands moved to his jeans. Then he returned them to her waist, to pull her down to him. As he filled her, she felt the current that moved through both of them. Twining her arms around his neck, burying her face there, she sank lower. He clasped her hips, lifting her, lowering her again, plunging deeper inside her with every thrust.

Her lips caressed his neck, and her need mounted, beginning to build as she'd known it would. Every step she took toward fulfillment fired the hunger. She tasted the salt of his skin, felt the blood rushing beneath it.

He moved faster. Ecstasy hovered just beyond her reach, and the thirst raged. She tore her head away from his muscled neck, averting her face.

His hands slid up over her back, captured her face and turned it toward him again. He kissed her, deeply, desperately. "It's all right, Cuyler." His lips moved over hers as he whispered. He guided her head to his neck once more. "It's all right. Do it."

Her lips trembled on his skin, then parted. Only a sip, only one small taste of his essence. Just enough to get her through this night.

He stiffened, moaning deep and hoarse as her teeth pierced his throat. His hands pressed to the back of her head even as his body rocked harder and faster in time with hers. The climax claimed her, held her in its shattering grip for an instant, and forever.

As it slowly faded, the ripples of pleasure smoothing and stilling, Cuyler lifted her head away and closed her eyes to prevent the tears from spilling over. "God, what have I done?" She couldn't look at him, couldn't bear to see condemnation in his eyes. She began to rise, but he held her to him.

"You had to, Cuyler. You needed—"

Her sudden stare stopped his words. She searched his face, not believing what she was thinking, not wanting to think it. "You knew, didn't you? You knew the way desire would heighten the need until I couldn't fight it?"

He nodded once. "Yeah. I knew. And I also knew you couldn't take another night on the run without it." He shrugged, his hands moving into her hair, stroking it. "I offered earlier. You refused. I couldn't think of any other way."

That's all it was, then. Physical needs that needed fulfillment, just as he'd said. Only he'd been referring to hers, not to his own.

She slid to the floor, pulling from his grasp when he tried to keep her with him. Without a word, she picked up the clothes and began to dress. He got up, as well, but she didn't look at him. She couldn't. Making love to him had filled her heart to overflowing. Realizing how little it meant to him had broken it in two, and she could almost feel the fragile contents spilling onto the floor.

Cuyler heard him moving around, packing up his treasures, she imagined. Then he stood still, and she felt his gaze on her.

"I hurt you," he said softly. "I didn't mean to."

Blinking her eyes dry, she fixed her face into a smiling mask, and turned to face him. "No, Ramsey. It was physical, right? No feelings involved."

His eyes probed hers, reaching through the darkness, it seemed, into the depths of her soul. "Maybe…" He stopped speaking, his head coming up slowly. "What is that? Sounds like a flock of geese, or…"

Cuyler listened, and then her broken heart froze inside her. "Dogs! God, they've got dogs!" The crying of what sounded like a hundred hounds filled the night, louder when she flung the door open and ran outside.

Ramsey grasped her hand and headed for the street. She knew there was no use creeping through the woods, not now. Speed was what mattered. Calming one family pet with the power of her mind was a simple trick. She knew better than to try it with an entire pack of vicious hounds.

Cuyler's heart hammered with fear as she ran beside Ramsey. The baying drew nearer, louder. In moments the dogs would burst out of the woods where they were searching. They'd be on them seconds later, and it would be over. Everything—life—would be over.

"There! Look!" Ramsey didn't slow down. He kept running, but veered into a driveway, only stopping when he came to a mean-looking black motorcycle leaning on its kickstand. Releasing her hand, he straddled the seat. One kick, two. The motor roared and Ramsey twisted the accelerator, revving it. Puffs of black smoke belched from twin pipes at the back. Cuyler leapt on behind him, clinging to his waist as he released the clutch and the bike lurched into motion. Inexpertly, he turned it around, lowering one foot for balance. Then he shifted, gunned it, and they shot out of the driveway and down the street.

She might be killed on this suicide machine, she thought vaguely. But at least she couldn't hear those damn dogs anymore.

Okay, so he'd hurt her…again. He could only pray there would be time to make it up later.

When he'd decided to make love to Cuyler, he'd told himself he was doing it for her, so she wouldn't wilt and die of her brand of starvation before he could get her to safety. The problem was, what he'd told himself had been a lie. And not even a very convincing one. He'd wanted her. Hell, he still wanted her. Instead of dulling this rampant lust he felt, being with her had only sharpened it to a razor's edge. It hadn't been physical, dammit. It had been something more, something deeper, almost…almost spiritual. And when she'd finally done what he'd wanted her to do…

He shook his head in wonder. For a few brief seconds he'd felt everything she was feeling. He'd experienced her thoughts, known her emotions, felt every sensation that rippled through her body. It had been as if their minds had melded into one. He'd had the shocking sensation of her heart beating beside his within his own chest.

All of that had combined with the passion he felt for her and exploded into something he'd never felt before. It wasn't like sex with a…with a normal woman. It was above and beyond, a whole other world.

And so what had he done with all this newfound knowledge about her? Nothing. He'd ignored it, pretended it hadn't happened, let her go on thinking the entire exchange had been his own clever plot to get her to drink.

She was hurting over that, now. There was a real, physical pain where her heart lived. She felt as if her soul was bleeding, and she was battling tears.

Ramsey blinked in shock as those emotions flicked through his mind just as clearly as if they were his own. What the hell?

A police car blocked the road ahead. Ramsey leaned left, turning the handlebars and heading the bike over someone's back lawn. They bounded up and down on the seat as he drove over what felt like a washboard, up a shallow hill, and onto another road, then continued in the direction he'd been going. The ploy worked. The police couldn't get ahead of him in time to block his way, and he realized he could get to the road that ran parallel to the highway in the same manner.

This time, though, he didn't wait for a cruiser with flashing lights to force him off. He drove across a farmer's field, rutted and rough all the way, and he had to struggle to keep the bike upright. The cops would converge on the road where he'd been. But he would zip right past them by another route. For the first time tonight he thought they just might get out of this mess alive.

Cuyler was beginning to think so, too.

Ramsey frowned, glancing at her behind him. Her arms tightened a little at his waist, and her head rested against his back. He supposed he could no longer doubt that she had feelings and emotions. Not when he was experiencing everything she thought, everything she felt. This must have been what she'd meant when she'd told him that the connection between them would be even more powerful if she drank from him.

He felt her emotions. She was scared. But beyond that, a profound sadness made her keep fighting back tears. She thought that maybe she'd been wrong about him, all along. She thought that he'd never be able to see that his mistrust of her kind was a mistake, a product of the hatred he'd nurtured for so long. And she thought...

Ramsey blinked in shock and nearly dumped the bike. She thought she might be falling in love with him.

"Have we lost them?" She had to yell close to his ear to make herself heard over the motorcycle.

"Only for the moment," he shouted back. "Once they get a chopper up, they'll spot us again." The road they were on veered away from the highway, but he followed it anyway. It took her a moment to realize where he was going, but when she saw the sign, she stiffened. Limestone 5 Miles.

"Ramsey, you're going the wrong way! This is where we started!"

"Exactly what they'll be thinking," he told her. He took a turn, then another, and within a few minutes they were on a road Cuyler recognized. Ramsey stopped the bike, and when they both got off, he pushed it into the trees at the roadside. Taking her hand, he pulled her along beside him, right up to the gates of the house where she'd been held prisoner such a short time ago.

Chapter Eleven

She shivered uncontrollably as Ramsey pulled her through the gates, along the path, right through the front door. He knew what she must be thinking. That he'd lost his mind, or that he'd decided to turn her over to DPI after all. It amazed him that she didn't argue with him, just came along, completely trusting a man who'd given her nothing but reasons not to.

Sensing her turmoil, he gave her hand a reassuring squeeze as he closed the door behind them. "It's gonna be all right, Cuyler. This is the safest place we could be right now. The last place they'd think to look for us. And you can bet Fuller and his men won't be back here as long as they think they're on our trail."

She bit her lip, her gaze scanning the living room. The place looked like the home of a wealthy, tasteless individual. Not a branch office for a government agency. But then, that was the whole idea. DPI's anonymity was vital to its success.

Ramsey armed the security device, then began fiddling with the buttons, programming a new entry code, one Fuller wouldn't know. Cuyler walked slowly away from him, and he heard her exhausted sigh. Fortunately, though, her wounds had healed with the daytime rest. Her wrists were no longer cut and bruised. The purple mark on her face had vanished, and her cut lip had healed.

But some wounds were tougher to heal than others. And he still felt her pain, the one he'd caused himself. He'd have to find a way to remedy that soon, or he'd lose her. He wasn't sure they could get out of this alive, but if they did, and if they went their separate ways the way Cuyler seemed to have decided they must, he was going to hurt for a very long time.

He paused in punching buttons, to slant her a glance. "Cuyler, you're wrung out. Why don't you go upstairs, take a nice hot bath, relax for a while?"

She blinked slowly, and he knew she was tempted by the suggestion. "No, Ramsey. Two sets of eyes are better than one. Suppose I go up there and a swarm of agents kick the door in?"

"I don't think that's likely to happen anytime soon."

He finished punching in the new entry code. No one would open this door, or the front gate, without him knowing about it. Then he turned to her again, saw the uncertainty in her eyes. "Go on, Cuyler. Ask me."

"Ask you what?" Her chin lifted a little, and he saw her trying to mask her doubts.

"Why I brought you here," he said softly. He ran one hand over the side of her face, cupped her cheek. God, her skin was soft. "Not to give you up, Cuyler. If they want you, they'll have to go through me."

She bit her lower lip, nodding, but he knew she wasn't as sure of that as he was.

"You don't believe it?"

"I…" She shook her head, paced away from him. "How can I believe you'd lay your life on the line to protect someone you still see as some kind of inferior species?"

"That isn't—"

"I know. That isn't what you meant to say." She shook her head, turning to face him again, her gaze steady, strong. "But it's how you feel."

He shook his head slowly. "You're wrong, Cuyler. There's nothing inferior about you."

"Just the rest of my kind, right, Ramsey? So what does that make me? An exception? A freak?"

He lifted his hands, palms up, struggling to find words that would convince her how wrong she was, but she gave him a single glance that told him it would do no good. She wouldn't listen. He let his hands fall to his sides, sighing in defeat.

"So, why *did* you bring me here?"

Ramsey closed his eyes, tried to find some patience. It would take time to get her to trust him again. She'd believed so strongly in him before, and his fall from grace must have been a damaging one. But not fatal. "Come here. I'll show you."

He took her hand in his and laced his fingers with hers. Such a small hand, silky soft, steady now, despite her fears. He thought about the way that hand had felt tangled in his hair, those fingertips sinking into his shoulders. He glanced down at her, caught her staring up at him, but she looked away fast. He cleared his throat and pulled her with him to the door at the far end of the room. When he stepped through, he waved an arm at the equipment that covered every inch of the counters that lined the room. Computers, faxes, phones, radios, an entire bank of video screens, each showing a steady view of a different room within this house.

He heard the air escape her in a rush, heard her murmured exclamation. Ignoring it, he moved forward, snapping on the police band receiver, and then the more sophisticated radio. The one DPI used to keep in touch. He listened for a minute, heard nothing but static. Then he sank into a chair and flicked on a computer.

"What are you doing?"

He glanced sideways at her, but his attention shot right back to the screen. "I'll know everything they do, every move they make from here on in, Cuyler. We'll figure a safe way out of here before morning. Meanwhile, this system is a direct link to the main one in White Plains. I'd like to see what they have on me, find out why Fuller's been doubting my loyalty."

He heard her move, then turned to see her leaning against a wall, chewing her lower lip. "There's not much you can do here, really. I'll be on top of things. Take that bath."

Cuyler bathed. She didn't do as Ramsey had suggested, though, and lounge around in steaming water for hours. She made it quick and efficient. Then she scoured the house for extra clothes, finding none. She made do with the jeans and sweater she'd been wearing. After she'd towel dried her hair, she wandered back down to the first floor, located the kitchen, and brewed a pot of coffee.

With a cup in her hand, she went back to the room, tapped once, and walked in. Ramsey's face did a lousy job of hiding his emotions, and the look it wore made her heart trip over itself. He faced her when he heard her come in, tried to mask his bewildered expression, but still failed miserably.

She crossed to where he sat, pressed the mug into his hand. "How bad is it?"

He licked his lips, lowering his eyes. "Pretty bad."

"Tell me."

He glanced at the screen in front of him. It showed a spider web of lines that looked like a map, with little red lights glowing at intervals. He pointed to one of them. "These are the roadblocks. There's not one route out of here they haven't plugged tight. They're checking every vehicle that passes."

"So we can't get out by car. We can go on foot."

"They have choppers up, scanning the ground for us. And the dogs are working the woods. Cuyler, I don't think—"

The front door slammed and both of them went stiff, whirling toward the sound.

"You don't *think* at all, Bachman. That's part of the problem."

The deep voice was one Ramsey had heard before. He recognized it, and rose slowly.

The dark form filled the doorway, nodding once to Ramsey. "Hello again, Agent Bachman."

Ramsey tried to swallow, but found his throat blocked by a brick of hatred. This man was a killer, a killer Ramsey had been sent to bring in. But he'd failed. "Damien."

"Aren't you glad to see me, Bachman? Thought you'd be over-joyed, after chasing me all those months, trying to capture me for your bosses at DPI."

Ramsey took a single step forward. "You killed two women, you bastard. And you—"

Damien glared at him, his black eyes glittering with unconcealed dislike. "I killed one man. A vampire. The one responsible for the two murders you were sent to investigate."

"Liar!" Ramsey lunged toward him, only to have Cuyler leap in front of him, her palms flat to his chest.

"It's true, Ramsey! There were witnesses. I've read the whole account, and he's telling you the truth."

Ramsey glanced down at her, then at the man he'd spent months trying to capture, the man who'd made a beautiful young woman into a creature like himself.

Damien blinked and held his gaze. Some of the fury left the vampire's eyes. "She was dying," he said simply. "I loved her, Bachman. I couldn't just stand by and let her go."

Ramsey narrowed his eyes and shook his head.

"Check your precious DPI files, if you don't believe me." Damien lowered his head and paced in a small circle. "They know now it wasn't me who murdered those two. They know it was Anthar, the vampire I killed. Yet the hunt for me continues." He stood still, shot Ramsey a glare. "Go on, check. You have the information at your fingertips. Or are you afraid of what you'll find?"

Ramsey blinked twice, and stared at him, stunned speechless. "Anthar?" he finally managed. He glanced toward Cuyler, and she nodded confirmation. Sighing hard, Ramsey sank back into his chair. He closed his eyes. "All right. I believe you."

Cuyler sighed in relief, but Damien only cocked his brows in surprise. "You don't need to see the proof?"

"No." Ramsey shook his head slowly. "No. I've found quite a few surprises in my own DPI files. Enough to show me what they're really about." He shook his head, meeting Cuyler's gaze. "You were right all along. I just wish I'd believed you sooner."

Cuyler blinked moisture away from her eyes, and faced Damien. If she looked a bit awed, Ramsey figured it was natural. She was in the same room with the man reputed to be the oldest of all of them, the first. "Why are you here?" she asked him.

"To get you out."

"But how did you know—"

"No time for that, child. You must come with me now." He took her hand and tugged her toward the doorway.

She pulled free. "I'm not leaving him."

Damien's eyes took on a feral gleam. "He's not worth your devotion, Cuyler. He's one of them, those same bastards who make our very existence a game of hide-and-seek. The ones who see to it we never know peace. If they've turned on him now, then all the better. Poetic justice, if you ask me."

"I didn't ask you!"

His glare grew sharper still.

"They had me, Damien. He got me out. He risked his life to do it."

"Too little, too late. What good did it do? He's one of them, Cuyler! Leave him here and be rid of him for good."

"*Damn* you with your us-and-them mentality! Don't you see that's exactly the bigotry that got us to this point in the first place! Damien, your way of thinking is just as twisted as DPI's. Can't you see that?"

Ramsey touched her shoulder, his hands squeezing gently, but his gaze remained on Damien. "Can you get her out?"

"There's no doubt."

"No!" She twisted her head to stare into Ramsey's eyes just before he slammed them shut.

"Go with him, Cuyler."

"I won't! Dammit, I won't!"

"There's no time to argue," Damien said softly, though his eyes had lost some of their anger, and a frown that might have been one of confusion had taken up residence between his brows. "Have you noticed the radio silence, Ramsey? The sudden stop in all radio contact?"

Ramsey opened his eyes and turned slowly to stare at the computer screen that glowed like an all-seeing oracle.

"They knew the second you turned it on and began accessing information," Damien said softly. "They're probably already on their—"

A bullhorn-enhanced voice apparently shattered the slight grip Cuyler had on her composure. She screamed at the first words, but Ramsey still heard them.

"Bachman, we have the house surrounded. There's no way out. Give yourselves up."

Ramsey lowered his head. "Can you still get her out, Damien?"

"Ramsey—"

"If we can get to the roof," Damien replied, cutting her off.

She threw her arms around Ramsey's neck. "No! I won't do it. I love you—"

The bullhorn-enhanced voice came again. "We'll give you ten minutes, Bachman. Then we come in shooting."

The sharpshooter in the tallest pine tree whistled, and when he had Fuller's attention, he whispered loudly, "There's a third person in there, Fuller. A man, tall, very dark complexion."

"How the hell—" Fuller nodded, and hurried toward the DPI van, glancing as he did at the miniature dish on the top. "Can you get this thing up and operational? I need to hear what's being said inside."

The technician only held up one hand for patience, adjusting his headset and fiddling with dials. Finally he nodded and smiled. He handed the headset to Fuller, who held it up to one ear. Then his eyes widened, and he smiled.

"It's *him!*" He shook his head slowly. "We've hit the damn jackpot this time, fellas. Get me a line to Bachman. It's time to make a deal."

Chapter Twelve

Damien studied Ramsey as if seeing him for the first time. "Hard to believe we have one common goal, after all this. We both want to see Cuyler get out of this alive."

Ramsey lowered his eyes. "We have more in common than you know, Damien."

The other man frowned, parted his lips to ask something, but Ramsey cut him off. "Look, it's no secret that I don't like you."

"You're not exactly my favorite person, either, Ramsey."

"Unpleasant as you are, though, you're not a killer."

"Thanks so much for informing me."

Ramsey blew air through his teeth. "You want to shut the hell up and let me apologize!"

"Is that what you were doing?"

Damien's stare was as hateful as ever, and Ramsey knew the one he sent back was as bad, or worse. Ramsey wanted to deck the guy, but he restrained himself. There was another part of him that wanted to shake Damien's hand, call him friend.

"The one you killed, Anthar..." Ramsey swallowed the lump in his throat and shook his head.

"What about him?"

Clearing his throat, stiffening his spine, Ramsey answered. "He was the one who murdered my mother." He heard Cuyler catch her breath. "DPI knew all along. It's in my files, along with a lot of other…" He bit his lip, shook his head. "Doesn't matter now, I guess. I just thought you ought to know."

"Know?"

"That you're not quite the bastard I had you pegged as being, all right? Now, if you don't mind, can we quit talking and get Cuyler out of here?"

Damien tilted his head to one side. "You aren't a bit afraid of me, are you?"

"Oh, *hell* yes, Damien. Scared witless. Don't you see my knees knocking?"

Damien chewed his inner cheek, eyes narrow. "You're an unusual mortal."

"You're both idiots!" Cuyler shouted the words as she crossed into the living room and peered through a curtain. "And insane, to boot, if you think I'm leaving here without you, Ramsey." There were tears glittering in her eyes. "We go together or not at all."

He went to her, unable to stop himself. Vaguely he was aware of Damien tactfully slipping out of the room, but his mind was focused on Cuyler. Her heart was breaking. He could feel it. Or was that his own? His hands slipped around her waist as she turned to him and he pulled her close.

"I'm not worth dying for," he whispered. "Cuyler, you have to go with him."

She threaded her fingers in his hair. "You love me, don't you, Ramsey?"

His eyes devoured her face. Her turned-up nose, her huge, dark eyes. That ruffly jet hair.

"Say it, just once, say it."

He nodded, his mind reeling with the force of what he felt. "I don't think love is a strong enough word. Hell, Cuyler, you've turned me inside out. Before you, I swear there was ice running in my veins instead of blood. A big hunk of granite hatred where my heart ought to be. You changed that." He lowered his head, captured her sweet mouth one last time, kissed her the way he'd been wanting to all night long. When he pulled away, he licked the taste of her from his lips. "Yes, Cuyler. I love you."

Tears flowed like rivers on her cheeks. "Then don't ask me to go on without you." She sniffed, swallowed, her voice became tight and thin. "'Cause I don't think I can."

"You'd have to sooner or later anyway." His thumbs swept the moisture from her cheeks. "You're immortal. I'm not and there's no way I can be." God, how it tore him apart to utter that lie. There was a way. He knew that now, was still jolted by the knowledge. But he couldn't tell her. She'd never leave if she knew.

She shook her head fast and hard, but he caught her face between his palms, held it still. "It's the truth. We would have had to face it eventually."

"I don't want to hear this!" She whirled away from him.

Damien reentered the room, clearing his throat to announce his presence. Ramsey met his probing gaze. It was knowing, that look.

"There's a door to the roof through the attic," Ramsey said, fighting for a level tone. "I want you to go with Damien now. They won't wait patiently much longer."

Damien went to Cuyler, took a gentle hold on her arm, and started for the stairs. The telephone jangled and Ramsey went rigid. It rang again, and this time the voice on the bullhorn shouted at him to pick it up.

His hands damp with sweat, he did.

"Bachman?"

His lips thinned. The voice belonged to Wes Fuller, his trusted superior. "What the hell do you want?"

"Wouldn't be a good idea for your two pals to go up on the roof, Bachman. We have sharpshooters high enough to hit them there."

He swore his heart turned to ice in his chest. He covered the mouth piece with one hand, waved to get Damien's attention. Damien halted halfway up the stairs and waited, watching Ramsey's face intently.

Ramsey cleared his throat. "What makes you think anyone was thinking about going to the roof?"

"Oh, we don't think. We *know*. I've been listening in on your touching little conversation."

"Maybe you'd like to meet me one on one, Fuller? Maybe you need a little dental work done, hmm?"

Fuller's laugh was low and throaty. "No, thanks. Look, I know you've been sniffing around in your files...among other things. How much do you know?"

"About what?"

The other man hesitated, then went on. "Your diabetes, for starters."

"I know I don't have it. Never did."

"And your insulin?"

"An experiment. To mask..." Ramsey glanced toward Cuyler on the stairs, and decided not to say any more.

"Go on, Bachman. Tell me, do you know about your blood type?"

"I know," he said softly, slowly.

"So you know all that crap you just fed the...*lady* was bull. You could join the ranks and live happily ever after with her. You realize that?"

Ramsey stiffened. "What's your point, Fuller?"

"I could let you go. Her, too. I could pull back and let you both walk out of here, right now. I have the authority."

Just like that. Fuller let the words hang in the air for a long moment. But Ramsey wasn't stupid. There was more. It was either a trick to get them to let their guard down, or Fuller wanted something. He wasn't certain which.

"What's the catch?" He tried not to let the sudden surge of hope come through in his voice.

"Finish the assignment you had before this one. That's all. Not so much to ask, is it, Bachman?"

Ramsey closed his eyes, knowing exactly what Fuller wanted. The job before this one had been the capture of Damien Namtar, the most powerful, the oldest, probably the first of all vampires.

Ramsey had had no qualms about hunting him down a year ago, when he'd believed with everything in him that the man was a heartless predator, a killer. But now he knew better. He'd wronged Damien with his persecution. And he owed the man. More than ever, Ramsey knew what would happen to Damien if he were turned over to DPI. *They* were the heartless killers, not him. God, it was all so clear now. Why had it taken so long?

"How do you expect me to do that?" he asked, just to stall, trying to think of some way out of this trap.

"The tranquilizer, Bachman. There are filled syringes in the desk, bottom drawer. Just stick him, and leave the rest to us. You and your pet can walk away and never look back."

Ramsey turned and met Damien's steady gaze. Not looking away, he replied, "It might take a little while."

"I can give you an hour, Bachman. Not a minute longer." The connection was broken.

Ramsey licked his lips and put the phone back in its cradle.

"What?" Cuyler whispered. "What's going on?"

"Nothing." His gaze shifted to Damien's and he got the odd feeling the man knew every word that had been said. "I bought us some time, is all." He reached for a piece of paper and a pencil, and scribbled quickly. "They can hear every word we say, so be careful."

When he held it up, Damien and Cuyler came back down the stairs. Cuyler looked at it, blinked in surprise, and showed it to Damien.

Ramsey looked around the house, feeling more trapped and helpless than he ever had before. More, even, than when he'd awakened in Cuyler's castlelike hideaway. The thought made him close his eyes and wince inwardly. He'd give a limb to be there with her right now. He'd let so much time go to waste, time when he'd been alone with her in that magical place.

They could never go back there now.

Inspiration struck, and Ramsey tilted his head so they'd follow, and headed for the basement. The place was solid, lead-lined and secure. Ramsey didn't think they'd be heard down here. Still, he whispered what he had to say.

"Damien, we need to exchange clothes."

Damien lifted one brow, then lowered it, his eyes narrowing in understanding. "Why?"

"There's no time to go into it," Ramsey lied. "Look, there are sharpshooters out there. If you head for the roof, they'll pick you off so fast it'll make your head spin. I have a plan."

Damien nodded thoughtfully and lowered himself to the bottom step. "Tell me about it."

"I told you, there isn't time."

Cuyler looked from one to the other. "I don't like this, Ramsey. Tell me the truth, what did that bastard say to you on the phone?"

Ramsey looked away, chewing his lip. "Nothing you need to be concerned about."

"No," Damien agreed. "He simply offered to let you and Cuyler go free, in exchange for my capture. That's it, isn't it?"

Ramsey's head came up and his eyes flashed angrily. The jerk was going to ruin everything.

"And you planned to put on my clothes, pretend to be me, and give Cuyler and me time to escape."

"Ramsey, you can't!"

Ramsey clasped her hands in his, squeezing to calm her, while glaring at Damien. "You had to spill it all? You couldn't just take her and go?"

Damien gave his head an almost imperceptible shake. "An unusual mortal," he said again, as if to himself.

"I've had enough of both of you!" Cuyler tugged her hands from Ramsey's and stalked through the basement, peering through the narrow windows, whose bottoms were level with the ground outside. One after another, pacing back to the first again as Damien and Ramsey continued their silent battle of wills.

"Here!" Her shout caught both men's attention. "Okay, see that DPI car right there? It's the closest one to the house."

Damien glanced at Ramsey. Ramsey only shook his head.

"I won't bother trying to explain to you two. You're too busy

with your own tug-of-war to listen. Ramsey, get Fuller on the line
again. Tell him you agree to his terms, but he has to pull all the
police off the highways. The chopper has to land. Tell him you'll
surrender Damien only to him and those two clowns he has with
him. Everyone else has to leave. Especially those sharpshooters.
I can see one from here, up in a tree. We won't stand a chance
unless we get rid of them.''

Ramsey frowned, rising, gripping her shoulders. "Honey, I
don't know what—"

"We'll need a distraction. Then we make a run for that car.
We'll squeeze through this window, and…" Her words came to
a stop as she pulled free of Ramsey, clambered onto a wooden
box, and pried the window from its opening. Ramsey could only
watch in wonder as she wrestled it free, and very quietly climbed
down, setting it aside.

"Look," she whispered, even more softly than before. She
pointed to the shrubs growing between the house and the car.
There would only be a few yards without cover.

She nudged Ramsey's shoulder. "Go on, get up there and make
that call.''

Chapter Thirteen

They hovered at the open window as Ramsey conversed via the cordless phone with Fuller. No one was in sight outside now. Only two DPI cars and three agents. They must want Damien very badly, Cuyler mused, to take such a chance.

Either that or they were playing a huge bluff. Maybe the others were only out of sight, waiting. Maybe Fuller and DPI had no intention of letting any of them go.

"He's out cold, Fuller," Ramsey said into the phone. "Apparently your tranquilizer works. Cuyler and I want transportation out of here. Now."

Ramsey held the phone away from his ear, and Cuyler leaned in close to hear the reply. Damien didn't bother. Cuyler wondered if perhaps he didn't need to. She had no idea the extent of his powers.

"You and *Cuyler* stay put. We're coming in. When we see for ourselves that he's incapacitated, we'll let you go."

Ramsey covered the mouthpiece with his hand. "Lying through his teeth." Removing his hand, he said, "All right, Fuller. But you better keep your word."

They waited, all of them pressed to the opening in the window. Cuyler knew Damien could leave if he wanted to. He had the ability. But he stayed, all the same.

When they heard the front door open, and Fuller calling Ramsey's name, Ramsey made a stirrup of his hands, and bent. Cuyler stepped up, pushing herself through the window. She emerged kneeling, concealed by the shrubbery, still close enough to hear Fuller's voice raised in alarm.

"Where the hell are you, Bachman?" Then, "Dammit, he's up to something. Search the place."

Damien was beside her a second later. Then Ramsey himself crawled through. She bit her lip as Damien reached back, offering a hand, which Ramsey took. Sandwiched between the two men, she glanced toward the car.

"We move as one," Ramsey said, his body shielding hers on one side. Damien nodded. Bending low, they ran toward the car. Just as they reached the end of the shrub cover, the front door of the house burst open and several shots rang out.

She felt Ramsey stiffen beside her, but he never faltered. One arm came around her and he moved faster, around the far side of the car. Ramsey opened the back door, bending over her body as she threw herself inside, facedown on the floor. The window above her exploded and glass rained down into her hair. She tried to turn, tried to see Ramsey and Damien, but the bullets whizzed near her face, bringing back a flood of horrifying memories, until she could only lower her head again, covering it with her hands. She heard the door slam and felt the car jerk into motion. And then the bullets stopped ringing in her ears. She chanced lifting her head, only to see Damien on the back seat, sitting calmly amid the gunfire, his gaze so intense...and then glowing as he stared at something behind them.

Curious, even while shaking all over, she sat up a bit, following his gaze. She saw the DPI men running toward their car. But before they reached it, it exploded in a ball of blinding white flame.

Shielding her eyes and gasping, she glanced at Damien. But he didn't notice, still too focused on what was behind them. He stared at the house now, even as the confused men turned to scramble toward it.

All three flew backward when it exploded. This time, the ground beneath the car rocked with the impact. She heard Ramsey swear, saw him twist in the driver's seat to look at the sight. Then she was looking, too. The entire house was nothing but a flaming framework, rapidly disintegrating to ash. Great beam-shaped lengths of fire fell in slow motion, disappearing into the mouth of the inferno waiting below to devour them.

She still felt the vibrations of the explosion, and the house was all but gone already.

My God.

They rounded a bend. The car weaved in and out of its lane and steadily lost speed. Cuyler frowned, clambering over the seat. "Ramsey, what's wrong? What's—"

She bit off the rest of her words, seeing the blood that soaked the front of him. His grip on the steering wheel was white-knuckled, his eyes steadily glazing over, his back bowing more and more as his right leg began a spastic dance. The car jerked with his foot's movements on the accelerator.

"Ramsey!" She swung her leg over his, jamming her foot down on the brake and jerking the gearshift into Neutral. She gripped the wheel, guided the car to the roadside, slammed it into Park, and grabbed Ramsey's shoulders, shaking him. "Dammit, Ramsey, don't do this to me! Ramsey! *Ramsey!*"

He focused on her eyes, and she could see it was a struggle. One side of his mouth pulled into that half smile of his, and he managed to wink. "Maybe Damien oughta drive, hmm?" Both his legs trembled now. Then they stopped, and his eyelids fell closed.

Cuyler buried her face in the crook of his neck, crying uncontrollably. "It isn't over, Ramsey. Damn you, it isn't over. Not yet, not like this!"

A firm hand on her shoulder drew her gaze upward to look into Damien's solemn eyes. "No, Cuyler. It isn't over. Not yet." He got out of the car, opened the front door, hauled Ramsey out, then carefully placed him across the back seat. Cuyler got back there, too, and lifted Ramsey's head as she slid in, so she could cradle it in her lap. Damien got behind the wheel. "Hold on to him, Cuyler. I'll drive you somewhere safe. And the rest..." He glanced over his shoulder at the man she held, his eyes narrow. "The rest, I guess, will be up to Ramsey."

Ramsey woke to the most incredible, burning pain he'd ever felt in his life. But at least he woke. He supposed he ought to be grateful for small favors.

His chest was bandaged. His legs had gone numb. But there was warmth, softness. His head was pillowed on what felt like satin. Small hands were running over his face, through his hair. A musical voice, like the wind, begged him to wake up. Salty tears rained down on his face. Trembling lips pressed to his over and over again.

He opened his eyes. Hazy, everything was so hazy. His body felt weak, drained. And there was this incredible urge to just close his eyes again and float away.

"Ramsey?"

God, but he didn't want to float away. Not if "away" meant away from Cuyler.

"Right here." That didn't sound like his voice. It sounded far away, echoing back to his ears from the other end of a hollow tunnel. Man, he was fading fast. He tried to look around, but could only make out several halos of golden light. Candles? And one bigger one, a fireplace, maybe. He felt the warmth, smelled the fragrance. Yes, a fireplace. And he thought he was on a bed, but he couldn't be sure. "Where are we?"

"Damien's house...one of his houses, as he put it. We're safe here, Ramsey. Damien went to get rid of the car. When he comes back, I'm sending him for a doctor."

"A doctor can't help, Cuyler." He knew it, somewhere deep in his soul. Just the same way he knew her devastation. She sensed him slipping away, just as he did. And she was dying a little bit, right along with him.

He struggled to sit up, and she helped him. "I can't stand this, Ramsey. I can't stand losing you." She propped pillows at his back.

He caught her hands, brought them to his lips. "I've been a fool."

"You saved our lives, Ramsey. Even Damien knows what you did back there."

"A fool," he whispered. God, it was getting harder and harder to speak, to string words together. He had to focus every ounce of strength on saying what he had to say. "He's a decent man, Damien. I was wrong...about him. About...about everything."

"It doesn't matter now—"

"Yes. Yes, it does. I'm not..." He drew a painful breath, grated his teeth. "I'm not what you think I am, Cuyler. The insulin...all this time...they tricked me."

She sank onto the edge of the bed, running her hands through his hair. "Don't try to talk. Just rest—"

"I don't deserve...to be...to live. But I'm not ready to die, either."

She choked on a sob. Shaking all over, she lowered her head to his chest, clung to him.

"But I'll...make it up to you...to all of you."

She lifted her head and stared into his eyes. "What do you mean?"

"I want to live, Cuyler." He wanted to stop. He was panting, out of breath as if he'd just run a marathon, but he had to continue. "I want to be able...to love you...the way you deserve." The pain in his chest was unbearable. But the pain in his heart was worse. "I want it. I want you to do it to me, Cuyler. Right now."

Her brows drew together as she searched his face, desperation etched in her every feature. "Do... Ramsey, what are you saying? I can't transform you. The antigen—"

"I have it." He inhaled, but it was too shallow. His voice grew weaker with every word. "I have...all along. The insulin..." That was it. It was the end. He felt himself slipping steadily away from her. He tried to tighten his hold on her, but didn't have the strength. With supreme effort, he gasped, and in a harsh whisper, went on. "I love you, Cuyler..."

His eyes fell closed and the breath slowly escaped his lungs.

"Ramsey! Ramsey, no..."

But she knew the end was here. And she knew he'd been telling her something...something she didn't understand.

Go on, Cuyler. Damien's soft, deep voice floated across the boundaries of time and space. *He's one of us. Always has been. It's all in the files. They've masked it with some new drug or other. Told him it was insulin and that he was diabetic. They've brainwashed him through most of his life, and still he found his way to you. Go on, bring him over. If ever a man was worthy of the gift, it's him.*

Cuyler felt her eyes widen. She was shocked beyond belief, and half wondered if the voice in her mind might have been her own imagination. But if there was a chance...

She bent her head and kissed Ramsey's slack mouth. Then she bent lower, sliding her lips over his bristly jaw, to his throat. "Come back to me, love," she whispered, her lips moving over his salty skin.

When Ramsey opened his eyes a long while later, there were a hundred new and unbelievable sensations coursing through him. Things he'd never felt before, didn't understand, a sense of elation and strength and vitality he'd never had before.

But all of that paled beside the joy he felt at finding Cuyler cradling him in her arms. He looked up at her, saw the uncertainty in her huge onyx eyes as they searched his face.

"You did it, didn't you?" he asked her, and even his voice seemed different. Or maybe it was his hearing that had taken on a new intensity.

She nodded. "You said... I thought..." She bit her lip. "Don't hate me for it, Ramsey. It seemed to be what you wanted. If I misunderstood, then—"

"It's what I wanted."

"But—"

He lifted his head, silencing her by pressing his lips to hers. "I love you, Cuyler Jade. You know that, don't you?"

The worry fled her eyes and she smiled. "Of course I do. I knew it before you did. And it's a good thing."

"Why's that?"

She kissed his forehead, then his mouth. "Because, Ramsey, I love you, and I wouldn't settle for anything less in return. Especially since I have to put up with you for the rest of eternity."

"Eternity with Tinkerbell," he said, grinning. He gathered her into his arms and held her close. "I can't think of a sweeter fate."

*   *   *   *   *

And the story continues...

In March 2002.
Mira Books is proud to present a brand-new,
compelling story that returns to
Maggie Shayne's vampire world,

TWILIGHT HUNGER

Turn the page to catch a glimpse into this original
world of the night...

Chapter 1

W̲e children were supposed to be asleep....

But we woke, as if in response to some silent summons. We crept to the entrances of our tents and wagons, drawn like moths to the snapping flames of the central fire and the dark, leaping shadows the strange woman cast as she danced.

There was no music. I knew there was none, but it seemed to me that music filled my head all the same as I peered around the painted flap and watched her. She whirled, scarves trailing like colorful ghosts in her wake, her hair black as the night, yet gleaming blue in the fire's glow. She arched and twisted and spun around again. And then she stopped still, and her eyes, like shining bits of coal, fixed right on mine. Scarlet lips curved in a terrifying smile, and she crooked a finger at me.

I tried to swallow, but the lump of cold dread in my throat wouldn't let me. Licking my lips, I glanced sideways, at the tents and painted wagons of my kin, and saw the other children of our band.

We were Gypsies all, and proud. The dancing woman... she was a Gypsy, too. I knew that at a glance. She was one of our own.

And crooking her finger at me still.

I stiffened my spine and stepped out of my mother's tent. As I crept closer, the others, taking courage in mine, began to come out, too. Slowly we gathered around the beautiful stranger like sinners come to worship at the feet of a goddess. And as we did, her smile grew wider. She beckoned us closer, a finger to her lips, and then she sat down on a log near the fire.

"Who is she?" I whispered to my cousin Dimitri.

"Stupid, do you know nothing? She is our aunt. Her name is Sarafina. She's not supposed to be here, though. When the grown-ups find out, there will be trouble."

"Why?" I was entranced by the mysterious stranger as she lowered herself to the log, spreading the layers of her colorful skirts around her, opening her arms to welcome the young ones who crowded closer to sit on the ground all around her. I sat closest of all, right at her feet. Never had I seen a woman so beautiful. But there was something else about her, as well. Something…unearthly. Something frightening.

And there was the way her eyes kept meeting mine. There was a secret in that black gaze—a secret I could not quite see. Something shadowed, hidden.

"Why will there be trouble?" I whispered again.

"Because! She is outcast!"

My brows drew together. I was about to ask why, but the woman—my aunt Sarafina, whom I had never seen before in my life—began to speak. And her voice was like a song. Mesmerizing, deep, beguiling.

"Come, little ones. Oh, how I've missed you." Her gaze swept the faces of the children, the look in her eyes almost painful to see, so intense was the emotion there. "But most of you do not remember me at all, do you?" Her smile faltered. "You, little Dante. You are…how old now?"

"Seven," I told her, my voice a mere whisper.

"Seven years," she replied with a heavy sigh. "I was there the day you were born, you know."

"No. I…didn't know."

"No matter. Oh, children, I've so much to tell you. But first..."
She tugged open a drawstring sack that dangled from the sash
around her waist, and from it she began to draw glorious things,
which she handed around to one and all. Sweets and confections
such as we had never tasted, wrapped in brightly colored paper.
Shiny baubles on chains, and glittering stones of all kinds, carved
into the shapes of animals and birds.

The one she gave to me was a stone of black onyx in the shape
of a bat.

Reaching down, she stroked a path through my hair and leaned
close to me, whispering into my ear. "You are my very special
boy, Dante. You and I share a bond more powerful even than the
one you share with your own mother. Remember my words. I'll
come back for you someday. When you need me, I will come."

I shivered and didn't know why.

MAGGIE SHAYNE

*He is every woman's fantasy, yet he remains alone
and untouched. His world is one of secrecy and
solitude, darkness and danger. Now one woman has
found his journal. She has told his secrets.
He must stop her, and there is only one way....*

When struggling screenwriter Morgan DeSilva uncovers the ancient
diaries in the attic of an old house in Maine, she is swept into the
seductive world of a long-dead madman who had believed himself a
vampire. Now, though Dante's story has made her famous, Morgan is
wasting away. At night she dreams of him, an erotic fantasy so real
she can see the marks on her neck, feel her life's blood draining
from her. Almost as if he were real…

**Return with Maggie Shayne to the dark,
erotic world of *Wings in the Night*.**

TWILIGHT HUNGER

**His touch promises ecstasy.
His kiss offers immortality.**

*Available the first week
of March 2002
wherever paperbacks
are sold!*

MIRA®

MERLINE
LOVELACE

spent twenty-three years as an air force officer, serving tours at
the Pentagon and at bases all over the world before she began
a new career as a novelist. When she's not tied to her keyboard,
she and her own handsome hero, Al, enjoy traveling, golf and
long lively dinners with friends and family.

A *USA Today* bestselling author with over five million copies
of her books in print, Merline is known for her mainstream
military thrillers and her historical novels for MIRA as well
as her category romances. Merline is a five-time nominee for
the Romance Writers of America prestigious RITA Award,
and is proud to have been named the 1998 Oklahoma
Author of the Year.

Merline enjoys hearing from readers and can be reached by
e-mail via Internet through the Silhouette/Harlequin Web site
at www.eHarlequin.com or at her own Web site
www.merlinelovelace.com.

Silhouette®

Where love comes alive ™

PSDTH-TR